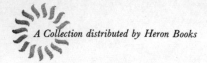 *A Collection distributed by Heron Books*

JOHN GALSWORTHY

Collected Works

JOHN GALSWORTHY
1867–1933

JOHN GALSWORTHY

The Burning Spear
Villa Rubein

Original Illustrations by
SANDRA ARCHIBALD

Distributed by
HERON BOOKS

Published by arrangement with
William Heinemann Ltd

The Burning Spear

"With a heart of furious fancies,
  Whereof I am commander,
  With a burning spear and a horse of air
  In the wilderness I wander;
  With a night of ghosts and shadows
  I summoned am to tourney
  Ten leagues beyond the wide world's end
  For me it is no journey."

TOM O'BEDLAM.

I

THE HERO

In the year —— there dwelt on Hampstead Heath a small thin gentleman of fifty-eight, gentle disposition, and independent means, whose wits had become somewhat addled from reading the writings and speeches of public men. The castle which, like every Englishman, he inhabited was embedded in lilac bushes and laburnums, and was attached to another castle, embedded, in deference to our national dislike of uniformity, in acacias and laurustinus. Our gentleman, whose name was John Lavender, had until the days of the Great War passed one of those curious existences which are sometimes to be met with, in doing harm to nobody. He had been brought up to the Bar, but like most barristers had never practised, and had spent his time among animals and the wisdom of the past. At the period in which this record opens he owned a young female sheep-dog called Blink, with beautiful eyes obscured by hair ; and was attended to by a thin and energetic housekeeper, in his estimation above all weakness, whose name was Marian Petty, and by her husband, his chauffeur, whose name was Joe.

It was the ambition of our hero to be, like all public men, without fear and without reproach. He drank not, abstained from fleshly intercourse, and habitually spoke the truth. His face was thin, high cheek-boned, and not unpleasing, with one loose eyebrow over

3

which he had no control; his eyes, bright and of
hazel hue, looked his fellows in the face without seeing
what was in it. Though his moustache was still dark,
his thick waving hair was permanently white, for his
study was lined from floor to ceiling with books,
pamphlets, journals, and the recorded utterances of
great mouths. He was of a frugal habit, ate what was
put before him without question, and if asked what
he would have, invariably answered : " What is there ?'
without listening to the reply. For at mealtimes it
was his custom to read the writings of great men.

" Joe," he would say to his chauffeur, who had a
slight limp, a green wandering eye, and a red face,
with a rather curved and rather redder nose, " you
must read this."

And Joe would answer: " Which one is that, sir ? "

" Hummingtop ; a great man, I think, Joe."

" A brainy chap, right enough, sir."

" He has done wonders for the country. Listen
to this." And Mr. Lavender would read as follows :
" If I had fifty sons I would give them all. If I had
forty daughters they should nurse and scrub and weed
and fill shells ; if I had thirty country-houses they
should all be hospitals ; if I had twenty pens I would
use them all day long ; if I had ten voices they should
never cease to inspire and aid my country."

" If 'e had nine lives," interrupted Joe, with a
certain suddenness, " 'e'd save the lot."

Mr. Lavender lowered the paper.

" I cannot bear cynicism, Joe ; there is no quality
so unbecoming to a gentleman."

" Me and 'im don't put in for that, sir."

" Joe," Mr. Lavender would say, " you are incorrig-
ible. . . . "

Our gentleman, in common with all worthy of the name, had a bank-book, which, in hopes that it would disclose an unsuspected balance, he would have " made up " every time he read an utterance exhorting people to invest and save their country.

One morning at the end of May, finding there was none, he called in his housekeeper and said :

" Mrs. Petty, we are spending too much ; we have again been exhorted to save. Listen ! ' Every penny diverted from prosecution of the war is one more spent in the interest of the enemies of mankind. No patriotic person, I am confident, will spend upon him or herself a stiver which could be devoted to the noble ends so near to all our hearts. Let us make every spare copper into bullets to strengthen the sinews of war ! ' A great speech. What can we do without ? "

" The newspapers, sir."

" Don't be foolish, Mrs. Petty. From what else could we draw our inspiration and comfort in these terrible days ? "

Mrs. Petty sniffed.

" Well, you can't eat less than you do," she said ; " but you might stop feedin' Blink out of your rations—that I do think."

" I have not found that forbidden as yet in any public utterance," returned Mr. Lavender ; " but when the Earl of Betternot tells us to stop, I shall follow his example, you may depend on that. The country comes before everything."

Mrs. Petty tossed her head and murmured darkly :

" Do you suppose he's got an example, sir ? "

" Mrs. Petty," replied Mr. Lavender, " that is quite unworthy of you. But tell me, what *can* we do without ? "

5

"I could do without Joe," responded Mrs. Petty, "now that you're not using him as chauffeur."

"Please be serious. Joe is an institution; besides, I am thinking of offering myself to the Government as a speaker now that we may use gas."

"Ah!" said Mrs. Petty.

"I am going down about it to-morrow."

"Indeed, sir!"

"I feel my energies are not fully employed."

"No, sir?"

"By the way, there was a wonderful leader on potatoes yesterday. We must dig up the garden. Do you know what the subsoil is?"

"Brickbats and dead cats, I expect, sir."

"Ah! We shall soon improve that. Every inch of land reclaimed is a nail in the coffin of our common enemies."

And going over to a bookcase, Mr. Lavender took out the third from the top of a pile of newspapers. "Listen!" he said. "'The problem before us is the extraction of every potential ounce of food. No half measures must content us. Potatoes! Potatoes! No matter how, where, when—the prime national necessity is now the growth of potatoes. All Britons should join in raising a plant which may be our very salvation.'"

"Fudge!" murmured Mrs. Petty.

Mr. Lavender read on, and his eyes glowed. 'Ah!' he thought, 'I, too, can do my bit to save England. . . . It needs but the spark to burn away the dross of this terrible horse-sense which keeps the country back.'

"Mrs. Petty!" But Mrs. Petty was already not.

.   .   .   .

6

II

The grass never grew under the feet of Mr. Lavender. No sooner had he formed his sudden resolve than he wrote to what he conceived to be the proper quarter, and, receiving no reply, went down to the centre of the official world. It was at a time of change and no small national excitement ; brooms were sweeping clean, and new offices had arisen everywhere. Mr. Lavender passed bewildered among large stone buildings and small wooden buildings, not knowing where to go. He had bought no clothes since the beginning of the war, except the various Volunteer uniforms which the exigencies of a shifting situation had forced the authorities to withdraw from time to time ; and his small shrunken figure struck somewhat vividly on the eye, with elbows and knees shining in the summer sunlight. Stopping at last before the only object which seemed unchanged, he said :

" Can you tell me where the Ministry is ? "

The officer looked down at him.

" What for ? "

" For speaking about the country."

" Ministry of Propagation ? First on the right, second door on the left."

" Thank you. The Police are wonderful."

" None of that," said the officer coldly.

" I only said you were wonderful."

" I 'eard you."

" But you are. I don't know what the country would do without you. Your solid qualities, your imperturbable bonhomie, your truly British tenderness towards——"

7

" Pass away ! " said the officer.

" I am only repeating what we all say of you," rejoined Mr. Lavender reproachfully.

" Did you 'ear me say ' Move on,' " said the officer ; " or must I make you an example ? "

" *You* are the example," said Mr. Lavender warmly.

" Any more names," returned the officer, " and I take you to the station." And he moved out into the traffic. Puzzled by his unfriendliness Mr. Lavender resumed his search, and, arriving at the door indicated, went in. A dark, dusty, deserted corridor led him nowhere, till he came on a little girl in a brown frock, with her hair down her back.

" Can you tell me, little one—— " he said, laying his hand on her head.

" Chuck it ! " said the little girl.

" No, no ! " responded Mr. Lavender, deeply hurt. " Can you tell me where I can find the Minister ? "

" 'Ave you an appointment ? "

" No ; but I wrote him. He should expect me."

" Wot nyme ? "

" John Lavender. Here is my card."

" I'll tyke it in. Wyte 'ere ! "

' Wonderful ! ' mused Mr. Lavender ; ' the patriotic impulse already stirring in these little hearts ! What was the stanza of that patriotic poet ?

> ' " *Lives not a babe who shall not feel the pulse*
> *Of Britain's need beat wild in Britain's wrist.*
> *And, sacrificial, in the world's convulse*
> *Put up its lips to be by Britain kissed.*"

So young to bring their lives to the service of the country ! '

" Come on," said the little girl, reappearing suddenly ;
" 'e'll see you."

Mr. Lavender entered a room which had a considerable resemblance to the office of a lawyer save for the
absence of tomes. It seemed furnished almost exclusively by the Minister, who sat with knees crossed, in a
pair of large round tortoiseshell spectacles, which did
not, however, veil the keenness of his eyes. He was a
man with close-cropped grey hair, a broad yellow,
clean-shaven face, and thrusting grey eyes.

" Mr. Lavender," he said, in a raw, forcible voice ;
" sit down, will you ? "

" I wrote to you," began our hero, " expressing the
wish to offer myself as a speaker."

" Ah ! " said the Minister. " Let's see—Lavender,
Lavender. Here's your letter." And extracting a
letter from a file he read it, avoiding with difficulty his
tortoiseshell spectacles. " You want to stump the
country ? M.A., Barrister, and Fellow of the Zoologi-
cal. Are you a good speaker ? "

" If zeal——" began Mr. Lavender.

" That's it ; spark ! We're out to win this war, sir."

" Quite so," began Mr. Lavender. " If devotion——"

" You'll have to use gas," said the Minister ; " and
we don't pay."

" Pay ! " cried Mr. Lavender with horror ; " no,
indeed ! "

The Minister bent on him a shrewd glance " What's
your line ? Anything particular, or just general
patriotism ? I recommend that ; but you'll have to
put some punch into it, you know."

" I have studied all the great orators of the war, sir,"
said Mr. Lavender, " and am familiar with all the great

9

writers on it. I should form myself on them; and if enthusiasm——"

"Quite!" said the Minister. "If you want any atrocities we can give you them. No facts and no figures; just general pat."

"I shall endeavour——" began Mr. Lavender.

"Well, good-bye," said the Minister, rising. "When do you start?"

Mr. Lavender rose too. "To-morrow," he said; "if I can get inflated."

The Minister rang a bell.

"You're on your own, mind," he said. "No facts; what they want is ginger. Yes, Mr. Japes?"

And seeing that the Minister was looking over his tortoiseshell spectacles at somebody behind him, Mr. Lavender turned and went out. In the corridor he thought, 'What terseness! How different from the days when Dickens wrote his "Circumlocution Office"! Punch!' And opening the wrong door, he found himself in the presence of six little girls in brown frocks, sitting against the walls with their thumbs in their mouths.

"Oh!" he said, "I'm afraid I've lost my way."

The eldest of the little girls withdrew a thumb. "What d'yer want?"

"The door," said Mr. Lavender.

"Second on the right."

"Good-bye," said Mr. Lavender.

The little girls did not answer. And he went out thinking, 'These children are really wonderful! What devotion one sees! And yet the country is not yet fully roused!'

II

THE VALET

JOE PETTY stood contemplating the car which, purchased some fifteen years before, had not been used since the war began. Birds had nested in its hair. It smelled of mould inside; it creaked from rust. 'The Guv'nor must be cracked,' he thought, ' to think we can get anywhere in this old geyser. Well, well, it's summer; if we break down it won't break my 'eart. Government job—better than diggin' or drillin'. Good old Guv.!' So musing, he lit his pipe and examined the recesses beneath the driver's seat. ' A bottle or three,' he thought, ' in case our patriotism should get us stuck a bit off the beaten; a loaf or two, some 'oney in a pot, and a good old 'am. "A life on the rollin' road——" 'Ow they can give 'im the job I can't think !' His soliloquy was here interrupted by the approach of his wife, bearing a valise.

" Don't you wish you was comin', old girl?" he remarked to her lightly.

" I do not; I'm glad to be shut of you. Keep his feet dry. What have you got under there? "

Joe Petty winked.

" What a lumbering great thing it looks ! " said Mrs. Petty, gazing upwards.

" Ah ! " returned her husband thoughtfully, " we'll 'ave the population round us without advertising." And taking the heads of two small boys who had come

11

up, he knocked them together in an absent-minded fashion.

"Well," said Mrs. Petty, "I can't waste time. Here's his extra set of teeth. Don't lose them. Have you got your own toothbrush? Use it, and behave your-self. Let me have a line. And don't let him get excited." She tapped her forehead. "Go away, you boys; shoo!"

The boys, now six in number, raised a slight cheer; for at that moment Mr. Lavender, in a broad-brimmed grey felt hat and a holland dust-coat, came out through his garden-gate carrying a pile of newspapers and pamphlets so large that his feet, legs, and hat alone were visible.

"Open the door, Joe!" he said, and stumbled into the body of the vehicle. A shrill cheer rose from the eight boys, who could see him through the further window. Taking this for an augury of success, Mr. Lavender removed his hat, and putting his head through the window, thus addressed the ten boys:

"I thank you. The occasion is one which I shall ever remember. The Government has charged me with the great task of rousing our country in days which demand of each of us the utmost exertions. I am proud to feel that I have here, on the very threshold of my task, an audience of bright young spirits, each one of whom in this democratic country has in him perhaps the makings of a General or even of a Prime Minister. Let it be your earnest endeavour, boys——"

At this moment a piece of india-rubber rebounded from Mr. Lavender's forehead, and he recoiled into the body of the car.

"Are you right, sir?" said Joe, looking in; and without waiting for reply he started the engine. The

12

car moved out amid a volley of stones, balls, cheers, and other missiles from the fifteen boys who pursued it with frenzy. Swaying slightly from side to side, with billowing bag, it gathered speed, and, turning a corner, took road for the country. Mr. Lavender, somewhat dazed, for the india-rubber had been hard, sat gazing through the little back window at the great city he was leaving. His lips moved, expressing unconsciously the sentiments of innumerable Lord Mayors: " Greatest City in the world, Queen of Commerce, whose full heart I can still hear beating behind me, in mingled pride and regret I leave you. With the most sacred gratitude I lay down my office. I go to other work, whose—— Joe ! "

" Sir ? "

" Do you see that ? "

" I see your 'ead, that's all, sir."

" We seem to be followed by a little column of dust, which keeps ever at the same distance in the middle of the road. Do you think it can be an augury ? "

" No ; I should think it's a dog."

" In that case, hold hard ! " said Mr. Lavender, who had a weakness for dogs. Joe slackened the car's pace, and leaned his head round the corner. The column of dust approached rapidly.

" It *is* a dog," said Mr. Lavender ; " it's Blink."

The female sheep-dog, almost flat with the ground from speed, emerged from the dust, wild with hair and anxiety, white on the cheeks and chest and top of the head, and grey in the body and the very little tail, and passed them like a streak of lightning.

" Get on ! " cried Mr. Lavender, excited ; " follow her ; she's trying to catch us up ! "

13

Joe urged on the car, which responded gallantly, swaying from side to side, while the gasbag bellied and shook; but the faster it went the faster the sheep-dog flew in front of it.

"This is dreadful!" said Mr. Lavender in anguish, leaning far out. "Blink! Blink!"

His cries were drowned in the roar of the car.

"Damn the brute!" muttered Joe; "at this rate she'll be over the edge in 'alf a mo'. Wherever does she think we are?"

"Blink! Blink!" wailed Mr. Lavender. "Get on, Joe, get on! She's gaining on us!"

"Well, I never see anything like this," said Joe; "chasin' wot's chasing you! Hi! Hi!"

Urged on by their shouts and the noise of the pursuing car, the poor dog redoubled her efforts to rejoin her master, and Mr. Lavender, Joe, and the car, which had begun to emit the most lamentable creaks and odours, redoubled theirs.

"I shall bust her up," said Joe.

"I care not!" cried Mr. Lavender. "I must recover the dog."

They flashed through the outskirts of the Garden City. "Stop her, stop her!" called Mr. Lavender to such of the astonished inhabitants as they had already left behind. "This is a nightmare, Joe!"

"It's a blinkin' day-dream," returned Joe, forcing the car to an expiring spurt.

"If she gets to that 'ill before we ketch 'er, we're done; the old geyser can't 'alf crawl up 'ills."

"We're gaining," shrieked Mr. Lavender; "I can see her tongue."

As though it heard his voice, the car leaped forward and stopped with a sudden and most formidable jerk;

14

the door burst open, and Mr. Lavender fell out upon his sheep-dog.

Fortunately they were in the only bed of nettles in that part of the world, and its softness and that of Blink assuaged the severity of his fall, yet it was some minutes before he regained the full measure of his faculties. He came to himself sitting on a milestone, with his dog on her hind legs between his knees, licking his face clean, and panting down his throat.

" Joe," he said ; " where are you ? "

The voice of Joe replied from underneath the car : " Here, sir. She's popped."

" Do you mean that our journey is arrested ? "

" Ah ! We're in irons. You may as well walk 'ome, sir. It ain't two miles."

" No, no ! " said Mr. Lavender. " We passed the Garden City a little way back ; I could go there and hold a meeting. How long will you be ? "

" A day or two," said Joe.

Mr. Lavender sighed, and at this manifestation of grief his sheep-dog redoubled her efforts to comfort him. ' Nothing becomes one more than the practice of philosophy,' he thought. ' I have always admired those great public men who in moments of national peril can still dine with a good appetite. We will sit in the car a little, for I have rather a pain, and think over a speech.' So musing, he mounted the car, followed by his dog, and sat down in considerable discomfort. ' What subject can I choose for a Garden City ? ' he thought, and remembering that he had with him the speech of a bishop on the subject of babies, he dived into his bundle of literature, and extracting a pamphlet began to con its periods. A sharp blow from a hammer on the bottom of the car just below

where Blink was sitting caused him to pause and the
dog to rise and examine her tiny tail.

'Curious,' thought Mr. Lavender dreamily, 'how
Joe always does the right thing in the wrong place.
He is very English.' The hammering continued, and
the dog, who traced it to the omnipotence of her
master, got upon the seat where she could lick his
face. Mr. Lavender was compelled to stop.

"Joe," he said, leaning out and down; "must
you?"

The face of Joe, very red, leaned out and up.
"What's the matter now, sir?"

"I am preparing a speech; must you hammer?"

"No," returned Joe, "I needn't."

"I don't wish you to waste your time," said Mr.
Lavender.

"Don't worry about that, sir," replied Joe; "there's
plenty to do."

"In that case I shall be glad to finish my speech."

Mr. Lavender resumed his seat and Blink her position
on the floor, with her head on his feet. The sound
of his voice soon rose again in the car like the buzzing
of large flies. "'If we are to win this war we must
have an ever-increasing population. In town and
countryside, in the palace and the slum, above all in
the Garden City, we must have babies.'"

Here Blink who had been regarding him with
lustrous eyes, leaped on to his knees and licked his
mouth. Again Mr. Lavender was compelled to
stop.

"Down, Blink, down! I am not speaking to you.
'The future of our country depends on the little
citizens born now. I especially appeal to women.
It is to them we must look——' "

16

" Will you 'ave a glass, sir ? "

Mr. Lavender saw before him a tumbler containing a yellow fluid.

" Joe," he said sadly, " you know my rule——"

" 'Ere's the exception, sir."

Mr. Lavender sighed. "No, no ; I must practice what· I preach. I shall soon be rousing the people on the liquor question, too."

" Well, 'ere's luck," said Joe, draining the glass. " Will you 'ave a slice of 'am ? "

" That would not be amiss," said Mr. Lavender, taking Joe's knife with the slice of ham upon its point. " ' It is to them that we must look,' " he resumed, " ' to rejuvenate the Empire and make good the losses in the firing-line.' " And he raised the knife to his mouth. No result followed, while Blink wriggled on her base and licked her lips.

" Blink ! " said Mr. Lavender reproachfully " Joe ! "

" Sir ! "

" When you've finished your lunch and repaired the car you will find me in the Town Hall or market-place. Take care of Blink. I'll tie her up. Have you some string ? "

Having secured his dog to the handle of the door and disregarded the intensity of her gaze, Mr. Lavender walked back towards the Garden City with a pamphlet in one hand and a crutch-handled stick in the other. Restoring the ham to its nest behind his feet, Joe finished the bottle of Bass. ' This is a bit of all right ! ' he thought dreamily. " Lie down, you bitch ! Quiet, will you ? How can I get my nap while you make that row ? Lie down ! That's better."

Blink was silent, gnawing at her string. The smile

deepened on Joe's face, his head fell a little to one side ; his mouth fell open ; a fly flew into it. ' Ah ! ' he thought, spitting it out ; ' dog's quiet now.' He slept.

III

MR. LAVENDER ADDRESSES A CROWD OF HUNS

' " Give them ginger ! " ' thought Mr. Lavender, approaching the first houses. ' My first task, however, will be to collect them.'

" Can you tell me," he said to a dustman, " where the market-place is ? "

" Ain't none."

" The Town Hall, then ? "

" Likewise."

" What place is there, then," said Mr. Lavender " where people congregate ? "

" They don't."

" Do they never hold public meetings here ? "

" Ah ! " said the dustman mysteriously.

" I wish to address them on the subject of babies."

" Bill ! Gent abaht babies. Where'd he better go ? "

The man addressed, however, who carried a bag of tools, did not stop.

" You 'ear ? " said the dustman, and urging his horse, passed on.

' How rude ! ' thought Mr. Lavender. Something cold and wet was pressed against his hand, he felt a turmoil, and saw Blink moving round and round him, curved like a horseshoe, with a bit of string dangling from her white neck. At that moment of discouragement the sight of one who believed in him gave Mr.

19

Lavender nothing but pleasure. "How wonderful dogs are !" he murmured. The sheep-dog responded by bounds and ear-splitting barks, so that two boys and a little girl wheeling a perambulator stopped to look and listen.

'She is like Mercury,' thought Mr. Lavender; and taking advantage of her interest in his hat, which she had knocked off in her effusions, he placed his hand on her head and crumpled her ear. The dog passed into an hypnotic trance, broken by soft grumblings of pleasure. 'The most beautiful eyes in the world!' thought Mr. Lavender, replacing his hat; 'the innocence and goodness of her face are entrancing.'

In his long holland coat, with his wide-brimmed felt hat all dusty, and the crutch-handled stick in his hand, he had already arrested the attention of five boys, the little girl with the perambulator, a postman, a maid-servant, and three old ladies.

"What a beautiful dog yours is !" said one of the old ladies ; "dear creature ! Are you a shepherd ?"

Mr. Lavender removed his hat.

"No, madam," he said ; "a public speaker."

"How foolish of me !" replied the old lady.

"Not at all, madam ; the folly is mine." And Mr. Lavender bowed. "I have come here to give an address on babies."

The old lady looked at him shrewdly, and, saying something in a low voice to her companions, passed on, to halt again a little way off.

In the meantime the rumour that there was a horse down in the Clemenceau Road had spread rapidly, and more boys, several little girls, and three soldiers in blue, with red ties, had joined the group round Mr. Lavender, to whom there seemed something more than providential in this rapid assemblage. Looking round him for a platform from which to address them, he saw nothing but the low wall of the little villa garden outside which he was standing. Mounting on this, therefore, and firmly grasping the branch of a young acacia tree to steady himself, he stood upright, while Blink, on her hind legs, scratched at the wall, whining and sniffing his feet. Encouraged by the low murmur of astonishment, which swelled rapidly into a shrill cheer, Mr. Lavender removed his hat, and spoke as follows :

" Fellow Britons, at this crisis in the history of our country I make no apology for addressing myself to the gathering I see around me. Here, in the cradle of patriotism and the very heart of Movements, I may safely assume that you are aware of the importance of Man-power. At a moment when every man of a certain age and over is wanted at the front, and every woman of marriageable years is needed in hospitals, in factories, on the land, or where not, we see as never before the paramount necessity of mobilising the forces of racial progress and increasing the numbers of our population. Not a man, not a woman can be spared from the great task in which they are now engaged, of defeating the common enemy. Side by side with our American cousins, with la belle France, and the Queen of the Adriatic, we are fighting to avert the greatest menace which ever threatened civilisation. Our cruel enemies are strong and ruthless. While I have any say in this matter, no man or woman shall be withdrawn from the sacred cause of victory ; better they should die to the last unit than that we should take our hands from the plough. But, ladies and gentlemen, we must never forget that in the place of every one who dies we must put two. Do not be content with ordinary

21

measures ; these are no piping times of peace. Never was there in the history of this country such a crying need for—for twins, if I may put it picturesquely. In each family, in each home where there are no families, let there be two babies where there was one, for thus only can we triumph over the devastation of this war." At this moment the now considerable audience, which had hitherto been silent, broke into a shrill " 'Ear, 'ear ! " and Mr. Lavender, taking his hand from the acacia branch to silence them, fell off the wall into the garden. Seeing her master thus vanish, Blink, who had never ceased to whine and sniff his toes, leaped over and landed on his chest. Rising with difficulty, Mr. Lavender found himself in front of an elderly man with a commercial cast of countenance, who said : " You're trespassing ! "

" I am aware of it," returned Mr. Lavender politely ; " and I beg your pardon. It was quite inadvertent, however."

" Rubbish ! " said the man.

" I fell off the wall."

" Whose wall do you think it is ? " said the man.

" How should I know ? " said Mr. Lavender ; " I am a stranger."

" Out you go," said the man, applying his boot to Blink.

Mr. Lavender's eyes blazed. " You may insult me," he said, " but you must not kick my dog, or I shall do you an injury."

" Try ! " said the man.

" I will," responded Mr. Lavender, taking off his holland coat.

To what extremities he would have proceeded cannot be told, for at this moment the old lady who had taken him for a shepherd appeared on the garden path, tapping her forehead with a finger.

"All right!" said the owner of the garden; "take him away!"

The old lady placed her hand within Mr. Lavender's arm. "Come with me, sir," she said, "and your nice doggie."

Mr. Lavender, whose politeness to ladies was invariable, bowed, and resuming his coat accompanied her through the garden gate. "He kicked my dog," he said; "no action could be more despicable."

"Yes, yes," said the old lady soothingly. "Poor doggie!"

The crowd, who had hoped for better things, here gave vent to a prolonged jeer.

"Stop!" said Mr. Lavender; "I am going to take a collection."

"There, there!" said the old lady. "Poor man!"

"I don't know what you mean by that, madam," said Mr. Lavender, whose spirit was roused; "I shall certainly take a collection, in the interests of our population." So saying he removed his hat, and disengaging his arm from the old lady's hand, moved out into the throng, extending the hat. A boy took it from him at once, and placing it on his head, ran off, pursued by Blink, who, by barking and jumping up increased the boy's speed to one of which he could never have thought himself capable. Mr. Lavender followed, calling out "Blink!" at the top of his voice. The crowd followed Mr. Lavender, and the old lady followed the crowd. Thus they proceeded until the boy, arriving at a small piece of communal water, flung the hat into the middle of it, and, scaling the wall, made a strategic detour and became a disinterested spectator among the crowd,

The hat, after skimming the surface of the pond, settled like a water-lily, crown downward, while Blink, perceiving in all this the hand of her master, stood barking at it wildly. Mr. Lavender arrived at the edge of the pond slightly in advance of the crowd.

" Good Blink ! " he said. " Fetch it ! Good Blink ! "

Blink looked up into his face, and, with the acumen for which her breed is noted, perceiving that he desired her to enter the water, backed away from it.

" She is not a water dog," explained Mr. Lavender to the three soldiers in blue clothes. " Good dog ; fetch it ! " Blink backed into the three soldiers, who, bending down, took her by head and tail, threw her into the pond, and encouraged her on with small stones pitched at the hat. Having taken the plunge, the intelligent animal waded boldly to the hat, and endeavoured by barking and making little rushes at it with her nose, to induce it to return to shore.

" She thinks it's a sheep," said Mr. Lavender ; " a striking instance of hereditary instinct."

Blink, unable to persuade the hat, mounted it with her fore-paws and trod it under.

" 'Ooray ! " shouted the crowd.

" Give us a shilling, guv-nor, an' I'll get it for yer ? "

" Thank you, my boy," said Mr. Lavender, producing a shilling.

The boy—the same boy who had thrown it in—stepped into the water and waded towards the hat. But as he approached, Blink interposed between him and the hat, growling and showing her teeth.

" Does she bite ? " yelled the boy.

" Only strangers," cried Mr. Lavender. " Blink ! "

Excited by her master's appeal, Blink seized the

jacket of the boy, who made for the shore, while the hat rested in the centre of the pond, the cynosure of the stones with which the soldiers were endeavouring to drive it towards the bank. By this time the old lady had rejoined Mr. Lavender.

" Your nice hat ! " she murmured.

" I thank you for your sympathy, madam," said Mr. Lavender, running his hand through his hair ; " in moments like these one realises the deep humanity of the British people. I really believe that in no other race could you find such universal interest and anxiety to recover a hat. Say what you will, we are a great nation, who only need rousing to show our best qualities. Do you remember the words of the editor : ' In the spavined and spatch-cocked ruin to which our inhuman enemies have reduced civilisation, we of the island breed still shine with undimmed effulgence in all those qualities which mark man out from the ravening beast ' ? "

" But how are you going to get your hat ? " asked the old lady.

" I know not," returned Mr. Lavender, still under the influence of the sentiment he had quoted ; " but if I had fifteen hats I would take them all off to the virtues which have been ascribed to the British people by all those great men who have written and spoken since the war began."

" Yes," said the old lady soothingly. " But I think you had better come under my sunshade. The sun is very strong."

" Madam," said Mr. Lavender, " you are very good, but your sunshade is too small. To deprive you of even an inch of its shade would be unworthy of anyone in public life." So saying, he recoiled from the proffered sunshade into the pond, which he had forgotten was behind him.

"Oh, dear!" said the old lady; "now you've got your feet wet!"

"It is nothing," responded Mr. Lavender gallantly. And seeing that he was already wet, he rolled up his trousers, and holding up the tails of his holland coat, turned round and proceeded towards his hat, to the frantic delight of the crowd.

'The war is a lesson to us to make little of little things,' he thought, securing the hat and wringing it out. 'My feet are wet, but—how much wetter they would be in the trenches, if feet can be wetter than wet through,' he mused with some exactitude. "Down, Blink, down!" For Blink was plastering him with the watermarks of joy and anxiety. 'Nothing is quite so beautiful as the devotion of one's own dog,' thought Mr. Lavender, resuming the hat, and returning towards the shore. The by-now-considerable throng were watching him with every mark of acute enjoyment; and the moment appeared to Mr. Lavender auspicious for addressing them. Without, therefore, emerging from the pond, which he took for his platform, he spoke as follows:

"Circumstances over which I have no control have given me the advantage of your presence in numbers which do credit to the heart of the nation to which we all belong. In the midst of the greatest war which ever threatened the principle of Liberty, I rejoice to see so many people able to follow the free and spontaneous impulses of their inmost beings. For, while we must remember that our every hour is at the disposal of our country, we must not forget the maxim of our fathers : 'Britons never will be slaves.' Only by preserving the freedom of individual conscience, and at the same time surrendering it whole-heartedly to every call which the State makes on us, can we hope to defeat the machinations of the arch enemies of mankind."

At this moment a little stone hit him sharply on the hand.

" Who threw that stone ? " said Mr. Lavender. " Let him stand out."

The culprit, no other indeed than he who had thrown the hat in, and not fetched it out for a shilling, thus menaced with discovery made use of a masterly device, and called out loudly :

" Pro-German ! "

Such was the instinctive patriotism of the crowd that the cry was taken up in several quarters ; and for the moment Mr. Lavender remained speechless from astonishment.   The cries of " Pro-German ! " increased in volume, and a stone hitting her on the nose caused Blink to utter a yelp ; Mr. Lavender's eyes blazed.

" Huns ! " he cried ; " Huns !   I am coming out."

With this prodigious threat he emerged from the pond at the very moment that a car scattered the throng, and a well-known voice said :

" Well, sir, you 'ave been goin' it ! "

" Joe," said Mr. Lavender, " don't speak to me ! "

" Get in."

" Never ! "

" Pro-Germans ! " yelled the crowd.

" Get in ! " repeated Joe.

And seizing Mr. Lavender as if collaring him at football, he knocked off his hat, propelled him into the car, banged the door, mounted, and started at full speed, with Blink leaping and barking in front of them.

Debouching from Piave Parade into Bottomley Lane, he drove up it till the crowd was but a memory before he stopped to examine the condition of his master. Mr. Lavender was hanging out of the window, looking back, and shivering violently.

" Well, sir," said Joe. " I don't think ! "

" Joe," said Mr. Lavender, " that crowd ought not to be at large. They were manifestly Huns ! "

" The speakin's been a bit too much for you, sir," returned Joe. " But you've got it off your chest, anyway."

Mr. Lavender regarded him for a moment in silence ; then putting his hand to his throat, said hoarsely :

" No, on my chest, I think, Joe. All public speakers do. It is inseparable from that great calling."

" 'Alf a mo ' ! " grunted Joe, diving into the recesses beneath the driving-seat. " 'Ere, swig that off, sir."

Mr. Lavender raised the tumbler of fluid to his mouth, and drank it off ; only from the dregs left on his moustache did he perceive that it smelled of rum and honey.

" Joe," he said reproachfully, " you have made me break my pledge."

Joe smiled.

" Well, what are they for, sir ? You'll sleep at 'ome to-night."

" Never," said Mr. Lavender. " I shall sleep at High Barnet ; I must address them there to-morrow on abstinence during the war."

" As you please, sir. But try and 'ave a nap while we go along." And lifting Blink into the car, where she lay drenched and exhausted by excitement, with the petal of a purple flower clinging to her black nose, he mounted to his seat and drove off. Mr. Lavender,

for years unaccustomed to spirituous liquor, of which
he had swallowed nearly half a pint neat, passed rapidly
into a state of coma. Nor did he fully regain consciousness till he awoke in bed the next morning.

IV

FALLS INTO THE DANGERS OF A PUBLIC LIFE

'At what time is my meeting?' thought Mr. Lavender vaguely, gazing at the light filtering through the Venetian blind. "Blink!"

His dog, who was lying beside his bed gnawing a bone which with some presence of mind she had brought in, raised herself and regarded him with the innocence of her species. 'She has an air of divine madness,' thought Mr. Lavender, 'which is very pleasing to me. I have a terrible headache.' And seeing a bellrope near his hand, he pulled it.

A voice said : " Yes, sir."

" I wish to see my servant, Joe Petty," said Mr. Lavender. " I shall not require any breakfast, thank you. What is the population of High Barnet ? "

" I'm sure I don't know what you're talking about, sir," answered the voice, which seemed to be that of his housekeeper ; " but you can't see Joe ; he's gone out with a flea in his ear. The idea of his letting you get your feet wet like that ! "

" How is this ? " said Mr. Lavender. " I thought you were the chambermaid of the inn at High Barnet ? "

" No, indeed," said Mrs. Petty soothingly, placing a thermometer in his mouth. " Smoke that a minute, sir. Oh ! look at what this dog's brought in ! Fie ! " And taking the bone between thumb and finger she cast

it out of the window ; while Blink, aware that she was
considered in the wrong, and convinced that she was in
the right, spread out her left paw, laid her head on her
right paw, and pressed her chin hard against it.   Mrs.
Petty, returning from the window, stood above her
master, who lay gazing up with the thermometer jutting
out through the middle of his moustache.

" I thought so ! " she said, removing it ; " a hundred
and one.   No getting up for you, sir !   That Joe ! "

" Mrs. Petty," said Mr. Lavender rather feebly, for
his head pained him excessively, " bring me the morning papers."

" No, sir.   The thermometer bursts at an 'undred an'
ten.   I'll bring you the doctor."

Mr. Lavender was about to utter a protest when he
reflected that all public men had doctors.

" About the bulletin ? " he said faintly.

" What ? " ejaculated Mrs. Petty, whose face seemed
to Mr. Lavender to have become all cheek-bones, eyes,
and shadows.   " Joe never said a word about a bullet.
Where, and however did you get it in ? "

" I did not say ' bullet in,' " murmured Mr. Lavender,
closing his eyes ; " I said bulletin.   They have it."

At this mysterious sentence Mrs. Petty lifted her
hands, and muttering the word " Ravin' ! " hastened
from the room.   No sooner had she gone, however,
than Blink, whose memory was perfect, rose, and going
to the window placed her forepaws on the sill.   Seeing
her bone shining on the lawn below, with that disregard
of worldly consequence which she shared with all fine
characters, she leaped through.   The rattle of the
Venetian blind disturbed Mr. Lavender from the
lethargy to which he had reverted.   ' Mr. John Lavender passed a good night,' he thought, ' but his condition

is still critical.' And in his disordered imagination he seemed to see people outside Tube stations, standing stock-still in the middle of the traffic, reading that bulletin in the evening papers. ' Let me see,' he mused, ' how will they run ? To-morrow I shall be better, but not yet able to leave my bed ; the day after to-morrow I shall have a slight relapse, and my condition will still give cause for anxiety ; on the day following—— What is that noise ? ' For a sound like the whiffling of a wind through dry sticks combined with the creaking of a saw had impinged on his senses. It was succeeded by scratching. " Blink ! " said Mr. Lavender. A heartrending whine came from outside the door. Mr. Lavender rose and opened it. His dog came in carrying her bone, and putting it down by the bed divided her attention between it and her master's legs, revealed by the nightshirt which, in deference to the great Disraeli, he had never abandoned in favour of pyjamas. Having achieved so erect a posture, Mr. Lavender, whose heated imagination had now carried him to the convalescent stage of his indisposition, felt that a change of air would do him good, and going to the window, leaned out above a lilac-tree. " Mr. John Lavender," he murmured, " has gone to his country seat to recuperate before resuming his public duties."

While he stood there his attention was distracted by a tall young lady of fine build and joyous colouring, who was watering some sweet-peas in the garden of the adjoining castle. Naturally delicate, Mr. Lavender at once sought a jacket, and, having put it on, resumed his position at the window. He had not watched her more than two minutes before he saw that she was cultivating the soil, and, filled with admiration, he leaned still further out and said :

"My dear young madam, you are doing a great work."

Thus addressed, the young lady, who had those roving grey eyes which see everything and betoken a large nature not devoid of merry genius, looked up and smiled.

"Believe me," continued Mr. Lavender, "no task in these days is so important as the cultivation of the soil ; now that we are fighting to the last man and the last dollar every woman and child in these islands should put their hands to the plough." And at that word his vision became feverishly enlarged, so that he seemed to see not merely the young lady, but quantities of young ladies, filling the whole garden.

"This," he went on, raising his voice, "is the psychological moment, the turning-point in the history of these islands. The defeat of our common enemies imposes on us the sacred duty of feeding ourselves once more. ' There is a tide in the affairs of men which taken at the flood leads on to——' Oh ! " For in his desire to stir his audience, Mr. Lavender had reached out too far, and losing foothold on his polished bedroom floor, was slipping down into the lilac-bush. He was arrested by a jerk from behind ; where Blink, moved by this sudden elopement of her master, had seized him by the nightshirt tails, and was staying his descent.

"Is anything up ? " said the young lady.

"I have lost my balance," thickly answered Mr. Lavender, whose blood was running to his head, which was now lower than his feet. "Fortunately, my dog seems to be holding me from behind. But if someone could assist her it would be an advantage, for I fear that I am slipping."

" Hold on ! " cried the young lady.   And breaking through the low privet hedge which separated the domains, she vanished beneath him with a low gurgling sound.

Mr. Lavender, who dared not speak again for fear that Blink, hearing his voice, might let go to answer, remained suspended, torn with anxiety about his costume. ' If she comes in,' he thought, ' I shall die from shame.   And if she doesn't, I shall die from a broken neck.   What a dreadful alternative ! '   And he firmly grasped the most substantial lilac boughs within his reach, listening with the ears of a hare for any sound within the room, in which he no longer was to any appreciable extent.   Then the thought of what a public man should feel in his position came to his rescue. ' We die but once,' he mused ; ' rather than shock that charming lady let me seek oblivion.'   And the words of his obituary notice at once began to dance before his eyes.   " This great public servant honoured his country no less in his death than in his life."   Then striking out vigorously with his feet he launched his body forward. The words " My goodness ! " resounded above him, as all restraining influence was suddenly relaxed ; Mr. Lavender slid into the lilac-bush, turned heels over head, and fell bump on the ground.   He lay there at full length, conscious of everything, and especially of the faces of Blink and the young lady looking down on him from the window.

" Are you hurt ? " she called.

" No," said Mr. Lavender ; " that is—er—yes," he added, ever scrupulously exact.

" I'm coming down," said the young lady.   " Don't move ! "

With a great effort Mr. Lavender arranged his

costume, and closed his eyes. 'How many lie like this, staring at the blue heavens!' he thought.

"Where has it got you?" said a voice; and he saw the young lady bending over him.

"In the dorsal region, I think," said Mr. Lavender. "But I suffer more from the thought that I—that you——"

"That's all right," said the young lady; "I'm a V.A.D. It *was* a bump! Let's see if you can——" and taking his hands she raised him to a sitting posture. "Does it work?"

"Yes," said Mr. Lavender rather faintly.

"Try and stand," said the young lady, pulling.

Mr. Lavender tried, and stood; but no sooner was he on his feet than she turned her eyes away. Great tears rolled down her cheeks; and she writhed and shook all over.

"Don't!" cried Mr. Lavender, much concerned. "I beg you not to cry. It's nothing, I assure you—nothing!" The young lady with an effort controlled her emotion, and turned her large grey eyes on him.

"The angelic devotion of nurses!" murmured Mr. Lavender, leaning against the wall of the house with his hand to his back. "Nothing like it has been seen since the world began."

"I shall never forget the sight!" said the young lady, choking.

Mr. Lavender, who took the noises she made for sobbing, was unutterably disturbed.

"I can't bear to see you distressed on my account," he said. "I am quite well, I assure you; look—I can walk!" And he started forth up the garden in his nightshirt and Norfolk jacket. When he turned round she was no longer there, but sounds of uncontrollable

35

emotion were audible from the adjoining garden. Going to the privet hedge, he looked over. She was lying gracefully on the grass, with her face smothered in her hands, and her whole body shaking. 'Poor thing!' thought Mr. Lavender. 'No doubt she is one of those whose nerves have been destroyed by the terrible sights she has seen!' But at that moment the young lady rose and ran as if demented into her castle. Mr. Lavender stayed transfixed. 'Who would not be ill for the pleasure of drinking from a cup held by her hand?' he thought. 'I am fortunate to have received injuries in trying to save her from confusion. Down, Blink, down!'

For his dog, who had once more leaped from the window, was frantically endeavouring to lick his face. Soothing her, and feeling his anatomy, Mr. Lavender became conscious that he was not alone. An old lady was standing on the garden path which led to the front gate, holding in her hand a hat. Mr. Lavender sat down at once, and gathering his nightshirt under him, spoke as follows:

"There are circumstances, madam, which even the greatest public servants cannot foresee, and I, who am the humblest of them, ask you to forgive me for receiving you in this costume."

"I have brought your hat back," said the old lady with a kindling eye; "they told me you lived here, and I was anxious to know that you and your dear dog were none the worse."

"Madam," replied Mr. Lavender, "I am infinitely obliged to you. Would you very kindly hang my hat up on the—er—weeping willow tree?"

At this moment a little white dog, who accompanied the old lady, began sniffing round Mr. Lavender, and

36

Blink, wounded in her proprietary instincts, placed her paws at once on her master's shoulders, so that he fell prone. When he recovered a sitting posture neither the old lady nor the little dog was in sight, but his hat was hanging on a laurel bush. 'There seems to be something fateful about this morning,' he mused; 'I had better go in before the rest of the female population——' and recovering his feet with difficulty, he took his hat, and was about to enter the house when he saw the young lady watching him from an upper window of the adjoining castle. Thinking to relieve her anxiety, he said at once :

" My dear young lady, I earnestly beg you to believe that such a thing never happens to me, as a rule."

Her face was instantly withdrawn, and, sighing deeply, Mr. Lavender entered the house and made his way upstairs. ' Ah ! ' he thought, painfully recumbent in his bed once more, ' though my bones ache and my head burns I have performed an action not unworthy of the traditions of public life. There is nothing more uplifting than to serve Youth and Beauty at the peril of one's existence. Humanity and Chivalry have ever been the leading characteristics of the British race ' ; and, really half-delirious now, he cried aloud : " This incident will for ever inspire those who have any sense of beauty to the fulfilment of our common task. Believe me, we shall never sheathe the sword until the cause of humanity and chivalry is safe once more."

Blink, ever uneasy about sounds which seemed to her to have no meaning, stood up on her hind legs and endeavoured to stay them by licking his face ; and Mr. Lavender, who had become so stiff that he could not stir without great pain, had to content himself by moving his head feebly from side to side until his dog, having taken her fill, resumed the examination of her bone. Perceiving presently that whenever he began to talk she began to lick his face, he remained silent, with his mouth open and his eyes shut, in an almost unconscious condition, from which he was roused by a voice saying :

"He is suffering from alcoholic poisoning."

The monstrous injustice of these words restored his faculties, and seeing before him what he took to be a large concourse of people—composed in reality of Joe Petty, Mrs. Petty, and the doctor—he thus addressed them in a faint, feverish voice :

"The pressure of these times, ladies and gentlemen, brings to the fore the most pushing and obstreperous blackguards. We have amongst us persons who, under the thin disguise of patriotism, do not scruple to bring hideous charges against public men. Such but serve the blood-stained cause of our common enemies. Conscious of the purity of our private lives, we do not care what is said of us so long as we can fulfil our duty to our country. Abstinence from every form of spirituous liquor has been the watchword of all public men since this land was first threatened by the most stupendous cataclysm which ever hung over the heads of a great democracy. We have never ceased to preach the need for it, and those who say the contrary are largely Germans or persons lost to a sense of decency." So saying, he threw off all the bedclothes, and fell back with a groan.

"Easy, easy, my dear sir!" said the voice. "Have you a pain in your back?"

"I shall not submit," returned our hero, "to the ministrations of a Hun; sooner will I breathe my last."

"Turn him over," said the voice. And Mr. Lavender found himself on his face.

"Do you feel that?" said the voice.

Mr. Lavender answered faintly into his pillow:

"It is useless for you to torture me. No German hand shall wring from me a groan."

"Is there mania in his family?" asked the voice.

At this cruel insult Mr. Lavender, who was nearly smothered, made a great effort, and clearing his mouth of the pillow, said:

"Since we have no God nowadays, I call the God of my fathers to witness that there is no saner public man than I."

It was, however, his last effort, for the wriggle he had given to his spine brought on a kind of vertigo, and he relapsed into unconsciousness.

IS CONVICTED OF A NEW DISEASE

THOSE who were assembled round the bed of Mr. Lavender remained for a moment staring at him with their mouths open, while Blink growled faintly from underneath.

"Put your hand here," said the doctor at last. "There is a considerable swelling, an appearance of inflammation, and the legs are a curious colour. You gave him three-quarters of a tumbler of rum—how much honey?"

Thus addressed, Joe Petty, leaning his head a little to one side, answered:

"Not 'alf a pot, sir."

"Um! There are all the signs here of something quite new. He's not had a fall, has he?"

"Has he?" said Mrs. Petty severely to her husband.

"No," replied Joe.

"Singular!" said the doctor. "Turn him back again; I want to feel his head. Swoollen; it may account for his curious way of talking. Well, shove in quinine, and keep him quiet, with hot bottles to his feet. I think we have come on a new war disease. I'll send you the quinine. Good morning!"

"Wot oh!" said Joe to his wife, then they were left alone with the unconscious body of their master. "Poor old Guv.! Watch and pray!"

"However could you have given him such a thing?"

"Wet outside, wet your inside," muttered Joe sulkily, "'as always been my motto. Sorry I give 'im the honey. Who'd ha' thought the product of an 'armless insect could 'a done 'im in like this?"

"Fiddle!" said Mrs. Petty. "In my belief it's come on through reading those newspapers. If I had my way I'd burn the lot. Can I trust you to watch him while I go and get the bottles filled?"

Joe dropped his lids over his greenish eyes, and, with a whisk of her head, his wife left the room.

'Gawd 'elp us!' thought Joe, gazing at his unconscious master, and fingering his pipe; ''ow funny women are! If I was to smoke in 'ere she'd have a fit. I'll just 'ave a whiff in the window, though!' And, leaning out, he drew the curtains to behind him and lighted his pipe.

The sound of Blink gnawing her bone beneath the bed alone broke the silence.

'I could do with a pint o' bitter,' thought Joe; and, noticing the form of the weekly gardener down below, he said softly:

"'Ello, Bob!"

"'Ello?" replied the gardener.

"'Ow's yours?"

"Nicely."

"Goin' to 'ave some rain?"

"Ah!"

"What's the matter with that?"

"Good for the crops."

"Missis well?"

"So, so."

"Wish mine was."

"Wot's the matter with her?"

41

" Busy ! " replied Joe, sinking his voice. " Never
'ave a woman permanent ; that's my experience."

The gardener did not reply, but stood staring at the
lilac-bush below Joe Petty's face. He was a thin man,
rather like an old horse.

" Do you think we can win this war ? " resumed Joe.

" Dunno," replied the gardener apathetically. " We
seem to be goin' back nicely all the time."

Joe wagged his head. " You've 'it it," he said.
And, jerking his head back towards the room behind
him, " Gov'nor's got it now."

" What ? "

" The new disease."

" What new disease ? "

" Wy the Run-abaht-an-tell-'em-'ow-to-do-it."

" Ah ! "

" 'E's fair copped it. In bed."

" You don't say ! "

" Not 'alf ! " Joe sank his voice still lower. " Wot'll
you bet me I don't ketch it soon ? "

The gardener uttered a low gurgle.

" The cats 'ave been in that laylock," he replied,
twisting off a broken branch. " I'll knock off now
for a bit o' lunch."

But at that moment the sound of a voice speaking
as it might be from a cavern, caused him and Joe
Petty to stare at each other as if petrified.

" Wot is it ? " whispered Joe at last.

The gardener jerked his head towards a window on
the ground floor.

" Someone in pain," he said.

" Sounds like the Guv'nor's voice."

" Ah ! " said the gardener.

" 'Alf a mo' ! " And, drawing in his head, Joe

peered through the curtains. The bed was empty and the door open.

" Watch it ! 'E's loose ! " he called to the gardener, and descended the stairs at a run.

In fact, Mr. Lavender had come out of his coma at the words, " D'you think we can win the war ? " And, at once conscious that he had not read the morning papers, had got out of bed. Sallying forth just as he was he had made his way downstairs, followed by Blink. Seeing the journals lying on the chest in the hall, he took all five to where he usually went at this time of the morning, and sat down to read. Once there, the pain he was in, added to the disorder occasioned in his brain by the five leaders, caused him to give forth a summary of their contents, while Blink pressed his knees with her chin whenever the rising of his voice betokened too great absorption, as was her wont when she wanted him to feed her. Joe Petty joined the gardener in considerable embarrassment.

" Shan't I not 'alf cop it from the Missis ? " he murmured. " The door's locked."

The voice of Mr. Lavender maintained its steady flow, rising and falling with the tides of his pain and his feelings. " What, then, is our duty ? Is it not plain and simple ? We require every man in the Army, for that is the *sine qua non* of victory. . . . We must greatly reinforce the ranks of labour in our shipyards—ships, ships, ships, always more ships ; for without them we shall infallibly be defeated. We cannot too often repeat that we must see the great drama that is being played before our eyes steadily, and we must see it whole. . . . Not a man must be taken from the cultivation of our soil, for on that depends our

very existence as a nation. Without abundant labour
of the right sort on the land we cannot hope to cope
with the menace of the pirate submarine. We must
have the long vision, and not be scuppered by the fears
of those who would deplete our most vital industry. . . .
In munition works," wailed Mr. Lavender's voice, as
he reached the fourth leader, " we still require the
maximum of effort, and a considerable reinforcement
of man-power will in that direction be necessary to
enable us to establish the overwhelming superiority
in the air and in guns which alone can ensure the defeat
of our enemies." . . . He reached the fifth in what was
almost a scream. " Every man up to sixty must be
mobilised ; but here we would utter the most emphatic
caveat. In the end this war will be won by the country
whose financial position stands the strain best. The
last copper bullet will be the deciding factor. Our
economic strength must on no account be diminished.
We cannot at this time of day afford to deplete the
ranks of trade and let out the very life-blood in our
veins. We must see," groaned Mr. Lavender, " the
problem steadily, and see it whole."

" Poor old geyser ! " said the gardener ; " 'e do
seem bad."

" 'Old me ! " said Joe. " I'll get on the sill and
see what I can do through the top o' the window."

He got up, and, held by the gardener, put his arm
through. There was the sound of considerable disturbance, and through the barking of Blink, Mr.
Lavender's voice was heard again : " Stanch in the
middle of the cataclysm, unruffled by the waters of
heaven and hell, let us be captains of our souls. Down,
Blink, down ! "

" He's out ! " said Joe, rejoining the gardener.

" Now for it, before my missis comes ! " and he ran into the house.

Mr. Lavender was walking dazedly in the hall with the journals held out before him.

" Joe," he said catching sight of his servant, " gét the car ready. I must be in five places at once, for only thus can we defeat the greatest danger which ever threatened the future of civilisation."

" Right-o, sir," replied Joe ; and, waiting till his master turned round, he seized him round the legs, and lifting that thin little body ascended the stairs, while Mr. Lavender, with the journals waving fan-like in his hands, his white hair on end, and his legs kicking, endeavoured to turn his head to see what agency was moving him.

At the top of the stairs they came on Mrs. Petty, who, having Scotch blood in her veins, stood against the wall to let them pass, with a hot bottle in either hand. Having placed Mr. Lavender in his bed and drawn the clothes up to his eyes, Joe Petty passed the back of his hand across his brow and wrung it out.

" Phew ! " he gasped ; " he's artful ! "

His wife, who had followed them in, was already fastening her eyes on the carpet.

" What's that ? " she said sniffing.

" That ? " repeated Joe, picking up his pipe ; " why I had to run to ketch 'im, and it fell out o' me pocket."

" And lighted itself," said Mrs. Petty, darting at the floor and taking up a glowing quid which had burned a little round hole in the carpet. " You're a pretty one ! "

" You can't foresee those sort o' things," said Joe.

" You can't foresee anything," replied his wife ; " you might be a Government. Here ! hold the

45

clothes while I get the bottles to his feet. Well I never! If he hasn't got——" And from various parts of Mr. Lavender's body she recovered the five journals. "For putting things in the wrong place, Joe Petty, I've never seen your like!"

"They'll keep 'im warm," said Joe.

Mr. Lavender, who, on finding himself in bed, had once more fallen into a comatose condition, stirred, and some words fell from his lips. "Five in one, and one in five."

"What does he say?" said Mrs. Petty, tucking him up.

"It's the odds against Candelabra for the Derby."

"Only faith," cried Mr. Lavender, "can multiply exceedingly."

"Here, take them away!" muttered Mrs. Petty, and dealing the journals a smart slap, she handed them to Joe.

"Faith!" repeated Mr. Lavender, and fell into a doze.

"About this new disease," said Joe. "D'you think it's ketchin'? I feel rather funny meself."

"Stuff!" returned his wife. "Clear away those papers and that bone, and go and take Blink out, and sit on a seat; it's all you're fit for. Of all the happy-go-lucky's you're the worst."

"Well, I never could worry," said Joe from the doorway; "'tisn't in me. So long!"

And dragging Blink by the collar, he withdrew.

Alone with her patient, Mrs. Petty, an enthusiast for cleanliness and fresh air, went on her knees, and, having plucked out the charred rim of the little hole in the carpet, opened the window wider to rid the room of the smell of burning. 'If it wasn't for me,' she

46

thought, leaning out into the air, 'I don't know what'd become of them.'

A voice from a few feet away said : "I hope he's none the worse. What does the doctor say ? "

Looking round in astonishment, Mrs. Petty saw a young lady leaning out of a window on her right.

" We can't tell at present," she said, with a certain reserve ; " he is going on satisfactory."

" It's not hydrophobia, is it ? " asked the young lady. " You know he fell out of the window ? "

" What ! " ejaculated Mrs. Petty.

" Where the lilac's broken. If I can give you a hand I shall be very glad. I'm a V.A.D."

" Thank you, I'm sure," said Mrs. Petty stiffly, for the passion of jealousy to which she was somewhat prone, was rising in her ; " there is no call." And she thought, ' V.A. indeed ! I know them.'

" Poor dear ! " said the young lady. " He did come a bump. It was awfully funny ! Is he—er——? " And she touched her forehead, where tendrils of fair hair were blowing in the breeze.

Inexpressibly outraged by such a question concerning one for whom she had a proprietary reverence, Mrs. Petty answered acidly :

" Oh dear no ! He is much wiser than some people ! "

" It was only that he mentioned the last man and the last dollar, you know," said the young lady, as if to herself, " but, of course, that's no real sign." And she uttered a sudden silvery laugh.

Mrs. Petty became aware of something tickling her left ear, and turning round, found her master leaning out beside her, in his dressing-gown.

" Leave me, Mrs. Petty," he said with such dignity that she instinctively recoiled. " It may seem to you," continued Mr. Lavender, addressing the young lady, " indelicate on my part to resume my justification, but as a public man I suffer, knowing that I have committed a breach of decorum."

" Don't you think you ought to keep quiet in bed ? " Mrs. Petty heard the young lady ask.

" My dear young lady," Mr. Lavender replied, " the thought of bed is abhorrent to me at a time like this. What more ignoble fate than to die in one's bed ? "

" I'm only asking you to live in it," said the young lady, while Mrs. Petty grasped her master by the skirts of his gown.

" Down, Blink, down ! " said Mr. Lavender, leaning still further out.

" For pity's sake," wailed the young lady, " don't fall out again, or I shall burst."

" Ah, believe me," said Mr. Lavender in a receding voice, " I would not pain you further for the world."

Mrs. Petty, exerting all her strength, had hauled him in.

" Aren't you ashamed of yourself, sir," she said severely, " talking to a young lady like that in your dressing-gown ? "

" Mrs. Petty," said Mr. Lavender mysteriously, " it might have been worse. I should like some tea with a little lemon in it."

Taking this for a sign of returning reason Mrs. Petty drew him gently towards the bed, and, having seen him get in, tucked him up and said :

" Now, sir, you never break your word, do you ? "

" No public man——" began Mr. Lavender.

" Oh, bother ! Now promise me to stay quiet in bed while I get you that tea."

" I certainly shall," replied our hero, " for I feel rather faint."

" That's right," said Mrs. Petty. " I trust you." And bolting the window, she whisked out of the room and locked the door behind her.

Mr. Lavender lay with his eyes fixed on the ceiling, clucking his parched tongue. ' God,' he thought, ' for one must use that word when the country is in danger—God be thanked for Beauty ! But I must not allow it to unsteel my soul. Only when the cause of humanity has triumphed, and with the avenging sword and shell we have exterminated that criminal nation, only then shall I be entitled to let its gentle influence creep about my being.' And drinking off the tumbler of tea which Mrs. Petty was holding to his lips, he sank almost immediately into a deep slumber.

VI

MAKES A MISTAKE, AND MEETS A MOON-CAT

THE old lady, whose name was Sinkin, and whose interest in Mr. Lavender had become so deep, lived in a castle in Frognal; and with her lived her young nephew, a boy of forty-five, indissolubly connected with the Board of Guardians. It was entirely due to her representations that he presented himself at Mr. Lavender's on the following day, and, sending in his card, was admitted to our hero's presence.

Mr. Lavender, pale and stiff, was sitting in his study, with Blink on his feet, reading a speech.

"Excuse my getting up, sir," he said; "and pray be seated."

The nephew, who had a sleepy, hairless face and little Chinese eyes, bowed, and sitting down, stared at Mr. Lavender with a certain embarrassment.

"I have come," he said at last, "to ask you a few questions in behalf of——"

"By all means," said Mr. Lavender, perceiving at once that he was being interviewed. "I shall be most happy to give you my views. Please take a cigarette, for I believe that is usual. I myself do not smoke. If it is the human touch you want, you may like to know that I gave it up when that appeal in your contemporary flooded the trenches with cigarettes and undermined the nerves of our heroes. By setting an example of

50

abstinence, and at the same time releasing more tobacco for our men, I felt that I was but doing my duty. Please don't mention that, though. And while we are on the personal note, which I sincerely deprecate, you might like to stroll round the room and look at the portrait of my father, behind the door, and of my mother, over the fireplace. Forgive my not accompanying you. The fact is—this is an interesting touch—I have always been rather subject to lumbago." And seeing the nephew Sinkin, who had risen to his suggestion, standing somewhat irresolutely in front of him, he added: "Perhaps you would like to look a little closely at my eyes. Every now and then they flash with an almost uncanny insight." For by now he had quite forgotten his modesty in the identification he felt with the journal which was interviewing him. "I am fifty-eight," he added quickly; "but I do not look my years, though my hair, still thick and full of vigour, is prematurely white—so often the case with men whose brains are continually on the stretch. The little home, far from grandiose, which forms the background to this most interesting personality is embowered in trees. Cats have made their mark on its lawns, and its owner's love of animals was sharply illustrated by the sheep-dog which lay on his feet clad in Turkish slippers. Get up, Blink!"

Blink, disturbed by the motion of her master's feet, rose and gazed long into his face.

"Look!" said Mr. Lavender, "she has the most beautiful eyes in the world."

At this remark, which appeared to him no saner than the others he had heard—so utterly did he misjudge Mr. Lavender's character—the nephew put down the notebook he had taken out of his pocket, and said:

" Has there ever been anything—er—remarkable about your family ? "

" Indeed, yes," said Mr. Lavender. " Born of poor but lofty parentage in the city of Rochester, my father made a living as a publisher ; my mother was a true daughter of the bards, the scion of a stock tracing its decent from the Druids ; her name was originally Jones."

" Ah ! " said the nephew Sinkin, writing.

" She has often told me at her knee," continued Mr. Lavender, " that there was a strong vein of patriotism in her family."

" She did not die—in—in——"

" No, indeed," interrupted Mr. Lavender ; she is still living there."

" Ah ! " said the nephew. " And your brothers and sisters ? "

" One of my brothers," replied Mr. Lavender, with pardonable pride, " is the editor of *Cud Bits*. The other is a clergyman."

" Eccentric," murmured the nephew absently. " Tell me, Mr. Lavender, do you find your work a great strain ? Does it——" and he touched the top of his head, covered with moist black hair.

Mr. Lavender sighed. " At a time like this," he said, " we must all be prepared to sacrifice our health. No public man, as you know, can call his head his own for a moment. I should count myself singularly lacking if I stopped to consider—er—such a consideration."

" Consider—er—such a consideration," repeated the nephew, jotting it down.

" He carries on," murmured Mr. Lavender, once more identifying himself with the journal, " grappling with the intricacies of this enormous problem; happy in the thought that nothing—not even reason itself—is too precious to sacrifice on the altar of his duty to his country. The public may rest confident in the knowledge that he will so carry on till they carry him out on his shield." And aware subconsciously that the interview could go no further than that phrase, Mr. Lavender was silent, gazing up with rather startled eyes.

"I see," said the nephew; "I am very much obliged to you. Is your dog safe?" For Blink had begun to growl in a low and uneasy manner.

"The gentlest creature in the world," replied Mr. Lavender, "and the most sociable. I sometimes think," he went on in a changed voice, "that we have all gone mad, and that animals alone retain the sweet reasonableness which used to be esteemed a virtue in human society. Don't take that down," he added quickly, "we are all subject to moments of weakness. It was just an *obiter dictum*.

"Make your mind easy," said the nephew, rising, "it does not serve my purpose. Just one thing, Mr. Lavender."

At this moment Blink, whose instinct had long been aware of some sinister purpose in this tall and heavy man, whose trousers did not smell of dogs, seeing him approach too near, bit him gently in the calf.

The nephew started back. "She's bitten me!" he said in a hushed voice.

"My God!" ejaculated Mr. Lavender, rising, and falling back again, so stiff was he. "Is it possible? There must be some good reason. Blink!"

Blink wagged her little tail, thrust her nose into his hand, removed it, and growled again.

53

"She is quite well, I assure you," Mr. Lavender added hastily; "her nose is icy."

"She's bitten me," repeated the nephew, pulling up his trouser leg. "There's no mark, but she distinctly bit me."

"Treasure!" said Mr. Lavender, endeavouring to interest him in the dog. "Do you notice how dark the rims of her eyes are, and how clear the whites? Extraordinarily well bred. Blink!"

Aware that she was being talked of Blink continued to be torn between the desire to wag her tail and to growl. Unable to make up her mind, she sighed heavily and fell on her side against her master's legs.

"Wonderful with sheep, too," said Mr. Lavender; "at least, she would be if they would let her. You should see her with them on the heath. They simply can't bear her."

"You will hear from me again," said the nephew sourly.

"Thank you," said Mr. Lavender. "I shall be glad of a proof; it is always safer, I believe."

"Good morning," said the nephew.

Blink, who alone perceived the dark meaning in these words, seeing him move towards the door began to bark and run from side to side behind him, for all the world as if he had been a flock of sheep.

"Keep her off!" said the nephew anxiously. "Keep her off. I refuse to be bitten again."

"Blink!" called Mr. Lavender in some agony. Blink, whose obedience was excessive, came back to him at once, and stood growling from under her master's hand, laid on the white hair which flowed back from her collar, till the nephew's footsteps had died away. 'I cannot imagine,' thought Mr. Lavender,

' why she should have taken exception to that excellent journalist. Perhaps he did not smell quite right? One never knows.'

And with her moustachioed muzzle pressed to his chin Mr. Lavender sought for explanation in the innocent and living darkness of his dog's eyes. . . .

On leaving Mr. Lavender's the nephew forthwith returned to the castle in Frognal, and sought his aunt.

"Mad as a March hare, Aunt Rosie; and his dog bit me."

" That dear doggie ? "

" They're dangerous."

" You were always funny about dogs, dear," said his aunt soothingly. "Why, even Sealey doesn't really like you." And calling to the little low white dog she quite failed to attract his attention. " Did you notice his dress ? The first time I took him for a shepherd, and the second time——! What do you think ought to be done ? "

" He'll have to be watched," said the nephew. " We can't have lunatics at large in Hampstead."

" But, Wilfred," said the old lady, " will our man-power stand it ? Couldn't they watch each other ? Or, if it would be any help, I could watch him myself. I took such a fancy to his dear dog."

" I shall take steps," said the nephew.

" No, don't do that. I'll go and call on the people next door. Their name is Scarlet. They'll know about him, no doubt. We mustn't do anything inconsiderate."

The nephew, muttering and feeling his calf, withdrew to his study. And the old lady, having put on her bonnet, set forth placidly, unaccompanied by her little white dog.

On arriving at the castle embedded in acacias and laurustinus she asked of the maid who opened : " Can I see Mrs. Scarlet ? "

" No," replied the girl dispassionately ; " she's dead."

" Mr. Scarlet, then ? "

" No," replied the girl : " he's a major."

" Oh, dear ! " said the old lady.

" Miss Isabel's at home," said the girl, who appeared, like so many people in time of war, to be of a simple, plain-spoken nature ; " you'll find her in the garden." And she let the old lady out through a French window.

At the far end, under an acacia, Mrs. Sinkin could see the form of a young lady in a blue dress, lying in a hammock, with a cigarette between her lips and a yellow book in her hands. She approached her thinking, ' Dear me ! how comfortable, in these days ! ' And, putting her head a little on one side, she said with a smile : " My name is Sinkin, I hope I'm not disturbing you."

The young lady rose with a vigorous gesture.

" Oh, no ! Not a bit."

" I do admire some people," said the old lady ; " they seem to find time for everything."

The young lady stretched herself joyously.

" I'm taking it out before going to my new hospital. Try it," she said touching the hammock ; " it's not bad. Will you have a cigarette ? "

" I'm afraid I'm too old for both," said the old lady, " though I've often thought they must be delightfully soothing. I wanted to speak to you about your neighbour."

The young lady rolled her large grey eyes. "Ah!" she said, "he's perfectly sweet."

"I know," said the old lady, "and has such a dear dog. My nephew's very interested in them. You may have heard of him—Wilfred Sinkin—a very clever man; on so many Committees."

"Not really?" said the young lady.

"Oh, yes! He has one of those heads which nothing can disturb; so valuable in these days."

"And what sort of a heart?" asked the young lady, emitting a ring of smoke.

"Just as serene. I oughtn't to say so, but I think he's rather a wonderful machine."

"So long as he's not a doctor! You can't think how they get on your nerves when they're like that. I've bumped up against so many of them. They fired me at last!"

"Really! Where? I thought they only did that to the dear horses. Oh, what a pretty laugh you have! It's so pleasant to hear anyone laugh in these days."

"I thought no one did anything else! I mean, what else can you so, except die, don't you know?"

"I think that's *rather* a gloomy view," said the old lady placidly. "But about your neighbour. What is his name?"

"Lavender. But I call him Don Pickwixote."

"Dear me, do you indeed? Have you noticed anything very eccentric about him?"

"That depends on what you call eccentric. Wearing a nightshirt, for instance? I don't know what your standard is, you see."

The old lady was about to reply when a voice from the adjoining garden was heard saying:

"Blink! Don't touch that charming moon-cat!"

"Hush!" murmured the young lady; and seizing her visitor's arm, she drew her vigorously beneath the acacia tree. Sheltered from observation by those thick and delicate branches, they stooped, and applying their eyes to holes in the privet hedge, could see a very little cat, silvery-fawn in colour and far advanced in kittens, holding up its paw exactly like a dog, and gazing with sherry-coloured eyes at Mr. Lavender, who stood in the middle of his lawn, with Blink behind him.

"If you see me going to laugh," whispered the young lady, "pinch me hard."

"Moon-cat," repeated Mr. Lavender, "where have you come from? And what do you want, holding up your paw like that? What curious little noises you make, duckie." The cat, indeed, was uttering sounds rather like a duck. It came closer to Mr. Lavender, circled his legs, and rubbed itself against Blink's chest, while its tapered tail, barred with silver, brushed her mouth.

"This is extraordinary," they heard Mr. Lavender say; "I would stroke it if I wasn't so stiff. How nice of you little moon-cat to be friendly to my play-girl! For what is there in all the world so pleasant to see as friendliness between a cat and dog!"

At those words the old lady, who was a great lover of animals, was so affected that she pinched the young lady by mistake.

"Not yet!" whispered the latter in some agony. "Listen!"

"Moon-cat," Mr. Lavender was saying, "Arcadia is in your golden eyes. You have come, no doubt, to show us how far we have strayed away from it." And too stiff to reach the cat by bending, Mr.

Lavender let himself slowly down till he could sit. " Pan is dead," he said, as he arrived on the grass and crossed his feet, " and Christ is not alive. Moon-cat ! "

The little cat had put its head into his hand, while Blink was thrusting her nose into his mouth.

" I'm going to sneeze ! " whispered the old·lady, strangely affected.

" Pull your upper lip down hard, like the German Empress, and count nine ! " murmured the young.

While the old lady was doing this Mr. Lavender had again begun to speak.

" Life is now nothing but explosions. Gentleness has vanished, and beauty is a dream. When you have your kittens, moon-cat, bring them up in amity, to love milk, dogs, and the sun."

The moon-cat, who had now reached his shoulder, brushed the tip of her tail across his loose right eye-brow, while Blink's jealous tongue avidly licked his high left cheek-bone. With one hand Mr. Lavender was cuddling the cat's head, with the other twiddling Blink's forelock, and the watchers could see his eyes shining, and his white hair standing up all ruffled.

" Isn't it sweet ? " murmured the old lady.

" Now pinch me ! " whispered the young : " Lower, harder ! Oo ! "

" Ah ! moon-cat," went on Mr. Lavender, " come and live with us ! You shall have your kittens in the bathroom, and forget this age of blood and iron."

Both the old lady and the young were removing moisture from their eyes when the voice of Mr. Lavender, very changed, recalled them to their vigil. His face had become strained and troubled.

" Never," he was saying, " will we admit that doctrine of our common enemies. Might is not

59

right, gentlemen; those who take the sword shall perish by the sword. With blood and iron we will ourselves stamp out this noxious breed. No stone shall be left standing, and no babe sleeping in that abandoned country. We will restore the rule of humanity, if we have to wade through rivers of blood, across mountains of iron."

"Whom is he calling gentlemen?" whispered the old lady.

But Blink, by anxiously licking Mr. Lavender's lips, had produced a silence in which the young lady did not dare reply. The sound of the little cat's purring broke the hush.

"Down, Blink, down!" said Mr. Lavender. "Watch this little moon-cat and her perfect manners! We may all learn from her how not to be crude. See the light shining through her pretty ears!"

The little cat, who had seen a bird, had left Mr. Lavender's shoulder and was now crouching and moving the tip of its tail from side to side.

"She would like a bird inside her; but let us rather go and find her some milk instead," said Mr. Lavender, and he began to rise.

"Do you know, I think he's quite sane," whispered the old lady, "except, perhaps, at intervals. What do you?"

"Glorious print!" cried Mr. Lavender suddenly, for a journal had fallen from his pocket, and the sight of it lying there, out of his reach, excited him. "Glorious print! I can read you even from here. 'When the enemy of mankind uses the word God he commits blasphemy! How different from us!'" And rising his eyes from the journal Mr. Lavender fastened them, as it seemed to his anxious listeners, on the tree which

60

sheltered them. "Yes! Those unseen presences, who search out the workings of our heart, know that even the most jingo among us can say, ' I am not as they are! ' Come moon-cat! "

So murmuring, he turned and moved towards the house, clucking with his tongue, and followed by Blink.

"Did he mean *us* ? " said the old lady nervously.

"No ; that was one of his intervals. He's not mad ; he's just crazy."

"Is there any difference, my dear ? "

"Why, we're all crazy about something, you know ; it's only a question of what."

"But what is *his* what ? "

"He's got a message. They're in the air, you know."

"I haven't come across them," said the old lady. "I fear I live a very quiet life—except for picking over sphagnum moss."

"Oh, well! There's no hurry."

"Well, I shall tell my nephew what I've seen," said the old lady. "Good-bye."

"Good-bye," responded the young ; and, picking up her yellow book, she got back into the hammock and relighted her cigarette.

VII

SEES AN EDITOR AND FINDS A FARMER

Not for some days after his fall from the window did Mr. Lavender begin to regain the elasticity of body necessary to the resumption of public life. He spent the hours profitably, however, in digesting the newspapers and storing ardour. On Tuesday morning, remembering that no proof of his interview had yet been sent him, and feeling that he ought not to neglect so important a matter, he set forth to the office of the great journal from which, in the occult fashion of the faithful, he was convinced the reporter had come. While he was asking for the editor in the stony entrance, a young man who was passing looked at him attentively and said : " Ah, sir, here you are ! He's waiting for you. Come up, will you ? "

Mr. Lavender followed up some stairs, greatly gratified at the thought that he was expected. The young man led him through one or two swing doors into an outer office, where a young woman was typing.

" Half a moment," said the young man, and passed through a door. Mr. Lavender heard a voice speaking, and almost directly four gentlemen, exuding laughter, issued in single file, holding notebooks in their hands.

" Now, sir," said the young man, returning.

Mr. Lavender entered a room of excellent proportions, almost luxuriously furnished, where a man with grey hair, a long upper lip, and a veiled eye, was laying back in a chair at a bureau, smoking a cigar. He rose on seeing his visitor, and held out his hand.

" Glad to see you, sir," he said. " Sit down. Do you smoke ? "

Mr. Lavender shook his head, and sat down on the edge of a green leather chair. The editor, resuming his seat, crossed his legs deferentially, and sinking his chin again on his chest, began :

" About your article. My only trouble, of course, is that I'm running that stunt on British prisoners— great success ! You've seen it, I suppose ? "

" Yes, indeed," said Mr. Lavender ; " I read you every day."

The editor made a little movement which showed that he was flattered, and sinking his chin still further into his chest, resumed :

" It might run another week, or it might fall down to-morrow—you never can tell. But I'm getting lots of letters. Tremendous public interest."

" Yes, yes," assented Mr. Lavender ; " it's most important."

" Of course, we might run yours with it," said the editor. " But I don't know ; I think it'd kill the other. Still——"

" I shouldn't like——" began Mr. Lavender.

" I don't believe in giving them more than they want, you know," resumed the editor. " I think I'll have my news editor in," and he blew into a tube. " Send me Mr. Crackamup. This thing of yours is very important, sir. Suppose we began to run it on Thursday. Yes, I should think they'll be tired of British prisoners by then."

" Don't let me——" began Mr. Lavender.

The editor's eye became unveiled for the moment.

" You'll be wanting to take it somewhere else if we——
Quite ! Well, I think we *could* run them together.
See here, Mr. Crackamup "—Mr. Lavender saw a small
man like Beethoven frowning from behind spectacles—
" could we run this German prisoner stunt alongside
the British, or d'you think it would kill it ? "

Mr. Lavender almost rose from his chair in surprise.
" Are you——" he said ; " is it——"

The small man hiccoughed, and said in a raw voice :
" The letters are falling off."

" Ah ! " murmured the editor, " I thought we should
be through by Thursday. We'll start this new stunt
Thursday. Give it all prominence, Crackamup. It'll
focus fury. All to the good—all to the good.
Opinion's ripe." Then for a moment he seemed to
hesitate, and his chin sank back on his chest. " I don't
know," he murmured ; " of course it may——"

" Please," began Mr. Lavender, rising, while the
small man hiccoughed again. The two motions
seemed to determine the editor.

" That's all right, sir," he said, rising also; " that's
quite all right. We'll say Thursday, and risk it.
Thursday, Crackamup." And he held out his hand to
Mr. Lavender. " Good morning, sir, good morning.
Delighted to have seen you. You wouldn't put your
name to it ? Well, well, it doesn't matter ; only *you*
could have written it. The turn of phrase—immense !
They'll tumble all right ! " And Mr. Lavender found
himself, with Mr. Crackamup, in the lobby. ' It's
bewildering,' he thought, ' how quickly he settled that.
And yet he had such repose. But is there some mistake ? ' He was about to ask his companion, but with a
distant hiccough the small man had vanished. Thus
deserted, Mr. Lavender was in two minds whether to

ask to be readmitted, when the four gentlemen with notebooks repassed him in single file into the editor's room.

"My name is Lavender," he said resolutely to the young woman. "Is that all right?"

"Quite," she answered, without looking up.

Mr. Lavender went out slowly, thinking, ' I may perhaps have said more in that interview than I remember. Next time I really will insist on having a proof. Or have they taken me for some other public man?' This notion was so disagreeable, however, that he dismissed it, and passed into the street.

On Thursday, the day fixed for his fresh tour of public speaking, he opened the great journal eagerly. Above the third column was the headline: "OUR VITAL DUTY: BY A GREAT PUBLIC MAN." ' That must be it,' he thought. The article, which occupied just a column of precious space, began with an appeal so moving that before he had read twenty lines Mr. Lavender had identified himself completely with the writer; and if anyone had told him that he had not uttered these sentiments, he would have given him the lie direct. Working from heat to heat the article finished in a glorious outburst with a passionate appeal to the country to starve all German prisoners. Mr. Lavender put it down in a glow of exultation. ' I shall translate words into action,' he thought; ' I shall at once visit a rural district where German prisoners are working on the land, and see that the farmers do their duty.' And, forgetting in his excitement to eat his breakfast, he put the journal in his pocket, wrapped himself in his dust-coat and broad-brimmed hat and went out to his car, which was drawn up, with Blink, who had not forgotten her last experience, inside.

"We will go to a rural district, Joe," he said, getting in.

"Very good, sir," answered Joe; and, unnoticed by the population, they glided into the hazy heat of the June morning.

"Well, what abaht it, sir?" said Joe, after they had proceeded for some three hours. "Here we are."

Mr. Lavender, who had been lost in the beauty of the scenes through which he was passing, awoke from reverie, and said:

"I am looking for German prisoners, Joe; if you see a farmer, you might stop."

"Any sort of farmer?" asked Joe.

"Is there more than one sort?" returned Mr. Lavender, smiling.

Joe cocked his eye. "Ain't you never lived in the country, sir?"

"Not for more than a few weeks at a time, Joe, unless Rochester counts. Of course, I know Eastbourne very well."

"I know Eastbourne from the inside," said Joe discursively. "I was a waiter there once."

"An interesting life, a waiter's, Joe, I should think."

"Ah! Everything comes to 'im who waits, they say. But abaht farmers—you've got a lot to learn, sir."

"I am always conscious of that, Joe; the ramifications of public life are innumerable."

"I could give you some rummikins abaht farmers. I once travelled in breeches."

"You seem to have done a great many things, Joe."

"That's right, sir. I've been a sailor, a 'traveller,' a waiter, a scene-shifter, and a shover, and I don't know which was the cushiest job. But, talking of farmers : there's the old English type that wears Bedfords—don't you go near 'im, 'e bites. There's the modern scientific farmer, but it'll take us a week to find *'im*. And there's the small-'older, wearin' trahsers, likely as not ; I don't think 'e'd be any use to you."

" What am I to do then ? " asked Mr. Lavender.

" Ah ! " said Joe, " 'ave lunch."

Mr. Lavender sighed, his hunger quarrelling with his sense of duty. " I should like to have found a farmer first," he said.

" Well, sir, I'll drive up to that clump o' beeches, and you can have a look round for one while I get lunch ready."

" That will do admirably."

" There's just one thing, sir," said Joe, when his master was about to start ; " don't you take any house you come across for a farm. They're mostly cottages o' gentility nowadays, in'abited by lunatics."

" I shall be very careful," said Mr. Lavender.

' This glorious land ! ' he thought, walking away from the beech clump, with Blink at his heels ; ' how wonderful to see it being restored to its former fertility under pressure of the war ! The farmer must be a happy man, indeed, working so nobly for his country, without thought of his own prosperity. How flowery those beans look already ! ' he mused, glancing at a field of potatoes. " Now that I am here I shall be able to combine my work on German prisoners with an effort to stimulate food production. Blink ! " For Blink was lingering in a gateway. Moving back to her Mr. Lavender saw that the sagacious animal was staring through the gate at a farmer who was standing in a field perfectly still, with his back turned, about thirty yards away.

"Have you——" Mr. Lavender began eagerly; "is it—are you employing any German prisoners, sir?"

The farmer did not seem to hear. 'He must,' thought Mr. Lavender, 'be of the old stolid English variety.'

The farmer, who was indeed attired in a bowler hat and Bedford cords, continued to gaze over his land, unconscious of Mr. Lavender's presence.

"I am asking you a question, sir," resumed the latter in a louder voice. "And however patriotically absorbed you may be in cultivating your soil, there is no necessity for rudeness."

The farmer did not move a muscle.

"Sir," began Mr. Lavender again, very patiently, "though I have always heard that the British farmer is of all men least amenable to influence and new ideas, I have never believed it, and I am persuaded that if you will but listen I shall be able to alter your whole outlook about the agricultural future of this country." For it had suddenly occurred to him that it might be a long time before he had again such an opportunity of addressing a rural audience on the growth of food, and he was loth to throw away the chance. The farmer, however, continued to stand with his back to the speaker, paying no more heed to his voice than to the buzzing of a fly.

"You *shall* hear me," cried Mr. Lavender, unconsciously miming a voice from the past, and catching, as he thought, the sound of a titter, he flung his hand out, and exclaimed:

"Grass, gentlemen, grass is the hub of the matter. We have put our hand to the plough"—and, his imagination taking flight at those words, he went on in a voice calculated to reach the great assembly of farmers which he now saw before him with their backs turned—" and never shall we take it away till we have reduced every acre in the country to an arable condition. In the future not only must we feed ourselves, but our dogs, our horses, and our children, and restore the land to its pristine glory in the front rank of the world's premier industry. But me no buts," he went on with a winning smile, remembering that geniality is essential in addressing a country audience, " and butter me no butter, for in future we shall require to grow our margarine as well. Let us, in a word, put behind us all prejudice and pusillanimity till we see this country of ours once more blooming like one great cornfield, covered with cows. Sirs, I am no iconoclast; let us do all this without departing in any way from those great principles of Free Trade, Industrialism, and Individual Liberty which have made our towns the largest, most crowded, and wealthiest under that sun which never sets over the British Empire. We do but need to see this great problem steadily and to see it whole, and we shall achieve this revolution in our national life without the sacrifice of a single principle or a single penny. Believe me, gentlemen, we shall yet eat our cake and have it."

Mr. Lavender paused for breath, the headlines of his great speech in to-morrow's paper dancing before his eyes : " THE CLIMACTERIC—EATS CAKE AND HAS IT—A GREAT CONCLUSION." The wind, which had risen somewhat during Mr. Lavender's speech, fluttered the farmer's garments at this moment, so that they emitted a sound like the stir which runs through an audience at a moment of strong emotion.

" Ah ! " cried Mr. Lavender, " I see that I move you, gentlemen. Those have traduced you who call you unimpressionable. After all, are you not the backbone of this country up which runs the marrow which feeds the brain ; and shall you not respond to an appeal at once so simple and so fundamental ? I assure you, gentlemen, it needs no thought ; indeed, the less you think about it the better, for to do so will but weaken your purpose and distract your attention. Your duty is to go forward with stout hearts, firm steps, and kindling eyes ; in this way alone shall we defeat our common enemies." And at those words, which he had uttered at the top of his voice, Mr. Lavender stood like a clock which has run down, rubbing his eyes. For Blink, roaming the field during the speech, and encountering the quadruped called rabbit, which she had never seen before, had backed away from it in dismay, brushed against the farmer's legs and caused his breeches to fall down, revealing the sticks on which they had been draped. When Mr. Lavender saw this he called out in a loud voice : " Sir, you have deceived me. I took you for a human being. I now perceive that you are but a selfish automaton, rooted to your own business, without a particle of patriotic sense. Farewell ! "

VIII

STARVES SOME GERMANS

AFTER parting with the scarecrow Mr. Lavender, who felt uncommonly hungry, was about to despair of finding any German prisoners when he saw before him a gravel-pit, and three men working therein. Clad in dungaree, and very dusty, they had a cast of countenance so unmistakably Teutonic that Mr. Lavender stood still. They paid little or no attention to him, however, but went on sadly and silently with their work, which was that of sifting gravel. Mr. Lavender sat down on a milestone opposite, and his heart contracted within him. ' They look very thin and sad,' he thought; ' I should not like to be a prisoner myself, far from my country, in the midst of a hostile population, without a woman or a dog to throw me a wag of the tail. Poor men ! For, though it is necessary to hate the Germans, it seems impossible to forget that we are all human beings. This is weakness,' he added to himself, ' which no editor would tolerate for a moment. I must fight against it if I am to fulfil my duty of rousing the population to the task of starving them. How hungry they look already— their cheeks are hollow ! I must be firm. Perhaps they have wives and families at home, thinking of them at this moment. But, after all, they are Huns. What did the great writer say ? " Vermin—creatures no more worthy of pity than the tiger or the rat."

71

How true! And yet—Blink!' For his dog, seated on her haunches, was looking at him with that peculiarly steady gaze which betokened in her the desire for food. 'Yes,' mused Mr. Lavender, 'pity is the mark of the weak man. It is a vice which was at one time rampant in this country; the war has made one beneficial change at least—we are moving more and more towards the manly and unforgiving vigour of the tiger and the rat. To be brutal! This is the one lesson that the Germans can teach us, for we had almost forgotten the art. What danger we were in! Thank God, we have past masters again among us now!' A frown became fixed between his brows. 'Yes, indeed, past masters. How I venerate those good journalists and all the great crowd of witnesses who have dominated the mortal weakness, pity. "The Hun must and shall be destroyed—root and branch—hip and thigh—bag and baggage—man, woman, and babe —this is the sole duty of the great and humane British people. Roll up, ladies and gentlemen, roll up!" Great thought—great language! And yet——'

Here Mr. Lavender broke into a gentle sweat, while the Germans went on sifting gravel in front of him, and Blink continued to look up into his face with her fixed, lustrous eyes. 'What an awful thing,' he thought, 'to be a man.' If only I were just a public man and could, as they do, leave out the human and individual side of everything, how simple it would be! It is the being a man as well which is so troublesome. A man has feelings; it is wrong—wrong! There should be no connection whatever between public duty and the feelings of a man. One ought to be able to starve one's enemy without a quiver, to watch him drown without a wink. In fact, one ought to be a

German. We ought all to be Germans. Blink, we ought all to be Germans, dear! I must steel myself!' And Mr. Lavender wiped his forehead, for, though a great idea had come to him, he still lacked the heroic savagery to put it into execution. 'It is my duty,' he thought, 'to cause those hungry, sad-looking men to follow me and watch me eat my lunch. It is my duty. God give me strength! For unless I make this sacrifice of my gentler nature I shall be unworthy to call myself a public man, or to be reported in the newspapers. *En avant, de Bracy!*' So musing, he rose, and Blink with him. Crossing the road, he clenched his fists, and said in a voice which anguish made somewhat shrill:

"Are you hungry, my friends?"

The Germans stopped sifting gravel, looked up at him, and one of them nodded.

"And thirsty."

This time they all three nodded.

"Come on, then," said Mr. Lavender.

And he led the way back along the road, followed by Blink and the three Germans. Arriving at the beech clump whose great trees were already throwing shadows denoting that it was long past noon, Mr. Lavender saw that Joe had spread food on the smooth ground, and was, indeed, just finishing his own repast.

'What is there to eat?' thought Mr. Lavender, with a sort of horror. 'For I feel as if I were about to devour a meal of human flesh.' And he looked round at the three Germans slouching up shamefacedly behind him.

"Sit down, please," he said. The three men sat down.

"Joe," said Mr. Lavender to his surprised chauffeur,

" serve my lunch. Give me a large helping, and a glass of ale." And, paler than his holland dust-coat, he sat resolutely down on the bole of a beech, with Blink on her haunches beside him. While Joe was filling a plate with pigeon-pie and pouring out a glass of foaming Bass, Mr. Lavender stared at the three Germans and suffered the tortures of the damned. 'I will not flinch,' he thought; 'God helping me, I certainly will not flinch. Nothing shall prevent my going through with it.' And his eyes, more prominent than a hunted rabbit's, watched the approach of Joe with the plate and glass. The three men also followed the movements of the chauffeur, and it seemed to Mr. Lavender that their eyes were watering. ' Courage ! ' he murmured to himself, transfixing a succulent morsel with his fork and conveying it to his lips. For fully a minute he revolved the tasty mouthful, which he could not swallow, while the three men's eyes watched him with a sort of lugubrious surprise. 'If,' he thought with anquish, 'if I were a prisoner in Germany ! Come, come ! One effort, it's only the first mouthful ! ' and with a superhuman effort he swallowed. " Look at me ! " he cried to the three Germans, "look at me ! I—I—I'm going to be sick ! " and putting down his plate, he rose and staggered forward. " Joe," he said in a dying voice, " feed these poor men, feed them ; make them drink, feed them ! " And rushing headlong to the edge of the grove, he returned what he had swallowed—to the great interest of Blink. Then, waving away the approach of Joe, and consumed with shame and remorse at his lack of heroism, he ran and hid himself in a clump of hazel bushes, trying to sink into the earth. ' No,' he thought; ' no ; I am not for public life. I have failed at the first test. Was ever so squeamish an exhibition? I have betrayed my country and the honour of public life. These Germans are now full of beer and pigeon-pie. What am I but a poltroon, unworthy to lace the shoes of the great leaders of my land? The sun has witnessed my disgrace.'

How long he stayed there lying on his face he did not know before he heard the voice of Joe saying, " Wot oh, sir ! "

" Joe," replied Mr. Lavender faintly, " my body is here, but my spirit has departed."

" Ah ! " said Joe, " a rum upset—that there. Swig this down, sir ! " and he held out to his master a flask-cup filled with brandy. Mr. Lavender swallowed it.

" Have they gone ? " he said, gasping.

" They 'ave, sir," replied Joe, " and not 'alf full neither. Where did you pick 'em up ? "

" In a gravel-pit," said Mr. Lavender. " I can never forgive myself for this betrayal of my King and country. I have fed three Germans. Leave me, for I am not fit to mingle with my fellows."

" Well, I don't think ! " said Joe. " Germans ? "

Gazing up into his face Mr. Lavender read the unmistakable signs of uncontrolled surprise.

" Why do you look at me like that ? " he said.

" Germans ? " repeated Joe ; " what Germans ? Three blighters workin' on the road, as English as you or me. Wot are you talkin' about, sir ? "

" What ! " cried Mr. Lavender ; " do you tell me they were not Germans ? "

" Well, their names was Tompkins, 'Obson and Brown, and they 'adn't an aitch in their 'eads."

" God be praised ! " said Mr. Lavender. " I am,

then, still an English gentleman. Joe, I am very hungry ; is there nothing left ? "

" Nothin' whatever, sir," replied Joe.

" Then take me home," said Mr. Lavender ; " I care not, for my spirit has come back to me."

So saying, he rose, and supported by Joe, made his way towards the car, praising God in his heart that he had not disgraced his country.

IX

CONVERSES WITH A CONSCIENTIOUS OBJECTOR

" Yes," said Mr. Lavender, when they had proceeded some twenty miles along the road for home, " my hunger is excessive. If we come across an hotel, Joe, pull up."

" Right-o, sir," returned Joe. " 'Otels ain't what they were, but we'll find something. I've got your coupons."

Mr. Lavender, who was seated beside his chauffeur on the driving seat, while Blink occupied in solitude the body of the car, was silent for a minute, revolving a philosophic thought.

" Do you find," he said suddenly, " that compulsory sacrifice is doing you good, Joe ? "

" It's good for my thirst, sir," replied Joe. " Never was so powerful thirsty in me life as I've been since they watered beer. There's just enough in it to tickle you. That bottle o' Bass you would 'ave 'ad at lunch is the last of the old stock at 'ome, sir ; an' the sight of it fair gave me the wind up. To think those blighters 'ad it ! Wish *I'd* known they was Germans—*I* wouldn't 'ave weakened at it."

" Do not, I beg," said Mr. Lavender, " remind me of that episode. I sometimes think," he went on as dreamily as his hunger would permit, " that being forced to deprive oneself awakens one's worst passions ;

that is, of course, speaking rather as a man than a public man. What do you think will happen, Joe, when we are no longer obliged to sacrifice ourselves ? "

" Do wot we've been doin' all along—sacrifice someone else," said Joe lightly.

" Be serious, Joe," said Mr. Lavender.

" Well," returned Joe, " I don't know what'll 'appen to you, sir, but I shall go on the bust permanent."

Mr. Lavender sighed. " I do so wonder whether I shall too," he said.

Joe looked round at him, and a gleam of compassion twinkled in his greenish eyes. " Don't you worry, sir," he said ; " it's a question of constitootion. A week'd sew you up."

" A week ! " said Mr. Lavender with watering lips. " I trust I may not forget myself so long as that. Public men do not go ' on the bust,' Joe, as you put it."

" Be careful, sir ! I can't drive with one eye."

" How can they, indeed ? " went on Mr. Lavender ; " they are like athletes, ever in training for their unending conflict with the national life."

" Well," answered Joe indulgently, " they 'as their own kind of intoxication, too—that's true ; and the fumes is permanent ; they're gassed all the time, and chloroformed the rest."

" I don't know to what you allude, Joe," said Mr. Lavender severely.

" 'Aven't you never noticed, sir, that there's two worlds—the world as it is, and the world as it seems to the public man ? "

" That may be," said Mr. Lavender with some excitement. " But which is the greater, which is the nobler, Joe ? And what does the other matter ? Surely that which flourishes in great minds, and by

78

their utterances is made plain. Is it not better to live in a world where nobody shrinks from being starved or killed so long as they can die for their kings and countries, rather than in a world where people merely wish to live?"

"Ah!" said Joe; "we're all ready to die for our countries if we've got to. But we don't look on it, like the public speakers, as a picnic. They're a bit too light-'earted."

"Joe," said Mr. Lavender, covering his ears, and instantly uncovering them again, "this is the most horrible blasphemy I have ever listened to."

"I can do better than that, sir," answered Joe. "Shall I get on with it?"

"Yes," said Mr. Lavender, clenching his hands, "a public man shrinks from nothing—not even from the gibes of his enemies."

"Well, wot abaht it, sir? Look at the things they say, and at what really is. Mind you, I'm not speakin' particular of the public men in this country—or any other country; I'm speakin' of the lot of 'em in every country. They're a sort of secret society, brought up on gas. And every now and then someone sets a match to it, and we get it in the neck. Look 'ere, sir. Dahn squats one on his backside an' writes something in 'igh words. Up pops another and says something in 'igher; an' so they go on poppin' up an' squattin' dahn till you get an atmosphere where you can't breathe; and all the time all we want is to be let alone, and 'uman kindness do the rest. All these fellers 'ave got two weaknesses—one's ideas, and the other's their own importance. They've got to be conspicuous, and without ideas they can't, so it's a vicious circle. When I see a man bein' conspicuous, I says to meself: 'Gawd

79

'elp us, we shall want it!' And sooner or later we
always do. I'll tell you what's the curse of the world,
sir; it's the gift of expressin' what ain't your real
feeling. And—Lord! what a lot of us 'ave got it!"

"Joe," said Mr. Lavender, whose eyes were almost
starting from his head, "your words are the knell of
poetry, philosophy, and prose—especially of prose.
They are the grave of history, which, as you know, is
made up of the wars and intrigues which have originated
in the brains of public men. If your sordid views were
true, how do you suppose for one minute that in this
great epic struggle we could be consoled by the thought
that we are 'making history'? Has there been a single
utterance of any note which has not poured the balm
of those words into our ears? Think how they have
sustained the widow and the orphan, and the wounded
lying out in agony under the stars. 'To make history,'
'to act out the great drama'—that thought, ever kept
before us, has been our comfort and their stay. And
you would take it from us? Shame—shame!" repeated Mr. Lavender. "You would destroy all
glamour, and be the death of every principle."

"Give me facts," said Joe stubbornly, "an' you
may 'ave my principles. As to the other thing, I don't
know what it is, but you may 'ave it, too. And 'ere's
another thing, sir: haven't you never noticed that
when a public man blows off and says something, it
does 'im in? No matter what 'appens afterwards,
he's got to stick to it or look a fool."

"I certainly have not," said Mr. Lavender. "I
have never, or very seldom, noticed that narrowness in
public men, nor have I ever seen them 'looking fools'
as you rudely put it."

"Where are your eyes, sir?" answered Joe;

" where *are* your eyes ? I give you my word it's one or the other, though I admit they've brought camouflage to an 'igh art. But, speaking soberly, sir, if that's possible, public men are a good thing, and you can 'ave too much of it. But you began it, sir," he added soothingly, " and 'ere's your hotel. You'll feel better with something inside you."

So saying, he brought the car to a standstill before a sign which bore the words, " Royal Goat."

Mr. Lavender, deep sunk in the whirlpool of feeling which had been stirred in him by his chauffeur's cynicism, gazed at the square red-brick building with bewildered eyes.

" It's quite O.K.," said Joe ; " I used to call 'ere regular when I was travellin' in breeches. Where the commercials are gathered together the tap is good," he added, laying a finger against the side of his nose. " And they've a fine brand of pickles. Here's your coupon."

Thus encouraged, Mr. Lavender descended from the car, and, accompanied by Blink, entered the hotel and sought the coffee-room.

A maid of robust and comely appearance, with a fine free eye, divested him of his overcoat and the coupon, and pointed to a table and a pale and intellectual-looking young man in spectacles who was eating.

" Have you any more beef ? " said the latter, without looking up.

" No, sir," replied the maid.

" Then bring me the ham and eggs," he added. " Here's another coupon—and anything else you've got."

Mr. Lavender, whose pangs had leaped in him at the

word " beef," gazed at the bare bone of the beef-joint and sighed.

" I, too, will have some ham and a couple of poached eggs," he said.

" You can have ham, sir," replied the maid, " but there are only eggs enough for one."

" And I am the one," said the young man, looking up for the first time.

Mr. Lavender at once conceived an aversion from him ; his appearance was unhealthy, and his eyes ravened from behind the spectacles beneath his high forehead.

" I have no wish to deprive you of your eggs, sir," he said, " though I have had nothing to eat all day."

" I have had nothing to eat to speak of for six months," replied the young man ; " and in a fortnight's time I shall have nothing to eat again for two years."

Mr. Lavender, who habitually spoke the truth, looked at him with a sort of horror. But the young man had again concentrated his attention on his plate. ' How deceptive are appearances,' thought Mr. Lavender ; ' one would say an intellectual, not to say a spiritual type, and yet he eats like a savage, and lies like a trooper ! ' And the pinchings of his hunger again attacking him, he said rather acidly :

" May I ask you, sir, whether you consider it amusing to tell such untruths to a stranger ? "

The young man, who had finished what was on his plate, paused, and with a faint smile said :

" I spoke figuratively. You, sir, I expect have never been in prison."

At the word " prison " Mr. Lavender's natural kindliness reasserted itself at once. " Forgive me," he said gently ; " please eat all the ham. I can easily do with bread and cheese. I am extremely sorry you have had that misfortune, and would on no account do anything which might encourage you to incur it again. If it is a question of money or anything of that sort," he went on timidly, "please command me. I abhor prisons; I consider them inhuman; people should only be confined upon their honours."

The young man's eyes kindled behind his spectacles. "*I* have been confined," he said, "not upon my honour, but because of my honour; to break it in."

"How is that?" cried Mr. Lavender, aghast; "to break it in?"

"Yes," said the young man, cutting a large slice of bread, "there's no other way of putting it with truth. They want me to go back on my word, to go back on my faith, and I won't. In a fortnight's time they'll gaol me again, so I *must* eat—excuse me. I shall want all my strength." And he filled his mouth too full to go on speaking.

Mr. Lavender stared at him, greatly perturbed. 'How unjustly I judged him,' he thought; and seeing that the maid had placed the end of a ham before him, he began carving off what little there was left on it, and, filling a plate, placed it before the young man. The latter thanked him, and without looking up ate rapidly on. Mr. Lavender watched him with beaming eyes. 'It's lovely to see him!' he thought; 'poor fellow!'

"Where are the eggs?" said the young man suddenly.

Mr. Lavender got up and rang the bell.

"Please bring those eggs for him," he said.

"Yes, sir," said the maid. "And what are *you* going to have? There's nothing in the house now."

"Oh!" said Mr. Lavender, startled. "A cup of

coffee and a slice of bread, thank you. I can always eat at any time."

The maid went away muttering to herself, and bringing the eggs, plumped them down before the young man, who ate them more hastily than words could tell.

" I mean," he said, " to do all I can in this fortnight to build up my strength. I shall eat almost continuously. They shall never break me." And, reaching out, he took the remainder of the loaf.

Mr. Lavender watched it disappear with a certain irritation which he subdued at once. ' How selfish of me,' he thought, ' even to think of eating while this young hero is still hungry.'

" Are you, then," he said, " the victim of some religious or political plot ? "

" Both," replied the young man, leaning back with a sigh of repletion, and wiping his mouth. " I was released to-day, and, as I said, I shall be court-martialled again to-day fortnight. It'll be two years this time. But they can't break me."

Mr. Lavender grasped, for at the word " court-martialled " a dreadful doubt had assailed him.

" Are you," he stammered—" you are not—you cannot be a Conscientious Objector ? "

" I can," said the young man.

Mr. Lavender half rose in horror.

" I don't approve," he ejaculated ; " I do *not* approve of you."

" Of course not," said the young man with a little smile at once proud and said; " who does ? If you did I shouldn't have to eat like this, nor should I have the consciousness of spiritual loneliness to sustain me. You look on me as a moral outcast, as a leper. That is

84

my comfort and my strength. For though I have a genuine abhorrence of war, I know full well that I could not stick this if it were not for the feeling that I must not and will not lower myself to the level of mere opportunists like you, and sink myself in the herd of men in the street."

At hearing himself thus described Mr. Lavender flushed.

" I yield to no one," he said, " in my admiration of principle. It is because of my principles that I regard you as a——"

" Shirker," put in the young man calmly. " Go on ; don't mince words ; we're used to them."

" Yes," said Mr. Lavender, kindling, " a shirker. Excuse me ! A renegade from the camp of Liberty, a deserter from the ranks of Humanity, if you will pardon me."

" Say, a Christian, and have done with it ! " said the young man.

" No," said Mr. Lavender, who had risen to his feet, " I will not go so far as that. You are not a Christian, you are a Pharisee. I abhor you."

" And I abhor you," said the young man suddenly. " I am a Christian Socialist, but I refuse to consider you my brother. And I can tell you this : Some day when through our struggle the triumph of Christian Socialism and of Peace is assured, we shall see that you firebrands and jingoes get no chance to put up your noxious heads and disturb the brotherhood of the world. We shall stamp you out. We shall do you in. We who believe in love will take jolly good care that you apostles of hate get all we've had and more—if you provoke us enough that is."

He stopped, for Mr. Lavender's figure had rigidified

on the other side of the table into the semblance of one who is about to address the House of Lords.

"I can find here," he cried, "no analogy with religious persecution. This is a simple matter. The burden of defending his country falls equally on every citizen. I know not, and I care not, what promises were made to you, or in what spirit the laws of compulsory service were passed. You will either serve or go to prison till you do. I am a plain Englishman, expressing the view of my plain countrymen."

The young man, tilting back in his chair, rapped on the table with the handle of his dinner-knife.

"Hear, hear!" he murmured.

"And let me tell you this," continued Mr. Lavender, "you have no right to put a mouthful of food between your lips so long as you are not prepared to die for it. And if the Huns came here to-morrow I would not lift a finger to save you from the fate you would undoubtedly receive."

During this colloquy their voices had grown so loud that the maid, entering in dismay, had gone into the bar and informed the company that a Conscientious Objector had eaten all the food and was "carrying on outrageous" in the coffee-room. On hearing this report those who were assembled—being four commercial travellers far gone in liquor—taking up the weapons which came nearest to hand—to wit, four syphons—formed themselves two deep and marched into the coffee-room. Aware at once from Mr. Lavender's white hair and words that he was not the Objector in question, they advanced upon the young man, who was still seated, and taking up the four points of the compass, began squirting him unmercifully with soda-water. Blinded and dripping, the unfortunate young fellow tried desperately to elude the cordon of his persecutors, only to receive a fresh stream in his face at each attempt. Seeing him thus tormented, amid the coarse laughter of these half-drunken " travellers," Mr. Lavender suffered a moment of the most poignant struggle between his principles and his chivalry. Then, almost unconsciously grasping the ham-bone, he advanced and called out loudly :

" Stop ! Do not persecute that young man. You are four and he is one. Drop it, I tell you—Huns that you are ! "

The commercial fellows, however, laughed ; and this infuriating Mr. Lavender, he dealt one of them a blow with the ham-bone, which, lighting on the funny point of his elbow, caused him to howl and spin round the room. One of the others promptly avenged him with a squirt of syphon in Mr. Lavender's left eye ; whereon he incontinently attacked them all, whirling the ham-bone round his head like a shillelagh. And had it not been that Blink and the maid seized his coat-tails he would have done them severe injury. It was at this moment that Joe Petty, attracted by the hullabaloo, arrived in the doorway, and running up to his master, lifted him from behind and carried him from the room, still brandishing the ham-bone and kicking out with his legs. Dumping him into the car, Joe mounted hastily and drove off. Mr. Lavender sat for two or three minutes coming to his senses before full realisation of what he had done dawned on him. Then, flinging the ham-bone from him, he sank back among the cushions, with his chin buried on his chest. ' What have I done ? ' he thought over and over again. ' What *have* I done ? Taken up the bone for a Conscientious Objector—defended a renegade against great odds ! My God ! I am indeed less than a public man ! '

And in this state of utter dejection, inanition, and collapse, with Blink asleep on his feet, he was driven back to Hampstead.

X

DREAMS A DREAM AND SEES A VISION

THOUGH habitually abstemious, Mr. Lavender was so very hungry that evening when he sat down to supper that he was unable to leave the lobster which Mrs. Petty had provided until it was reduced to mere integument. Since his principles prevented his lightening it with anything but ginger-beer he went to bed in some discomfort, and, tired out with the emotions of the day, soon fell into a heavy slumber, which at dawn became troubled by a dream of an extremely vivid character. He fancied himself, indeed, dressed in khaki, with a breastplate composed of newspapers containing reports of speeches which he had been charged to deliver to soldiers at the front. He was passing in a winged tank along those scenes of desolation of which he had so often read in his daily papers, and which his swollen fancy now coloured even more vividly than had those striking phrases of the past, when presently the tank turned a somersault, and shot him out into a morass lighted up by countless star-shells whizzing round and above. In this morass were hundreds and thousands of figures sunk like himself up to the waist, and waving their arms above their heads. 'These,' thought Mr. Lavender, 'must be the soldiers I have come to speak to,' and he tore a sheet off his breastplate; but before he could speak from its columns it became thin air in his hand; and he went on tearing off sheet after sheet;

hoping to find a speech which would stay solid long enough for him to deliver it. At last a little corner stayed substantial in his hand, and he called out in a loud voice : " Heroes ! " But at the word the figures vanished with a wail, sinking into the mud, which was left covered with bubbles iridescent in the light of the star-shells. At this moment one of these, bursting over his head, turned into a large bright moon ; and Mr. Lavender saw to his amazement that the bubbles were really butterflies, perched on the liquid moon-lit mud, fluttering their crimson wings, and peering up at him with tiny human faces. " Who are you ? " he cried ; " oh ! who are you ? " The butterflies closed their wings ; and on each of their little faces came a look so sad and questioning that Mr. Lavender's tears rolled down into his breastplate of speeches. A whisper rose from them. " We are the dead." And they flew up suddenly in swarms, and beat his face with their wings.

Mr. Lavender woke up sitting in the middle of the floor, with light shining in on him through a hole in the curtain, and Blink licking off the tears which were streaming down his face.

" Blink," he said, " I have had a horrible dream." And still conscious of that weight on his chest, as of many undelivered speeches, he was afraid to go back to bed ; so, putting on some clothes, he went carefully downstairs and out of doors into the morning. He walked with his dog towards the risen sun, alone in the silvery light of Hampstead, meditating deeply on his dream. ' I have evidently,' he thought, ' not yet acquired that felicitous insensibility which is needful for successful public speaking. This is undoubtedly the secret of my dream. For the subconscious know-

ledge of my deficiency explains the weight on my chest
and the futile tearing of sheet after sheet, which vanished
as I tore them away. I lack the self-complacency
necessary to the orator in any surroundings, and that
golden certainty which has enchanted me in the out-
pourings of great men, whether in ink or speech. This
is, however, a matter which I can rectify with practice.'
And coming to a little may-tree in full blossom, he thus
addressed it :

" Little tree, be my audience, for I see in you, tipped
with the sunlight, a vision of the tranquil and beautiful
world, which, according to every authority, will emerge
out of this carnival of blood and iron."

And the little tree lifted up its voice and answered
him with the song of a blackbird.

Mr. Lavender's heart, deeply responsive to the voice
of Nature, melted within him.

" What are the realms of this earth, the dreams of
statesmen, and all plots and policies," he said, " com-
pared with the beauty of this little tree ? She—or is it
a he ?—breathes, in her wild and simple dress, just to
be lovely and loved. He harbours the blackbird, and
shakes fragrance into the morning ; and with her
blossom catches the rain and the sun drops of heaven.
I see in him the witchery of God ; and of her prettiness
would I make a song of redemption."

So saying he knelt down before the little tree, while
Blink on her haunches, very quiet beside him, looked
wiser than many dogs. A familiar gurgling sound
roused him from his devotions, and turning his head he
saw his young neighbour in the garb of a nurse, standing
on the path behind him. ' She has dropped from
heaven,' he thought : ' for all nurses are angels.' And,
taking off his hat, he said :

" You surprised me at a moment of which I am not ashamed; I was communing with Beauty. And behold! Aurora is with me."

" Say, rather, Borealis," said the young lady. " I was so fed-up with hospital that I had to have a scamper before turning in. If you're going home we might go together ? "

" It would, indeed, be a joy," said Mr. Lavender. " The garb of mercy becomes you."

" Do you think so? " replied the young lady, in whose cheeks a lovely flush had not deepened. " I call it hideous. Do you always come out and pray to that tree ? "

" I am ashamed to say," returned Mr. Lavender, " that I do not. But I intend to do so in future, since it has brought me such a vision." And he looked with such deferential and shining eyes at his companion that she placed the back of her hand before her mouth, and her breast rose.

" I'm most fearfully sleepy," she said. " Have you had any adventures lately—you and Samjoe ? "

" Samjoe ? " repeated Mr. Lavender.

" Your chauffeur—I call him that. He's very like Sam Weller and Sancho Panza, don't you think, Don Pickwixote ? "

" Ah ! " said Mr. Lavender, bewildered ; " Joe, you mean. A good fellow. He has in him the sort of heroism which I admire more than any other."

" Which is that ? " asked the young lady.

" That imperturbable humour in the face of adverse circumstances for which our soldiers are renowned."

" You are a great believer in heroics, Don Pick-wixote," said the young lady.

" What would life be without them ? " returned

Mr. Lavender. "The war could not go on for a minute."

"You're right there," said the young lady bitterly.

"You surely," said Mr. Lavender, aghast, "cannot wish it to stop until we have destroyed our common enemies?"

"Well," said the young lady, "I'm not a Pacifist; but when you see as many people without arms and legs as I do, heroics get a bit off, don't you know." And she increased her pace until Mr. Lavender, who was not within four inches of her stature, was almost compelled to trot. "If I were a Tommy," she added, "I should want to shoot every man who uttered a phrase. Really, at this time of day, they are the limit."

"Aurora," said Mr. Lavender, "if you will permit me, who am old enough—alas!—to be your father, to call you that, you must surely be aware that phrases are the very munitions of war, and certainly not less important than mere material explosives. Take the word 'Liberty,' for instance; would you deprive us of it?"

The young lady fixed on him those large grey eyes which had in them the roll of genius. "Dear Don Pickwixote," she said, "I would merely take it from the mouths of those who don't know what it means; and how much do you think would be left? Not enough to butter the parsnips of a Borough Council, or fill one leader in a month of Sundays. Have you not discovered, Don Pickwixote, that Liberty means the special form of tyranny which one happens to serve under; and that our form of tyranny is GAS?"

"High heaven!" cried Mr. Lavender, "that I should hear such words from so red lips!"

"I've not been a Pacifist, so far," continued the young lady, stifling a yawn, "because I hate cruelty,

I hate it enough to want to be cruel to it. I want the Huns to lap their own sauce. I don't want to be revengeful, but I just can't help it."

" My dear young lady," said Mr. Lavender soothingly, " you are not—you cannot be revengeful ; for every great writer and speaker tells us that revengefulness is an emotion alien to the Allies, who are merely just."

" Rats ! "

At this familiar word, Blink who had been following their conversation quietly, threw up her nose and licked the young lady's hand so unexpectedly that she started and added :

" Darling ! "

Mr. Lavender, who took the expression as meant for himself, coloured furiously.

" Aurora," he said in a faint voice, " the rapture in my heart prevents my taking advantage of your sweet word. Forgive me, and let us go quietly in, with the vision I have seen, for I know my place."

The young lady's composure seemed to tremble in the balance, and her lips twitched ; then holding out her hand she took Mr. Lavender's and gave it a good squeeze.

" You really *are* a dear," she said. " I think you ought to be in bed. My name's Isabel, you know."

" Not to me," said Mr. Lavender. " You are the Dawn ; nothing shall persuade me to the contrary. And from henceforth I swear to rise with you every morning."

" Oh, no ! " cried the young lady ; " please don't imagine that I sniff the matutinal as a rule. I just happened to be in a night shift."

" No matter," said Mr. Lavender ; " I shall see you with the eye of faith, in your night shifts, and draw

94

from the vision strength to continue my public work beckoned by the fingers of the roseate future."

"Well," murmured the young lady, "so long for now; and do go back to bed. It's only about five." And waving the tips of those fingers, she ran lightly up the garden-path and disappeared into her house.

Mr. Lavender remained for a moment as if transfigured; then, entering his garden, he stood gazing up at her window, until the thought that she might appear there was too much for him, and he went in.

XI

BREAKS UP A PEACE MEETING

WHILE seated at breakfast on the morning after he had seen this vision, Mr. Lavender, who read his papers as though they had been Holy Writ, came on an announcement that a meeting would be held that evening at a chapel in Holloway under the auspices of the " Free Speakers' League," an association which his journals had often branded with a reputation for desiring Peace. On reading the names of the speakers Mr. Lavender felt at once that it would be his duty to attend. ' There will,' he thought, ' very likely be no one there to register a protest. For in this country we have pushed the doctrine of free speech to a limit which threatens the noble virtue of patriotism. This is no doubt a recrudescence of that terrible horse-sense in the British people which used to permit everybody to have his say, no matter what he said. Yet I would rather stay at home,' he mused, ' for they will do me violence, I expect ; cowardice, however, would not become me, and I must go.'

He was in a state of flurry all day, thinking of his unpleasant duty towards those violent persons, and furbishing up his memory by reading such past leaders in his five journals as bore on the subject. He spoke no word of his intentions, convinced that he ran a considerable risk at the hands of the Pacifists, but too sensible of his honour to assist anyone to put that spoke in his wheel which he could not help longing for.

At six o'clock he locked Blink into his study, and arming himself with three leaders, set forth on his perilous adventure. Seven o'clock saw him hurrying along the dismal road to the chapel, at whose door he met with an unexpected check.

" Where is your ticket ? " said a large man.

" I have none," replied Mr. Lavender, disconcerted ; " for this is a meeting of the Free Speakers' League, and it is for that reason that I have come."

The large man looked at him attentively. " No admittance without ticket," he said.

" I protest," said Mr. Lavender. " How can you call yourself by that name and not let me in ? "

The large man smiled.

" Well," he said, " you haven't the strength of a rabbit—in you go ! "

Mr. Lavender found himself inside and in some indignation.

The meeting had begun, and a tall man at the pulpit end, with the face of a sorrowful bull, was addressing an audience composed almost entirely of women and old men, while his confederates sat behind him trying to look as if they were not present. At the end of a row, about half-way up the chapel, Mr. Lavender composed himself to listen, thinking, ' However eager I may be to fulfil my duty and break up this meeting, it behoves me as a fair-minded man to ascertain first what manner of meeting it is that I am breaking up.' But as the speaker progressed, in periods punctuated by applause from what, by his experience at the door, Mr. Lavender knew to be a packed audience, he grew more and more uneasy. It cannot be said that he took in

what the speaker was saying, obsessed as he was by the
necessity of formulating a reply, and of revolving, to
the exclusion of all else, the flowers and phrases of the
leaders which during the day he had almost learned by
heart.   But by nature polite he waited till the orator
was sitting down before he arose, and, with the three
leaders firmly grasped in his hand, walked deliberately
up to the seated speakers.   Turning his back on them,
he said, in a voice to which nervousness and emotion
lent shrillness :

" Ladies and gentlemen, it is now your turn, in ac-
cordance with the tradition of your society, to listen to
me.   Let us not mince matters with mealy mouths.
There are in our midst certain viperous persons, like
that notorious gentleman who had the sulphurous impudence to have a French father—French ! gentlemen ;
not German, ladies—mark the cunning and audacity
of the fellow ; like that renegade Labour leader, who
has never led anything, yet, if he had his will, would
lead us all into the pit of destruction ; like those other
high-brow emasculates who mistake their pettifogging
pedantry for pearls of price, and plaster the plain issue
before us with perfidious and Pacifistic platitudes.   We
say at once, and let them note it, we will have none
of them ; we will have——"   Here his words were
drowned by an interruption greater even than that
which was fast gathering among the row of speakers
behind him, and the surprised audience in front ; and
he could see the large man being forced from the door
and up the aisle by a posse of noisy youths, till he stood
with arms pinioned, struggling to turn round, just in
front of Mr. Lavender.   Seeing his speech thus endangered, the latter cried out at the top of his voice :
" Free speech, gentlemen, free speech ; I have come

here expressly to see that we have nothing of the sort."
At this the young men, who now filled the aisle, raised
a mighty booing.

"Gentlemen," shouted Mr. Lavender, waving his
leaders, "gentlemen——" But at this moment the
large man was hurled into contact with what served
Mr. Lavender for stomach, and the two fell in confusion. An uproar ensued of which Mr. Lavender was
more than vaguely conscious, for many feet went over
him. He managed, however, to creep into a corner,
and, getting up, surveyed the scene. The young men
who had invaded the meeting, much superior in
numbers and strength to the speakers, to the large man,
and the three or four other able-bodied persons who had
rallied to them from among the audience, were taking
every advantage of their superiority; and it went to Mr.
Lavender's heart to see how they thumped and mal-
treated their opponents. The sight of their brutality,
indeed, rendered him so furious that, forgetting all his
principles and his purposes in coming to the meeting,
he climbed on to a form, and folding his arms tightly
on his breast, called out at the top of his voice : "Cads !
Do not thus take advantage of your numbers. Cads ! "
Having thus defended what in his calmer moments he
would have known to be the wrong, he awaited his
own fate calmly. But in the hubbub his words had
passed unnoticed. 'It is in moments like these,' he
thought, ' that the great speaker asserts his supremacy,
quells the storm, and secures himself a hearing.' And
he began to rack his brains to remember how they did
it. ' It must require the voice of an ox,' he thought,
' and the skin of an alligator. Alas ! How deficient
I am in public qualities ! ' But his self-depreciation
was here cut off with the electric light. At this sheer

intervention of Providence Mr. Lavender, listening to the disentangling sounds which rose in the black room, became aware that he had a chance such as he had not yet had of being heard.

" Stay, my friends ! " he said ; " here in darkness we can see better the true proportions of this great question of free speech. There are some who contend that in a democracy every opinion should be heard ; that, just because the good sense of the majority will ever lead the country into the right paths, the minority should be accorded full and fair expression, for they cannot deflect the country's course, and because such expression acts as a healthful safety-valve. Moreover, they say there is no way of preventing the minority from speaking save that of force, which is unworthy of a majority, and the negation of what we are fighting for in this war. But *I* say, following the great leader-writers, that in a time of national danger nobody ought to say anything except what is in accord with the opinions of the majority ; for only in this way can we present a front which will seem to be united to our common enemies. I say, and since I am the majority I must be in the right, that no one who disagrees with me must say anything if we are to save the cause of freedom and humanity. I deprecate violence, but I am thoroughly determined to stand no nonsense, and shall not hesitate to suppress by every means in the power of the majority—including, if need be, Prussian measures —any whisper from those misguided and unpatriotic persons whose so-called principles induce them to assert their right to have opinions of their own. This has ever been a free country, and they shall not imperil its freedom by their volubility and self-conceit." Here Mr. Lavender paused for breath, and in the darkness a faint noise, as of a mouse scrattling at a wainscot, attracted his attention. 'Wonderful,' he thought, elated by the silence, ' that I should so have succeeded in riveting their attention as to be able to hear a mouse gnawing. I must have made a considerable impression.' And, fearing to spoil it by further speech, he set to work to grope his way round the chapel wall in the hope of cóming to the door. He had gone but a little way when his outstretched hand came into contact with something warm, which shrank away with a squeal.

" Oh ! " cried Mr. Lavender, while a shiver went down his spine, " what is that ? "

" Me," said a stifled voice. " Who are you ? "

" A public speaker, madam," answered Mr. Lavender, unutterably relieved. " Don't be alarmed."

" Ouch ! " whispered the voice. " That madman ! "

" I assure you, madam," replied Mr. Lavender, striving to regain contact, " I wouldn't harm you for the world. Can you tell me in what portion of the hall we are ? " And crouching down he stretched out his arms and felt about him. No answer came ; but he could tell that he was between two rows of chairs, and, holding to the top of one, he began to sidle along, crouching, so as not to lose touch with the chairs behind him. He had not proceeded the length of six chairs in the pitchy darkness when the light was suddenly turned up, and he found himself glaring over the backs of the chairs in front into the eyes of a young woman, who was crouching and glaring back over the same chairs.

" Dear me ! " said Mr. Lavender, as with a certain dignity they both rose to their full height, " I had no conception——"

Without a word, the young woman put her hand up to her back hair, sidled swiftly down the row of chairs, ran down the aisle, and vanished. There was no one else in the chapel. Mr. Lavender, after surveying the considerable wreckage, made his way to the door and passed out into the night. ' Like a dream,' he thought ; ' but I have done my duty, for no meeting was ever more completely broken up. With a clear conscience and a good appetite I can now go home.'

XII

SPEEDS UP TRANSPORT, AND SEES A DOCTOR

GREATLY cheered by his success at the Peace meeting, Mr. Lavender searched his papers next morning to find a new field for his activities; nor had he to read far before he came on this paragraph:

"Every thing is dependent on transport, and we cannot sufficiently urge that this should be speeded up by every means in our power."

'How true!' he thought. And, finishing his breakfast hastily, he went out with Blink to think over what he could do to help. 'I can exhort,' he mused, 'any one engaged in transport who is not exerting himself to the utmost. It will not be pleasant to do so, for it will certainly provoke much ill-feeling. I must not, however, be deterred by that, for it is the daily concomitant of public life, and hard words break no bones, as they say, but rather serve to thicken the skins and sharpen the tongues of us public men, so that we are able to meet our opponents with their own weapons. I perceive before me, indeed, a liberal education in just those public qualities wherein I am conscious of being as yet deficient.' And his heart sank within him, thinking of the carts on the hills of Hampstead and the boys who drove them. 'What is lacking to them,' he mused, ' is the power of seeing this problem steadily and seeing it whole. Let me endeavour to impart this habit to all who have any connection with transport.' He had just completed this reflection when, turning a corner, he came on a large van standing stockstill at the top of an incline. The driver was leaning idly against the hind wheel filling a pipe. Mr. Lavender glanced at the near horse, and seeing that he was not distressed, he thus addressed the man :

" Do you not know, my friend, that every minute is of importance in this national crisis ? If I could get you to see the question of transport steadily, and to see it whole, I feel convinced that you would not be standing there lighting your pipe when perhaps this half-hour's delay in the delivery of your goods may mean the death of one of your comrades at the front."

The man, who was wizened, weathered, and old, with but few teeth, looked up at him from above the curved hands with which he was coaxing the flame of a match into the bowl of his pipe. His brow was wrinkled, and moisture stood at the corners of his eyes.

" I assure you," went on Mr. Lavender, " that we have none of us the right in these days to delay for a single minute the delivery of anything—not even of speeches. When I am tempted to do so, I think of our sons and brothers in the trenches, and how every shell and every word saves their lives, and I deliver."

The old man, who had finished lighting his pipe, took a long pull at it, and said hoarsely : " Go on ! "

" I will," said Mr. Lavender, " for I perceive that I can effect a revolution in your outlook, so that instead of wasting the country's time by leaning against that wheel you will drive on zealously and help to win the war."

The old man looked at him, and one side of his face became drawn up in a smile, which seemed to Mr. Lavender so horrible that he said :

" Why do you look at me like that ? "

" Cawn't 'elp it," said the man.

" What makes you," continued Mr. Lavender, " pause here with your job half finished ? It is not the hill which keeps you back, for you are at the top, and your horses seem rested."

" Yes," said the old man, with another contortion of his face, " they're rested—leastways, one of 'em."

" Then what delays you—if not that British sluggish-ness which we in public life find such a terrible handicap to our efforts in conducting the war ? "

" Ah ! " said the old man. " But out of one you don't make two, guv'nor. Git on the offside, and you'll see it a bit steadier and a bit 'oler than you 'ave 'itherto."

Struck by his words, which were accompanied by a painful puckering of the cheeks, Mr. Lavender moved round the van looking for some defect in its machinery, and suddenly became aware that the off horse was lying on the ground, with the traces cut. It lay on its side, and did not move.

" Oh ! " cried Mr. Lavender ; " oh ! " And going up to the horse's head he knelt down. The animal's eye was glazing.

" Oh ! " he cried again, " poor horse ! Don't die ! " And tears dropped out of his eyes on to the horse's cheek. The eye seemed to give him a look, and became quite glazed.

" Dead ! " said Mr. Lavender, in an awed whisper.

" This is horrible ! What a thin horse—nothing but bones ! " And his gaze haunted the ridge and furrow of the horse's carcase, while the living horse looked round and down at its dead fellow, from whose hollow face a ragged forelock drooped in the dust.

" I must go and apologise to that old man," said Mr. Lavender aloud, " for no doubt he is even more distressed than I am.".

" Not 'e, guv'nor," said a voice, and looking up he saw the aged driver standing beside him ; " not 'e ; for of all the crool jobs I ever 'ad—drivin' that 'orse these last three months 'as been the croolest. There 'e lies, and 'e's aht of it ; and that's where they'd all like to be. Speed, guv'nor—speed done 'im in, savin' 'is country's time an' 'is country's oats ; that done 'im in. A good old 'orse, a willin' old 'orse, 'as broke 'is 'eart tryin' to do 'is bit on 'alf rations. There 'e lies ; and I'm glad 'e does." And with the back of his hand the old fellow removed some brown moisture which was trembling on his jaw. Mr. Lavender rose from his knees.

" Dreadful !—monstrous ! " he cried ; " poor horse ! Who is responsible for this ? "

" Why," said the old driver, " the gents as sees it steady and sees it 'ole from one side o' the van, same as you."

So smitten to the heart was Mr. Lavender by those words that he covered his ears with his hands and almost ran from the scene, nor did he stop till he had reached the shelter of his study, and was sitting in his arm-chair with Blink upon his feet. ' I will buy a go-cart,' he thought ; ' Blink and I will pull our weight and save the poor horses. We can at least deliver our own milk and vegetables.'

He had not been sitting there for half-an-hour revolving the painful complexities of national life before the voice of Mrs. Petty recalled him from that sad reverie.

" Dr. Gobang to see you, sir."

At sight of the doctor who had attended him for alcoholic poisoning Mr. Lavender experienced one of those vaguely disagreeable sensations which follow on half-realised insults.

" Good-morning, sir," said the doctor ; " I thought I'd just look in and make my mind easy about you. That was a nasty attack. Do you still feel your back ? "

" No," said Mr. Lavender rather coldly, while Blink growled.

" Nor your head ? "

" I have never felt my head," replied Mr. Lavender, still more coldly.

" I seem to remember——" began the doctor.

" Doctor," said Mr. Lavender with dignity, " surely you know that public men do not feel their heads—it would not do. They sometimes suffer from their throats, but otherwise they have perfect health, fortunately."

The doctor smiled.

" Well, what do you think of the war ? " he asked chattily.

" Be quiet, Blink," said Mr. Lavender. Then in a far-away voice, he added : " Whatever the clouds which have gathered above our heads for the moment, and whatever the blows which Fate may have in store for us, we shall not relax our efforts till we have attained our aims and hurled our enemies back. Nor shall we stop there," he went on, warming at his own words. " It is but a weak-kneed patriotism which would be content with securing the objects for which we began to fight. We shall not hesitate to sacrifice the last of our men, the last of our money, in the sacred task of achieving the complete ruin of the fiendish Power which has brought this great calamity on the world. Even if our enemies surrender we will fight on till we have dictated terms on the doorsteps of Potsdam."

The doctor, who, since Mr. Lavender began to speak, had been looking at him with strange intensity, dropped his eyes.

" Quite so," he said heartily, " quite so. Well, good-morning. I only just ran in ! " And leaving Mr. Lavender to the exultation he was evidently feeling, this singular visitor went out and closed the door. Outside the garden-gate he rejoined the nephew Sinkin.

" Well ? " asked the latter.

" Sane as you or me," said the doctor. " A little pedantic in his way of expressing himself, but quite all there, really."

" Did his dog bite you ? " muttered the nephew.

" No," said the doctor absently. " I wish to heaven everyone held his views. So long. I must be getting on." And they parted.

But, Mr. Lavender, after pacing the room six times, had sat down again in his chair, with a cold feeling in the pit of his stomach, such as other men feel on mornings after a debauch.

XIII

ADDRESSES SOME SOLDIERS ON THEIR FUTURE

On pleasant afternoons Mr. Lavender would often take his seat on one of the benches which adorned the Spaniard's Road to enjoy the beams of the sun and the towers of the city confused in smoky distance. And strolling forth with Blink on the afternoon of the day on which the doctor had come to see him he sat down to read a periodical, which enjoined on everyone the necessity of taking the utmost interest in soldiers disabled by the war. ' Yes,' he thought, ' it is indeed our duty to force them, no matter what their disablements, to continue and surpass the heroism they displayed out there, and become superior to what they once were.' And it seemed to him a distinct dispensation of Providence when the rest of his bench was suddenly occupied by three soldiers in the blue garments and red ties of hospital life. They had been sitting there for some minutes, divided by the iron bars necessary to the morals of the neighbourhood, while Mr. Lavender cudgelled his brains for an easy and natural method of approach, before Blink supplied the necessary avenue by taking her stand before a soldier and looking up into his eye.

" Lord ! " said the one thus accosted, " what a fyce ! Look at her moustache ! Well, cocky, 'oo are you starin' at ? "

" My dog," said Mr. Lavender, perceiving his chance, " has an eye for the strange and beautiful."

" Wow ! " said the soldier, whose face was bandaged, " she'll get it 'ere, won't she ? "

Encouraged by the smiles of the soldier and his comrades, Mr. Lavender went on in the most natural voice he could assume.

" I'm sure you appreciate, my friends, the enormous importance of your own futures ? "

The three soldiers, whose faces were all bandaged, looked as surprised as they could between them, and did not answer. Mr. Lavender went on, dropping unconsciously into the diction of the article he had been reading : " We are now at the turning-point of the ways, and not a moment is to be lost in impressing on the disabled man the paramount necessity of becoming again the captain of his soul. He who was a hero in the field must again lead us in those qualities of enterprise and endurance which made him the admiration of the world."

The three soldiers had turned what was visible of their faces towards Mr. Lavender, and, seeing that he had riveted their attention, he proceeded : " The apathy which hospital produces, together with the present scarcity of labour, is largely responsible for the dangerous position in which the disabled man now finds himself. Only we who have not to face his future can appreciate what that future is likely to be if he does not make the most strenuous efforts to overcome it. Boys," he added earnestly, remembering suddenly that this was the word which those who had the personal touch ever employed, " are you making those efforts ? Are you equipping your minds ? Are you taking advantage of your enforced leisure to place yourselves upon some path of life in which you can largely hold your own against all comers ? "

He paused for a reply.

The soldiers, silent for a moment, in what seemed to Mr. Lavender to be sheer astonishment, began to fidget ; then the one next him turned to his neighbour, and said :

" Are we, Alf ? Are we doin' what the gentleman says ? "

" I can answer that for you," returned Mr. Lavender brightly ; " for I can tell by your hospitalised faces that you are living in the present ; a habit which, according to our best writers, is peculiar to the British. I assure you," he went on with a winning look, " there is no future in that. If you do not at once begin to carve fresh niches for yourselves in the temple of industrialism you will be engulfed by the returning flood, and left high and dry upon the beach of fortune."

During these last few words the half of an irritated look on the faces of the soldiers changed to fragments of an indulgent and protective expression.

" Right you are, guv'nor," said the one in the middle. " Don't you worry, we'll see you 'ome all right."

" It is you," said Mr. Lavender, " that I must see home. For that is largely the duty of us who have not had the great privilege of fighting for our country."

These words, which completed the soldier's conviction that Mr. Lavender was not quite all there, caused them to rise.

" Come on then," said one ; " we'll see each other home. We've got to be in by five. You don't have a string to your dog, I see."

" Oh no ! " said Mr. Lavender, puzzled ; " I am not blind."

" Balmy," said the soldier soothingly. " Come on, sir, an' we can talk abaht it on the way."

Mr. Lavender, delighted at the impression he had made, rose and walked beside them, taking insensibly the direction for home.

" What do you advise us to do, then, guv'nor ? " said one of the soldiers.

" Throw away all thought of the present," returned Mr. Lavender, with intense earnestness ; " forget the past entirely, wrap yourselves wholly in the future. Do nothing which will give you immediate satisfaction. Do not consider your families, or any of those transient considerations such as pleasure, your homes, your condition of health, or your economic position ; but place yourself unreservedly in the hands of those who by hard thinking on this subject are alone in the condition to appreciate the individual circumstances of each of you. For only by becoming a flock of sheep can you be conducted into those new pastures where the grass of your future will be sweet and plentiful. Above all, continue to be the heroes which you were under the spur of your country's call, for you must remember that your country is still calling you."

" That's right," said the soldier on Mr. Lavender's left. " Puss, puss ! Does your dog swot cats ? "

At so irrelevant a remark Mr. Lavender looked suspiciously from left to right, but what there was of the soldiers' faces told him nothing.

" Which is your hospital ? " he asked.

" Down the 'ill, on the right," returned the soldier. " Which is yours ? "

" Alas ! it is not a hospital that I——"

112

"I know," said the soldier delicately, "don't give it a name; no need. We're all friends 'ere. Do you get out much?"

"I always take an afternoon stroll," said Mr. Lavender, "when my public life permits. If you think your comrades would like me to come and lecture to them on their future I should be only too happy."

"D'you 'ear, Alf?" said the soldier. "D'you think they would?"

The soldier addressed put a finger to the sound side of his mouth and uttered a cat-call.

"I might effect a radical change in their views," continued Mr. Lavender, a little puzzled. "Let me leave you this periodical. Read it, and you will see how extremely vital all that I have been saying is. And then, perhaps, if you would send me a round robin, such as is usual in a democratic country, I could pop over almost any day after five. I sometimes feel"— and here Mr. Lavender stopped in the middle of the road, overcome by sudden emotion—"that I have really no right to be alive when I see what you have suffered for me."

"That's all right, old bean," said the soldier on his left; "you'd 'a done the same for us but for your disabilities. We don't grudge it you."

"Boys," said Mr. Lavender, "you are men. I cannot tell you how much I admire and love you."

"Well, give it a rest, then; 'tain't good for yer. And, look 'ere! Any time they don't treat you fair in there, tip us the wink, and we'll come over and do in your 'ousekeeper."

Mr. Lavender smiled.

"My poor housekeeper!" he said. "I thank you all the same for your charming goodwill. This is where I live," he added, stopping at the gate of the little house smothered in lilac and laburnum. " Can I offer you some tea ? "

The three soldiers looked at each other, and Mr. Lavender, noticing their surprise, attributed it to the word tea.

" I regret exceedingly that I am a total abstainer," he said.

The remark, completing the soldiers' judgment of his case, increased their surprise at the nature of his residence ; it remained unanswered, save by a shuffling of the feet.

Mr. Lavender took off his hat.

" I consider it a great privilege," he said, " to have been allowed to converse with you. Good-bye, and God bless you ! "

So saying, he opened the gate and entered his little garden, carrying his hat in his hand, and followed by Blink.

The soldiers watched him disappear within, then continued on their way down the hill in silence.

" Blimy ! " said one suddenly, " some of these old civilians *'ave* come it balmy on the crumpet since the war began. Give me the trenches ! "

XIV

ENDEAVOURS TO INTERN A GERMAN

AGLOW with satisfaction at what he had been able to do for the wounded soldiers, Mr. Lavender sat down in his study to drink the tea which he found there. 'There is nothing in life,' he thought, 'which gives one such pleasure as friendliness and being able to do something for others. Moon-cat!'

The moon-cat, who, since Mr. Lavender had given her milk, abode in his castle, awaiting her confinement, purred loudly, regarding him with burning eyes, as was her fashion when she wanted milk. Mr. Lavender put down the saucer and continued his meditations. 'Everything is vain; the world is full of ghosts and shadows; but in friendliness and the purring of a little cat there is solidity.'

"A lady has called, sir."

Looking up, Mr. Lavender became aware of Mrs. Petty.

"How very agreeable!"

"I don't know, sir," returned his housekeeper in her decisive voice; "but she wants to see you. Name of Pullbody."

"Pullbody," repeated Mr. Lavender dreamily; "I don't seem—— Ask her in, Mrs. Petty, ask her in."

"It's on your head, sir," said Mrs. Petty, and went out.

Mr. Lavender was immediately conscious of a

presence in dark green silk, with a long upper lip, a loose lower lip, and a fixed and faintly raddled air, moving stealthily towards him.

" Sit down, madam, I beg. Will you have some tea ? "

The lady sat down. " Thank you, I have had tea. It was on the recommendation of your next-door neighbour, Miss Isabel Scarlet——"

" Indeed ! " replied Mr. Lavender, whose heart began to beat ; " command me, for I am entirely at her service."

" I have come to see you," began the lady with a peculiar sinuous smile, " as a public man and a patriot."

Mr. Lavender bowed, and the lady went on :

" I am in very great trouble. The fact is, my sister's husband's sister is married to a German."

" Is it possible, madam ? " murmured Mr. Lavender, crossing his knees, and joining the tips of his fingers.

" Yes," resumed the lady, " and what's more, he is still at large."

Mr. Lavender, into whose mind there had instantly rushed a flood of public utterances, stood gazing at her haggard face in silent sympathy.

" You may imagine my distress, sir, and the condition of my conscience," pursued the lady, " when I tell you that my sister's husband's sister is a very old friend of mine—and, indeed, so was this German. The two are a very attached young couple, and, being childless, are quite wrapped up in each other. I have come to you feeling it my duty to secure his internment."

Mr. Lavender, moved by the human element in her words, was about to say, " But why, madam ? " when the lady continued :

" I have not myself precisely heard him speak well of

116

his country. But the sister of a friend of mine who was having tea in their house distinctly heard him say that there were two sides to every question, and that he could not believe all that was said in the English papers."

" Dear me ! " said Mr. Lavender, troubled ; " that is serious."

" Yes," went on the lady ; " and on another occasion my sister's husband himself heard him remark that a man could not help loving his country and hoping that it would win."

" But that is natural," began Mr. Lavender.

" What ! " said the lady, nearly rising, " when that country is Germany ? " The word revived Mr. Lavender's sense of proportion.

" True," he said, " true. I was forgetting for the moment. It is extraordinary how irresponsible one's thoughts are sometimes. Have you reason to suppose that he is dangerous ? "

" I should have thought that what I have said might have convinced you," replied the lady reproachfully ; " but I don't wish you to act without satisfying yourself. It is not as if you knew him, of course. I have easily been able to get up an agitation among his friends, but I should not expect an outsider—so I thought if I gave you his address you could form your own opinion."

" Yes," murmured Mr. Lavender, " yes. It is in the last degree undesirable that any man of German origin should remain free to work possible harm to our country. There is no question in this of hatred or of mere rabid patriotism," he went on in a voice growing more and more far-away ; " it is largely the A.B.C. of common prudence."

" I ought to say," interrupted his visitor, " that we

all thought him, of course, an honourable man until this war, or we should not have been his friends. He is a dentist," she added, " and, I suppose, may be said to be doing useful work, which makes it difficult. I suggest that you go to him to have a tooth out."

Mr. Lavender quivered, and insensibly felt his teeth.

" Thank you," he said ; " I will see if I can find one. It is certainly a matter which cannot be left to chance. We public men, madam, often have to do very hard and even inhumane things for no apparent reason. Our consciences alone support us. An impression, I am told, sometimes gets abroad that we yield to clamour. Those alone who know us realise how un-founded that aspersion is."

" This is his address," said the lady, rising, and handing him an envelope. " I shall not feel at rest until he is safely interned. You will not mention my name, of course. It is tragic to be obliged to work against one's friends in the dark. Your young neighbour spoke in enthusiastic terms of your zeal, and I am sure that in choosing you for my public man she was not pulling—er—was not making a mistake."

Mr. Lavender bowed. " I hope not, madam," he said humbly ; " I try to do my duty."

The lady smiled her sinuous smile and moved towards the door, leaving on the air a faint odour of vinegar and sandalwood.

When she was gone Mr. Lavender sat down on the edge of his chair before the tea-tray and extracted his teeth, while Blink, taking them for a bone, gazed at them lustrously, and the moon-cat between his feet purred from repletion. ' There is reason in all things,' he thought, running his finger over what was left in his mouth, 'but not in patriotism, for that would prevent us from consummating the destruction of our common enemies. It behoves us public men ever to set an example. Which one can I spare, I wonder ?' And he fixed upon a large rambling tooth on the left wing of his lower jaw. " It will hurt horribly, I'm afraid ; and if I have an anæsthetic there will be someone else present ; and not improbably I shall feel ill afterwards, and be unable to form a clear judgment. I must steel myself. Blink ! "

For Blink was making tremulous advances to the teeth. ' How pleasant to be a dog ! ' thought Mr. Lavender, ' and know nothing of Germans and teeth. I shall be very unhappy till this is out ; but Aurora recommended me, and I must not complain, but rather consider myself the most fortunate of public men.' And, ruffling his hair till it stood up all over his head, while his loose eyebrow worked up and down, he gazed at the moon-cat.

" Moon-cat," he said suddenly, " we are but creatures of chance, unable to tell from one day to another what Fate has in store for us. My tooth is beginning to ache already. That is, perhaps, as it should be, for I shall not forget which one it is." So musing he resumed his teeth ; and, going to his bookcase, sought fortitude and inspiration in the records of a Parliamentary debate on enemy aliens. . . .

It was not without considerable trepidation, however, on the following afternoon that he made his way up Welkin Street, and rang at the number on the envelope in his hand

" Yes, sir, doctor is at home," said the maid

Mr. Lavender's heart was about to fail him when, conjuring up the vision of Aurora, he said in a faint voice: "I wish to see him professionally." And, while the maid departed up the stairs, he waited in the narrow hall, alternately taking his hat off and putting it on again, so great was his spiritual confusion.

"Doctor will see you at once, sir."

Putting his hat on hastily, Mr. Lavender followed her upstairs, feeling at his tooth to make quite sure that he remembered which it was. His courage mounted as he came nearer to his fate, and he marched into the room behind the maid holding his hat on firmly with one hand and his tooth in firmly with the other. There, beside a red velvet dentist's chair, he saw a youngish man dressed in a white coat, with round eyes and a domestic face, who said in good English:

"What can I do for you, my dear sir? I fear you are in bain."

"In great pain," replied Mr. Lavender faintly, "in great pain." And, indeed, he was; for the nervous crisis from which he was suffering had settled in the tooth, on which he still pressed a finger through his cheek.

"Sit down, sir, sit down," said the young man; "and perhaps it would be better if you should remove your hat. We shall not hurd you—no, no, we shall not hurd you."

At those words, which seemed to cast doubt on his courage, Mr. Lavender recovered all his presence of mind. He took off his hat, advanced resolutely to the chair, sat down in it, and, looking up, said:

"Do to me what you will; I shall not flinch, nor depart in any way from the behaviour of those whose duty it is to set an example to others."

So saying, he removed his teeth, and placing them in a bowl on the little swinging table which he perceived on his left hand, he closed his eyes, put his finger in his mouth, and articulated : " 'Ith one."

" Excuse me, sir," said the young German, " but do you wish a dooth oud ? "

" 'At ish my deshire," said Mr. Lavender, keeping his finger on his tooth, and his eyes closed. " 'At one."

" I cannot give you gas without my anæsthedist."

" I dow," said Mr. Lavender ; " be wick."

And, feeling the little cold spyglass begin to touch his gums, he clenched his hands and thought : ' This is the moment to prove that I, too, can die for a good cause. If I am not man enough to bear for my country so small a woe I can never again look Aurora in the face.'

The voice of the young dentist dragged him rudely from the depth of his resignation.

" Excuse me, but which dooth did you say ? "

Mr. Lavender again inserted his finger, and opened his eyes.

The dentist shook his head. " Imbossible," he said ; " that dooth is perfectly sound. The other two are rotten. But they do not ache ? "

Mr. Lavender shook his head and repeated : " 'At one."

" You are my first client this week, sir," said the young German calmly, " but I cannot that dooth dake oud."

At those words Mr. Lavender experienced a sensation as if his soul were creeping back up his legs ; he spoke as it reached his stomach.

" Noc ? " he said.

" No," replied the young German. " It is nod the dooth which causes you the bain."

Mr. Lavender, suddenly conscious that he had no pain, took his finger out.

" Sir," he said, " I perceive that you are an honourable man. There is something sublime in your abnegation, if, indeed, you have had no other client this week."

" No fear," said the young German. " Haf I, Cicely ? "

Mr. Lavender became conscious for the first time of a young woman leaning up against the wall, with a pair of tweezers in her hand.

" Take it out, Otto," she said in a low voice, " if he wants it."

" No, no," said Mr. Lavender sharply, resuming his teeth ; " I would not for the world burden your conscience."

" My clients are all batriots," said the young dentist, " and my bractice is Kaput. We are in a bad way, sir," he added, with a smile, " but we try to do the correct ting."

Mr. Lavender saw the young woman move the tweezers in a manner which caused his blood to run a little cold.

" We must live," he heard her say.

" Young madam," he said, " I honour the impulse which makes you desire to extend your husband's practice. Indeed, I perceive you both to be so honourable that I cannot but make you a confession. My tooth is indeed sound, though, since I have been pretending that it isn't, it has caused me much discomfort. I came here largely to form an opinion of your husband's character, with a view to securing his internment."

At that word the two young people shrank together till they were standing side by side, staring at Mr. Lavender with eyes full of anxiety and wonder. Their hands, which still held the implements of dentistry, insensibly sought each other.

"Be under no apprehension," cried Mr. Lavender, much moved ; "I can see that you are greatly attached, and even though your husband is a German, he is still a man, and I could never bring myself to separate him from you."

"Who are you ? " said the young woman in a frightened voice, putting her arm round her husband's waist.

"Just a public man," answered Mr. Lavender. "I came here from a sense of duty ; nothing more, I assure you."

"Who put you up to it ? "

"That," said Mr. Lavender, bowing as best he could from the angle he was in, "I am not at liberty to disclose. But, believe me, you have nothing to fear from this visit ; I shall never do anything to distress a woman. And please charge me as if the tooth had been extracted."

The young German smiled, and shook his head.

"Sir," he said, "I am grateful to you for coming, for it shows us what danger we are in. The hardest ting to bear has been the uncertainty of our bosition, and the feeling that our friends were working behind our backs. Now we know that this is so we shall vordify our souls to bear the worst. But, tell me," he went on, "when you came here, surely you must have subbosed that to tear me away from my wife would be very bainful to her and to myself. You say now you never could do that—how was it, then, you came ? "

"Ah, sir ! " cried Mr. Lavender, running his hands through his hair and staring at the ceiling, "I feared this might seem inconsistent to your logical German

123

mind. But there are many things we public men would never do if we could see them being done. Fortunately, as a rule we cannot. Believe me, when I leave you I shall do my best to save you from a fate which I perceive to be unnecessary."

So saying, he rose from the chair, and, picking up his hat, backed towards the door.

" I will not offer you my hand," he said, " for I am acutely conscious that my position is neither dignified nor decent. I owe you a tooth that I shall not readily forget. Good-bye ! "

And backing through the doorway he made his way down the stairs and out into the street, still emotionalised by the picture of the two young people holding each other by the waist. He had not, however, gone far before reason resumed its sway, and he began to see that the red velvet chair in which he had been sitting was in reality a wireless apparatus reaching to Berlin, or at least concealed a charge of dynamite to blow up some King or Prime Minister ; and that the looking-glasses, of which he had noticed two at least, were surely used for signalling to Gothas or Zeppelins. This plunged him into a confusion so poignant that, rather by accident than design, he found himself again at Hampstead instead of at Scotland Yard. ' In the society of Aurora alone,' he thought, ' can I free myself from the goadings of conscience, for it was she who sent me on that errand.' And, instead of going in, he took up a position on his lawn whence he could attract her attention by waving his arms. He had been doing this for some time, to the delight of Blink, who thought it a new game, before he saw her in her nurse's dress coming out of a French-window with her yellow book in her hand. Redoubling his efforts till he had arrested her attention, he went up to the privet hedge, and said, in a deep and melancholy voice :

"Aurora, I have failed in my duty, and the errand on which you sent me is unfulfilled. Mrs. Pullbody's sister's husband's sister's husband is still, largely speaking, at large."

"I knew he would be," replied the young lady, with her joyous smile ; "that's why I put her on to you— the cat ! "

At a loss to understand her meaning, Mr. Lavender, who had bent forward above the hedge in his eagerness to explain, lost his balance, and, endeavouring to save the hedge, fell over into some geranium pots.

"Dear Don Pickwixote," cried the young lady, assisting him to rise, "have you hurt your nose ? "

"It is not that," said Mr. Lavender, removing some mould from his hair, and stilling the attentions of Blink ; "but rather my honour, for I have allowed my duty to my country to be overridden by the common emotion of pity ! "

"Hurrah ! " cried the young lady. "It'll do you ever so much good."

"Aurora ! " cried Mr. Lavender aghast, walking at her side. But the young lady only uttered her enchanting laugh.

"Come and lie down in the hammock ! " she said ; "you're looking like a ghost. I'll cover you up with a rug, and smoke a cigarette to keep the midges off you. Tuck up your legs ; that's right ! "

"No ! " said Mr. Lavender from the recesses of the hammock, feeling his nose, "let the bidges bide me. I deserve they should devour me alive."

"All right," said the young lady. "But have a

nap, anyway ! " And sitting down in a low chair, she opened her book and lit a cigarette.

Mr. Lavender remained silent, watching her with the eyes of an acolyte, and wondering whether he was in his senses to have alighted on so rare a fortune. Nor was it long before he fell into a hypnotic doze.

XV

ENCOUNTERS A PRUSSIAN

How long Mr. Lavender had been asleep he could not of course tell before he dreamed that he was caught in a net, the meshes of which were formed of the cries of newspaper boys announcing atrocities by land and sea. He awoke looking into the eyes of Aurora, who, to still his struggles, had taken hold of his ankles.

"My goodness! You are thin!" were the first words he heard. "No wonder you're light-headed."

Mr. Lavender, whose returning chivalry struggled with unconscious delight, murmured with difficulty:

"Let me go, let me go; it is too heavenly!"

"Well, have you finished kicking?" asked the young lady.

"Yes," returned Mr. Lavender in a fainting voice— "alas!"

The young lady let go of his ankles, and, aiding him to rise from the hammock, said: "I know what's the matter with you now—you're starving yourself. You ought to be kept on your back for three months at least, and fed on butter."

Mr. Lavender, soothing the feelings of Blink, who, at his struggles, had begun to pant deeply answered with watering lips:

"Everyone in these days must do twice as much as he ought, and eat half, for only in this way can we compass the defeat of our common enemies." The young lady's answer, which sounded like " Bosh ! " was lost in Mr. Lavender's admiration of her magnificent proportions while she bent to pick up her yellow book.

" Aurora," he said, " I know not what secret you share with the goddesses ; suffer me to go in and give thanks for this hour spent in your company."

And he was about to recross the privet hedge when she caught him by the coat-tail saying :

" No, Don Pickwixote, you must dine with us. I want you to meet my father. Come along ! " And, linking her arm in his, she led him towards her castle. Mr. Lavender, who had indeed no option but to obey, such was the vigour of her arm, went with a sense of joy not unmingled with consternation lest the personage she spoke of should have viewed him in the recent extravagance of his dreaming moments.

" I don't believe," said the young lady, gazing down at him, " that you weigh an ounce more than seven stone.   It's appalling ! "

" Not," returned Mr. Lavender, " by physical weight and force shall we win this war, for it is at bottom a question of morale.   Right is ever victorious in the end, and though we have infinitely greater material resources than our foes, we should still triumph were we reduced to the last ounce, because of the inherent nobility of our cause."

" You'll be reduced to the last ounce if we don't feed you up somehow," said the young lady.   " Would you like to wash your hands ? "

Mr. Lavender having signified his assent, she left him alone in a place covered with linoleum.   When, at length, followed by Blink, he emerged from dreamy ablutions, Mr. Lavender saw that she had changed her

128

dress to a flowing blue garment of diaphanous character, which made her appear like an emanation of the sky. He was about to say so when he noticed a gentleman in khaki scrutinising him with lively eyes slightly injected with blood.

" Don Pickwixote," said the young lady; " my father, Major Scarlet."

Mr. Lavender's hand was grapsed by one which seemed to him made of iron.

" I am honoured, sir," he said painfully, " to meet the father of my charming young neighbour."

The Major answered in a voice as clipped as his grey bottle-brush moustache: " Delighted! Dinner's ready. Come along! "

Mr. Lavender saw that he had a mouth which seemed to have a bitt in it; several hairs on a finely rounded head; and an air of efficient and truculent bonhomie tanned and wrinkled by the weather.

The table at which they became seated seemed to one accustomed to frugality to groan with flowers and china and glass; and Mr. Lavender had hardly supped his rich and steaming soup before his fancy took fire; nor did he notice that he was drinking from a green glass in which was a yellow fluid.

" I get Army rations," said the Major, holding a morsel of fillet of beef towards Blink.   " Nice dog, Mr. Lavender."

" Yes," replied Mr. Lavender, ever delighted that his favourite should receive attention: " she is an angel."

" Too light," said the Major, " and a bit too narrow in front; but a nice dog.   What's your view of the war ? "

Before Mr. Lavender could reply he felt Aurora's foot pressing his, and heard her say:

" Don Pickwixote's views are after your own heart, Dad; he's for the complete destruction of the Hun."

" Indeed, yes," cried Mr. Lavender with shining eyes. " Right and Justice demand it. We seek to gain nothing——"

" But we'll take all we can get," said the Major. " They'll never get their Colonies back. We'll stick to *them* fast enough."

Mr. Lavender stared at him for a moment, then, remembering what he had so often read, he murmured :

" Aggrandisement is not our object; but we can never forget that so long as any territory remains in the hands of our treacherous foe the arteries of our far-flung Empire are menaced at the roots."

" Right-o," said the Major; " we've got the chance of our lives, and we're going to take it."

Mr. Lavender sat forward a little on his chair. " I shall never admit," he said, " that we are going to take anything, for that would be contrary to the principles which we are pledged to support, and to our avowed intention of seeking only the benefit of the human race ; but our inhuman foes have compelled us to deprive them of the power to injure others.".

" Yes," said the Major, " we must just go on killing Germans and collaring every bit of their property we can."

Mr. Lavender sat a little further forward on his chair, and the trouble in his eyes grew.

" After all's said and done," continued the Major ; " it's a simple war—us or them ! And in the long run it's bound to be us. We've got the cards." Mr. Lavender started, and said in a weak and wavering voice :

" We shall never sheathe the sword until——"

" The whole bag of tricks is in our hands.   Might isn't Right, but Right's Might, Mr. Lavender : ha, ha ! "

Mr. Lavender's eyes lighted on his glass, and he emptied it in his confusion.   When he looked up again he could not see the Major very well, but could distinctly hear the truculent bonhomie of his voice.

" Every German ought to be interned ; all their property ought to be confiscated ; all their submarines' and Zeppelins' crews ought to be hung ; all German prisoners ought to be treated as they treat our men. We ought to give 'em no quarter.   We ought to bomb their towns out of existence.   I draw the line at their women.   Short of that there's nothing too bad for them.   I'd treat 'em like rabbits.   Vermin they were and vermin they remain."

During this speech the most astounding experience befell Mr. Lavender, so that his eyes nearly started from his head.   It seemed to him, indeed, that he was seated at dinner with a Prussian, and the Major's voice had no sooner ceased its genial rasping than with a bound forward on his chair he ejaculated :

" Behold the man—the Prussian in his jack-boot ! " And, utterly oblivious of the fact that he was addressing Aurora's father, he went on with almost terrible incoherence : " Although you have conquered this country, sir, never shall you subdue in my breast the sentiments of liberty and generosity which make me an Englishman.   I abhor you—invader of the world—trampler underfoot of the humanities—enemy of mankind— apostle of force !   You have blown out the sparks of love and kindliness, and have for ever robbed the Universe.   Prussian ! "

The emphasis with which he spoke that word caused his chair, on the edge of which he was sitting, to tilt up under him so that he slid under the table, losing the vision of that figure in helmet and field-grey which he had been apostrophising.

"Hold up!" said a voice, while Blink joined him nervously beneath the board.

"Never!" cried Mr. Lavender. "Imprison, mal-treat me—do what you will. You have subdued her body, but never will I admit that you have conquered the honour of Britain and trodden her gentle culture into the mud."

And, convinced that he would now be dragged away to be confined in some dungeon on bread and water, he clasped the leg of the dining-table with all his might, while Blink, sagaciously aware that something peculiar was occurring to her master, licked the back of his neck. He had been sitting there perhaps half a minute, with his ears stretched to catch the half-whispered sounds above, when he saw a shining object appear under the table, the head, indeed, of the Prussian squatting there to look at him.

"Go up, thou bald-head," he called out at once; "I will make no terms with the destroyer of justice and humanity."

"All right, my dear sir," replied the head. "Will you let my daughter speak to you?"

"Prussian blasphemer," responded Mr. Lavender, shifting his position so as to be further away, and clasping instead of the table leg some soft silken objects, which he was too excited to associate with Aurora, "you *have* no daughter, for no woman would own one whose hated presence poisons this country."

"Well, well," said the Major. "How shall we get him out?"

Hearing these words, and believing them addressed

132

to a Prussian guard, Mr. Lavender clung closer to the objects, but finding them wriggle in his clasp let go, and, bolting forward like a rabbit on his hands and knees, came into contact with the Major's head. The sound of the concussion, the Major's oaths, Mr. Lavender's moans, Blink's barking, and the peals of laughter from Aurora made up a noise which might have been heard in Portugal. The situation was not eased until Mr. Lavender crawled out, and taking up a dinner-knife, rolled his napkin round his arm, and prepared to defend himself against the German Army.

" Well, I'm damned," said the Major when he saw these preparations ; " I *am* damned."

Aurora, who had been leaning against the wall from laughter, here came forward, gasping :

" Go away, Dad, and leave him to me."

" To you ! " cried the Major. " He's not safe ! "

" Oh yes, he is ; it's only you that are exciting him. Come along ! "

And taking her father by the arm she conducted him from the room. Closing the door behind him, and putting her back against it, she said gently :

" Dear Don Pickwixote, all danger is past. The enemy has been repulsed, and we are alone in safety. Ha, ha, ha ! "

Her voice recalled Mr. Lavender from his strange hallucination. " What ? " he said weakly. " Why ? Who ? Where ? When ? "

" You have been dreaming again. Let me take you home, and tuck you into bed." And taking from him the knife and napkin, she opened the French-window, and passed out on to the lawn. Mr. Lavender, who now that his reason had come back, would have fol-lowed her to the death, passed out also, accompanied by Blink, and watched by the Major, who had put his head in again at the door. Unfortunately, the spirit moved Mr. Lavender to turn round at this moment, and seeing the head he cried out in a loud voice :

" He is there ! He is there ! Arch enemy of mankind ! Let me go and die under his jack-boot, for never over my living body shall he rule this land ! " And the infatuated gentleman would certainly have rushed at his host had not Aurora stayed him by the slack of his nether garments. The Major withdrawing his head, Mr. Lavender's excitement again passed from him, and he suffered himself to be led dazedly away and committed to the charge of Mrs. Petty and Joe, who did not leave him till he was in bed with a strong bromide to keep him company.

XVI

FIGHTS THE FIGHT OF FAITH

THE strenuous experiences through which Mr. Lavender had passed resulted in what Joe Petty called " a fair knock-out " ; and he was forced to spend three days in the seclusion of his bed, deprived of his newspapers. He instructed Mrs. Petty, however, on no account to destroy or mislay any journal, but to keep them in a pile in his study. This she did, for though her first impulse was to light the kitchen fire with the five of them every morning, deliberate reflection convinced her that twenty journals read at one sitting would produce on him a more soporific effect than if he came down to a mere five.

Mr. Lavender passed his three days, therefore, in perfect repose, feeding Blink, staring at the ceiling, and conversing with Joe. An uneasy sense that he had been lacking in restraint caused his mind to dwell on life as seen by the monthly rather than the daily papers, and to hold with his chauffeur discussions of a somewhat philosophical character.

" As regards the government of this country, Joe," he said, on the last evening of his retirement, " who do you consider really rules ? For it is largely on this that our future must depend."

" Can't say, sir," answered Joe, " unless it's Botty."

" I do not know whom or what you signify by that

135

word," replied Mr. Lavender; "I am wondering if it is the People who rule."

"The People!" replied Joe; "the People's like a gent in a lunatic asylum, allowed to 'ave instinks but not to express 'em. One day it'll get aht, and we shall all step lively."

"It is, perhaps, Public Opinion," continued Mr. Lavender to himself, "as expressed in the Press."

"Not it," said Joe; "the nearest opinion the Press gets to expressin' is that of Mayors. 'Ave you never noticed, sir, that when the Press is 'ard up for support of an opinion that the public don't 'old, they go to the Mayors, and get 'em in two columns?"

"Mayors are most valuable public men," said Mr. Lavender.

"I've nothing against 'em," replied Joe; "very average lot in their walk of life; but they ain't the People."

Mr. Lavender sighed. "What, then, is the People, Joe?"

"I am," replied Joe; "I've got no opinions on anything except that I want to live a quiet life—just enough beer and 'baccy, short hours, and no worry."

"If you compare that with the aspiration of Mayors you will see how sordid such a standard is," said Mr. Lavender gravely.

"Sordid it may be, sir," replied Joe; "but there's a thing abaht it you 'aven't noticed. I don't want to sacrifice nobody to satisfy my aspirations. Why? Because I've got none. That's priceless. Take the Press, take Parlyment, take Mayors—all mad on aspirations. Now it's Free Trade, now it's Imperialism; now its Liberty in Europe; now it's Slavery in Ireland;

now it's sacrifice of the last man an' the last dollar. You never can tell what aspiration 'll get 'em next. And the 'ole point of an aspiration is the sacrifice of someone else. Don't you make a mistake, sir. I defy you to make a public speech which 'asn't got that at the bottom of it."

" We are wandering from the point, Joe," returned Mr. Lavender. " Who is it that governs the country ? "

" A Unseen Power," replied Joe promptly.

" How ? "

" Well, sir, we're a democratic country, ain't we ? Parlyment's elected by the People, and Gover'ment's elected by Parlyment. All right so far ; but what 'appens ? Gover'ment says ' I'm going to do this.' So long as it meets with the approval of the Unseen Power, well an' good. But what if it don't ? The U.P. gets busy ; in an 'undred papers there begins to appear what the U.P. calls Public Opinion, that's to say the opinion of the people that agree with the U.P. There you 'ave it, sir, only them—and it appears strong. Attacks on the Gover'ment policy, nasty things said abaht members of it that's indiscreet enough to speak aht what they think—German fathers, and other secret vices ; an' what's more than all, not a peep at any opinion that supports the Gover'ment. Well, that goes on day after day, playin' on the mind of Parlyment, if they've got any, and gittin' on the Gover'ment's nerves, which they've got weak, till they says : ' Look 'ere, it's no go ; Public Opinion won't stand it. We shall be outed ; and that'll never do, because there's no other set of fellows that can save this country.' Then they 'ave a meetin' and change their policy. And what they've never seen is that they've never seen Public Opinion at all. All they've seen is what the U.P. let

137

'em. Now if I was the Gover'ment, I'd 'ave it out once for all with the U.P."

" Ah ! " cried Mr. Lavender, whose eyes were starting from his head, so profoundly was he agitated by what was to him a new thought.

" Yes," continued Joe, " if I was the Gover'ment, next time it 'appened, I'd say : ' All right, old cock, do your damnedest. I ain't responsible to you. Attack, suppress, and all the rest of it. We're goin' to do what we say, all the same ! ' And then I'd do it. And what'd come of it ? Either the U.P. would go beyond the limits of the Law—and then I'd jump on it, suppress its papers, and clap it into quod—or it'd take it lyin' down. Whichever 'appened it'd be all up with the U.P. I'd a broke its chain off my neck for good. But I ain't the Gover'ment, an' Gover'ment's got tender feet. I ask you, sir, wot's the good of havin' a Constitooshion, and all the bother of electing these fellows, if they can't act according to their judgment for the short term of their natural lives ? The U.P. may be patriotic and estimable, and 'ave the best intentions and all that, but its outside the Constitooshion ; and what's more, I'm not goin' to spend my last blood an' my last money in a democratic country to suit the tastes of any single man, or triumpherate, or wotever it may be made of. If the Gover'ment's uncertain wot the country wants they can always ask it in the proper way, but they never ought to take it on 'earsay from the papers. That's wot I think."

While he was speaking Mr. Lavender had become excited to the point of fever, for, without intending it, Joe had laid bare to him a yawning chasm between his worship of public men and his devotion to the Press. And no sooner had his chauffeur finished than he cried :

" Leave me, Joe, for I must think this out."

" Right, sir," answered Joe with his smile, and taking the tea-tray from off his master, he set it where it must infallibly be knocked over, and went out.

' Can it be possible,' thought Mr. Lavender, when he was alone, ' that I am serving God and Mammon ? And which is God and which is Mammon ? ' he added, letting his thoughts play over the countless speeches and leading articles which had formed his spiritual diet since the war began. ' Or, indeed, are they not both God or both Mammon ? If what Joe says is true, and nothing is recorded save what seems good to this Unseen Power, have I not been listening to ghosts and shadows ; and am I, indeed, myself anything but the unsubstantial image of a public man ? For it is true that I have no knowledge of anything save what is recorded in the papers.' And perceiving that the very basis of his faith was endangered, he threw off the bedclothes, and began to pace the room. ' Are we, then, all,' he thought, ' being bounded like india-rubber balls by an unseen hand ; and is there no one of us strong enough to bounce into the eye of our bounder and overthrow him ? My God, I am unhappy ; for it is a terrible thing not to know which my God is, and whether I am a public man or an india-rubber ball.' And the more he thought the more dreadful it seemed to him, now that he perceived that all those journals, pamphlets, and reports with which his study walls were lined might not be the truth, but merely authorised versions of it.

" This," he said aloud " is a nightmare from which I must awaken or lose all my power of action and my ability to help my country in its peril."

And sudden sweat broke out on his brow, for he

perceived that he had now no means of telling even whether there *was* a peril, so strangely had Joe's words affected his powers of credulity.

' But surely,' he thought, steadying himself by gripping his washstand, ' there was, at least, a peril once. And yet, how do I know even that, for I have only been told so ; and the tellers themselves were only told so by this Unseen Power ; and suppose it has made a mistake or has some private ends to serve ! Oh ! it is terrible, and there is no end to it.' And he shook the crockery in the spasms which followed the first awakenings of these religious doubts. " Where, then, am I to go," he cried, " for knowledge of the truth ? For even books would seem dependent on the good opinion of this Unseen Power, and would not reach my eyes unless they were well spoken of by it."

And the more he thought the more it seemed to him that nothing could help him but to look into the eyes of this Unseen Power, so that he might see for himself whether it was the Angel of Truth or some Demon jumping on the earth. No sooner had this conviction entered his brain than he perceived how in carrying out such an enterprise he would not only be setting his own mind at rest, and re-establishing or abolishing his faith, but he would be doing the greatest service which he could render to his country and to all public men. ' Thus,' he thought, ' shall I cannonise my tourney, and serve Aurora, who is the dawn of truth and beauty in the world. I am not yet worthy, however, of this adventure, which will, indeed, be far more arduous and distressing to accomplish than any which I have yet undertaken. What can I do to brighten and equip my mind and divest it of all those prejudices in which it may unconsciously have become steeped ? If

I could leave the earth for a short space and commune. with the clouds it might be best. I will go to Hendon and see if someone will take me up for a consideration ; for on earth I can no longer be sure of anything.' And having rounded off his purpose with this lofty design, he went back to bed with his head lighter than a puff-ball.

XVII

ADDRESSES THE CLOUDS

On the morning following his resurrection, Mr. Lavender set out very early for the celebrated flying ground without speaking of his intention to anyone. At the bottom of the hill he found to his annoyance that Blink had divined his purpose and was following. This, which compelled him to walk, greatly delayed his arrival. But chance now favoured him, for he found he was expected, and at once conducted to a machine which was about to rise. A taciturn young man, with a long jaw, and wings on his breast, was standing there gazing at it with an introspective eye.

" Ready, sir ? " he said.

" Yes," replied Mr. Lavender, enveloped to the eyes in a garment of fur and leather. " Will you kindly hold my dog ? " he added, stroking Blink with the feeling that he was parting for ever with all that was most dear to him.

An attendant having taken hold of her by the collar, Mr. Lavender was heaved into the machine, where the young airman was already seated in front of him.

" Shall I feel sick ? " asked Mr. Lavender.

" Probably," said the young airman.

" That will not deter me, for the less material I become the better it will be."

The young airman turned his head, and Mr. Lavender caught the surprised yellow of his eye.

" Hold on," said the airman, " I'm going to touch her off."

Mr. Lavender held on, and the machine moved ; but at this moment Blink, uttering a dismal howl, leapt forward, and, breaking from the attendant's grasp, landed in the machine against Mr. Lavender's chest.

" Stop ! stop ! " he cried. " My dog."

" Stuff her down," said the unmoved airman, " between your legs. She's not the first to go up, and won't be the last to come down."

Mr. Lavender stuffed her down as best he could. ' If we are to be killed,' he thought, ' it will be together. Blink ! ' The faithful creature, who bitterly regretted her position now that the motion had begun, looked up with a darkened eye at Mr. Lavender, who was stopping his ears against the horrible noises which had now begun. He, too, had become aware of the pit of his stomach ; but this sensation soon passed away in the excitement he felt at getting away from the earth, for they were already at the height of a house, and rising rapidly.

' It is not at all like a little bird,' he thought, ' but rather resembles a slow train on the surface of the sea, or a horse on a switchback merry-go-round. I feel, however, that my spirit will soon be free, for the earth is becoming like a board whereon a game is played by an unseen hand, and I am leaving it.' And craning his head out a little too far he felt his chin knock against his spine. Drawing it in with difficulty he concentrated his attention upon that purification of his spirit which was the object of his journey. ' I am now,' he thought, ' in the transcendent ether. It should give me an amazing power of expression such as only the greatest writers and orators attain ; and, divorced as I am rapidly becoming from all sordid reality, truth will appear to me like one of those stars towards which I am undoubtedly flying though I cannot as yet see it.'

Blink, who between his legs had hitherto been unconscious of their departure from the earth, now squirmed irresistibly up till her forepaws were on her master's chest, and gazed lugubriously at the fearful prospect. Mr. Lavender clasped her convulsively. They were by now rapidly nearing a flock of heavenly sheep, which as they approached became ever more gigantic till they were transformed into monstrous snow-fleeces intersected by wide drifts of blue.

'Can it be that we are to adventure above them?' thought Mr. Lavender. 'I hope not, for they seem to me fearful.' His alarm was soon appeased, for the machine began to take a level course a thousand feet, perhaps, below the clouds, whence little wraiths wandering out now and again dimmed Mr. Lavender's vision and moistened his brow.

Blink having retired again between her master's legs, a sense of security and exaltation was succeeding to the natural trepidation of Mr. Lavender's mood. 'I am now,' he thought, 'lifted above all petty plots and passions on the wings of the morning. Soon will great thoughts begin to jostle in my head, and I shall see the truth of all things made clear at last.'

But the thoughts did not jostle, a curious lethargy began stealing over him instead, so that his head fell back, and his mouth fell open. This might have endured until he returned to earth had not the airman stopped the engines so that they drifted ruminantly in space below the clouds. With the cessation of the noise Mr. Lavender's brain regained its activity, and he was enchanted to hear the voice of his pilot saying:

" How are you getting on, sir ? "

" As regards the sensation," Mr. Lavender replied, " it is marvellous, for after the first minute or two, during which the unwonted motion causes a certain inconvenience, one grasps at once the exhilaration and joy of this great adventure. To be in motion towards the spheres, and see the earth laid out like a chess-board below you ; to feel the lithe creature beneath your body responding so freely to every call of its gallant young pilot ; to be filled with the scream of the engines, as of an eagle at sport ; to know that at the least aberration of the intrepid airman we should be dashed into a million pieces ; all this is largely to experience an experience so unforgettable that one will never—er——forget it."

" Gosh ! " said the young airman.

" Yes," pursued Mr. Lavender, who was now unconsciously reading himself in his morning's paper, " one can only compare the emotion to that which the disembodied spirit might feel passing straight from earth to heaven. We saw at a great depth below us on a narrow white riband of road two crawling black specks, and knew that they were human beings, the same and no more than we had seen before we left that great common place called Earth."

" Gum ! " said the young airman, as Mr. Lavender paused, " you're getting it fine, sir ! Where will it appear ? "

" Those great fleecy beings the clouds," went on Mr. Lavender, without taking in the interruption, " seemed to await our coming in the morning glory of their piled-up snows ; and we, with the rarefied air in our lungs, felt that we must shout to them." And so carried away was Mr. Lavender by his own style that he really did begin to address the clouds : " Ghosts of the sky, who creep cold about this wide blue air, we small adventuring mortals great-hearted salute you. Humbly proud of our daring have we come to sport with you and the winds of Ouranos, and, in the rapturous corridors between you, play hide-and-seek, avoiding your glorious moisture with the dips and curves and skimming of our swallow flights—we, the little unconquerable Spirits of the Squirth ! "

The surprise which Mr. Lavender felt at having uttered so peculiar a word in the middle of such a flow of poetry reduced him to sudden silence.

" Golly ! " said the airman, with sudden alarm in his voice. " Hold tight ! " And they began to shoot towards earth faster than they had risen.

They came down, by what seemed a miracle to Mr. Lavender, who was still contemplative, precisely where they had gone up. A little group was collected there, and as they stepped out a voice said, " I beg your pardon," in a tone so dry that it pierced even the fogged condition in which Mr. Lavender alighted. The gentleman who spoke had a dark moustache and thick white hair, and, except that he wore a monocle, and was perhaps three inches taller, bore a striking resemblance to himself.

" Thank you," he replied, " certainly."

" No," said the gentleman, " not at all—on the contrary. Who the hell are you ? "

" A public man," said Mr. Lavender, surprised ; " at least," he added conscientiously, " I am not quite certain."

" Well," said the gentleman, " you've jolly well stolen my stunt."

" Who, then, are you ? " asked Mr. Lavender.

"I?" replied the gentleman, evidently intensely surprised that he was not known; "I—my name——"

But at this moment Mr. Lavender's attention was diverted by the sight of Blink making for the horizon, and crying out in a loud voice: "My dog!" he dropped the coat in which he was still enveloped and set off running after her at full speed, without having taken in the identity of the gentleman or disclosed his own. Blink, indeed, scenting another flight in the air, had made straight for the entrance of the enclosure, and finding a motor cab there with the door open had bolted into it, taking it for her master's car. Mr. Lavender sprang in after her. At the shake which this imparted to the cab, the driver, who had been dozing, turned his head.

"Want to go back, sir?" he said.

"Yes," replied Mr. Lavender, breathless; "London."

XVIII

SEES TRUTH FACE TO FACE

'I FEAR,' thought Mr. Lavender, as they sped towards town, 'that I have inadvertently taken a joy-ride which belonged to that distinguished person with the eye-glass. No matter, my spirit is now bright for the adventure I have in hand. If only I knew where I could find the Unseen Power—but possibly its movements may be recorded in these journals.' And taking from his pocket his morning papers, which he had not yet had time to peruse, he buried himself in their contents. He was still deeply absorbed when the cab stopped, and the driver knocked on the window. Mr. Lavender got out, followed by Blink, and was feeling in his pocket for the fare when an exclamation broke from the driver :

"Gorblimy ! I've brought the wrong baby ! "

And before Mr. Lavender had recovered from his surprise, he had whipped the car round and was speeding back towards the flying ground.

'How awkward ! ' thought Mr. Lavender, who was extremely nice in money matters ; 'what shall I do now ? ' And he looked around him. There, as it were by a miracle, was the office of a great journal, whence obviously his distinguished colleague had set forth to the flying grounds, and to which he had been returned in error by the faithful driver.

148

Perceiving in all this the finger of Providence, Mr. Lavender walked in. Those who have followed his experiences so far will readily understand how no one could look on Mr. Lavender without perceiving him to be a man of extreme mark, and no surprise need be felt when he was informed that the Personage he sought was on the point of visiting Brighton to open a hospital, and might yet be overtaken at Victoria Station.

With a beating heart he took up the trail in another taxi-cab, and, arriving at Victoria, purchased tickets for himself and Blink, and inquired for the Brighton train.

" Hurry up ! " replied the official. Mr. Lavender ran, searching the carriage windows for any indication of his objective. The whistle had been blown, and he was in despair, when his eye caught the label " Reserved " on a first-class window, and looking in he saw a single person evidently of the highest consequence smoking a cigar, surrounded by papers. Without a moment's hesitation he opened the door, and, preceded by Blink, leaped in. " This carriage is reserved, sir," said the Personage, as the train moved out.

" I know," said Mr. Lavender, who had fallen on to the edge of the seat opposite ; " and only the urgency of my business would have caused me to violate the sanctity of your retreat, for, believe me, I have the instincts if not the habits of a gentleman."

The Personage, who had made a move of his hand as if to bring the train to a standstill, abandoning his design, replaced his cigar, and contemplated Mr. Lavender from above it.

The latter remained silent, returning that remarkable stare, while Blink withdrew beneath the seat and pressed

149

her chin to the ground, savouring the sensation of another new motion.

' Yes,' he thought, ' those eyes have an almost superhuman force and cunning. They are the eyes of a spider in the centre of a great web. They seem to draw me.'

" You are undoubtedly the Unseen Power, sir," he said suddenly, " and I have reached the heart of the mystery. From your own lips I shall soon know whether I am a puppet or a public man."

The Personage, who by his movements was clearly under the impression that he had to do with a lunatic, sat forward with his hands on his knees ready to rise at a moment's notice ; he kept his cigar in his mouth, however, and an enforced smile on the folds of his face.

" What can I do for you, sir ? " he said. " Will you have a cigar ? "

" No, thank you," replied Mr. Lavender, " I must keep the eyes of my spirit clear, and come to the point. Do you rule this country or do you not ? For it is largely on the answer to this that my future depends. In telling others what to do am I speaking as *my* conscience or as *your* conscience dictates ; and, further, if indeed I am speaking as your conscience dictates, have you a conscience ? "

The Personage, who had evidently made up his mind to humour the intruder, flipped the ash off his cigar.

" Well, sir," he said, " I don't know who the devil you may be, but my conscience is certainly as good as yours."

" That," returned Mr. Lavender with a sigh, " is a great relief, for whether you rule the country or not, you are undoubtedly the source from which I, together with the majority of my countrymen, derive our inspirations. You are the fountain-head at which we draw and drink. And to know that your waters are pure, unstained by taint of personal prejudice and the love of power, will fortify us considerably. Am I to assume, then, that above all passion and pettiness, you are an impersonal force whose innumerable daily editions reflect nothing but abstract truth, and are in no way the servants of a preconceived and personal view of the situation ? "

" You want to know too much, don't you think ? " said the Personage with a smile.

" How can that be, sir ? " asked Mr. Lavender : " If you are indeed the invisible king swaying the currents of national life, and turning its tides at will, it is essential that we should believe in you ; and before we can believe in you must we not know all about you?"

" By Jove, sir," replied the Personage, " that strikes me as being contrary to all the rules of religion. I thought faith was the ticket."

By this answer Mr. Lavender was so impressed that he sat for a moment in silence, with his eyebrow working up and down.

" Sir," he said at last, " you have given me a new thought. If you are right, to disbelieve in you and the acts which you perform, or rather the editions which you issue, is blasphemy."

" I should think so," said the Personage, emitting a long whiff of smoke. " Hadn't that ever occurred to you before ? "

" No," replied Mr. Lavender, naïvely, " for I have never yet disbelieved anything in those journals."

The Personage coughed heartily.

" I have always regarded them," went on Mr.

151

Lavender, "as I myself should wish to be regarded, 'without fear and without reproach.' For that is, as I understand it, the principle on which a gentleman must live, ever believing of others what he would wish believed of himself. With the exception of Germans," he added hastily.

"Naturally," returned the Personage. "And I'll defy you to find anything in them which disagrees with that formula. Everything they print refers to Germans if not directly then obliquely. Germans are the *idée fixe*, and without an *idée fixe*, as you know, there's no such thing as religion. Do you get me?"

"Yes, indeed," cried Mr. Lavender, enthused, for the whole matter now seemed to him to fall into coherence, and, what was more, to coincide with his preconceptions, so that he had no longer any doubts. "You, sir—the Unseen Power—are but the crystallised embodiment of the national sentiment in time of war; in serving you, and fulfilling the ideas which you concrete in your journals, we public men are servants of the general animus, which in its turn serves the blind and burning instinct of Justice. This is eminently satisfactory to me, who would wish no better fate than to be a humble lackey in that house." He had no sooner, however, spoken those words than Joe Petty's remarks about Public Opinion came back to him, and he added: "But are you really the general animus, or are you only the animus of Mayors, that is the question?"

The Personage seemed to follow this thought with difficulty. "What's that?" he said.

Mr. Lavender ran his hands through his hair.

"All turns," he said, "on what is the unit of national feeling and intelligence? Is it or is it not a Mayor?"

The Personage smiled. " Well, what do you think ? " he said. " Haven't you ever heard them after dinner ? There's no question about it. Make your mind easy if that's your only trouble."

Mr. Lavender, greatly cheered by the genial certainty in this answer, said : " I thank you, sir. I shall go back and refute that common scoffer, that caster of doubts. I have seen the Truth face to face, and am greatly encouraged to further public effort. With many apologies I can now get out," he added, as the train stopped at South Croydon. " Blink ! " And, followed by his dog, he stepped from the train.

The Personage, who was indeed no other than the private secretary of the private secretary of It whom Mr. Lavender had designated as the Truth watched him from the window.

" Well, that *was* a treat, dear papa ! " he murmured to himself, emitting a sigh of smoke after his retreating interlocutor.

XIX

IS IN PERIL OF THE STREET

On the Sunday following this interview with the Truth Mr. Lavender, who ever found the day of rest irksome to his strenuous spirit, left his house after an early supper. It had been raining all day, but the sinking sun had now emerged and struck its level light into the tree tops from a still cloudy distance. Followed by Blink, he threaded the puddled waste which lies to the west of the Spaniard's Road, nor was it long before the wild beauty of the scene infected his spirit, and he stood still to admire the world spread out. The smoke rack of misted rain was still drifting above the sunset radiance in an apple-green sky; and behind Mr. Lavender, while he gazed at those clouds symbolical of the world's unrest, a group of tall, dark pine-trees, wild and witch-like, had collected as if in audience of his cosmic mood. He formed a striking group for a painter, with the west wind flinging back his white hair, and fluttering his dark moustache along his cheeks, while Blink, a little in front of him, pointed at the prospect and emitted barks whose vigour tossed her charming head now to this side now to that.

' How beautiful is this earth ! ' thought Mr. Lavender, ' and how simple to be good and happy thereon. Yet must we journey ten leagues beyond the wide world's end to find justice and liberty. There are dark powers like lions ever in the path. Yes,' he continued, turning round to the pine-trees, who were creaking slightly in the wind, ' hate and oppression, greed, lust, and ambition ! There you stand malevolently regarding me. Out upon you, dark witches of evil ! If I had but an axe I would lay you lower than the dust. But the poor pine-trees paid no attention save to creak a little louder. And so incensed was Mr. Lavender by this insensibility on the part of those which his own words had made him perceive where the powers of darkness that he would very likely have barked his knuckles on them if Blink by her impatience had not induced him to resume his walk and mount on to the noble rampart of the Spaniard's Road.

Along this he wandered and down the hill with the countless ghosts and shadows of his brain, liberating the world in fancy from all the hindrances which beset the paths of public men, till dark fell, and he was compelled to turn towards home. Closely attended by the now sobered Blink he had reached the Tube Station when he perceived in the inky wartime dusk that a woman was following him. Dimly aware that she was tall and graceful he hurried to avoid her, but before long could but note that she was walking parallel and turning her face towards him. Her gloved hand seemed to make a beckoning movement, and perceiving at once that he was the object of that predatory instinct which he knew from the many letters and protests in his journals to be one of the most distressing features of the war, he would have broken into a run if he had not been travelling up-hill; being deprived of this means of escape, his public nature prevailed, and he saw that it was his duty to confront the woman, and strike a blow at the national evil stalking beside him. But he was in a difficulty, for his natural delicacy towards women seemed to preclude him from treating her as if she were what she evidently was, while his sense of duty urged him with equal force to do so.

A whiff of delicious scent determined him. "Madam," he said, without looking in her face, which, indeed, was not visible—so great was the darkness, "it is useless to pursue one who not only has the greatest veneration for women but regards you as a public danger at a time when all the energies of the country should be devoted to the defeat of our common enemies."

The woman, uttering a sound like a laugh, edged towards him, and Mr. Lavender edged away, so that they proceeded up the street crabwise, with Blink adhering jealously to her master's heels.

"Do you know," said Mr. Lavender, with all the delicacy in his power, "how terribly subversive of the national effort it is to employ your beauty and grace to snare and slacken the sinews of our glorious youth? The mystery of a woman's glance in times like these should be used solely to beckon our heroes on to death in the field. But you, madam, than whom no one indeed has a more mysterious glance, have turned it to ends which, in the words of a great public man, profane the temple of ou—our——"

Mr. Lavender stopped, for his delicacy would not allow him even in so vital a cause to call bodies bodies. The woman here edged so close that he bolted across her in affright, and began to slant back towards the opposite side of the street.

"Madam," he said, "you must have perceived by now that I am, alas! not privileged by age to be one of the defenders of my country; and though I am prepared to yield to you, if by so doing I can save some young hero from his fate, I wish you to clearly under-

156

stand that only my sense of duty as a public man would induce me to do any such thing." At this he turned his eyes dreadfully upon her graceful form still sidling towards him, and conscious again of that delightful scent, felt a swooning sensation which made him lean against a lamp-post. "Spare me, madam," he said in a faint voice; "for my country's sake I am ready to do anything, but I must tell you that I worship another of your sex from afar, and if you are a woman you will not seek to make me besmirch that adoration or imperil my chivalry."

So saying he threw his arms around the lamp-post and closed his eyes, expecting every moment to be drawn away against his will into a life of vice. A well-known voice, strangled to the pitch almost of inaudibility, said in his ear: "Oh, Don Pickwixote, Don Pickwixote, you will be the death of me!"

Electrified, Mr. Lavender opened his eyes, and in the dull orange rays of the heavily shaded lamp he saw beside him no other than the writhing, choking figure of Aurora herself. Shocked beyond measure by the mistake he had made, Mr. Lavender threw up his hands and bolted past her through the gateway of his garden; nor did he cease running till he had reached his bedroom and got under the bed, so terribly was he upset. There, in the company of Blink, he spent perhaps the most shame-stricken hours of his existence, cursing the memory of all those bishops and novelists who had caused him to believe that every woman in a dark street was a danger to the State; nor could the persuasion of Mrs. Petty or Joe induce him to come out, so that in despair they were compelled to leave him to pass the night in this penetential position, which he did without even taking out his teeth.

RECEIVES A REVELATION

FULLY a week elapsed before Mr. Lavender recovered
from the effects of the night which he had spent under
his bed and again took his normal interest in the course
of national affairs.   That which at length tore him from
his torpid condition and refixed his imagination was an
article in one of his journals on the League of Nations,
which caused him suddenly to perceive that this was
the most important subject of the day.   Carefully
extracting the address of the society who had the
matter in hand, he determined to go down forthwith
and learn from their own lips how he could best induce
everybody to join them in their noble undertaking.
Shutting every window, therefore, and locking Blink
carefully into his study, he set forth and took the tube to
Charing Cross.

Arriving at the premises indicated he made his way
in lifts and corridors till he came to the name of this
great world undertaking upon the door of Room 443,
and paused for a moment to recover from the astonishment he felt that the whole building at least was not
occupied by the energies of such a prodigious association.

' Appearances, however, are deceptive,' he thought ;
' and from a single grain of mustard-seed whole fields
will flower.'   He knocked on the door, therefore, and
receiving the reply, " Cub id," in a female voice, he

entered a room where two young ladies with bad colds were feebly tapping type-writers.

" Can I see the President ? " asked Mr. Lavender.

" Dot at the bobent," said one of the young ladies. " Will the Secretary do ? "

" Yes," replied Mr. Lavender, " for I seek information."

The young ladies indulged in secret confabulation, from which the perpetual word " He " alone escaped to Mr. Lavender's ears.

Then one of them slipped into an inner room, leaving behind her a powerful trail of eucalyptus. She came back almost directly, saying, " Go id."

The room which Mr. Lavender entered contained two persons, one seated at a bureau and the other pacing up and down and talking in a powerful bass voice. He paused, looked at Mr. Lavender from under bushy brows, and at once went on walking and talking, with a sort of added zest.

' This must be He,' thought Mr. Lavender, sitting down to listen, for there was something about the gentleman which impressed him at once. He had very large red ears, and hardly a hair on his head, while his full, bearded face and prominent eyes were full of force and genius.

" It won't do a little bit, Titmarsh," he was saying, " to allow the politicians to meddle in this racket. We want men of genius, whose imaginations carry them beyond the facts of the moment. This is too big a thing for those blasted politicians. They haven't shown a sign so far of paying attention to what I've been telling them all this time. We must keep them out, Titmarsh. Machinery without mechanism, and a change of heart in the world. It's very simple.

A single man of genuis from each country, no petti-fogging opposition, no petty prejudices."

The other gentleman, whom Mr. Lavender took for the Secretary, and who was leaning his head rather wearily on his hand, interjected : " Quite so ! And whom would you choose besides yourself ? In France, for instance ? "

He who was walking stopped a moment, again looked at Mr. Lavender intently, and again began to speak as if he were not there.

" France ? " he said. " There isn't anybody— Anatole's too old—there isn't anybody."

" America, then ? " hazarded the Secretary.

" America ! " replied the other ; " they haven't got even half a man. There's that fellow in Germany that I used to influence ; but I don't know—no, I don't think he'd be any good."

" D'Annunzio, surely——" began the Secretary.

" D'Annunzio ? My God ! D'Annunzio ! No ! There's nobody in Italy or Holland—she's as bankrupt as Spain ; and there's not a cat in Austria. Russia might, perhaps, give us someone, but I can't at the moment think of him. No, Titmarsh, it's difficult."

Mr. Lavender had been growing more and more excited at each word he overheard, for a scheme of really stupendous proportions was shaping itself within him. He suddenly rose, and said : " I have an idea."

The Secretary sat up as if he had received a Faradic shock, and he who was walking up and down stood still. " The deuce you have, sir," he said.

" Yes," cried Mr. Lavender ; " and in concentration and marvellous simplicity it has, I am sure, never been surpassed. It is clear to me, sir, that you, and you alone, must be this League of Nations. For if it is entirely in your hands there will be no delay. The plan will spring full fledged from the head of Jove, and this great and beneficial change in the lot of mankind will at once become an accomplished fact. There will be no need for keeping in touch with human nature, no call for patience and all that laborious upbuilding stone by stone which is so apt to discourage mankind and imperil the fruition of great reforms. No, sir; you—you must be this League, and we will all work to the end that to-morrow at latest there may be perfected this crowning achievement of the human species."

The gentleman, who had commenced to walk again, looked furtively from Mr. Lavender to the Secretary, and said :

" By Jingo ! some idea ! "

" Yes," cried Mr. Lavender, entranced that his grand notion should be at once accepted ; " for it is only men like you who can both soaringly conceive and immediately concrete in action ; and, what is more, there will be no fear of your tiring of this job and taking up another, for you will be IT ; and one cannot change oneself."

The gentleman looked at Mr. Lavender very suddenly at the words " tiring of this job," and transferred his gaze to the Secretary, who had bent his face down to his papers, and was smothering a snigger with his hand.

" Who *are* you, sir ? " he said sharply.

" Merely one," returned Mr. Lavender, " who wishes to do all in his power to forward a project so fraught with beneficence to all mankind. I count myself fortunate beyond measure to have come here this morning and found the very Heart of the matter, the grain of mustard-seed."

The gentleman, who had begun to walk again, here

161

muttered words which would have sounded like " Damned impudence " if Mr. Lavender had not been too utterly carried away by his idea to hear them.

" I shall go forth at once," he said, " and make known the good tidings that the fields are sown, the League formed. Henceforth there are no barriers between nations, and the reign of perpetual Peace is assured. It is colossal."

The gentleman abruptly raised his boot, but, seeming to think better of it, lowered it again, and turned away to the window.

Mr. Lavender, having bowed to his back, went out, and urged on by his enthusiasm, directed his steps at once towards Trafalgar Square.

Arriving at this hub of the universe he saw that Chance was on his side, for a meeting was already in progress, and a crowd of some forty persons assembled round one of the lions. Owing to his appearance Mr. Lavender was able without opposition to climb up on to the plinth and join the speaker, a woman of uncertain years. He stood there awaiting his turn and preparing his oration, while she continued her discourse, which seemed to be a protest against any interference with British control of the freedom of the seas. A Union Jack happened to be leaning against the monument, and when she had at last finished, Mr. Lavender seized it and came forward to the edge.

" Great tidings ! " he said at once, waving the flag, and without more ado plunged into an oration, which, so far as it went, must certainly be ranked among his masterpieces. " Great tidings, Friends ! I have planted the grain of mustard-seed ; or, in common parlance, have just come from the meeting which has incepted the League of Nations ; and it will be my

task this morning briefly to make known to you the principles which in future must dominate the policy of the world. Since it is for the closer brotherhood of man and the reign of perpetual peace that we are struggling, we must first secure the annihilation of our common enemies. Those members of the human race whose infamies have largely placed them beyond the pale must be eliminated once for all." Loud cheers greeted this utterance, and stimulated by the sound Mr. Lavender proceeded : " What, however, must the civilised nations do when at last they have clean sheets ? In the first place, all petty prejudices and provincial aspirations must be set aside; and though the world must be firmly founded upon the principle of nationality it must also act as one great people. This, my fellow-countrymen, is no mere contradiction in terms, for though in their new solidarities each nation will be prouder of itself, and more jealous of its good name and independence than ever, that will not prevent it sacrificing its inalienable rights for the good of the whole human nation of which it is a member. Friends, let me give you a simple illustration, which in a nutshell will make the whole thing clear. We, here in Britain, are justly proud and tenacious of our sea power—in the words of the poet, ' We hold all the gates of the water.' Now it is abundantly and convincingly plain that this reinforced principle of nationality bids us to retain and increase them, while internationalism bids us give them up."

His audience, which had hitherto listened with open mouths, here closed them, and a strident voice exclaimed : " Give it a name, gov'nor. D'you say we ought to give up Gib ? "

This word pierced Mr. Lavender, standing where he

163

was, to the very marrow, and he fell into such confusion of spirit that his words became inaudible.

'My God!' he thought, appalled; 'is it possible that I have not got to the bottom of this question?' And, turning his back on the audience, he gazed in a sort of agony at the figure of Nelson towering into the sky above him. He was about to cry out piteously: 'Countrymen, I know not what I think. Oh! I am unhappy!' when he inadvertently stepped back over the edge of the plinth, and, still entangled in the flag, was picked up by two policemen and placed in a dazed condition and a deserted spot opposite the National Gallery.

It was while he was standing there, encircled by pigeons and forgotten by his fellow man, that there came to him a spiritual revelation. 'Strange!' he thought; 'I notice a certain inconsistency in myself, and even in my utterances. I am two men, one of whom is me and one not me; and the one which is not me is the one which causes me to fall into the arms of policemen and other troubles. The one which is me loves these pigeons, and desires to live quietly with my dog, not considering public affairs, which, indeed, seem to be suited to persons of another sort. Whence, then, comes the one which is not me? Can it be that it is derived from the sayings and writings of others, and is but a spurious spirit only meet to be outcast? Do I, to speak in the vernacular, care any buttons whether we stick to Gibraltar, or not so long as men do but live in kindness? And if that is so, have I the right to say I do? Ought I not, rather, to be true to my private self and leave the course of public affairs to those who have louder voices and no private selves?' The thought was extremely painful, for it seemed to disclose to him grave inconsistency in the recent management of his life. And, thoroughly mortified, he turned round with a view of entering the National Gallery and soothing his spirit with art, when he was arrested by the placard which covered it announcing which town had taken which sum of bonds. This lighted up such a new vista of public utility that his brain would certainly have caught fire again if one of the policemen who had conducted him across the Square had not touched him on the arm, and said : " How are you now, sir ? "

" I am pretty well, thank you, policeman," replied Mr. Lavender, " and sorry that I occasioned so much disturbance."

" Don't mention it, sir," answered the policeman ; " you came a nasty crump."

" Tell me," said Mr. Lavender, suddenly looking up into his face, " do you consider that a man is justified in living a private life ? For, as regards my future, it is largely on your opinion that I shall act."

The policeman, whose solid face showed traces of astonishment, answered slowly : " As a general thing, a man's private life don't bear lookin' into, as you know, sir."

" I have not lived one for some time," said Mr. Lavender.

" Well," remarked the policeman, " if you take my advice you won't try it again. I should say you 'adn't the constitution."

" I fear you do not catch my meaning," returned Mr. Lavender, whose whole body was aching from his fall ; " it is my public life which tries me."

" Well, then, I should chuck it," said the policeman.

" Really ? " murmured Mr. Lavender eagerly ; " would you ? "

" Why not ? " said the policeman.

So excited was Mr. Lavender by this independent confirmation of his sudden longing that he took out half a crown.

" You will oblige me greatly," he said, " by accepting this as a token of my gratitude."

" Well, sir, I'll humour you," answered the policeman ; " though it was no trouble, I'm sure ; you're as light as a feather. Goin' anywhere in particular ? " he added.

" Yes," said Mr. Lavender, rather faintly, " the Tube Station."

" Come along with me, then."

Mr. Lavender went along, not sorry to have the protection of that stalwart form, for his nerve was shaken, not so much by physical suffering as by the revelation he had received.

" If you'll take *my* tip, sir," said the policeman, parting from him, " you won't try no private life again ; you don't look strong."

" Thank you, policeman," said Mr. Lavender musingly ; " it is kind of you to take an interest in me. Good-bye ! "

Safely seated in the Tube for Hampstead he continued the painful struggle of his meditations. ' If, indeed,' he thought, ' as a public man I do more harm than good, I am prepared to sacrifice all for my country's sake and retire into private life. But the policeman said that would be dangerous for me. What, then, is left ? To live neither a public nor a private life ! '

This thought, at once painful and heroic, began to take such hold of him that he arrived at his house in a high fever of the brain.

XXI

AND ASCENDS TO PARADISE

Now when Mr. Lavender once slept over an idea it became so strong that no power on earth could prevent his putting it into execution, and all night long he kept Blink awake by tramping up and down his bedroom and planning the details of such a retirement as would meet his unfortunate case. For at once he perceived that to retire from both his lives without making the whole world know of it would be tantamount to not retiring. 'Only by a public act,' he thought, 'of so striking a character that nobody can miss it can I bring the moral home to all public and private men.' And a hundred schemes swarmed like ants in his brain. Nor was it till the cock crew that one adequate to this final occasion occurred to him.

'It will want very careful handling,' he thought, 'for otherwise I shall be prevented, and perhaps even arrested in the middle, which will be both painful and ridiculous.' So sublime, however, was his idea that he shed many tears over it, and often paused in his tramping to regard the unconscious Blink with streaming eyes. All the next day he went about the house and heath taking a last look at objects which had been dear, and at meal times ate and drank even less than usual, absorbed by the pathos of his coming renunciation. He determined to make his preparations for the final act during the night, when Mrs. Petty would be prevented by Joe's snoring from hearing the necessary sounds; and at supper he undertook the delicate and harrowing task of saying good-bye to his devoted housekeeper without letting her know that he was doing it.

"Mrs. Petty," he said, trifling with a morsel of cheese, " it is useless to disguise from you that I may be going on a journey, and I feel that I shall not be able to part from all the care you have bestowed on me without recording in words my heartfelt appreciation of your devotion. I shall miss it, I shall miss it terribly, if, that is, if I am permitted to miss anything."

Mrs. Petty, whose mind instantly ran to his bed-socks, answered : " Don't you worry, sir ; I won't forget them. But wherever are you going now ? "

"Ah ! " said Mr. Lavender subtly, " it is all in the air at present ; but now that the lime-trees are beginning to smell a certain restlessness is upon me, and you may see some change in my proceedings. Whatever happens to me, however, I commit my dear Blink to your care ; feed her as if she were myself, and love her as if she were Joe, for it is largely on food and affection that dogs depend for happiness."

"Why, good gracious, sir," said Mrs. Petty, " you talk as if you were going for a month of Sundays. Are you thinking of Eastbourne ? "

Mr. Lavender sighed deeply at that word, for the memory of a town where he had spent many happy days added to the gentle melancholy of his feelings on this last evening.

" As regards that I shall not inform you at present ; for, indeed, I am by no means certain what my destination will be. Largely speaking, no pub-public man, he stammered, doubtful whether he was any longer that, " knows where he will be going to-morrow. Sufficient unto the day are the intentions in his head."

" Well, sir," said Mrs. Petty frankly, " you can't go anywhere without Joe or me, that's flat."

Mr. Lavender smiled.

" Dear Mrs. Petty," he murmured, " there are sacrifices one cannot demand even of the most faithful friends, But," he went on with calculated playfulness, " we need not consider that point until the day after to-morrow at least, for I have much to do in the meantime."

Reassured by those words and the knowledge that Mr. Lavender's plans seldom remained the same for more than two days, Mrs. Petty tossed her head slightly, and went to the door. " Well, it *is* a mystery, I'm sure," she said.

" I should like to see Joe," said Mr. Lavender, with a lingering look at his devoted housekeeper.

" The beauty ! " muttered Mrs. Petty ; " I'll send him," and withdrew.

Giving the morsel of cheese to Blink, who, indeed, had eaten practically the whole of this last meal, Mr. Lavender took the moon-cat on his shoulder, and abandoned himself for a moment to the caresses of his two favourites.

" Blink," he said in a voice which trembled slightly, " be good to this moon-cat while I am away ; and if I am longer than you expect, darling, do not be unhappy. Perhaps some day you will rejoin me ; and even if we are not destined to meet again, I would not, in the fashion of cruel men, wish to hinder your second marriage, or to stand in the way of your happy forgetfulness of me. Be as light-hearted as you can, my dear, and wear no mourning for your master."

So saying, he flung his arms round her, and embraced her warmly, inhaling with the most poignant emotion her sheep-like odour. He was still engaged with her when the door was opened, and Joe came in.

" Joe," said Mr. Lavender resolutely, " sit down and light your pipe. You will find a bottle of pre-war port in the sideboard. Open it, and drink my health ; indeed, I myself will drink it too, for it may give me courage. We have been good friends, Joe," he went on while Joe was drawing the cork, " and have participated in pleasant and sharp adventures. I have called you in at this moment, which may some day seem to you rather solemn, partly to shake your hand and partly to resume the discussion on public men which we held some days ago, if you remember."

" Ah ! " said Joe, with his habitual insouciance, " when I told you that they give me the 'ump. Yes, what abaht it, sir ? 'Ave they been sayin' anything particular vicious ? " His face flying up just then with the cork which he was extracting encountered the expression on Mr. Lavender's visage, and he added : " Don't take wot I say to 'eart, sir ; try as you like *you'll* never be a public man."

Those words, which seemed to Mr. Lavender to seal his doom, caused a faint pink flush to invade his cheeks.

" No," continued Joe, pouring out the wine ; " you 'aven't got the brass in times like these. I dare say you've noticed, sir, that the times is favourable for bringing out the spots on the body politic. 'Ere's 'ealth ! "

" Joe," said Mr. Lavender, raising his glass to his lips with solemnity, " I wish you a most happy and prosperous life. Let us drink to all those qualities which make you *par excellence* one of that great race, the best hearted in the world, which never thinks of to-morrow, never knows when it is beaten, and seldom loses its sense of humour."

" Ah ! " returned Joe enigmatically, half-closing one of his greenish eyes, and laying the glass to one side of his reddish nose. Then, with a quick move-ment, he swallowed its contents and refilled it before Mr. Lavender had succeeded in absorbing more than a drop. "I don't say," he continued, "but what there's a class o' public man that's got its uses, like the little 'un that keeps us all alive, or the perfect English gentleman what did his job and told nobody nothin' abaht it. You can 'ave confidence in a man like that —that's why 'e's gone an' retired ; 'e's civilised, you see, the finished article ; but all this raw material, this ' get-on ' or ' get-out ' lot, that's come from 'oo knows where, well, I wish they'd stayed there with their tell-you-how-to-do-it and their 'ymns of 'ate."

" Joe," said Mr. Lavender, "are you certain that therein does not speak the snob inherent in the national bosom ? Are you not unconsciously paying deference to the word gentleman ? "

" Why not, sir ? " replied Joe, tossing off his second glass. "It'd be a fine thing for the country if we was all gentlemen—straight, an' a little bit stupid, and 'ad 'alf a thought for others." And he refilled his master's glass. "I don't measure a gentleman by 'is money, or 'is title, not even by 'is clothes—I measure 'im by whether he can stand 'avin' power in 'is 'ands without gettin' unscrupled or swollen 'eaded, an' whether 'e can do what he thinks right without payin' attention to clamour. But, mind you, 'e's got to 'ave right thoughts too, and a feelin' 'eart. 'Ere's luck, sir."

Mr. Lavender, who, absorbed in his chauffeur's

sentiments, had now drunk two glasses, rose from his chair, and clutching his hair said : " I will not conceal from you, Joe, that I have always assumed every public man came up to that standard, at least."

" Crickey ! " said Joe. " 'Ave you really, sir ? My Gawd ! Got any use for the rest of this bottle ? "

" No, Joe, no: I shall never have use for a bottle again."

" In that case I might as well," said Joe, pouring what remained into a tumbler and drinking it off. " Is there any other topic you'd like to mention ? If I can 'ave any influence on you, I shall be very glad."

" Thank you, Joe," returned Mr. Lavender, " what I have most need of at this moment is solitude and your good wishes. And will you kindly take Blink away, and when she has had her run, place her in my bedroom, with the window closed. Good-night, Joe. Call me late to-morrow morning."

" Certainly, sir. Good-night, sir."

" Good-night, Joe. Shake hands."

When Joe was gone, accompanied by the unwilling Blink, turning her beautiful dark eyes back to the last, Mr. Lavender sat down at his bureau, and drawing a sheet of paper to him, wrote at the top of it.

" My last Will and Testament."

It was a long time before he got any further, and then entirely omitted to leave anything in it, completely preoccupied by the preamble, which gradually ran as follows :

" I, John Lavender, make known to all men by these presents that the act which I contemplate is symbolical, and must in no sense be taken as implying either weariness of life or that surrender to misfortune which is unbecoming to an English public gentleman."

172

(Over this description of himself Mr. Lavender was
obliged to pause some time hovering between the two
designations, and finally combining them as the only
way out of his difficulty.) " Long and painful experience has convinced me that only by retiring from the
former can I retain the latter character, and only retiring
from both can I point the moral ever demanded by
my countrymen. Conscious, indeed, that a mere act
of private resignation would have no significance to
the body politic, nor any deflecting influence on the
national life, I have chosen rather to disappear in blue
flame, so that every Englishman may take to heart
my lesson, and learn from my strange fate how to be
himself uninfluenced by the verbiage of others. At the
same time, with the utmost generosity, I wish to
acknowledge in full my debt towards all those great
writers and speakers on the war who have exercised
so intoxicating an influence on my mind." (Here
followed an alphabetical list of names beginning with
B and ending with S.) " I wish to be dissociated
firmly from the views of my chauffeur Joe Petty, and to
go to my last account with an emphatic assertion that
my failure to become a perfect public gentleman is
due to private idiosyncrasies rather than to any conviction that it is impossible, or to anything but
admiration of the great men I have mentioned. If
anybody should wish to paint me after I am dead, I
desire that I may be represented with my face turned
towards the Dawn ; for it is at that moment—so
symptomatic of a deep adoration which I would
scorn to make the common property of gossiping
tongues—that I intend to depart. If there should be
anything left of me—which is less than probable
considering the inflammatory character of the material

173

I design for my pyre—I would be obliged if, without giving anybody any trouble, it could be buried in my garden, with the usual Hampstead tablet.

" ' JOHN LAVENDER,
THE PUBLIC MAN, WHO DIED FOR
HIS COUNTRY'S GOOD, LIVED HERE.'

" In conclusion, I would say a word to that land I have loved and served : ' Be not extreme ! Distrust the words of others. To yourself be true ! As you are strong be gentle, as you are brave be modest ! Beloved country, farewell ! ' "

Having written that final sentence he struggled long with himself before he could lay down the pen. But by this time the port he had drunk had begun to have its usual effect, and he fell into a doze, from which he was awakened five hours later by the beams of a full moon striking in on him.

' The hour has come,' he thought, and, opening the French-window, he went out onto the lawn, where the dew lay white. The freshness in the air, the glamour of the moonlight, and the fumes of the port combined to make him feel strangely rhumantic, and if he had possessed a musical instrument he would very likely have begun to play on it. He spent some moments tracking to and fro in the dew before he settled on the centre of the lawn as the most suitable spot for the act which he contemplated, for thence he would be able to turn his last looks towards Aurora's bedroom-window without interference from foliage. Having drawn a twelve-foot circle in the dew with his toe he proceeded in the bright moonlight to the necessary accumulation of his funeral pile, conveying from his

174

study, book by book, journal by journal, pamphlet
by pamphlet, the hoarded treasures of the last four
years ; and as he carefully placed each one, building up
at once a firm and cunning structure, he gave a little
groan, thinking of the intoxications of the past, and
all the glorious thoughts embodied in that literature.
Underneath, in the heart of the pile, he reserved a space
for the most inflammable material, which he selected
from a special file of a special journal, and round the
circumference of the lofty and tapering mound he
carefully deposited the two hundred and four war
numbers of a certain weekly, so that a ring of flame
might lick well up the sides and permeate the more
solid matter on which he would be sitting. For two
hours he worked in the waning moonlight, till he had
completed this weird and heroic erection ; and just
before the dawn, sat down by the light of the candle
with which he meant to apply the finishing touch, to
compose that interview with himself whereby he intended to convey to the world the message of
his act.

" I found him," he began, in the words of the inter-
viewer, " sitting upon a journalistic pile of lovely
leaves of thought, which in the dawning of a new day
glowed with a certain restrained flamboyance, as
though the passion stored within those exotic pages
gave itself willingly to the *éclaircissement* of the situation,
and of his lineaments in which suffering had already
set their stamp.

" ' I should like,' I said, approaching as near as I
could, for the sparks, like little fireflies on a Riviera
evening, were playing profoundly round my trousers,
' I should like to hear from your own lips the reasons
which have caused you to resign.'

" ' Certainly,' he replied, with the courtesy which I have always found characteristic of him in moments which would try the suavity of more ordinary men ; and with the utmost calm and clarity he began to tell me the inner workings of his mind, while the growing dawn-light irradiated his wasted and expressive features, and the flames slowly roasted his left boot.

" ' Yes,' he said quietly, and his eyes turned inwards, ' I have at last seen the problem clearly, and seen it whole. It is largely because of this that I have elected to seek the seclusion of another world. What that world contains for me I know not, though so many public men have tried to tell me ; but it has never been my way to recoil from the Unknown, and I am ready for my journey beyond the wide world's end.'

" I was greatly struck by the large-hearted way in which he spoke those words, and I interrupted him to ask whether he did not think that there was something fundamental in the British character which would leap as one man at such an act of daring sacriffce and great adventure.

" ' As regards that,' he replied fearlessly, while in the light of the ever-brightening dawn I could see the suspender on his right leg gradually charring, so that he must already have been in great pain, ' as regards that, it is largely the proneness of the modern British to leap to verbal extremity which is inducing me to afford them this object-lesson in restraint and commonsense. Ouch ! '

" This momentary ejaculation seemed to escape him in spite of all his iron control ; and the smell of burning flesh brought home to me as nothing else, perhaps, could have done the tortures he must have been suffering.

" ' I feel,' he went on very gravely, ' that extravagance of word and conduct is fatal to my country,
and having so profoundly experienced its effects upon
myself, I am now endeavouring by a shining example
to supply a remedy for a disease which is corroding the
vitals and impairing the sanity of my countrymen and
making them a race of second-hand spiritual drunkards.
Ouch ! '

" I confess that at this moment the tears started to
my eyes, for a more sublime show than the spectacle
of this devoted man slowly roasting himself to death
before my eyes for the good of his country I had seldom
seen. It had a strange, an appalling interest, and for
nothing on earth could I have torn my gaze away. I
now realised to the full for the first time the will-power
and heroism of the human species, and I rejoiced with
a glorious new feeling that I was of the same breed
as this man, made of such stern stuff that not even a
tear rolled down his cheeks to quench the flames that
leaped around him ever higher and higher. And the
dawn came up in the eastern sky ; and I knew that a
great day was preparing for mankind ; and with my
eyes fixed upon him as he turned blacker and blacker
I let my heart loose in a great thanksgiving that I had
lived to see this moment. It was then that he cried out
in a loud voice :

" ' I call Aurora to witness that I have died without
a falter, grasping a burning spear to tilt at the mal-
practice which has sent me mad ! ' And I saw that he
held in his fast-consuming hand a long roll of journals
sharpened to a point of burning flame.

" ' Aurora ! ' he cried again, and with that enigmatic
word on his lips was incinerated in the vast and towering belch of the devouring element.

" It was among the most inspiring sights I have ever witnessed."

When Mr. Lavender had completed that record, whose actuality and wealth of moving detail had greatly affected him, and marked it " For the Press— Immediate," he felt very cold. It was, in fact, that hour of dawn when a shiver goes through the world ; and, almost with pleasurable anticipation he took up his lighted candle and stole shivering out of his pile, rising ghostly to the height of some five feet in the middle of the dim lawn whereon a faint green tinge was coming with the return of daylight. Having reached it, he walked round it twice, and readjusted four volumes of the history of the war as stepping-stones to the top ; then lowering the candle, whose flame burned steadily in the stillness, he knelt down in the grey dew and set fire to an article in a Sunday paper. Then, sighing deeply, he returned to his little ladder and, with some difficulty preserving his balance, mounted to the top, and sat down with his legs towards the house and his eyes fixed on Aurora's bedroom-window. He had been there perhaps ten minutes before he realised that nothing was happening below him, and, climbing down again, proceeded to the aperture where he had inserted the burning print. There by the now considerable day-light, he saw that the flame had gone out at the words " The Stage is now set for the last act of this colossal world drama." And convinced that Providence had intended that heartening sentence to revive his some-what drooping courage, he thought, ' I, too, shall be making history this morning,' and relighting the journal, went on his hands and knees and began manfully to blow the flames. . . .

Now the young lady in the adjoining castle, who had

got out of bed, happened, as she sometimes did, to go to the window to look at the sun rising over Parliament Hill. Attracted by the smell of burning paper she saw Mr. Lavender in this act of blowing up the flames.

' What on earth is the poor dear doing now ? ' she thought. ' This is really the limit ! ' And slipping on her slippers and blue dressing-gown she ensconced herself behind the curtain to await developments.

Mr. Lavender had now backed away from the flames at which he had been blowing, and remained on his hands and knees, apparently assuring himself that they had really obtained hold. He then rose, and to her intense surprise began climbing up onto the pile. She watched him at first with an amused astonishment, so ludicrous was his light little figure, crowned by stivered-up white hair, and the expression of eager melancholy on his thin, high-cheekboned face upturned towards her window. Then, to her dismay, she saw that the flame had really caught, and, suddenly persuaded that he had some crazy intention of injuring himself with the view, perhaps, of attracting her attention, she ran out of her room and down the stairs, and emerging from the back door just as she was, circled her garden, so that she might enter Mr. Lavender's garden from behind him, ready for any eventuality. She arrived within arm's reach of him without his having heard her, for Blink, whose anxious face as she watched her master wasting, could be discerned at the bedroom-window, was whining, and Mr. Lavender himself had now broken into a strange and lamentable chantey, which in combination with the creeping flutter of the flames in the weekly journals encircling the base of the funeral pyre, wellnigh made her blood curdle. " Aurora," sang Mr. Lavender, in that most dolorous voice,

179

"Aurora, my heart I bring,
For I know well it will not burn,
Oh ! when the leaves puff out in Spring
And when the leaves in Autumn turn
  Think, think of me !
Aurora, I pass away !
Upon my horse of air I ride ;
Here let my grizzled ashes stay,
But take, ah ! take my heart inside !
  Aurora ! Aurora ! "

At this moment, just as a fit of the most uncontrollable laughter was about to seize her, she saw a flame which had just consumed the word Horatio reach Mr. Lavender's right calf.

" Oh ! " he cried out in desperate tones, stretching up his arms to the sky. " Now is my hour come ! Sweet sky, open and let me see her face ! Behold ! I behold her with the eyes of faith. It is enough. Courage, brother ; let me now consume in silence ! " So saying, he folded his arms tightly across his breast and closed his lips. The flame rising to the bottom of the weekly which had indeed been upside down, here nipped him vigorously, so that with a wholly unconscious movement he threw up his little legs, and, losing his balance, fell backwards into the arms of Aurora, watchfully outstretched to receive him. Uplifted there, close to that soft blue bosom away from the reek of the flame, he conceived that he was consumed and had passed already from his night of ghosts and shadows into the arms of the morning, and through his swooning lips came forth the words : " I am in Paradise."

1918.

Villa Rubein

TO
MY SISTER
BLANCHE LILIAN SAUTER

I

WALKING along the river wall at Botzen, Edmund Dawney said to Alois Harz : " Would you care to know the family at that pink house, Villa Rubein ? "

Harz answered with a smile :

" Perhaps."

" Come with me then this afternoon."

They had stopped before an old house with a blind, deserted look, that stood by itself on the wall ; Harz pushed the door open.

" Come in, you don't want breakfast yet. I'm going to paint the river to-day."

He ran up the bare broad stairs, and Dawney followed leisurely, his thumbs hooked in the armholes of his waistcoat, and his head thrown back.

In the attic which filled the whole top story, Harz had pulled a canvas to the window. He was a young man of middle height, square-shouldered, active, with an angular face, high cheek-bones, and a strong, sharp chin. His eyes were piercing and steel-blue, his eyebrows very flexible, nose long and thin with a high bridge ; and his dark, unparted hair fitted him like a cap. His clothes looked as if he never gave them a second thought.

This room, which served for studio, bedroom, and sitting-room, was bare and dusty. Below the window

183

the river in spring flood rushed down the valley, a stream of molten bronze. Harz dodged before the canvas like a fencer finding his distance; Dawney took his seat on a packing-case.

"The snows have gone with a rush this year," he drawled. "The Talfer comes down brown, the Eisack comes down blue; they flow into the Etsch and make it green; a parable of the Spring for you, my painter."

Harz mixed his colours.

"I've no time for parables," he said, "no time for anything. If I could be guaranteed to live to ninety-nine, like Titian—he had a chance. Look at that poor fellow who was killed the other day! All that struggle, and then—just at the turn!"

He spoke English with a foreign accent; his voice was rather harsh, but his smile very kindly.

Dawney lit a cigarette.

"You painters," he said, "are better off than most of us. You can strike out your own line. Now if I choose to treat a case out of the ordinary way and the patient dies, I'm ruined."

"My dear Doctor—if I don't paint what the public likes, I starve; all the same I'm going to paint in my own way; in the end I shall come out on top."

"It pays to work in the groove, my friend, until you've made your name; after that—do what you like, they'll lick your boots all the same."

"Ah, you don't love your work."

Dawney answered slowly: "Never so happy as when my hands are full. But I want to make money, to get known, to have a good time, good cigars, good wine. I hate discomfort. No, my boy, I must work it on the usual lines; I don't like it, but I must lump it. One starts in life with some notion of the ideal—it's gone by the board with me. I've got to shove along until I've made my name, and then, my little man—then——"

" Then you'll be soft ! You pay dearly for that first period ! "

" Take my chance of that ; there's no other way."

" Make one ! "

" Humph ! "

Harz poised his brush, as though it were a spear :

" A man must do the best in him. If he has to suffer—let him ! "

Dawney stretched his large soft body ; a calculating look had come into his eyes.

" You're a tough little man ! " he said.

" I've *had* to be tough."

Dawney rose ; tobacco smoke was wreathed round his unruffled hair.

" Touching Villa Rubein," he said, " shall I call for you ? It's a mixed household, English mostly—very decent people."

" No, thank you. I shall be painting all day. Haven't time to know the sort of people who expect one to change one's clothes."

" As you like ; ta-ta ! " And, puffing out his chest, Dawney vanished through a blanket looped across the doorway.

Harz set a pot of coffee on a spirit-lamp, and cut himself some bread. Through the window the freshness of the morning came ; the scent of sap and blossom and young leaves ; the scent of earth, and the mountains freed from winter ; the new flights and songs of birds ; all the odorous, enchanted, restless Spring.

There suddenly appeared through the doorway a white rough-haired terrier dog, black-marked about the face, with shaggy tan eyebrows. He sniffed at Harz, showed the whites round his eyes, and uttered a sharp bark. A young voice called :

" Scruff ! Thou naughty dog ! " Light footsteps were heard on the stairs ; from the distance a thin, high voice called :

" Greta ! You mustn't go up there ! "

A little girl of twelve, with long fair hair under a wide-brimmed hat, slipped in.

Her blue eyes opened wide, her face flushed up. That face was not regular ; its cheek-bones were rather prominent, the nose was flattish ; there was about it an air, innocent, reflecting, quizzical, shy.

" Oh ! " she said.

Harz smiled : " Good-morning ! This your dog ? "

She did not answer, but looked at him with soft bewilderment ; then running to the dog seized him by the collar.

" Scr-ruff ! Thou naughty dog—the baddest dog ! " The ends of her hair fell about him ; she looked up at Harz, who said :

" Not at all ! Let me give him some bread."

" Oh no ! You must not—I will beat him—and tell him he is bad ; then he shall not do such things again. Now he is sulky ; he looks so always when he is sulky. Is this your home ? "

" For the present ; I am a visitor."

" But I think you are of this country, because you speak like it."

" Certainly, I am a Tyroler."

" I have to talk English this morning, but I do not like it very much—because, also I am half Austrian,

186

and 1 like it best; but my sister, Christian, is all English. Here is Miss Naylor; she shall be very angry with me."

And pointing to the entrance with a rosy-tipped forefinger, she again looked ruefully at Harz.

There came into the room with a walk like the hopping of a bird an elderly, small lady, in a grey serge dress, with narrow bands of claret-coloured velveteen; a large gold cross dangled from a steel chain on her chest; she nervously twisted her hands, clad in black kid gloves, rather white about the seams.

Her hair was prematurely grey; her quick eyes brown; her mouth twisted at one corner; she held her face, kind-looking, but long and narrow, rather to one side, and wore on it a look of apology. Her quick sentences sounded as if she kept them on strings, and wanted to draw them back as soon as she had let them forth.

"Greta, how *can* you do such things? I don't know what your father would say! I am sure I don't know how to—so extraordinary——"

"Please!" said Harz.

"You must come at once—so very sorry—so awkward!"

They were standing in a ring: Harz with his eyebrows working up and down; the little lady fidgeting her parasol; Greta, flushed and pouting, her eyes all dewy, twisting an end of fair hair round her finger.

"Oh, look!" The coffee had boiled over. Little brown streams trickled spluttering from the pan; the dog, with ears laid back and tail tucked in, went scurrying round the room. A feeling of fellowship fell on them at once.

"Along the wall is our favourite walk, and Scruff—

so awkward, so unfortunate—we did not think any one lived here—the shutters are cracked, the paint is peeling off so dreadfully. Have you been long in Botzen ? Two months ? Fancy ! You are not English ? You are Tyrolese ? But you speak English so well—there for seven years ? Really ? So fortunate !—It is Greta's day for English."

Miss Naylor's eyes darted bewildered glances at the roof where the crossing of the beams made such deep shadows ; at the litter of brushes, tools, knives, and colours on a table made out of packing-cases ; at the big window, innocent of glass, and flush with the floor, whence dangled a bit of rusty chain—relic of the time when the place had been a store-loft ; her eyes were hastily averted from an unfinished figure of the nude.

Greta, with feet crossed, sat on a coloured blanket, dabbling her finger in a little pool of coffee, and gazing up at Harz. And he thought : ' I should like to paint her like that. " A forget-me-not." '

He took out his chalks to make a sketch of her.

" Shall you show me ? " cried out Greta, scrambling to her feet.

" ' Will,' Greta—' will ' ; how often must I tell you ? I think we should be going—it is very late—your father—so very kind of you, but I think we should be going. Scruff ! " Miss Naylor gave the floor two taps. The terrier backed into a plaster cast which came down on his tail, and sent him flying through the doorway. Greta followed swiftly, crying :

" *Ach !* poor *Scruffee !* "

Miss Naylor crossed the room ; bowing, she murmured an apology, and also disappeared.

Harz was left alone, his guests were gone ; the little girl with the fair hair and the eyes like forget-me-nots, the little lady with kindly gestures and bird-like walk, the terrier. He looked round him ; the room seemed very empty. Gnawing his moustache, he muttered at the fallen cast. Then taking up his brush, stood before his picture, smiling and frowning. Soon he had forgotten it all in his work.

II

It was early morning four days later, and Harz was loitering homewards. The shadows of the clouds passing across the vines were vanishing over the jumbled roofs and green-topped spires of the town. A strong sweet wind was blowing from the mountains, there was a stir in the branches of the trees, and flakes of the late blossom were drifting down. Amongst the soft green pods of a kind of poplar chafers buzzed, and numbers of their little brown bodies were strewn on the path.

He passed a bench where a girl sat sketching. A puff of wind whirled her drawing to the ground ; Harz ran to pick it up. She took it from him with a bow ; but, as he turned away, she tore the sketch across.

" Ah ! " he said ; " why did you do that ? "

This girl, who stood with a bit of the torn sketch in either hand, was slight and straight ; and her face earnest and serene. She gazed at Harz with large, clear, greenish eyes ; her lips and chin were defiant, her forehead tranquil.

" I don't like it."

" Will you let me look at it ? I am a painter."

" It isn't worth looking at, but—if you wish—— "

He put the two halves of the sketch together.

" You see ! " she said at last ; " I told you."

Harz did not answer, still looking at the sketch.   The girl frowned.

Harz asked her suddenly :

" Why do you paint ? "

She coloured, and said :

" Show me what is wrong."

" I cannot show you what is wrong, there is nothing wrong—but why do you paint ? "

" I don't understand."

Harz shrugged his shoulders.

" You've no business to do that," said the girl in a hurt voice ;   " I want to know."

" Your *heart* is not in it," said Harz.

She looked at him, startled ;   her eyes had grown thoughtful.

" I suppose that *is* it.   There are so many other things——"

" There should be nothing else," said Harz.

She broke in :   " I don't want always to be thinking of myself.   Suppose——"

" Ah !   When you begin supposing ! "

The girl confronted him ;   she had torn the sketch again.

" You mean that if it does not matter enough, one had better not do it at all.   I don't know if you are right —I think you are."

There was the sound of a nervous cough, and Harz saw behind him his three visitors—Miss Naylor offering him her hand ;   Greta, flushed, with a bunch of wild flowers, staring intently in his face ;   and the terrier, sniffing at his trousers.

Miss Naylor broke an awkward silence.

" We wondered if you would still be here, Christian.

I am sorry to interrupt you—I was not aware that you knew Mr.—Herr——"

" Harz is my name—we were just talking——"

" About my sketch. Oh, Greta, you do tickle ! Will you come and have breakfast with *us* to-day, Herr Harz ? It's our turn, you know."

Harz, glancing at his dusty clothes, excused himself.

But Greta in a pleading voice said : " Oh ! do come ! Scruff likes you. It is so dull when there is nobody for breakfast but ourselves."

Miss Naylor's mouth began to twist. Harz hurriedly broke in :

" Thank you. I will come with pleasure ; you don't mind my being dirty ? "

" Oh no ! we do not mind ; then we shall none of us wash, and afterwards I shall show you my rabbits."

Miss Naylor, moving from foot to foot, like a bird on its perch, exclaimed :

" I hope you won't regret it, not a very good meal— the girls are so impulsive—such informal invitation ; we shall be very glad."

But Greta pulled softly at her sister's sleeve, and Christian, gathering her things, led the way.

Harz followed in amazement ; nothing of this kind had come into his life before. He kept shyly glancing at the girls ; and, noting the speculative innocence in Greta's eyes, he smiled. They soon came to two great poplar-trees, which stood, like sentinels, one on either side of an unweeded gravel walk leading through lilac bushes to a house painted dull pink, with green-shuttered windows, and a roof of greenish slate. Over the door in faded crimson letters were written the words, " Villa Rubein."

" That is to the stables," said Greta, pointing down a

path, where some pigeons were sunning themselves on a wall. " Uncle Nic keeps his horses there : Countess and Cuckoo—his horses begin with C, because of Chris—they are quite beautiful. He says he could drive them to Kingdom-Come and they would not turn their hair. Bow, and say ' Good-morning ' to our house ! "

Harz bowed.

" Father said all strangers should, and *I* think it brings good luck." From the doorstep she looked round at Harz, then ran into the house.

A broad, thick-set man, with stiff, brushed-up hair, a short, brown, bushy beard parted at the chin, a fresh complexion, and blue glasses across a thick nose, came out, and called in a bluff voice :

" Ha ! my good dears, kiss me quick—prrt ! How goes it then this morning ? A good walk, *hein ?* " The sound of many loud rapid kisses followed.

" Ha, Fräulein, good ! " He became aware of Harz's figure standing in the doorway : " *Und der Herr ?* "

Miss Naylor hurriedly explained.

" Good ! An artist ! *Kommen Sie herein*, I am delight. You will breakfast ? I too—yes, yes, my dears—I too breakfast with you this morning. I have the hunter's appetite."

Harz, looking at him keenly, perceived him to be of middle height and age, stout, dressed in a loose holland jacket, a very white, starched shirt, and blue silk sash ; that he looked particularly clean, had an air of belonging to Society, and exhaled a really fine aroma of excellent cigars and the best hairdresser's essences.

The room they entered was long and rather bare ; there was a huge map on the wall, and below it a pair of globes on crooked supports, resembling two in-

flated frogs erect on their hind legs. In one corner was
a cottage piano, close to a writing-table heaped with
books and papers ; this nook, sacred to Christian,
was foreign to the rest of the room, which was
arranged with supernatural neatness. A table was
laid for breakfast, and the sun-warmed air came in
through French windows.

The meal went merrily ; Herr Paul von Morawitz
was never in such spirits as at table. Words streamed
from him. Conversing with Harz, he talked of Art
as who should say : " One does not claim to be a
connoisseur—*pas si bête*—still, one has a little knowledge, *que diable !* " He recommended him a man in
the town who sold cigars that were " not so very bad."
He consumed porridge, ate an omelette ; and bending
across to Greta gave her a sounding kiss, muttering :
" Kiss me quick ! "—an expression he had picked up
in a London music-hall, long ago, and considered *chic*.
He asked his daughters' plans, and held out porridge to
the terrier, who refused it with a sniff.

" Well," he said suddenly, looking at Miss Naylor,
" here is a gentleman who has not even heard our
names ! "

The little lady began her introductions in a breathless
voice.

" Good ! " Herr Paul said, puffing out his lips :
" Now we know each other ! " and, brushing up the
ends of his moustaches, he carried off Harz into another
room, decorated with pipe-racks, prints of dancing-
girls, spittoons, easy-chairs well-seasoned by cigar
smoke, French novels, and newspapers.

The household at Villa Rubein was indeed of a mixed
and curious nature. Cut on both floors by corridors,
the Villa was divided into four divisions ; each of

which had its separate inhabitants, an arrangement which had come about in the following way :

When old Nicholas Treffry died, his estate, on the boundary of Cornwall, had been sold and divided up among his three surviving children—Nicholas, who was much the eldest, a partner in the well-known firm of Forsyte and Treffry, teamen, of the Strand ; Constance, married to a man called Decie ; and Margaret, at her father's death engaged to the curate of the parish, John Devorell, who shortly afterwards became its rector. By his marriage with Margaret Treffry the rector had one child called Christian. Soon after this he came into some property, and died, leaving it unfettered to his widow. Three years went by, and when the child was six years old, Mrs. Devorell, still young and pretty, came to live in London with her brother Nicholas. It was there that she met Paul von Morawitz—the last of an old Czech family, who had lived for many hundred years on their estates near Budweiss. Paul had been left an orphan at the age of ten, and without a solitary ancestral acre. Instead of acres, he inherited the faith that nothing was too good for a von Morawitz. In later years his *savoir faire* enabled him to laugh at faith, but it stayed quietly with him all the same. The absence of acres was of no great consequence, for through his mother, the daughter of a banker in Vienna, he came into a well-nursed fortune. It befitted a von Morawitz that he should go into the Cavalry, but, unshaped for soldiering, he soon left the Service ; some said he had a difference with his Colonel over the quality of food provided during some manœuvres ; others that he had retired because his chargers did not fit his legs, which were, indeed, rather round.

He had an admirable appetite for pleasure ; a man-about-town's life suited him. He went his genial, unreflecting, costly way in Vienna, Paris, London. He loved exclusively those towns, and boasted that he was as much at home in one as in another. He combined exuberant vitality with fastidiousness of palate, and devoted both to the acquisition of a special taste in women, weeds, and wines ; above all he was blessed with a remarkable digestion. He was thirty when he met Mrs. Devorell ; and she married him because he was so very different from anybody she had ever seen. People more dissimilar were never mated. To Paul—accustomed to stage doors—freshness, serene tranquillity, and obvious purity were the baits ; he had run through more than half his fortune, too, and the fact that she had money was possibly not overlooked. Be that as it may, he was fond of her ; his heart was soft, he developed a domestic side.

Greta was born to them after a year of marriage. The instinct of the " freeman " was, however, not dead in Paul ; he became a gambler. He lost the remainder of his fortune without being greatly dis-turbed. When he began to lose his wife's fortune too things naturally became more difficult. Not too much remained when Nicholas Treffry stepped in, and caused his sister to settle what was left on her daughters, after providing a life-interest for herself and Paul. Losing his supplies, the good man had given up his cards. But the instinct of the " freeman " was still living in his breast ; he took to drink. He was never grossly drunk, and rarely very sober. His wife sorrowed over this new passion ; her health, already much enfeebled, soon broke down. The doctors sent her to the Tyrol. She seemed to benefit by this, and settled down at Botzen. The following year, when Greta was just ten, she died. It was a shock to Paul. He gave up excessive drinking; became a constant smoker, and lent full rein to his natural domesticity. He was fond of both the girls, but did not at all understand them; Greta, his own daughter, was his favourite. Villa Rubein remained their home; it was cheap and roomy. Money, since Paul became housekeeper to himself, was scarce.

About this time Mrs. Decie, his wife's sister, whose husband had died in the East, returned to England; Paul invited her to come and live with them. She had her own rooms, her own servant; the arrangement suited Paul—it was economically sound, and there was some one always there to take care of the girls. In truth he began to feel the instinct of the " freeman " rising again within him; it was pleasant to run over to Vienna now and then; to play piquet at a Club in Gries, of which he was the shining light; in a word, to go " on the tiles " a little   One could not always mourn—even if a woman were an angel; moreover, his digestion was as good as ever.

The fourth quarter of this Villa was occupied by Nicholas Treffry, whose annual sojourn out of England perpetually surprised himself. Between him and his young niece Christian, there existed, however, a rare sympathy; one of those affections between the young and old, which, mysteriously born like everything in life, seems the only end and aim to both, till another feeling comes into the younger heart.

Since a long and dangerous illness, he had been ordered to avoid the English winter, and at the commencement of each spring he would appear at Botzen, driving his own horses by easy stages from the Italian

Riviera, where he spent the coldest months. He always stayed till June before going back to his London Club, and during all that time he let no day pass without growling at foreigners, their habits, food, drink, and raiment, with a kind of big dog's growling that did nobody any harm. The illness had broken him very much; he was seventy, but looked more. He had a servant, a Luganese, named Dominique, devoted to him. Nicholas Treffry had found him overworked in an hotel, and had engaged him with the caution : " Look—here, Dominique ! I swear ! " To which Dominique, dark of feature, saturnine and ironical, had only replied : " *Tres bien, M'sieur !* "

III

Harz and his host sat in leather chairs ; Herr Paul's square back was wedged into a cushion, his round legs crossed. Both were smoking, and they eyed each other furtively, as men of different stamp do when first thrown together. The young artist found his host extremely new and disconcerting ; in his presence he felt both shy and awkward. Herr Paul, on the other hand, very much at ease, was thinking indolently : ' Good-looking young fellow—comes of the people, I expect, not at all the manner of the world ; wonder what he talks about.'

Presently noticing that Harz was looking at a photograph, he said : " Ah ! yes ! that was a woman ! They are not to be found in these days. She *could* dance, the little Coralie ! Did you ever see such arms ? Confess that she is beautiful, *hein ?* "

" She has individuality," said Harz. " A fine type ! "

197

Herr Paul blew out a cloud of smoke.

"Yes," he murmured, "she was fine all over!" He had dropped his eyeglasses, and his full brown eyes, with little crow's-feet at the corners, wandered from his visitor to his cigar.

' He'd be like a Satyr if he wasn't too clean,' thought Harz. ' Put vine leaves in his hair, paint him asleep, with his hands crossed, so!'

"When I am told a person has individuality," Herr Paul was saying in a rich and husky voice, "I generally expect boots that bulge, an umbrella of improper colour; I expect a creature of ' bad form ' as they say in England; who will shave some days and some days will not shave; who sometimes smells of india-rubber, and sometimes does not smell, which is discouraging!"

"You do not approve of individuality?" said Harz shortly.

"Not if it means doing, and thinking, as those who know better do not do, or think."

"And who are those who know better?"

"Ah! my dear, you are asking me a riddle? Well, then—Society, men of birth, men of recognised position, men above eccentricity, in a word, of reputation."

Harz looked at him fixedly. "Men who haven't the courage of their own ideas, not even the courage to smell of india-rubber; men who have no desires, and so can spend all their time making themselves flat!"

Herr Paul drew out a red silk handkerchief and wiped his beard. "I assure you, my dear," he said, "it is easier to be flat; it is more respectable to be flat. *Himmel!* why not, then, be flat?"

"Like any common fellow?"

"*Certes;* like any common fellow—like me, *par*

198

exemple ! " Herr Paul waved his hand. When he exercised unusual tact, he always made use of a French expression.

Harz flushed. Herr Paul followed up his victory. " Come, come ! " he said. " Pass me my men of repute ! *que diable !* we are not anarchists."

" Are you sure ? " said Harz.

Herr Paul twisted his moustache. " I beg your pardon," he said slowly. But at this moment the door was opened; a rumbling voice remarked : " Morning, Paul. Who's your visitor ? " Harz saw a tall, bulky figure in the doorway.

" Come in," called out Herr Paul. " Let me present to you a new acquaintance, an artist : Herr Harz—Mr. Nicholas Treffry. Psumm bumm ! All this introducing is dry work." And going to the sideboard he poured out three glasses of a light, foaming beer.

Mr. Treffry waved it from him : " Not for me," he said : " Wish I could ! They won't let me look at it." And walking over to the window with a heavy tread, which trembled like his voice, he sat down. There was something in his gait like the movements of an elephant's hind legs. He was very tall (it was said, with the customary exaggeration of family tradition, that there never had been a male Treffry under six feet in height), but now he stooped, and had grown stout. There was something at once vast and unobtrusive about his personality.

He wore a loose brown velvet jacket, and waistcoat, cut to show a soft frilled shirt and narrow black ribbon tie ; a thin gold chain was looped round his neck and fastened to his fob. His heavy cheeks had folds in them like those in a bloodhound's face. He wore big, drooping, yellow-grey moustaches, which he had a habit of sucking, and a goatee beard. He had long loose ears that might almost have been said to flap. On his head there was a soft black hat, large in the brim and low in the crown. His grey eyes, heavy-lidded, twinkled under their busy brows with a queer, kind cynicism. As a young man he had sown many a wild oat; but he had also worked and made money in business; he had, in fact, burned the candle at both ends; but he had never been unready to do his fellows a good turn. He had a passion for driving, and his reckless method of pursuing this art had caused him to be nicknamed: "The notorious Treffry."

Once, when he was driving tandem down a hill with a loose rein, the friend beside him had said: "For all the good you're doing with those reins, Treffry, you might as well throw them on the horses' necks."

"Just so," Treffry had answered. At the bottom of the hill they had gone over a wall into a potato patch. Treffry had broken several ribs; his friend had gone unharmed.

He was a great sufferer now, but, constitutionally averse to being pitied, he had a disconcerting way of humming, and this, together with the shake in his voice, and his frequent use of peculiar phrases, made the understanding of his speech depend at times on intuition rather than intelligence.

The clock began to strike eleven. Harz muttered an excuse, shook hands with his host, and bowing to his new acquaintance, went away. He caught a glimpse of Greta's face against the window, and waved his hand to her. In the road he came on Dawney, who was turning in between the poplars, with thumbs as usual hooked in the armholes of his waistcoat.

"Hallo!" the latter said.

200

"Doctor!" Harz answered slyly; "the Fates out-witted me, it seems."

"Serve you right," said Dawney, "for your con-founded egoism! Wait here till I come out, I shan't be many minutes."

But Harz went on his way. A cart drawn by cream-coloured oxen was passing slowly towards the bridge. In front of the brushwood piled on it two peasant girls were sitting with their feet on a mat of grass—the picture of contentment.

"I'm wasting my time!" he thought. "I've done next to nothing in two months. Better get back to London! That girl will never make a painter!" She would never make a painter, but there was something in her that he could not dismiss so rapidly. She was not exactly beautiful, but she was sympathetic. The brow was pleasing, with dark-brown hair softly turned back, and eyes so straight and shining. The two sisters were very different! The little one was innocent, yet mysterious; the elder seemed as clear as crystal! . . .

He had entered the town, where the arcaded streets exuded their peculiar pungent smell of cows and leather, wood-smoke, wine-casks, and drains. The sound of rapid wheels over the stones made him turn his head. A carriage drawn by red-roan horses was passing at a great pace. People stared at it, standing still, and looking alarmed. It swung from side to side and vanished round a corner. Harz saw Mr. Nicholas Treffry in a long, whitish dust-coat; his Italian servant, perched behind, was holding to the seat-rail, with a nervous grin on his dark face.

'Certainly,' Harz thought, 'there's no getting away from these people this morning—they are everywhere.'

In his studio he began to sort his sketches, wash his

brushes, and drag out things he had accumulated during his two months' stay. He even began to fold his blanket door. But suddenly he stopped. Those two girls ! Why not try ? What a picture ! The two heads, the sky and leaves ! Begin to-morrow ! Against that window—no, better at the Villa ! Call the picture—Spring ! . . .

IV

The wind, stirring among trees and bushes, flung the young leaves skywards. The trembling of their silver linings was like the joyful flutter of a heart at good news. It was one of those Spring mornings when everything seems full of a sweet restlessness—soft clouds chasing fast across the sky ; soft scents floating forth and dying ; the notes of birds, now shrill and sweet, now hushed in silences ; all nature striving for something, nothing at peace.

Villa Rubein withstood the influence of the day, and wore its usual look of rest and isolation. Harz sent in his card, and asked to see " *der Herr.*" The servant, a grey-eyed, clever-looking Swiss with no hair on his face, came back saying :

" *Der Herr, mein Herr,* is in the Garden gone." Harz followed him.

Herr Paul, a small white flannel cap on his head, gloves on his hands, glasses on his nose, was watering a rosebush, and humming the serenade from *Faust*.

This aspect of the house was very different from the other. The sun fell on it, and over a veranda creepers clung and scrambled in long scrolls. There was a lawn, with freshly mown grass ; flower-beds were laid out, and at the end of an avenue of young acacias stood an arbour covered with wisteria.

In the east, mountain peaks—fingers of snow—glittered above the mist. A grave simplicity lay on that scene, on the roofs and spires, the valleys and the dreamy hillsides, with their yellow scars and purple bloom, and white cascades, like tails of grey horses swishing in the wind.

Herr Paul held out his hand : " What can we do for you ? " he said.

" I have to beg a favour," replied Harz. " I wish to paint your daughters. I will bring the canvas here—they shall have no trouble. I would paint them in the garden when they have nothing else to do."

Herr Paul looked at him dubiously—ever since the previous day he had been thinking : ' Queer bird, that painter—thinks himself the devil of a swell ! Looks a determined fellow too ! ' Now—staring in the painter's face—it seemed to him, on the whole, best if some one else refused this permission.

" With all the pleasure, my dear sir," he said. " Come, let us ask these two young ladies ! " and putting down his hose, he led the way towards the arbour, thinking : ' You'll be disappointed, my young conqueror, or I'm mistaken.'

Miss Naylor and the girls were sitting in the shade, reading La Fontaine's fables. Greta, with one eye on her governess, was stealthily cutting a pig out of orange peel.

" Ah ! my dear dears ! " began Herr Paul, who in the presence of Miss Naylor always paraded his English. " Here is our friend, who has a very flattering request to make ; he would paint you, yes—both together, *al*

203

fresco, in the air, in the sunshine, with the birds, the little birds ! "

Greta, gazing at Harz, flushed deep pink, and furtively showed him her pig.

Christian said : " Paint us ? Oh no ! "

She saw Harz looking at her, and added, slowly : " If you really wish it, I suppose we could ! " then dropped her eyes.

" Ah ! " said Herr Paul raising his brows till his glasses fell from his nose : " And what says Gretchen ? Does she want to be handed up to posterities a little peacock along with the other little birds ? "

Greta, who had continued staring at the painter, said : " Of-course-I-want-to-be."

" Prrt ! " said Herr Paul, looking at Miss Naylor. The little lady indeed opened her mouth wide, but all that came forth was a tiny squeak, as sometimes happens when one is anxious to say something, and has not arranged beforehand what it shall be.

The affair seemed ended ; Harz heaved a sigh of satisfaction. But Herr Paul had still a card to play.

" There is your Aunt," he said ; " there are things to be considered—one must certainly inquire—so, we shall see." Kissing Greta loudly on both cheeks, he went towards the house.

" What makes you want to paint us ? " Christian asked, as soon as he was gone.

" I think it very wrong," Miss Naylor blurted out.

" Why ? " said Harz, frowning.

" Greta is so young—there are lessons—it is such a waste of time ! "

His eyebrows twitched : " Ah ! You think so ! "

" I don't see why it is a waste of time," said Christian

quietly ; " there are lots of hours when we sit here and do nothing."

" And it is very dull," put in Greta, with a pout.

" You are rude, Greta," said Miss Naylor in a little rage, pursing her lips, and taking up her knitting.

" I think it seems always rude to speak the truth," said Greta. Miss Naylor looked at her in that concentrated manner with which she was in the habit of expressing displeasure.

But at this moment a servant came, and said that Mrs. Decie would be glad to see Herr Harz. The painter made them a stiff bow, and followed the servant to the house. Miss Naylor and the two girls watched his progress with apprehensive eyes ; it was clear that he had been offended.

Crossing the veranda, and passing through an open window hung with silk curtains, Harz entered a cool dark room. This was Mrs. Decie's sanctum, where she conducted correspondence, received her visitors, read the latest literature, and sometimes, when she had bad headaches, lay for hours on the sofa, with a fan, and her eyes closed. There was a scent of sandalwood, a suggestion of the East, a kind of mystery, in here, as if things like chairs and tables were not really what they seemed, but something much less commonplace.

The visitor looked twice, to be quite sure of anything ; there were many plants, bead curtains, and a deal of silverwork and china.

Mrs. Decie came forward in the slightly rustling silk which—whether in or out of fashion—always accompanied her. A tall woman, over fifty, she moved as if she had been tied together at the knees. Her face was long, with broad brows, from which her sandy-grey hair was severely waved back ; she had pale eyes, and a perpetual, pale, enigmatic smile. Her complexion had been ruined by long residence in India, and might unkindly have been called fawn-coloured. She came close to Harz, keeping her eyes on his, with her head bent slightly forward.

"We are so pleased to know you," she said, speaking in a voice which had lost all ring. "It is charming to find some one in these parts who can help us to remember that there is such a thing as Art. We had Mr. C—— here last autumn, such a charming fellow. He was so interested in the native customs and dresses. You are a subject painter, too, I think? Won't you sit down?"

She went on for some time, introducing painters' names, asking questions, skating round the edge of what was personal. And the young man stood before her with a curious little smile fixed on his lips. 'She wants to know whether I'm worth powder and shot,' he thought.

"You wish to paint my nieces?" Mrs. Decie said at last, leaning back on her settee.

"I wish to have that honour," Harz answered with a bow.

"And what sort of picture did you think of?"

"That," said Harz, "is in the future. I couldn't tell you." And he thought: 'Will she ask me if I get my tints in Paris, like the woman Tramper told me of?'

The perpetual pale smile on Mrs. Decie's face seemed to invite his confidence, yet to warn him that his words would be sucked in somewhere behind those broad fine brows, and carefully sorted. Mrs. Decie, indeed, was thinking: 'Interesting young man, regular Bohemian—no harm in that at his age; something Napoleonic in his face; probably has no dress clothes.

206

Yes, should like to see more of him ! ' She had a fine
eye for points of celebrity ; his name was unfamiliar,
would probably have been scouted by that famous
artist Mr. C——, but she felt her instinct urging her
on to know him. She was to do her justice, one of
those " lion " finders who seek the animal for pleasure,
not for the glory it brings them ; she had the courage
of her instincts—leonentities were indispensable to her,
but she trusted to divination to secure them ; nobody
could foist a " lion " on *her*.

" It will be very nice. You will stay and have some
lunch ? The arrangements here are rather odd. Such
a mixed household—but there is always lunch at two
o'clock for anyone who likes, and we all dine at seven.
You would have your sittings in the afternoons, perhaps ? I should so like to see your sketches. You
are using the old house on the wall for studio ; that is
so original of you ! "

Harz would not stay to lunch, but asked if he might
begin work that afternoon ; he left a little suffocated
by the sandalwood and sympathy of this sphinx-like
woman.

Walking home along the river wall, with the singing
of the larks and thrushes, the rush of waters, the humming of the chafers in his ears, he felt that he would
make something fine of this subject. Before his eyes
the faces of the two girls continually started up, framed
by the sky, with young leaves fluttering against their
cheeks.

<h1 style="text-align:center">V</h1>

Three days had passed since Harz began his picture,
when early in the morning, Greta came from Villa
Rubein along the river dyke and sat down on a bench

from which the old house on the wall was visible. She had not been there long before Harz came out.

" I did not knock," said Greta, " because you would not have heard, and it is so early, so I have been waiting for you a quarter of an hour."

Selecting a rosebud, from some flowers in her hand, she handed it to him. " That is my first rosebud this year," she said ; " it is for you because you are painting me. To-day I am thirteen, Herr Harz ; there is not to be a sitting, because it is my birthday ; but, instead, we are all going to Meran to see the play of Andreas Hofer. You are to come too, please ; I am here to tell you, and the others shall be here directly."

Harz bowed : " And who are the others ? "

" Christian, and Dr. Edmund, Miss Naylor, and Cousin Teresa. Her husband is ill, so she is sad, but to-day she is going to forget that. It is not good to be always sad, is it, Herr Harz ? "

He laughed : " *You* could not be."

Greta answered gravely : " Oh yes, I could. I too am often sad. You are making fun. You are not to make fun to-day, because it is my birthday. Do you think growing up is nice, Herr Harz ? "

" No, Fraulein Greta, it is better to have all the time before you."

They walked on side by side.

" I think," said Greta, " you are very much afraid of losing time. Chris says that time is nothing."

" Time is everything," responded Harz.

" She says that time is nothing, and thought is everything," Greta murmured, rubbing a rose against her cheek, " but *I* think you cannot have a thought unless you have the time to think it in. There are the others ! Look ! "

A cluster of sunshades on the bridge glowed for a moment and was lost in shadow.

"Come," said Harz, "let's join them!"

At Meran, under Schloss Tirol, people were streaming across the meadows into the open theatre. Here were tall fellows in mountain dress, with leather breeches, bare knees, and hats with eagles' feathers, here were fruit-sellers, burghers and their wives, mountebanks, actors, and every kind of visitor. The audience, packed into an enclosure of high boards, sweltered under the burning sun. Cousin Teresa, tall and thin, with hard, red cheeks, shaded her pleasant eyes with her hand.

The play began. It depicted the rising in the Tyrol of 1809 : the village life, dances and yodelling ; murmurings and exhortations, the warning beat of drums ; then the gathering, with flint-locks, pitchforks, knives ; the battle and victory ; the homecoming, and festival. Then the second gathering, the roar of cannon ; betrayal, capture, death. The impassive figure of the patriot Andreas Hofer always in front, black-bearded, leathern-girdled, under the blue sky, against a screen of mountains.

Harz and Christian sat behind the others. He seemed so intent on the play that she did not speak, but watched his face, rigid with a kind of cold excitement ; he seemed to be transported by the life passing before them. Something of his feeling seized on her ; when the play was over she too was trembling. In pushing their way out they became separated from the others.

"There's a short cut to the station here," said Christian ; "let's go this way."

The path rose a little ; a narrow stream crept alongside the meadow, and the hedge was spangled with wild roses. Christian kept glancing shyly at the painter. Since their meeting on the river wall her thoughts had never been at rest. This stranger, with his keen face, insistent eyes, and ceaseless energy, had roused a strange feeling in her; his words had put shape to something in her not yet expressed. She stood aside at a stile to make way for some peasant boys, dusty and rough-haired, who sang and whistled as they went by.

"I was like those boys once," said Harz.

Christian turned to him quickly. "Ah! that was why you felt the play, so much."

"It's my country up there. I was born amongst the mountains. I looked after the cows, and slept in hay-cocks, and cut the trees in winter. They used to call me a ' black sheep,' a ' loafer ' in my village."

."Why?"

"Ah! why? I worked as hard as any of them. But I wanted to get away. Do you think I could have stayed there all my life?"

Christian's eyes grew eager.

"If people don't understand what it is you want to do, they always call you a loafer!" muttered Harz.

"But you did what you meant to do in spite of them," Christian said.

For herself it was so hard to finish or decide. When in the old days she told Greta stories, the latter, whose instinct was always for the definite, would say: "And what came at the end, Chris? Do finish it this morning!" but Christian never could. Her thoughts were deep, vague, dreamy, invaded by both sides of every question. Whatever she did, her needlework, her verse-making, her painting, all had its charm; but it was not always what it was intended for at the beginning. Nicholas Treffry had once said of her: "When

Chris starts out to make a hat, it may turn out an altar-cloth, but you may bet it won't be a hat." It was her instinct to look for what things meant; and this took more than all her time. She knew herself better than most girls of nineteen, but it was her reason that had informed her, not her feelings. In her sheltered life, her heart had never been ruffled except by rare fits of passion—" tantrums " old Nicholas Treffry dubbed them—at what seemed to her mean or unjust.

" If I were a man," she said, " and going to be great, I should have wanted to begin at the very bottom as you did."

" Yes," said Harz quickly, " one should be able to feel *everything*."

She did not notice how simply he assumed that he was going to be great. He went on, a smile twisting his mouth unpleasantly beneath its dark moustache :

" Not many people think like you ! It's a crime not to have been born a gentleman."

" That's a sneer," said Christian ; " I didn't think *you* would have sneered ! "

" It is true. What is the use of pretending that it isn't ? "

" It may be true, but it is finer not to say it ! "

" By Heavens ! " said Harz, striking one hand into the other, " if more truth were spoken there would not be so many shams."

Christian looked down at him from her seat on the stile.

" You are right all the same, Fräulein Christian," he added suddenly ; " that's a very little business. Work is what matters, and trying to see the beauty in the world."

Christian's face changed. She understood, well

enough, this craving after beauty. Slipping down from the stile, she drew a slow deep breath.

" Yes ! " she said. Neither spoke for some time, then Harz said shyly :

" If you and Fräulein Greta would ever like to come and see my studio, I should be so happy. I would try and clean it up for you ! "

" I should like to come. I could learn something. I want to learn."

They were both silent till the path joined the road.

" We must be in front of the others ; it's nice to be in front—let's dawdle. I forgot—you never dawdle, Herr Harz."

" After a big fit of work, I can dawdle against any one ; then I get another fit of work—it's like appetite."

" I'm always dawdling," answered Christian.

By the roadside a peasant woman screwed up her sun-dried face, saying in a low voice : " Please, gracious lady, help me to lift this basket ! "

Christian stooped, but before she could raise it, Harz hoisted it up on his back.

" All right," he nodded ; " this good lady doesn't mind."

The woman, looking very much ashamed, walked along by Christian ; she kept rubbing her brown hands together, and saying : " Gracious lady, I would not have wished. It is heavy, but I would not have wished."

" I'm sure he'd rather carry it," said Christian.

They had not gone far along the road, however, before the others passed them in a carriage, and at the strange sight Miss Naylor could be seen pursing her lips ; Cousin Teresa nodding pleasantly ; a smile on

Dawney's face; and beside him Greta, very demure
Harz began to laugh.

"What are you laughing at?" asked Christian.

"You English are so funny. You mustn't do this
here, you mustn't do that there, it's like sitting in a
field of nettles. If I were to walk with you without
my coat, that little lady would fall off her seat." His
laugh infected Christian; they reached the station
feeling that they knew each other better.

The sun had dipped behind the mountains when the
little train steamed down the valley. All were subdued, and Greta, with a nodding head, slept fitfully.
Christian, in her corner, was looking out of the window,
and Harz kept studying her profile.

He tried to see her eyes. He had remarked indeed
that, whatever their expression, the brows, arched and
rather wide apart, gave them a peculiar look of understanding. He thought of his picture. There was
nothing in her face to seize on, it was too sympathetic,
too much like light. Yet her chin was firm, almost
obstinate.

The train stopped with a jerk; she looked round at
him. It was as though she had said: "You are my
friend."

At Villa Rubein, Herr Paul had killed the fatted calf
for Greta's *Fest*. When the whole party were
assembled, he alone remained standing; and waving
his arm above the cloth, cried: "My dears! Your
happiness! There are good things here—Come!"
And with a sly look, the air of a conjurer producing
rabbits, he whipped the cover off the soup tureen:

"Soup—turtle, fat, green fat!" He smacked his lips.

No servants were allowed, because, as Greta said to
Harz:

" It is that we are to be glad this evening."

Geniality radiated from Herr Paul's countenance, mellow as a bowl of wine. He toasted everybody, exhorting them to pleasure.

Harz passed a cracker secretly behind Greta's head, and Miss Naylor, moved by a mysterious impulse, pulled it with a sort of gleeful horror ; it exploded, and Greta sprang off her chair. Scruff, seeing this, appeared suddenly on the side-board with his forelegs in a plate of soup ; without moving them, he turned his head, and appeared to accuse the company of his false position. It was the signal for shrieks of laughter. Scruff made no attempt to free his forelegs ; but sniffed the soup, and finding that nothing happened, began to lap it.

" Take him out ! Oh ! take him out ! " wailed Greta, " he shall be ill ! "

" *Allons ! Mon cher !* " cried Herr Paul, " *c'est magnifique, mais, vous savez, ce n'est guere la guerre !* " Scruff, with a wild spring, leaped past him to the ground.

" Ah ! " cried Miss Naylor, " the carpet ! " Fresh moans of mirth shook the table ; for having tasted the wine of laughter, all wanted as much more as they could get. When Scruff and his traces were effaced, Herr Paul took a ladle in his hand.

" I have a toast," he said, waving it for silence ; " a toast we will drink all together from our hearts ; the toast of my little daughter, who to-day has thirteen years become ; and there is also in our hearts," he continued, putting down the ladle and suddenly becoming grave, " the thought of one who is not to-day with us to see this joyful occasion ; to her, too, in this our happiness we turn our hearts and glasses because it is her joy that we should yet be joyful. I drink to my little daughter ; may God her shadow bless ! "

All stood up, clinking their glasses, and drank : then, in the hush that followed, Greta, according to custom, began to sing a German carol ; at the end of the fourth line she stopped, abashed.

Herr Paul blew his nose loudly, and, taking up a cap that had fallen from a cracker, put it on.

Every one followed his example, Miss Naylor attaining the distinction of a pair of donkey's ears, which she wore, after another glass of wine, with an air of sacrificing to the public good.

At the end of supper came the moment for the offering of gifts. Herr Paul had tied a handkerchief over Greta's eyes, and one by one they brought her presents. Greta, under forfeit of a kiss, was bound to tell the giver by the feel of the gift. Her swift, supple little hands explored noiselessly ; and in every case she guessed right.

Dawney's present, a kitten, made a scene by clawing at her hair.

" That is Dr. Edmund's," she cried at once. Christian saw that Harz had disappeared, but suddenly he came back breathless, and took his place at the end of the rank of givers.

Advancing on tiptoe, he put his present into Greta's hands. It was a small bronze copy of a Donatello statue.

" Oh, Herr Harz ! " cried Greta ; " I saw it in the studio that day. It stood on the table, and it is lovely."

Mrs. Decie, thrusting her pale eyes close to it, murmured : " Charming ! "

Mr. Treffry took it in his fingers.

"Rum little toad! Cost a pot of money, I expect!"
He eyed Harz doubtfully.

They went into the next room now, and Herr Paul,
taking Greta's bandage, transferred it to his own eyes.

"Take care—take care, all!" he cried; "I am a
devil of a catcher," and, feeling the air cautiously, he
moved forward like a bear about to hug. He caught
no one. Christian and Greta whisked under his arms
and left him grasping at the air. Mrs. Decie slipped
past with astonishing agility. Mr. Treffry, smoking
his cigar, and barricaded in a corner, jeered: "Bravo,
Paul! The active beggar! Can't he run! Go it,
Greta!"

At last Herr Paul caught Cousin Teresa, who,
flattened against the wall, lost her head and stood
uttering tiny shrieks.

Suddenly Mrs. Decie started playing *The Blue
Danube*. Herr Paul dropped the handkerchief, twisted
his moustache up fiercely, glared round the room, and
seizing Greta by the waist, began dancing furiously,
bobbing up and down like a cork in lumpy water.
Cousin Teresa followed suit with Miss Naylor, both
very solemn, and dancing quite different steps. Harz
went up to Christian.

"I can't dance," he said, "that is, I have only
danced once, but—if you would try with me!"

She put her hand on his arm, and they began. She
danced, light as a feather, eyes shining, feet flying, her
body bent a little forward. It was not a great success
at first, but as soon as the time had got into Harz's feet,
they went swinging on when all the rest had stopped.
Sometimes one couple or another slipped through the
window to dance on the veranda, and came whirling
in again. The lamplight glowed on the girls' white

dresses ; on Herr Paul's perspiring face. He constituted in himself a perfect orgy, and when the music stopped flung himself, full length, on the sofa gasping out :

"My God ! But, my God ! "

Suddenly Christian felt Harz cling to her arm. Glowing and panting she looked at him.

"Giddy ! " he murmured : "I dance so badly ; but I'll soon learn."

Greta clapped her hands : "Every evening we will dance, every evening we will dance."

Harz looked at Christian ; the colour had deepened in her face.

"I'll show you how they dance in my village, feet upon the ceiling ! " And running to Dawney, he said :

"Hold me here ! Lift me—so ! Now, one—two," he tried to swing his feet above his head, but, with an "Ouch ! " from Dawney, they collapsed, and sat abruptly on the floor. This untimely event brought the evening to an end. Dawney left, escorting Cousin Teresa, and Harz strode home humming *The Blue Danube*, still feeling Christian's waist against his arm.

In their room the two girls sat long at the window to cool themselves before undressing.

"Ah ! " sighed Greta, " this is the happiest birthday I have had."

Christian too thought : ' I have never been so happy in my life as I have been to-day. I should like every day to be like this ! ' And she leant out into the night, to let the air cool her cheeks.

VI

" Chris ! " said Greta some days after this, " Miss Naylór danced last evening ; I think she shall have a headache to-day. There is my French and my history this morning."

" Well, I can take them."

" That is nice ; then we can talk. I am sorry about the headache. I shall give her some of my *Eau de Cologne*."

Miss Naylor's headaches after dancing were things on which to calculate. The girls carried their books into the arbour ; it was a showery day, and they had to run for shelter through the raindrops and sunlight.

" The French first, Chris ! " Greta liked her French, in which she was not far inferior to Christian ; the lesson therefore proceeded in an admirable fashion. After one hour exactly by her watch (Mr. Treffry's birthday present—loved and admired at least once every hour) Greta rose.

" Chris, I have not fed my rabbits."

" Be quick ! there's not much time for history."

Greta vanished. Christian watched the bright water dripping from the roof ; her lips were parted in a smile. She was thinking of something Harz had said the night before. A discussion having been started as to whether average opinion did, or did not, safeguard Society, Harz, after sitting silent, had burst out : " I think one man in earnest is better than twenty half-hearted men who follow tamely ; in the end he does Society most good."

Dawney had answered : " If you had your way there would be no Society."

" I hate Society because it lives upon the weak."

" Bah ! " Herr Paul chimed in ; " the weak goes to the wall ; that is as certain as that you and I are here."

" Let them fall against the wall," cried Harz ; " don't push them there. . . ."

Greta reappeared, walking pensively in the rain.

" Bino," she said, sighing, " has eaten too much. I remember now, I did feed them before. *Must* we do the history, Chris ? "

" Of course ! "

Greta opened her book, and put a finger in the page. " Herr Harz is very kind to me," she said. " Yesterday he brought a bird which had come into his studio with a hurt wing ; he brought it very gently in his handkerchief—he is very kind, the bird was not even frightened of him. You did not know about that, Chris ? "

Chris flushed a little, and said in a hurt voice :

" I don't see what it has to do with me."

" No," assented Greta.

Christian's colour deepened. " Go on with your history, Greta."

" Only," pursued Greta, " that he always tells *you* all about things, Chris."

" He doesn't ! How can you say that ! "

" I think he does, and it is because you do not make him angry. It is very easy to make him angry ; you have only to think differently, and he shall be angry at once."

" You are a little cat ! " said Christian ; " it isn't true, at all. He hates shams, and can't bear meanness ; and it *is* mean to cover up dislikes and pretend that you agree with people."

" Papa says that he thinks too much about himself."

" Father ! " began Christian hotly ; biting her lips she stopped, and turned her wrathful eyes on Greta.

" *You* do not always show your dislikes, Chris."

" I ? What has that to do with it ? Because one is a coward that doesn't make it any better, does it ? "

" I think that he has a great many dislikes," murmured Greta.

" I wish you would attend to your own faults, and not pry into other people's," and pushing the book aside, Christian gazed in front of her.

Some minutes passed, then Greta leaning over, rubbed a cheek against her shoulder.

" I am very sorry, Chris—I only wanted to be talking. Shall I read some history ? "

" Yes," said Christian coldly.

" Are you angry with me, Chris ? "

There was no answer. The lingering raindrops pattered down on the roof. Greta pulled at her sister's sleeve.

" Look, Chris ! " she said. " There *is* Herr Harz ! "

Christian looked up, dropped her eyes again, and said : " Will you go on with the history, Greta ? "

Greta sighed.

" Yes, I will—but, oh ! Chris, there is the luncheon gong ! " and she meekly closed the book.

During the following weeks there was a " sitting " nearly every afternoon. Miss Naylor usually attended them ; the little lady was, to a certain extent, carried past objection. She had begun to take an interest in the picture, and to watch the process out of the corner of her eye ; in the depths of her dear mind, however, she never quite got used to the vanity and waste of time ; her lips would move and her knitting-needles click in suppressed remonstrances.

What Harz did fast he did best ; if he had leisure he " saw too much," loving his work so passionately that he could never tell exactly when to stop. He hated to lay things aside, always thinking : " I can get it better." Greta was finished, but with Christian, try as he would, he was not satisfied ; from day to day her face seemed to him to change, as if her soul were growing.

There were things too in her eyes that he could neither read nor reproduce.

Dawney would often stroll out to them after his daily visit, and lying on the grass, his arms crossed behind his head, and a big cigar between his lips, would gently banter everybody. Tea came at five o'clock, and then Mrs. Decie appeared armed with a magazine or novel, for she was proud of her literary knowledge. The sitting was suspended ; Harz, with a cigarette, would move between the table and the picture, drinking his tea, putting a touch in here and there ; he never sat down till it was all over for the day. During these " rests " there was talk, usually ending in discussion. Mrs. Decie was happiest in conversations of a literary order, making frequent use of such expressions as : " After all, it produces an illusion—does anything else matter ? " " Rather a *poseur*, is he not ? " " A question, that, of temperament," or " A matter of the definition of words " ; and other charming generalities, which sound well, and seem to go far, and are pleasingly irrefutable. Sometimes the discussion turned on Art —on points of colour or technique ; whether realism was quite justified ; and should we be pre-Raphaelites ? When these discussions started, Christian's eyes would grow bigger and clearer, with a sort of shining reasonableness ; as though they were trying to see into the depths. And Harz would stare at them. But the look in those eyes eluded him, as if they had no more meaning than Mrs. Decie's, which, with their pale, watchful smile, always seemed saying : " Come, let us take a little intellectual exercise."

Greta, pulling Scruff's ears, would gaze up at the speakers ; when the talk was over, she always shook herself. But if no one came to the " sittings," there would sometimes be very earnest, quick talk, sometimes long silences.

One day Christian said : " What is your religion ? "

Harz finished the touch he was putting on the canvas, before he answered : " Roman Catholic, I suppose ; I was baptised in that Church."

" I didn't mean that. Do you believe in a future life ? "

" Christian," murmured Greta, who was plaiting blades of grass, " shall always want to know what people think about a future life ; that is so funny ! "

" How can I tell ? " said Harz ; " I've never really thought of it—never had the time."

" How can you help thinking ? " Christian said : " I *have* to—it seems to me so awful that we might come to an end."

She closed her book, and it slipped off her lap. She went on : " There must be a future life, we're so incomplete. What's the good of your work, for instance ? What's the use of developing if you have to stop ? "

" I don't know," answered Harz. " I don't much care. All I know is, I've got to work."

" But why ? "

" For happiness—the real happiness is fighting— the rest is nothing. If you have finished a thing, does

222

it ever satisfy you ? You look forward to the next thing at once ; to wait is wretched ! "

Christian clasped her hands behind her neck ; sunlight flickered through the leaves on to the bosom of her dress.

" Ah ! Stay like that ! " cried Harz.

She let her eyes rest on his face, swinging her foot a little.

" You work because you must ; but that's not enough. Why do you feel you must ? I want to know what's behind. When I was travelling with Aunt Constance the winter before last we often talked —I've heard her discuss it with her friends. She says we move in circles till we reach Nirvana. But last winter I found I couldn't talk to her ; it seemed as if she never really meant anything. Then I started reading—Kant and Hegel——"

" Ah ! " put in Harz, " if they would teach me to draw better, or to see a new colour in a flower, or an expression in a face, I would read them all."

Christian leaned forward : " It must be right to get as near truth as possible ; every step gained is something. You believe in truth ; truth is the same as beauty—that was what you said—you try to paint the truth, you always see the beauty. But how can we know truth, unless we know what is at the root of it ? "

" I—think," murmured Greta, *sotto voce*, " you see one way—and he sees another—because—you are not one person."

" Of course ! " said Christian impatiently, " but why——"

A sound of humming interrupted her.

Nicholas Treffry was coming from the house, holding

the *Times* in one hand, and a huge meerschaum pipe in the other.

"Aha ! " he said to Harz : " how goes the picture ? " and he lowered himself into a chair.

"Better to-day, Uncle ? " said Christian softly.

Mr. Treffry growled. " Confounded humbugs, doctors ! " he said. " Your father used to swear by them ; why, his doctor killed him—made him drink such a lot of stuff ! "

"Why then do you *have* a doctor, Uncle Nic ? " asked Greta.

Mr. Treffry looked at her ; his eyes twinkled. " I don't know, my dear. If they get half a chance, they won't let go of you ! "

There had been a gentle breeze all day, but now it had died away ; not a leaf quivered, not a blade of grass was stirring ; from the house were heard faint sounds as of some one playing on a pipe. A black-bird came hopping down the path.

"When you were a boy, did you go after birds' nests, Uncle Nic ? " Greta whispered.

"I believe you, Greta." The blackbird hopped into the shrubbery.

"Your frightened him, Uncle Nic ! Papa says that at Schloss König, where he lived when he was young, he would always be after jackdaws' nests."

"Gammon, Greta. Your father never took a jackdaw's nest, his legs are much too round ! "

"Are you fond of birds, Uncle Nic ? "

"Ask me another, Greta ! Well, I s'pose so."

"Then why did you go bird-nesting ? *I* think it is cruel."

Mr. Treffry coughed behind his paper : " There you have me, Greta," he remarked.

Harz began to gather his brushes : " Thank you," he said, " that's all I can do to-day."

" Can I look ? " Mr. Treffry inquired.

" Certainly ! "

Uncle Nic got up slowly, and stood in front of the picture. " When it's for sale," he said at last, " I'll buy it."

Harz bowed ; but for some reason he felt annoyed, as if he had been asked to part with something personal.

" I thank you," he said. A gong sounded.

" You'll stay and have a snack with us ? " said Mr. Treffry ; " the doctor's stopping." Gathering up his paper, he moved off to the house with his hand on Greta's shoulder, the terrier running in front. Harz and Christian were left alone. He was scraping his palette, and she was sitting with her elbows resting on her knees ; between them, a gleam of sunlight dyed the path golden. It was evening already ; the bushes and the flowers, after the day's heat, were breathing out perfume ; the birds had started their evensong.

" Are you tired of sitting for your portrait, Fräulein Christian ? "

Christian shook her head.

" I shall get something into it that everybody does not see—something behind the surface, that will last."

Christian said slowly : " That's like a challenge. You were right when you said fighting is happiness— for yourself, but not for me. I'm a coward. I hate to hurt people, I like them to like me. If *you* had to do anything that would make them hate you, you would do it all the same, if it helped your work ; that's fine— it's what I can't do. It's—it's everything. Do you like Uncle Nic ? "

The young painter looked towards the house, where under the veranda old Nicholas Treffry was still in sight ; a smile came on his lips.

" If I were the finest painter in the world, he wouldn't think anything of me for it, I'm afraid ; but if I could show him handfuls of big cheques for bad pictures I had painted, he would respect me."

She smiled, and said : " I love him."

" Then I shall like him," Harz answered simply.

She put her hand out, and her fingers met his.

" We shall be late," she said, glowing, and catching up her book : " I'm always late ! "

VII

There was one other guest at dinner, a well-groomed person with pale, fattish face, dark eyes, and hair thin on the temples, whose clothes had a military cut. He looked like a man fond of ease, who had gone out of his groove, and collided with life. Herr Paul introduced him as Count Mario Sarelli.

Two hanging lamps with crimson shades threw a rosy light over the table, where, in the centre, stood a silver basket, full of irises.

Through the open windows the garden was all clusters of black foliage in the dying light. Moths fluttered round the lamps ; Greta, following them with her eyes, gave quite audible sighs of pleasure when they escaped. Both girls wore white, and Harz, who sat opposite Christian, kept looking at her, and wondering why he had not painted her in that dress.

Mrs. Decie understood the art of dining—the dinner, ordered by Herr Paul, was admirable ; the servants silent as their shadows; there was always a hum of conversation.

Sarelli, who sat on her right hand, seemed to partake of little except olives, which he dipped into a glass of sherry. He turned his black, solemn eyes silently from face to face, now and then asking the meaning of an English word. After a discussion on modern Rome, it was debated whether or no a criminal could be told by the expression of his face.

" Crime," said Mrs. Decie, passing her hand across her brow—" crime is but the hallmark of strong individuality."

Miss Naylor, flushing rather pink, stammered: " A great crime must show itself—a murder. Why, of course ! "

" If that were so," said Dawney, " we should only have to look about us—no more detectives."

Miss Naylor rejoined with slight severity : " I cannot conceive that such a thing can pass the human face by, leaving no impression ! "

Harz said abruptly : " There are worse things than murder."

" Ah ! *par exemple !* " said Sarelli.

There was a slight stir all round the table.

" Verry good," cried out Herr Paul, " *a vot' santé, cher*."

Miss Naylor shivered, as if someone had put a penny down her back; and Mrs. Decie, leaning towards Harz, smiled like one who has made a pet dog do a trick. Christian alone was motionless, looking thoughtfully at Harz.

" I saw a man tried for murder once," he said, " a murder for revenge ; I watched the judge, and I thought all the time : ' I'd rather be that murderer than you ;

I've never seen a meaner face ; you *crawl* through life ;
you're not a criminal, simply because you haven't the
courage.' "

In the dubious silence following the painter's speech,
Mr. Treffry could distinctly be heard humming. Then
Sarelli said : " What do you say to anarchists, who are
not men, but savage beasts, whom I would tear to
pieces ! "

" As to that," Harz answered defiantly, " it may be
wise to hang them, but then there are so many other
men that it would be wise to hang."

" How can we tell what they went through, what
their lives were ? " murmured Christian.

Miss Naylor, who had been rolling a pellet of bread,
concealed it hastily. " They are—always given a
chance to—repent—I believe," she said.

" ' For what they are about to receive,' " drawled
Dawney.

Mrs. Decie signalled with her fan : " We are trying
to express the inexpressible—shall we go into the
garden ? "

All rose ; Harz stood by the window, and in passing,
Christian looked at him.

He sat down again with a sudden sense of loss.
There was no white figure opposite now. Raising his
eyes he met Sarelli's. The Italian was regarding him
with a curious stare.

Herr Paul began retailing a piece of scandal he had
heard that afternoon.

" Shocking affair ! " he said ; " I could never have
believed it of her ! B——is quite beside himself.
Yesterday there was a row, it seems ! "

" There has been one every day for months,"
muttered Dawney.

" But to leave without a word, and go no one knows where! B—— is ' *viveur* ' no doubt, *mais, mon Dieu, que voulez-vous?* She was always a poor pale thing. Why I, when my——" he flourished his cigar; " I was not always—what I should have been—one lives in a world of flesh and blood—we are not all angels— *que diable !*—But this is a very vulgar business. She goes off; leaves everything—without a word; and B—— is very fond of her. These things are not done ! " the starched bosom of his shirt seemed swollen by indignation.

Mr. Treffry, with a heavy hand on the table, eyed him sideways. Dawney said slowly:

" B—— is a beast; I'm sorry for the poor woman; but what can she do alone ? "

" There is, no doubt, a man," put in Sarelli.

Herr Paul muttered: " Who knows ? "

" What is B—— going to do ? " said Dawney.

" Ah ! " said Herr Paul. " He is fond of her. He is a chap of resolution, he will get her back. He told me: ' Well, you know, I shall follow her wherever she goes till she comes back.' He will do it, he is a determined chap; he will follow her wherever she goes."

Mr. Treffry drank his wine off at a gulp, and sucked his moustache in sharply.

" She was a fool to marry him," said Dawney; " they haven't a point in common; she hates him like poison, and she's the better of the two. But it doesn't pay a woman to run off like that. B—— had better hurry up though. What do you think, sir ! " he said to Mr. Treffry.

" Eh ? " said Mr. Treffry; " how should I know ? Ask Paul there, he's one of your moral men, or Count Sarelli."

The latter said impassively : " If I cared for her I should very likely kill her—if not——" he shrugged his shoulders.

Harz, who was watching, was reminded of his other words at dinner, " wild beasts whom I would tear to pieces." He looked with interest at this quiet man who said these extremely ferocious things, and thought : ' I should like to paint that fellow.'

Herr Paul twirled his wine-glass in his fingers. " There are family ties," he said, " there is society, there is decency ; a wife should be with her husband. B—— will do quite right. He must go after her ; she will not perhaps come back at first ; he will follow her ; she will begin to think, ' I am helpless—I am ridiculous ! ' A woman is soon beaten. They will return. She is once more with her husband—Society will forgive, it will be all right "

" By Jove, Paul," growled Mr. Treffry, " wonderful power of argument ! "

" A wife is a wife," pursued Herr Paul ; " a man has a right to her society."

" What do you say to that, sir ? " asked Dawney.

Mr. Treffry tugged at his beard : " Make a woman live with you, if she don't want to ? I call it low."

" But, my dear," exclaimed Herr Paul, " how should you know ? You have not been married,"

" No, thank the Lord ! " Mr. Treffry replied.

" But looking at the question broadly, sir," said Dawney ; " if a husband always lets his wife do as she likes, how would the thing work out ? What becomes of the marriage tie ? "

" The marriage tie," growled Mr. Treffry, " is the biggest thing there is ! But, by Jove, Doctor, I'm a

Dutchman if hunting women ever helped the marriage tie ! "

" I am not thinking of myself," Herr Paul cried out, " I think of the community. There are rights."

" A decent community never yet asked a man to tread on his self-respect. If I get my fingers skinned over my marriage, which I undertake at my own risk, what's the community to do with it ? D'you think I'm going to whine to it to put the plaster on ? As to rights, it'd be a deuced sight better for us all if there wasn't such a fuss about 'em. Leave that to women ! I don't give a tinker's damn for men who talk about their rights in such matters."

Sarelli rose. " But your honour," he said, " there is your honour ! "

Mr. Treffry stared at him.

" Honour ! If huntin' women's your idea of honour, well—it isn't mine."

" Then you'd forgive her, sir, whatever happened," Dawney said.

" Forgiveness is another thing. I leave that to your sanctimonious beggars. But, hunt a woman ! Hang it, sir, I'm not a cad ! " and bringing his hand down with a rattle, he added : " This is a subject that don't bear talking of."

Sarelli fell back in his seat, twirling his moustaches fiercely. Harz, who had risen, looked at Christian's empty place.

' If I were married ! ' he thought suddenly.

Herr Paul, with a somewhat vinous glare, still muttered, " But your duty to the family ! "

Harz slipped through the window. The moon was like a wonderful white lantern in the purple sky ; there was but a smoulder of stars. Beneath

231

the softness of the air was the iciness of the snow ; it made him want to run and leap. A sleepy beetle dropped on its back ; he turned it over and watched it scurry across the grass.

Some one was playing Schumann's *Kinderscenen*. Harz stood still to listen. The notes came twining, weaving round his thoughts ; the whole night seemed full of girlish voices, of hopes and fancies, soaring away to mountain heights—invisible, yet present. Between the stems of the acacia-trees he could see the flicker of white dresses, where Christian and Greta were walking arm in arm. He went towards them ; the blood flushed up in his face, he felt almost surfeited by some sweet emotion. Then, in sudden horror, he stood still. He was in love ! With nothing done—with everything before him ! He was going to bow down to a face ! The flicker of the dresses was no longer visible. He would not be fettered, he would stamp it out ! He turned away ; but with each step, something seemed to jab at his heart.

Round the corner of the house, in the shadow of the wall, Dominique, the Luganese, in embroidered slippers, was smoking a long cherrywood pipe, leaning against a tree—Mephistopheles in evening clothes. Harz went up to him.

"Lend me a pencil, Dominique."

"*Bien M'sieur.*"

Resting a card against the tree Harz wrote to Mrs. Decie : "Forgive me, I am obliged to go away. In a few days I shall hope to return, and finish the picture of your nieces."

He sent Dominique for his hat. During the man's absence he was on the point of tearing up the card and going back into the house.

When the Luganese returned he thrust the card into his hand, and walked out between the tall poplars, waiting, like ragged ghosts, silver with moonlight.

VIII

Harz walked away along the road. A dog was howling. The sound seemed too appropriate. He put his fingers to his ears, but the lugubrious noise passed those barriers, and made its way into his heart. Was there nothing that would put an end to this emotion ? It was no better in the old house on the wall ; he spent the night tramping up and down.

Just before daybreak he slipped out with a knapsack, taking the road towards Meran.

He had not quite passed through Gries when he overtook a man walking in the middle of the road and leaving a trail of cigar smoke behind him.

" Ah ! my friend," the smoker said, " you walk early ; are you going my way ? "

It was Count Sarelli. The raw light had imparted a grey tinge to his pale face, the growth of his beard showed black already beneath the skin ; his thumbs were hooked in the pockets of a closely buttoned coat, he gesticulated with his fingers.

" You are making a journey ? " he said, nodding at the knapsack. " You are early—I am late ; our friend has admirable *kümmel*—I have drunk too much. You have not been to bed, I think ? If there is no sleep in one's bed it is no good going to look for it. You find that ? It is better to drink *kümmel* ! . . . Pardon ! You are doing the right thing : get away ! Get away as fast as possible ! Don't wait, and let it catch you ! "

Harz stared at him amazed.

" Pardon ! " Sarelli said again, raising his hat, " that girl—the white girl—I saw. You do well to get away ! " he swayed a little as he walked. " That old fellow—what is his name—Tr-r-reffr-ry ! What ideas of honour ! " He mumbled : " Honour is an abstraction ! If a man is not true to an abstraction, he is a low type ; but wait a minute ! "

He put his hand to his side as though in pain.

The hedges were brightening with a faint pinky glow ; there was no sound on the long, deserted road, but that of their footsteps ; suddenly a bird commenced to chirp, another answered—the world seemed full of these little voices. Sarelli stopped.

" That white girl," he said, speaking with rapidity. " Yes ! You do well ! get away ! Don't let it catch you ! I waited, it caught me—what happened ? Everything horrible—and now—*kümmel !* " Laughing a thick laugh, he gave a twirl to his moustache, and swaggered on.

" I was a fine fellow—nothing too big for Mario Sarelli ; the regiment looked to me. Then *she* came— with her eyes and her white dress, always white, like this one ; the little mole on her chin, her hands for ever moving—their touch as warm as sunbeams. Then no longer Sarelli this, and that ! The little house close to the ramparts ! Two arms, two eyes, and nothing here," he tapped his breast, " but flames that made ashes quickly—in *her* like this ash——! " he flicked the white flake off his cigar. " It's droll ! You agree, *hein ?* Some day I shall go back and kill her. In the meantime—*kümmel !* "

He stopped at a house close to the road, and stood still, his teeth bared in a grin.

" But I bore you," he said. His cigar, flung down, sputtered forth its sparks on the road in front of Harz. "I live here—good-morning! You are a man for work—your honour is your Art! *I* know, and you are young! The man who loves flesh better than his honour is a low type—I am a low type. I! Mario Sarelli, a low type! I love flesh better than my honour! "

He remained swaying at the gate with the grin fixed on his face ; then staggered up the steps, and banged the door. But before Harz had walked on, he again appeared, beckoning in the doorway. Obeying an impulse, Harz went in.

" We will make a night of it," said Sarelli ; " wine, brandy, *kümmel?* I am virtuous—*kümmel* it must be for me ! "

He sat down at a piano, and began to touch the keys. Harz poured out some wine. Sarelli nodded.

" You begin with that ? *Allegro—piu—presto !* Wine—brandy—*kümmel !* " he quickened the time of the tune : " it is not too long a passage, and *this* "—he took his hands off the keys—" comes after."

Harz smiled.

" Some men do not kill themselves," he said.

Sarelli, who was bending and swaying to the music of a tarantella, broke off, and letting his eyes rest on the painter, began playing Schumann's *Kinderscenen.* Harz leaped to his feet.

" Stop that ! " he cried.

" It pricks you ? " said Sarelli suavely ; " what do you think of *this ?* " he played again, crouching over the piano, and making the notes sound like the crying of a wounded animal.

" For me ! " he said, swinging round, and rising.

" Your health ! And so you don't believe in suicide, but in murder ? The custom is the other way ; but you don't believe in customs ? Customs are only for Society ? " He drank a glass of *kümmel*. " You do not love Society ? "

Harz looked at him intently ; he did not want to quarrel.

" I am not too fond of other people's thoughts," he said at last ; " I prefer to think my own."

" And is Society never right ? That poor Society ! "

" Society ! What is Society—a few men in good coats ? What has it done for me ? "

Sarelli bit the end off a cigar.

" Ah ! " he said ; " now we are coming to it. It is good to be an artist, a fine bantam of an artist ; where other men have their dis-ci-pline, he has his, what shall we say—his mound of roses ? "

The painter started to his feet.

" Yes," said Sarelli, with a hiccough, " you are a fine fellow ! "

" And you are drunk ! " cried Harz.

" A little drunk—not much, not enough to matter ! "

Harz broke into laughter. It was crazy to stay there listening to this mad fellow. What had brought him in ? He moved towards the door.

" Ah ! " said Sarelli, " but it is no good going to bed —let us talk. I have a lot to say—it is pleasant to talk to anarchists at times."

Full daylight was already coming through the chinks of the shutters.

" You are all anarchists, you painters, you writing fellows. You live by playing ball with facts. Images —nothing solid—*hein ?* You're all for new things too,

236

to tickle your nerves, No discipline! True anarchists, every one of you!"

Harz poured out another glass of wine and drank it off. The man's feverish excitement was catching.

"Only fools," he replied, "take things for granted. As for discipline, what do you aristocrats, or bourgeois know of discipline? Have you ever been hungry? Have you ever had your soul down on its back?"

"Soul on its back? That is good!"

"A man's no use," cried Harz, "if he's always thinking of what others think; he must stand on his own legs."

"He must not then consider other people?"

"Not from cowardice anyway."

Sarelli drank.

"What would you do," he said, striking his chest, "if you had a devil—here? Would you go to bed?"

A sort of pity seized on Harz. He wanted to say something that would be consoling but could find no words; and suddenly he felt disgusted. What link was there between him and this man; between his love and this man's love?"

"Harz!" muttered Sarelli; "Harz means 'tar,' *hein?* Your family is not an old one?"

Harz glared, and said: "My father is a peasant."

Sarelli lifted the *kümmel* bottle and emptied it into his glass, with a steady hand.

"You're honest—and we both have devils. I forgot; I brought you in to see a picture!"

He threw wide the shutters; the windows were already open, and a rush of air came in.

"Ah!" he said, sniffing, "smells of the earth, *nicht wahr, Herr Artist? You* should know—it belongs

237

to your father. . . . Come, here's my picture ; a Correggio ! What do you think of it ? "

" It is a copy."

" You think ? "

" I *know*."

" Then you have given me the lie, Signor," and drawing out his handkerchief Sarelli flicked it in the painter's face.

Harz turned white.

" Duelling is a good custom ! " said Sarelli. " I shall have the honour to teach you just this one, unless you are afraid. Here are pistols—this room is twenty feet across at least, twenty feet is no bad distance."

And pulling out a drawer he took two pistols from a case, and put them on the table.

" The light is good—but perhaps you are afraid."

" Give me one ! " shouted the infuriated painter ; " and go to the devil for a fool."

" One moment ! " Sarelli murmured : " I will load them, they are more useful loaded."

Harz leaned out of the window ; his head was in a whirl. ' What on earth is happening ? ' he thought. ' He's mad—or I am ! Confound him ! I'm not going to be killed ! ' He turned and went towards the table. Sarelli's head was sunk on his arms, he was asleep. Harz methodically took up the pistols, and put them back into the drawer. A sound made him turn his head ; there stood a tall, strong young woman in a loose gown caught together on her chest. Her grey eyes glanced from the painter to the bottles, from the bottles to the pistol-case. A simple reasoning, which struck Harz as comic.

" It is often like this," she said in the country patois ; " *der Herr* must not be frightened."

238

Lifting the motionless Sarelli as if he were a baby, she laid him on a couch.

" Ah ! " she said, sitting down and resting her elbow on the table ; " he will not wake ! "

Harz bowed to her ; her patient figure, in spite of its youth and strength, seemed to him pathetic. Taking up his knapsack, he went out.

The smoke of cottages rose straight ; wisps of mist were wandering about the valley, and the songs of the birds dropping like blessings. All over the grass the spiders had spun a sea of threads that bent and quivered to the presence of the air, like fairy tight-ropes.

All that day he tramped.

Blacksmiths, tall stout men with knotted muscles, sleepy eyes, and great fair beards, came out of their forges to stretch and wipe their brows, and stare at him.

Teams of white oxen, waiting to be harnessed, lashed their tails against their flanks, moving their heads slowly from side to side in the heat. Old women at chalet doors blinked and knitted.

The white houses, with gaping caves of storage under the roofs, the red church spire, the clinking of hammers in the forges, the slow stamping of oxen— all spoke of sleepy toil, without ideas or ambition. Harz knew it all too well ; like the earth's odour, it belonged to him, as Sarelli had said.

Towards sunset coming to a copse of larches, he sat down to rest. It was very still, but for the tinkle of cowbells, and, from somewhere in the distance, the sound of dropping logs.

Two barefooted little boys came from the wood, marching earnestly along, and looking at Harz as if he were a monster. Once past him, they began to run.

239

' At their age,' he thought, ' I should have done the same.' A hundred memories rushed into his mind.

He looked down at the village straggling below—white houses with russet tiles and crowns of smoke, vineyards where the young leaves were beginning to unfold, the red-capped spire, a thread of bubbling stream, an old stone cross. He had been fourteen years struggling up from all this ; and now just as he had breathing space, and the time to give himself wholly to his work—this weakness was upon him ! Better, a thousand times, to give her up !

In a house or two lights began to wink ; the scent of wood smoke reached him, the distant chimes of bells, the burring of a stream.

IX

Next day his one thought was to get back to work. He arrived at the studio in the afternoon, and, laying in provisions, barricaded the lower door. For three days he did not go out ; on the fourth day he went to Villa Rubein. . . .

Schloss Runkelstein—grey, blind, strengthless—still keeps the valley. The windows which once, like eyes, watched men and horses creeping through the snow, braved the splutter of guns and the gleam of torches, are now holes for the birds to nest in. Tangled creepers have spread to the very summits of the walls. In the keep, instead of grim men in armour, there is a wooden board recording the history of the castle and instructing visitors on the subject of refreshments. Only at night, when the cold moon blanches everything, the castle stands like the grim ghost of its old self, high above the river.

240

After a long morning's sitting the girls had started forth with Harz and Dawney to spend the afternoon at the ruin ; Miss Naylor, kept at home by headache, watched them depart with words of caution against sunstroke, stinging nettles, and strange dogs.

Since the painter's return Christian and he had hardly spoken to each other. Below the battlement on which they sat, in a railed gallery with little tables, Dawney and Greta were playing dominoes, two soldiers drinking beer, and at the top of a flight of stairs the Custodian's wife sewing at a garment. Christian said suddenly : " I thought we were friends."

" Well, Fräulein Christian, aren't we ? "

" You went away without a word ; friends don't do that."

Harz bit his lips.

" I don't think you care," she went on with a sort of desperate haste, " whether you hurt people or not. You have been here all this time without even going to see your father and mother."

" Do you think they would want to see me ? "

Christian looked up.

" It's all been so soft for you," he said bitterly ; " you don't understand."

He turned his head away, and then burst out : " I'm proud to come straight from the soil—I wouldn't have it otherwise ; but they are of ' the people,' everything is narrow with them—they only understand what they can see and touch."

" I'm sorry I spoke like that," said Christian softly ; " you've never told me about yourself."

There was something just a little cruel in the way the painter looked at her, then seeming to feel compunction, he said quickly : " I always hated the

241

peasant life—I wanted to get away into the world; I had a feeling in here—I wanted—I don't know what I wanted! I did run away at last to a house-painter at Meran. The priest wrote me a letter from my father—they threw me off; that's all."

Christian's eyes were very bright, her lips moved, like the lips of a child listening to a story.

" Go on," she said.

" I stayed at Meran two years, till I'd learnt all I could there, then a brother of my mother's helped me to get to Vienna; I was lucky enough to find work with a man who used to decorate churches. We went about the country together. Once when he was ill I painted the roof of a church entirely by myself; I lay on my back on the scaffold boards all day for a week—I was proud of that roof." He paused.

"When did you begin painting pictures ? "

" A friend asked me why I didn't try for the Académie. That started me going to the night schools; I worked every minute—I had to get my living as well, of course, so I worked at night. Then when the examination came, I thought I could do nothing—it was just as if I had never had a brush or pencil in my hand. But the second day a professor in passing me said, ' Good! Quite good! ' That gave me courage. I was sure I had failed though; but I was second out of sixty."

Christian nodded.

" To work in the schools after that I had to give up my business, of course. There was only one teacher who ever taught me anything; the others all seemed fools. This man would come and rub out what you'd done with his sleeve. I used to cry with rage—but I

242

told him I could only learn from him, and he was so astonished that he got me into his class."

" But how did you live without money ? " asked Christian.

His face burned with a dark flush.   " I don't know how I lived ; you must have been through these things to know, you would never understand."

" But I want to understand, please."

" What do you want me to tell you ?   How I went twice a week to eat free dinners !   How I took charity ! How I was hungry !   There was a rich cousin of my mother's—I used to go to him.   I didn't like it.   But if you're starving in the winter——"

Christian put out her hand.

" I used to borrow apronsful of coals from other students who were as poor—but I never went to the rich students."

The flush had died out of his face.

" That sort of thing makes you hate the world ! You work till you stagger ; you're cold and hungry ; you see rich people in their carriages, wrapped in furs, and all the time you want to do something great. You pray for a chance, any chance; nothing comes to the poor !   It makes you hate the world."

Christian's eyes filled with tears.   He went on :

" But I wasn't the only one in that condition ; we used to meet.   Garin, a Russian with a brown beard and patches of cheek showing through, and yellow teeth, who always looked hungry.   Paunitz, who came from *sympathy !*   He had fat cheeks and little eyes, and a big gold chain—the swine !   And little Misek.   It was in his room we met, with the paper peeling off the walls, and two doors with cracks in them, so that there was always a draught.   We used to sit on his bed, and

243

pull the dirty blankets over us for warmth; and smoke—tobacco was the last thing we ever went without. Over the bed was a Virgin and Child—Misek was a very devout Catholic; but one day when he had had no dinner and a dealer had kept his picture without paying him, he took the image and threw it on the floor before our eyes; it broke, and he trampled on the bits. Lendorf was another, a heavy fellow who was always puffing out his white cheeks and smiting himself, and saying: 'Cursed society!' And Schönborn, an aristocrat who had quarrelled with his family. He was the poorest of us all; but only he and I would ever have dared to do anything—they all knew that!"

Christian listened with awe. "Do you mean?" she said, "do you mean, that you—— ?"

"You see! you're afraid of me at once. It's impossible even for you to understand. It only makes you afraid. A hungry man living on charity, sick with rage and shame, is a wolf even to *you!*"

Christian looked straight into his eyes.

"That's not true. If I can't understand, I can feel. Would you be the same now if it were to come again?"

"Yes, it drives me mad even now to think of people fatted with prosperity, sneering and holding up their hands at poor devils who have suffered ten times more than the most those soft animals could bear. I'm older; I've lived—I know things can't be put right by violence—nothing will put things right, but that doesn't stop my feeling."

"Did you *do* anything? You must tell me all now."

"We talked—we were always talking."

"No, tell me everything!"

Unconsciously she claimed, and he seemed unconsciously to admit her right to this knowledge.

" There's not much to tell. One day we began talking in low voices—Garin began it; he had been in some affair in Russia. We took an oath; after that we never raised our voices. We had a plan. It was all new to me, and I hated the whole thing—but I was always hungry, or sick from taking charity, and I would have done anything. They knew that; they used to look at me and Schönborn; we knew that no one else had any courage. He and I were great friends, but we never talked of *that*; we tried to keep our minds away from the thought of it. If we had a good day and were not so hungry, it seemed unnatural; but when the day had not been good—then it seemed natural enough. I wasn't afraid, but I used to wake up in the night; I hated the oath we had taken, I hated every one of those fellows; the thing was not what I was made for, it wasn't my work, it wasn't my nature, it was forced on me—I hated it, but sometimes I was like a madman."

" Yes, yes," she murmured.

" All this time I was working at the Academie, and learning all I could. . . . One evening that we met, Paunitz was not there. Misek was telling us how the thing had been arranged. Schönborn and I looked at each other—it was warm—perhaps we were not hungry —it was springtime, too, and in the Spring it's different. There is something——"

Christian nodded.

" While we were talking there came a knock at the door. Lendorf put his eye to the keyhole, and made a sign. The police were there. Nobody said anything, but Misek crawled under the bed; we all followed; and the knocking grew louder and louder. In the wall at the back of the bed was a little door into

245

an empty cellar. We crept through. There was a trap-door behind some cases, where they used to roll barrels in. We crawled through that into the back street. We went different ways."

He paused, and Christian gasped.

" I thought I would get my money, but there was a policeman before my door. They had us finely. It was Paunitz; if I met him even now I should wring his neck. I swore I wouldn't be caught, but I had no idea where to go. Then I thought of a little Italian barber who used to shave me when I had money for a shave; I knew he would help. He belonged to some Italian Society; he often talked to me, under his breath, of course. I went to him. He was shaving himself before going to a ball. I told him what had happened; it was funny to see him put his back against the door. He was very frightened, understanding this sort of thing better than I did—for I was only twenty then. He shaved my head and moustache and put me on a fair wig. Then he brought me macaroni, and some meat, to eat. He gave me a big fair moustache, and a cap, and hid the moustache in the lining. He brought me a cloak of his own, and four *gulden*. All the time he was extremely frightened, and kept listening, and saying : ' Eat ! '

" When I had done, he just said : ' Go away, I refuse to know anything more of you.'

" I thanked him and went out. I walked about all that night; for I couldn't think of anything to do or anywhere to go. In the morning I slept on a seat in one of the squares. Then I thought I would go to the *Gallerien*; and I spent the whole day looking at the pictures. When the Galleries were shut I was very tired, so I went into a *café*, and had some beer. When

I came out I sat on the same seat in the Square. I meant to wait till dark and then walk out of the city and take the train at some little station, but while I was sitting there I went to sleep. A policeman woke me. He had my wig in his hand.

" ' Why do you wear a wig ? ' he said.

" I answered : ' Because I am bald.'

" ' No,' he said, ' you're not bald, you've been shaved. I can feel the hair coming.'

" He put his finger on my head. I felt reckless and laughed.

" ' Ah ! ' he said, ' you'll come with me and explain all this ; your nose and eyes are looked for.'

" I went with him quietly to the police-station." . . .

Harz seemed carried away by his story. His quick dark face worked, his steel-grey eyes stared as though he were again passing through all these long-past emotions.

The hot sun struck down ; Christian drew herself together, sitting with her hands clasped round her knees.

X

" I didn't care by then what came of it. I didn't even think what I was going to say. He led me down a passage to a room with bars across the windows and long seats, and maps on the walls. We sat and waited. He kept his eye on me all the time ; and I saw no hope. Presently the Inspector came. ' Bring him in here,' he said ; I remember feeling I could kill him for ordering me about ! We went into the next room. It had a large clock, a writing-table, and a window, without bars, looking on a courtyard. Long policemen's coats and caps were hanging from some pegs. The Inspector told me to take off my cap. I took it off, wig and all. . He asked me who I was, but I refused to answer. Just then there was a loud sound of voices in the room we had come from. The Inspector told the policeman to look after me, and went to see what it was. I could hear him talking. He called out : ' Come here, Becker ! ' I stood very quiet, and Becker went towards the door. I heard the Inspector say : ' Go and find Schwartz, I will see after this fellow.' The policeman went, and the Inspector stood with his back to me in the half-open door, and began again to talk to the man in the other room. Once or twice he looked round at me, but I stood quiet all the time. They began to disagree, and their voices got angry. The Inspector moved a little into the other room. ' Now ! ' I thought, and slipped off my cloak. I hooked off a policeman's coat and cap, and put them on. My heart beat till I felt sick. I went on tiptoe to the window. There was no one outside, but at the entrance a man was holding some horses. I opened the window a little and held my breath. I heard the Inspector say : ' I will report you for impertinence ! ' and slipped through the window. The coat came down nearly to my heels, and the cap over my eyes. I walked up to the man with the horses, and said : ' Good-evening.' One of the horses had begun to kick, and he only grunted at me. I got into a passing tram ; it was five minutes to the West Bahnhof ; I got out there. There was a train starting ; they were shouting ' *Einsteigen !* ' I ran. The collector tried to stop me. I shouted : ' Business—important ! ' He let me by. I jumped into a carriage. The train started."

He paused, and Christian heaved a sigh.

Harz went on, twisting a twig of ivy in his hands :
" There was another man in the carriage reading a
paper. Presently I said to him, ' Where do we stop
first ? ' ' St. Polten.' Then I knew it was the Munich
express—St. Polten, Amstetten, Linz, and Salzburg—
four stops before the frontier. The man put down his
paper and looked at me; he had a big fair moustache
and rather shabby clothes. His looking at me disturbed me, for I thought every minute he would say :
' You're no policeman ! ' And suddenly it came into
my mind that if they looked for me in this train, it
would be as a policeman !—they would know, of
course, at the station that a policeman had run past at
the last minute. I wanted to get rid of the coat and
cap, but the man was there, and I didn't like to move
out of the carriage for other people to notice. So I
sat on. We came to St. Polten at last. The man in
my carriage took his bag, got out, and left his paper on
the seat. We started again ; I breathed at last, and as
soon as I could took the cap and coat and threw them
out into the darkness. I thought : ' I shall get across
the frontier now.' I took my own cap out and found
the moustache Luigi gave me ; rubbed my clothes as
clean as possible ; stuck on the moustache, and with
some little ends of chalk in my pocket made my eyebrows light ; then drew some lines in my face to make
it older, and pulled my cap well down above my wig.
I did it pretty well—I was quite like the man who had
got out. I sat in his corner, took up his newspaper,
and waited for Amstetten. It seemed a tremendous
time before we got there. From behind my paper
I could see five or six policemen on the platform, one
quite close. He opened the door, looked at me, and
walked through the carriage into the corridor. I took

some tobacco and rolled up a cigarette, but it shook," Harz lifted the ivy twig, "like this. In a minute the conductor and two more policemen came. 'He was here,' said the conductor, 'with this gentleman.' One of them looked at me, and asked: 'Have you seen a policeman travelling on this train?' 'Yes,' I said. 'Where?' 'He got out at St. Polten.' The policeman asked the conductor: 'Did you see him get out there?' The conductor shook his head. I said: 'He got out as the train was moving.' 'Ah!' said the policeman, 'what was he like?' 'Rather short, and no moustache. Why?' 'Did you notice anything unusual?' 'No,' I said, 'only that he wore coloured trousers. What's the matter?' One policeman said to the other: 'That's our man! Send a telegram to St. Polten; he has more than an hour's start.' He asked me where I was going. I told him: 'Linz.' 'Ah!' he said, 'you'll have to give evidence; your name and address please?' 'Josef Reinhardt, 17 Donau Strasse.' He wrote it down. The conductor said: 'We are late, can we start?' They shut the door. I heard them say to the conductor: 'Search again at Linz, and report to the Inspector there.' They hurried on to the platform, and we started. At first I thought I would get out as soon as the train had left the station. Then, that I should be too far from the frontier; better to go on to Linz and take my chance there. I sat still and tried not to think. After a long time, we began to run more slowly. I put my head out and could see in the distance a ring of lights hanging in the blackness. I loosened the carriage door and waited for the train to run slower still; I didn't mean to go into Linz like a rat into a trap. At last I could wait no longer; I opened the door, jumped and fell into some bushes. I was not much hurt, but bruised, and the breath knocked out of me. As soon as I could, I crawled out. It was very dark. I felt heavy and sore, and for some time went stumbling in and out amongst trees. Presently I came to a clear space; on one side I could see the town's shape drawn in lighted lamps, and on the other a dark mass, which I think was forest; in the distance too was a thin chain of lights. I thought: 'They must be the lights of a bridge.' Just then the moon came out, and I could see the river shining below. It was cold and damp, and I walked quickly. At last I came out on a road, past houses and barking dogs, down to the river bank; there I sat against a shed and went to sleep. I woke very stiff. It was darker than before; the moon was gone. I could just see the river. I stumbled on, to get through the town before dawn. It was all black shapes—houses and sheds, and the smell of the river, the smell of rotting hay, apples, tar, mud, fish; and here and there on a wharf a lantern. I stumbled over casks and ropes and boxes; I saw I should never get clear—the dawn had begun already on the other side. Some men came from a house behind me. I bent, and crept behind some barrels. They passed along the wharf; they seemed to drop into the river. I heard one of them say: 'Passau before night.' I stood up and saw they had walked on board a steamer which was lying head up-stream, with some barges in tow. There was a plank laid to the steamer, and a lantern at the other end. I could hear the fellows moving below deck, getting up steam. I ran across the plank and crept to the end of the steamer. I meant to go with them to Passau! The rope which towed the barges was nearly taut; and I knew if I could get on to the barges

I should be safe. I climbed down on this rope and crawled along. I was desperate, I knew they'd soon be coming up, and it was getting light. I thought I should fall into the water several times, but I got to the barge at last. It was laden with straw. There was nobody on board. I was hungry and thirsty—I looked for something to eat; there was nothing but the ashes of a fire and a man's coat. I crept into the straw. Soon a boat brought men, one for each barge, and there were sounds of steam. As soon as we began moving through the water, I fell asleep. When I woke we were creeping through a heavy mist. I made a little hole in the straw and saw the bargeman. He was sitting by a fire at the barge's edge, so that the sparks and smoke blew away over the water. He ate and drank with both hands, and funny enough he looked in the mist, like a big bird flapping its wings; there was a good smell of coffee, and I sneezed. How the fellow started! But presently he took a pitchfork and prodded the straw. Then I stood up. I couldn't help laughing, he was so surprised—a huge, dark man, with a great black beard. I pointed to the fire and said: 'Give me some, brother!' He pulled me out of the straw; I was so stiff, I couldn't move. I sat by the fire, and ate black bread and turnips, and drank coffee; while he stood by, watching me and muttering. I couldn't understand him well—he spoke a dialect from Hungary. He asked me: How I got there—who I was—where I was from? I looked up in his face, and he looked down at me, sucking his pipe. He was a big man, he lived alone on the river, and I was tired of telling lies, so I told him the whole thing. When I had done he just grunted. I can see him now standing over me, with the mist hanging in his beard and his great naked arms. He drew me some water, and I washed and showed him my wig and moustache, and threw them overboard. All that day we lay out on the barge in the mist, with our feet to the fire, smoking; now and then he would spit into the ashes and mutter into his beard. I shall never forget that day. The steamer was like a monster with fiery nostrils, and the other barges were dumb creatures with eyes, where the fire were; we couldn't see the bank, but now and then a bluff and high trees, or a castle, showed in the mist. If I had only had paint and canvas that day!" He sighed.

"It was early Spring, and the river was in flood; they were going to Regensburg to unload there, take fresh cargo, and back to Linz. As soon as the mist began to clear, the bargeman hid me in the straw. At Passau was the frontier; they lay there for the night, but nothing happened, and I slept in the straw. The next day I lay out on the barge deck; there was no mist, but I was free—the sun shone gold on the straw and the green sacking; the water seemed to dance, and I laughed—I laughed all the time, and the bargeman laughed with me. A fine fellow he was! At Regensburg I helped them to unload; for more than a week we worked; they nicknamed me baldhead, and when it was all over I gave the money I earned for the unloading to the big bargeman. We kissed each other at parting. I had still three of the *gulden* that Luigi gave me, and I went to a house-painter and got work with him. For six months I stayed there to save money; then I wrote to my mother's cousin in Vienna, and told him I was going to London. He gave me an introduction to some friends there. I went to Hamburg, and from there to

253

London in a cargo steamer, and I've never been back till now."

XI

After a minute's silence Christian said in a startled voice : " They could arrest you then ! "

Harz laughed.

" If they knew ; but it's seven years ago."

" Why did you come here, when it's so dangerous ? "

" I had been working too hard, I wanted to see my country—after seven years, and when it's forbidden ! But I'm ready to go back now."   He looked down at her, frowning.

" Had you a hard time in London, too ? "

" Harder, at first—I couldn't speak the language. In my profession it's hard work to get recognised, it's hard work to make a living.   There are too many whose interest it is to keep you down—I shan't forget them."

" But every one is not like that ? "

" No ; there are fine fellows, too.   I shan't forget them either.   I can sell my pictures now ; I'm no longer weak, and I promise you I shan't forget.   If in the future I have power, and I shall have power—I shan't forget."

A shower of fine gravel came rattling on the wall. Dawney was standing below them with an amused expression on his upturned face.

" Are you going to stay there all night ? " he asked. " Greta and I have bored each other."

" We're coming," called Christian hastily.

On the way back neither spoke a word, but when they reached the Villa, Harz took her hand, and said :

" Fräulein Christian, I can't do any more with your picture. I shan't touch it again after this."

She made no answer, but they looked at each other, and both seemed to ask, to entreat, something more ; then her eyes fell. He dropped her hand, and saying, " Good-night," ran after Dawney.

In the corridor, Dominique, carrying a dish of fruit, met the sisters ; he informed them that Miss Naylor had retired to bed ; that Herr Paul would not be home to dinner ; his master was dining in his room ; dinner would be served for Mrs. Decie and the two young ladies in a quarter of an hour : " And the fish is good to-night ; little trouts ! try them, *Signorina !* " He moved on quickly, softly, like a cat, the tails of his dress-coat flapping, and the heels of his white socks gleaming.

Christian ran upstairs. She flew about her room, feeling that if she once stood still it would all crystallise in hard painful thought, which motion alone kept away. She washed, changed her dress and shoes, and ran down to her uncle's room. Mr. Treffry had just finished dinner, pushed the little table back, and was sitting in his chair, with his glasses on his nose, reading the *Times*. Christian touched his forehead with her lips.

" Glad to see you, Chris. Your stepfather's out to dinner, and I can't stand your aunt when she's in one of her talking moods—bit of a humbug, Chris, between ourselves, eh ; isn't she ? " His eyes twinkled.

Christian smiled. There was a curious happy restlessness in her that would not let her keep still.

" Picture finished ? " Mr. Treffry asked suddenly, taking up the paper with a crackle. " Don't go and fall in love with the painter, Chris."

Christian was still enough now.

'Why not?' she thought. 'What should *you* know about him? Isn't he good enough for me?' A gong sounded.

"There's your dinner," Mr. Treffry remarked.

With sudden contrition she bent and kissed him.

But when she had left the room Mr. Treffry put down the *Times* and stared at the door, humming to himself, and thoughtfully fingering his chin.

Christian could not eat; she sat, indifferent to the hoverings of Dominique, tormented by uneasy fear and longings. She answered Mrs. Decie at random. Greta kept stealing looks at her from under her lashes.

"Decided characters are charming, don't you think so, Christian?" Mrs. Decie said, thrusting her chin a little forward, and modelling the words. "That is why I like Mr. Harz so much; such an immense advantage for a man to know his mind. You have only to look at that young man to see that he knows what he wants, and means to have it."

Christian pushed her plate away. Greta, flushing, said abruptly: "Doctor Edmund is not a decided character, I think. This afternoon he said: 'Shall I have some beer—yes, I shall—no, I shall not'; then he ordered the beer, so, when it came, he gave it to the soldiers."

Mrs. Decie turned her enigmatic smile from one girl to the other.

When dinner was over they went into her room. Greta stole at once to the piano, where her long hair fell almost to the keys; silently she sat there fingering the notes, smiling to herself, and looking at her aunt, who was reading Pater's essays. Christian too had taken up a book, but soon put it down—of several

256

pages she had not understood a word. She went into the garden and wandered about the lawn, clasping her hands behind her head. The air was heavy; very distant thunder trembled among the mountains, flashes of summer lightning played over the trees; and two great moths were hovering about a rosebush. Christian watched their soft uncertain rushes. Going to the little summer-house she flung herself down on a seat, and pressed her hands to her heart.

There was a strange and sudden aching there. Was he going from her? If so, what would be left? How little and how narrow seemed the outlook of her life— with the world waiting for her, the world of beauty, effort, self-sacrifice, fidelity! It was as though a flash of that summer lightning had fled by, singeing her, taking from her all powers of flight, burning off her wings, as off one of those pale hovering moths. Tears started up, and trickled down her face. 'Blind!' she thought; 'how could I have been so blind?'

Some one came down the path.

"Who's there?" she cried.

Harz stood in the doorway.

"Why did you come out?" he said. "Ah! why did you come out?" He caught her hand; Christian tried to draw it from him, and to turn her eyes away, but she could not. He flung himself down on his knees and cried: "I love you!"

In a rapture of soft terror Christian bent her forehead down to his hand.

"What are you doing?" she heard him say. "Is it possible that *you* love me?" and she felt his kisses on her hair.

"My sweet! it will be so hard for you; you are so little, so little, and so weak." Clasping his hand closer to her face, she murmured: "I don't care."

There was a long, soft silence, that seemed to last for ever. Suddenly she threw her arms round his neck and kissed him.

" Whatever comes ! " she whispered, and gathering her dress, escaped from him into the darkness.

XII

Christian woke next morning with a smile. In her attitudes, her voice, her eyes, there was a happy and sweet seriousness, as if she were hugging some holy thought. After breakfast she took a book and sat in the open window, whence she could see the poplar-trees guarding the entrance. There was a breeze; the roses close by kept nodding to her; the cathedral bells were in full chime; bees hummed above the lavender; and in the sky soft clouds were floating like huge, white birds.

The sounds of Miss Naylor's staccato dictation travelled across the room, and Greta's sighs as she took it down, one eye on her paper, one eye on Scruff, who lay with a black ear flapped across his paw, and his tan eyebrows quivering. He was in disgrace, for Dominnique, coming on him unawares, had seen him " say his prayers " before a pudding, and take the pudding for reward.

Christian put her book down gently, and slipped through the window. Harz was coming in from the road. " I am all yours ! " she whispered. His fingers closed on hers, and he went into the house.

She slipped back, took up her book, and waited.

It seemed long before he came out, but when he did he waved her back, and hurried on ; she had a glimpse of his face, white to the lips.   Feeling faint and sick, she flew to her stepfather's room.

Herr Paul was standing in a corner with the utterly disturbed appearance of an easy-going man, visited by the unexpected.   His fine shirt-front was crumpled as if his breast had heaved too suddenly under strong emotion ; his smoked eyeglasses dangled down his back ; his fingers were embedded in his beard.   He was fixing his eye on a spot in the floor as though he expected it to explode and blow them to fragments. In another corner Mrs. Decie, with half-closed eyes, was running her finger-tips across her brow.

" What have you said to him ? " cried Christian.

Herr Paul regarded her with glassy eyes.

" *Mein Gott !* " he said.   " Your aunt and I ! "

" What have you said to him ? " repeated Christian.

" The impudence !   An anarchist !   A beggar ! "

" Paul ! " murmured Mrs. Decie.

" The outlaw !   The fellow ! "   Herr Paul began to stride about the room.

Quivering from head to foot, Christian cried : " How dared you ? " and ran from the room, pushing aside Miss Naylor and Greta, who stood blanched and frightened in the doorway.

Herr Paul stopped in his tramp, and, still with his eyes fixed on the floor, growled :

" A fine thing—*hein?*   What's coming !   Will you please tell me ?   An anarchist—a beggar ! "

" Paul ! " murmured Mrs. Decie.

" Paul !   Paul !   And you ! " he pointed to Miss Naylor—" Two women with eyes !—*hein !* "

" There is nothing to be gained by violence," Mrs.

Decie murmured, passing her handkerchief across her lips. Miss Naylor, whose thin brown cheeks had flushed, advanced towards him.

" I hope you do not——" she said ; " I am sure there was nothing that I could have prevented—I should be glad if that were understood." And, turning with some dignity, the little lady went away, closing the door behind· her.

" You hear ! " Herr Paul said, violently sarcastic : " nothing she could have prevented ! *Enfin !* Will you please tell me what I am to do ? "

" Men of the world "—whose philosophy is a creature of circumstance and accepted things—find any deviation from the path of their convictions dangerous, shocking, and an intolerable bore. Herr Paul had spent his life laughing at convictions ; the matter had but to touch him personally, and the tap of laughter was turned off. That any one to whom he was the lawful guardian should marry other than a well groomed man, properly endowed with goods, properly selected, was beyond expression horrid. From his point of view he had great excuse for horror ; and he was naturally unable to judge whether he had excuse for horror from other points of view. His amazement had in it a spice of the pathetic ; he was like a child in the presence of a thing that he absolutely could not understand. The interview had left him with a sense of insecurity which he felt to be particularly unfair.

The door was again opened, and Greta flew in, her cheeks flushed, her hair floating behind her, and tears streaming down her cheeks.

" Papa ! " she cried, " you have been cruel to Chris. The door is locked ; I can hear her crying—why have you been cruel ? " Without waiting to be answered, she flew out again.

Herr Paul seized his hair with both his hands : " Good ! Very good ! My own child, please ! What next then ? "

Mrs. Décie rose from her chair languidly. " My head is very bad," she said, shading her eyes and speaking in low tones : " It is no use making a fuss—nothing can come of this—he had not a penny. Christian will have nothing till you die, which will not be for a long time yet, if you can but avoid an apoplectic fit ! "

At these last words Herr Paul gave a start of real disgust. " Hum ! " he muttered ; it was as if the world were bent on being brutal to him. Mrs. Decie continued :

" If I know anything of this young man, he will not come here again, after the words you have spoken. As for Christian—you had better talk to Nicholas. I am going to lie down."

Herr Paul nervously fingered the shirt-collar round his stout, short neck.

" Nicholas ! Certainly—a good idea. *Quelle diable d'affaire !* "

' French ! ' thought Mrs Decie ; ' we shall soon have peace. Poor Christian ! I'm sorry ! After all, these things are a matter of time and opportunity.' This consoled her a good deal.

But for Christian the hours were a long nightmare of grief and shame, fear and anger. Would he forgive ? Would he be true to her ? Or would he go away without a word ? Since yesterday it was as if she had stepped into another world, and lost it again. In place of that new feeling, intoxicating as wine, what was coming ? What bitter, dreadful ending ?

A rude entrance this into the life of facts and primitive emotions !

She let Greta into her room after a time, for the child had begun sobbing ; but she would not talk, and sat hour after hour at the window with the air fanning her face, and the pain in her eyes turned to the sky and·trees. After one or two attempts at consolation, Greta sank on the floor, and remained there, humbly gazing at her sister in a silence only broken when Christian cleared her throat of tears, and by the song of birds in the garden. In the afternoon she slipped away and did not come back again.

After his interview with Mr. Treffry, Herr Paul took a bath, perfumed himself with precision, and caused it to be clearly understood that, under circumstances such as these, a man's house was not suited for a pig to live in. He shortly afterwards went out to the *Kurhaus*, and had not returned by dinner-time.

Christian came down for dinner. There were crimson spots in her cheeks, dark circles round her eyes ; she behaved, however, as though nothing had happened. Miss Naylor, affected by the kindness of her heart, and the shock her system had sustained, rolled a number of bread pills, looking at each as it came, with an air of surprise, and concealing it with difficulty. Mr. Treffry was coughing, and when he talked his voice seemed to rumble even more than usual. Greta was dumb, trying to catch Christian's eye; Mrs. Decie alone seemed at ease. After dinner Mr. Treffry went off to his room, leaning heavily on Christian's shoulder. As he sank into his chair, he said to her :

" Pull yourself together, my dear ! " Christian did not answer him.

Outside his room Greta caught her by the sleeve.

" Look ! " she whispered, thrusting a piece of paper into Christian's hand. " It is to me from Dr. Edmund, but you must read it."

Christian opened the note, which ran as follows :

" My PHILOSOPHER AND FRIEND,—I received your note, and went to our friend's studio ; he was not in, but half an hour ago I stumbled on him in the Plat. He is not quite himself ; has had a touch of the sun— nothing serious. I took him to my hotel, where he is in bed. If he will stay there he will be all right in a day or two. In any case he shall not elude my clutches for the present.

" My warm respects to Mistress Christian.— Yours in friendship and philosophy,

" EDMUND DAWNEY."

Christian read and re-read this note, then turned to Greta.

" What did you say to Dr. Dawney ? "

Greta took back the piece of paper, and replied : " I said :

" ' DEAR DR. EDMUND,—We are anxious about Herr Harz. We think he is perhaps not very well to-day. We (I and Christian) should like to know. You can tell us. Please shall you ?

" ' GRETA.'

" That is what I said."

Christian dropped her eyes. " What made you write ? "

Greta gazed at her mournfully : " I thought—O Chris ! come into the garden. I am so hot, and it is so dull without you ! "

263

Christian bent her head forward and rubbed her cheek against Greta's, then without another word ran upstairs and locked herself into her room. The child stood listening; hearing the key turn in the lock, she sank down on the bottom step and took Scruff in her arms.

Half an hour later Miss Naylor, carrying a candle, found her there fast asleep, with her head resting on the terrier's back, and tear stains on her cheeks. . . .

Mrs. Decie presently came out, also carrying a candle, and went to her brother's room. She stood before his chair, with folded hands.

" Nicholas, what is to be done ? "

Mr. Treffry was pouring whisky into a glass.

" Damn it, Con! " he answered; " how should I know ? "

" There's something in Christian that makes interference dangerous. I know very well that I've no influence with her at all."

" You're right there, Con," Mr. Treffry replied.

Mrs. Decie's pale eyes, fastened on his face, forced him to look up.

" I wish you would leave off drinking whisky and attend to me. Paul is an element——"

" Paul," Mr. Treffry growled, " is an ass ! "

" Paul," pursued Mrs. Decie, " is an element of danger in the situation; any ill-timed opposition of his might drive her to I don't know what. Christian is gentle, she is ' sympathetic ' as they say; but thwart her, and she is as obstinate as——"

" You or I ! Leave her alone ! "

" I understand her character, but I confess that I am at a loss what to do."

" Do nothing ! " He drank again.

Mrs. Decie took up the candle.

264

" Men ! " she said with a mysterious intonation ; shrugging her shoulders, she walked out.

Mr. Treffry put down his glass.

' Understand ? ' he thought ; ' no, you don't, and I don't. Who understands a young girl ? Vapourings, dreams, moonshine ! . . . What does she see in this painter fellow ? I wonder ! ' He breathed heavily. ' By heavens ! I wouldn't have had this happen for a hundred thousand pounds ! '

XIII

For many hours after Dawney had taken him to his hotel, Harz was prostrate with stunning pains in the head and neck. He had been all day without food, exposed to burning sun, suffering violent emotion. Movement of any sort caused him such agony that he could only lie in stupor, counting the spots dancing before his eyes. Dawney did everything for him, and Harz resented in a listless way the intent scrutiny of the doctor's calm, black eyes.

Towards the end of the second day he was able to get up ; Dawney found him sitting on the bed in shirt and trousers.

" My son," he said, " you had better tell me what the trouble is—it will do your stubborn carcase good."

" I must go back to work," said Harz.

" Work ! " said Dawney deliberately : " you couldn't if you tried."

" I must."

" My dear fellow, you couldn't tell one colour from another."

" I must be doing something ; I can't sit here and think."

Dawney hooked his thumbs into his waistcoat: " You won't see the sun for three days yet, if I can help it."

Harz got up.

" I'm going to my studio to-morrow," he said. " I promise not to go out. I must be where I can see my work. If I can't paint, I can draw ; I can feel my brushes, move my things about. I shall go mad if I do nothing."

Dawney took his arm, and walked him up and down.

" I'll let you go," he said, " but give me a chance ! It's as much to me to put you straight as it is to you to paint a decent picture. Now go to bed ; I'll have a carriage for you to-morrow morning."

Harz sat down on the bed again, and for a long time stayed without moving, his eyes fixed on the floor. The sight of him, so desperate and miserable, hurt the young doctor.

" Can you get to bed by yourself ? " he asked at last.

Harz nodded.

" Then, good-night, old chap ! " and Dawney left the room.

He took his hat and turned towards the Villa. Between the poplars he stopped to think. The farther trees were fretworked black against the lingering gold of the sunset ; a huge moth, attracted by the tip of his cigar, came fluttering in his face. The music of a concertina rose and fell, like the sighing of some dis-illusioned spirit. Dawney stood for several minutes staring at the house.

He was shown to Mrs. Decie's room. She was

holding a magazine before her eyes, and received him with as much relief as philosophy permitted.

"You are the very person I wanted to see," she said. He noticed that the magazine she held was uncut.

"You are a young man," pursued Mrs. Decie, "but as my doctor I have a right to your discretion."

Dawney smiled ; the features of his broad, clean-shaven face looked ridiculously small on such occasions, but his eyes retained their air of calculation.

"That is so," he answered.

"It is about this unfortunate affair. I understand that Mr. Harz is with you. I want you to use your influence to dissuade him from attempting to see my niece."

"Influence ! " said Dawney : "you know Harz ! "

Mrs. Decie's voice hardened.

"Everybody," she said, "has his weak points. This young man is open to approach from at least two quarters—his pride is one, his work another. I am seldom wrong in gauging character ; these are his vital spots, and they are of the essence of this matter. I'm sorry for him, of course—but at his age, and living a man's life, these things——" Her smile was extra pale. "I wish you could give me something for my head. It's foolish to worry. Nerves of course ! But I can't help it ! You know my opinion, Dr. Dawney. That young man will go far if he remains unfettered ; he will make a name. You will be doing him a great service if you could show him the affair as it really is—a drag on him, and quite unworthy of his pride ! *Do* help me ! You are just the man to do it ! "

Dawney threw up his head as if to shake off this impeachment ; the curve of his chin thus displayed was imposing in its fulness ; altogether he was imposing, having an air of capability.

She struck him, indeed, as really scared; it was as if her mask of smile had become awry, and failed to cover her emotion; and he was puzzled, thinking, ' I wouldn't have believed she had it in her.' . . . " It's not an easy business," he said; " I'll think it over."

" Thank you ! " murmured Mrs. Decie. " You are most kind."

Passing the schoolroom, he looked in through the open door. Christian was sitting there. The sight of her face shocked him, it was so white, so resolutely dumb. A book lay on her knees; she was not reading, but staring before her. He thought suddenly : ' Poor thing ! If I don't say something to her, I shall be a brute ! '

" Miss Devorell," he said : " You can reckon on him."

Christian tried to speak, but her lips trembled so that nothing came forth.

" Good-night," said Dawney, and walked out. . . .

Three days later Harz was sitting in the window of his studio. It was the first day he had found it possible to work, and now, tired out, he stared through the dusk at the slowly lengthening shadows of the rafters. A solitary mosquito hummed, and two house sparrows who had built beneath the roof, chirruped sleepily. Swallows darted by the window, dipping their blue wings towards the quiet water; a hush had stolen over everything. He fell asleep.

He woke, with a dim impression of some near presence. In the pale glimmer from innumerable stars, the room was full of shadowy shapes. He lit his lantern. The flame darted forth, flickered, then slowly lit up the great room.

" Who's there ? "

A rustling seemed to answer. He peered about, went to the doorway, and drew the curtain. A woman's cloaked figure shrank against the wall. Her face was buried in her hands; her arms, from which the cloak fell back, were alone visible.

" Christian ? "

She ran past him, and when he had put the lantern down was standing at the window. She turned quickly to him. " Take me away from here ! Let me come with you ! "

" Do you mean it ? "

" You said you wouldn't give me up ! "

" You know what you are doing ? "

She made a motion of assent.

" But you don't grasp what this means. Things to bear that you know nothing of—hunger perhaps ! Think, even hunger ! And your people won't forgive —you'll lose everything."

She shook her head.

" I must choose—it's one thing or the other. I can't give you up ! I should be afraid ! "

" But, dear ; how can you come with me ? We can't be married here."

" I am giving my life to you."

" You are too good for me," said Harz. " The life you're going into—may be dark, like that ! " he pointed to the window.

A sound of footsteps broke the hush. They could see a figure on the path below. It stopped, seemed to consider, vanished. They heard the sounds of groping hands, of a creaking door, of uncertain feet on the stairs.

Harz seized her hand.

" Quick ! " he whispered ; " behind this canvas ! "

Christian was trembling violently. She drew her hood across her face. The heavy breathing and ejaculations of the visitor were now plainly audible.

" He's there ! Quick ! Hide ! "

She shook her head.

With a thrill at his heart, Harz kissed her, then walked towards the entrance. The curtain was pulled aside.

XIV

It was Herr Paul, holding a cigar in one hand, his hat in the other, and breathing hard.

" Pardon ! " he said huskily, " your stairs are steep, and dark ! *mais enfin ! nous voilà !* I have ventured to come for a talk." His glance fell on the cloaked figure in the shadow.

" Pardon ! A thousand pardons ! I had no idea ! I beg you to forgive this indiscretion ! I may take it you resign pretensions then ? You have a lady here—I have nothing more to say ; I only beg a million pardons for intruding. A thousand times forgive me ! Good-night ! "

He bowed and turned to go. Christian stepped forward, and let the hood fall from her head,

" It's I ! "

Herr Paul pirouetted.

" Good God ! " he stammered, dropping cigar and hat. " Good God ! "

The lantern flared suddenly, revealing his crimson shaking cheeks.

" You came *here*, at night ! You, the daughter of my wife ! " His eyes wandered with a dull glare round the room.

270

"Take care!" cried Harz: "If you say a word against her——"

The two men stared at each other's eyes. And without warning, the lantern flickered and went out. Christian drew the cloak round her again. Herr Paul's voice broke the silence; he had recovered his self-possession.

"Ah! ah!" he said: "Darkness! *Tant mieux!* The right thing for what we have to say. Since we do not esteem each other, it is well not to see too much."

"Just so," said Harz.

Christian had come close to them. Her pale face and great shining eyes could just be seen through the gloom.

Herr Paul waved his arm; the gesture was impressive, annihilating.

"This is a matter, I believe, between two men," he said, addressing Harz. "Let us come to the point. I will do you the credit to suppose that you have a marriage in view. You know, perhaps, that Miss Devorell has no money till I die?"

"Yes."

"And I am passably young! You have money, then?"

"No."

"In that case, you would propose to live on air?"

"No, to work; it has been done before."

"It is calculated to increase hunger! You are prepared to take Miss Devorell a young lady accustomed to luxury, into places like—this!" he peered about him, "into places that smell of paint, into the *milieu* of ' the people,' into the society of Bohemians—who knows? of anarchists, perhaps?"

271

Harz clenched his hands : " I will answer no more questions."

" In that event, we reach the ultimatum," said Herr Paul. " Listen, Herr Outlaw ! If you have not left the country by noon to-morrow, you shall be introduced to the police ! "

Christian uttered a cry. For a minute in the gloom the only sound heard was the short, hard breathing of the two men.

Suddenly Harz cried : " You coward, I defy you ! "

" Coward ! " Herr Paul repeated. " That is indeed the last word. Look to yourself, my friend ! "

Stooping and fumbling on the floor, he picked up his hat. Christian had already vanished ; the sound of her hurrying footsteps was distinctly audible at the top of the dark stairs. Herr Paul stood still a minute. " Look to yourself, my dear friend ! " he said in a thick voice, groping for the wall. Planting his hat askew on his head, he began slowly to descend the stairs.

XV

Nicholas Treffry sat reading the paper in his room by the light of a lamp with a green shade ; on his sound foot the terrier Scruff was asleep and snoring lightly—the dog habitually came down when Greta was in bed, and remained till Mr. Treffry, always the latest member of the household, retired to rest.

Through the long window a little river of light shone out on the veranda tiles, and, flowing past, cut the garden in two.

There was a sound of hurried footsteps, a rustling of draperies ; Christian, running through the window stood before him.

Mr. Treffry dropped his paper, such a fury of passion and alarm shone in the girl's eyes.

" Chris ! What is it ? "

" Hateful ! "

" Chris ! "

" Oh ! Uncle ! He's insulted, threatened ! And I love his little finger more than all the world ? "

Her passionate voice trembled, her eyes were shining.

Mr. Treffry's profound discomfort found vent in the gruff words : " Sit down ! "

" I'll never speak to Father again ! Oh ! Uncle ! I love him ! "

Quiet in the extremity of his disturbance, Mr. Treffry leaned forward in his chair, rested his big hands on its arms, and stared at her.

Chris ! Here was a woman he did not know ! His lips moved under the heavy droop of his moustache. The girl's face had suddenly grown white. She sank down on her knees, and laid her cheek against his hand. He felt it wet ; and a lump rose in his throat. Drawing his hand away, he stared at it, and wiped it with his sleeve.

" Don't cry ! " he said.

She seized it again and clung to it ; that clutch seemed to fill him with sudden rage.

" What's the matter ? How the devil can I do anything if you don't tell me ? "

She looked up at him. The distress of the last days, the passion and fear of the last hour, the tide of that new life of the spirit and the flesh, stirring within her, flowed out in a stream of words.

When she had finished, there was so dead a silence that the fluttering of a moth round the lamp could be heard plainly.

Mr. Treffry raised himself, crossed the room, and touched the bell. " Tell the groom," he said to Dominique, " to put the horses to, and have 'em round at once ; bring my old boots ; we drive all night."

His bent figure looked huge, body and legs outlined by light, head and shoulders towering into shadow. " He shall have a run for his money ! " he said. His eyes stared down sombrely at his niece. " It's more than he deserves—it's more than *you* deserve, Chris. Sit down there and write to him ; tell him to put himself entirely in my hands." He turned his back on her, and went into his bedroom.

Christian rose, and sat down at the writing-table. A whisper startled her. It came from Dominique, who was holding out a pair of boots.

" M'mselle Chris, what is this ?—to run about all night ? " But Christian did not answer.

" M'mselle Chris, are you ill ? " Then seeing her face, he slipped away again.

She finished her letter and went out to the carriage. Mr. Treffry was seated under the hood.

" Shan't want you," he called out to the groom. " Get up, Dominique."

Christian thrust her letter into his hand. " Give him that," she said, clinging to his arm with sudden terror. " Oh ! Uncle ! do take care ! "

" Chris, if I do this for you——" They looked wistfully at one another. Then, shaking his head, Mr. Treffry gathered up the reins.

" Don't fret, my dear, don't fret ! Whoa, mare ! "

The carriage with a jerk plunged forward into darkness, curved with a crunch of wheels, and vanished, swinging between the black tree-pillars at the entrance.

Christian stood, straining to catch the failing sound of the hoofs.

Down the passage came a flutter of white garments ; soft limbs were twined about her, some ends of hair fell on her face.

"What is it, Chris ? Where have you been ? Where is Uncle Nic going ? Tell me ! "

Christian tore herself away. "I don't know," she cried, "I know nothing ! "

Greta stroked her face. "Poor Chris ! " she murmured. Her bare feet gleamed, her hair shone gold against her nightdress. "Come to bed, poor Chris ! "

Christian laughed. "You little white moth ! Feel how hot I am ! You'll burn your wings ! "

XVI

Harz had lain down, fully dressed. He was no longer angry, but felt that he would rather die than yield. Presently he heard footsteps coming up the stairs.

"M'sieu ! "

It was the voice of Dominique, whose face, illumined by a match, wore an expression of ironical disgust.

"My master," he said, "makes you his compliments ; he says there is no time to waste. You are to please come and drive with him ! "

"Your master is very kind. Tell him I'm in bed."

"Ah, M'sieu," said Dominique, grimacing, "I must not go back with such an answer. If you would not come, I was to give you this."

Harz broke the seal and read Christian's letter.

"I will come," he said.

A clock was striking as they went out through the

gate. From within the dark cave of the phaeton hood Mr. Treffry said gruffly : " Come along, sir ! "

Harz flung his knapsack in, and followed.

His companion's figure swayed, the whiplash slid softly along the flank of the off horse, and, as the carriage rattled forward, Mr. Treffry called out, as if by afterthought : " Hallo, Dominique ! " Dominique's voice, shaken and ironical, answered from behind : " *M' v'là, M'sieu !* "

In the long street of silent houses, men sitting in the lighted *cafés* turned with glasses at their lips to stare after the carriage. The narrow river of the sky spread suddenly to a vast, limpid ocean tremulous with stars. They had turned into the road for Italy.

Mr. Treffry took a pull at his horses. " Whoa, mare ! Dogged does it ! " and the near horse, throwing up her head, whinnied ; a fleck of foam drifted into Harz's face.

The painter had come on impulse ; because Christian had told him to, not of his own free will. He was angry with himself, wounded in self-esteem, for having allowed any one to render him this service. The smooth swift movement through velvet blackness splashed on either hand with the flying lamp-light ; the strong sweet air blowing in his face—air that had kissed the tops of mountains and stolen their spirit ; the snort and snuffle of the horses, and crisp rattling of their hoofs—all this soon roused in him another feeling. He looked at Mr. Treffry's profile, with its tufted chin ; at the grey road adventuring in darkness ; at the purple mass of mountains piled above it. All seemed utterly unreal.

As if suddenly aware that he had a neighbour, Mr. Treffry turned his head. " We 'shall do better than this

presently," he said, " bit of a slope coming. Haven't
had 'em out for three days. Whoa—mare ! Steady ! "

" Why are you taking this trouble for me ? " asked
Harz.

" I'm an old chap, Mr. Harz, and an old chap may
do a stupid thing once in a while ! "

" You are very good," said Harz, " but I want no
favours."

Mr. Treffry stared at him.

" Just so," he said drily, " but you see there's my
niece to be thought of. Look here ! We're not at
the frontier yet, Mr. Harz, by forty miles ; it's long odds
we don't get there—so, don't spoil sport ! " He
pointed to the left.

Harz caught the glint of steel. They were already
crossing the railway. The sigh of the telegraph wires
fluttered above them.

" Hear 'em," said Mr. Treffry, " but we if get away
up the mountains, we'll do yet ! " They had begun
to rise, the speed slackened. Mr. Treffry rummaged
out a flask.

" Not bad stuff, Mr. Harz—try it. You won't ?
Mother's milk ! Fine night, eh ? " Below them the
valley was lit by webs of milky mist like the glimmer of
dew on grass.

These two men sitting side by side—unlike in face,
age, stature, thought, and life—began to feel drawn
towards each other, as if, in the rolling of the wheels,
the snorting of the horses, the huge dark space, the
huge uncertainty, they had found something they could
enjoy in common. The steam from the horses' flanks
and nostrils enveloped them with an odour as of glue.

" You smoke, Mr. Harz ? "

Harz took the proffered weed, and lighted it from

277

the glowing tip of Mr. Treffry's cigar, by light of which his head and hat looked like some giant mushroom. Suddenly the wheels jolted on a rubble of loose stones ; the carriage was swung sideways. The scared horses, straining asunder, leaped forward, and sped downwards, in the darkness.

Past rocks, trees, dwellings, past a lighted house that gleamed and vanished. With a clink and clatter, a flirt of dust and pebbles, and the side lamps throwing out a frisky orange blink, the carriage dashed down, sinking and rising like a boat crossing billows. The world seemed to rock and sway ; to dance up, and be flung flat again. Only the stars stood still.

Mr. Treffry, putting on the brake, muttered apologetically : " A little out o' hand ! "

Suddenly with a headlong dive, the carriage swayed as if it would fly in pieces, slithered along, and with a jerk steadied itself. Harz lifted his voice in a shout of pure excitement. Mr. Treffry let out a short shaky howl, and from behind there rose a wail. But the hill was over and the startled horses were cantering with a free, smooth motion. Mr. Treffry and Harz looked at each other.

XVII

Mr. Treffry said with a sort of laugh : " Near go, eh ? You drive ? No ? That's a pity ! Broken most of my bones at the game—nothing like it ! " Each felt a kind of admiration for the other that he had not felt before. Presently Mr. Treffry began : " Look here, Mr. Harz, my niece is a slip of a thing, with all a young girl's notions ! What have you got to give her, eh ? Yourself ? That's surely not enough ;

mind this—six months after marriage we all turn out much the same—a selfish lot! Not to mention this anarchist affair! You're not of her blood, nor of her way of life, nor anything—it's taking chances—and ——" his hand came down on the young man's knee, " I'm fond of her, you see."

"If you were in my place," said Harz, " would *you* give her up ? "

Mr. Treffry groaned. " Lord knows ! "

" Men have made themselves before now. For those who don't believe in failure, there's no such thing. Suppose she does suffer a little ? Will it do her any harm ? Fair weather love is no good."

Mr. Treffry sighed.

"Brave words, sir ! You'll pardon me if I'm too old to understand 'em when they're used about my niece."

He pulled the horses up, and peered into the darkness. " We're going through this bit quietly ; if they lose track of us here so much the better. Dominique ! put out the lamps. Soho, my beauties ! " The horses paced forward at a walk ; the muffled beat of their hoofs in the dust hardly broke the hush. Mr. Treffry pointed to the left : " It'll be another thirty-five miles to the frontier."

They passed the whitewashed houses, and village church with its sentinel cypress-trees. A frog was croaking in a runlet ; there was a faint spicy scent of lemons. But nothing stirred.

It was wood now on either side, the high pines, breathing their fragrance out into the darkness, and, like ghosts amongst them, the silver stems of birch-trees.

Mr. Treffry said gruffly : " You won't give her up ? Her happiness means a lot to me."

" To you ! " said Harz : " to *him !* And I am nothing ! Do you think *I* don't care for her happiness ?
Is it a crime for me to love her ? "

" Almost, Mr. Harz—considering——"

" Considering that I've no money ! Always
money ! "

To this sneer Mr. Treffry made no answer, clucking
to his horses. " My niece was born and bred a lady,"
he said at last. " I ask you plainly : What position
have you got to give her ? "

" If she marries me," said Harz, " she comes into
my world. You think that I'm a common——"

Mr. Treffry shook his head : " Answer my question,
young man."

But the painter did not answer it, and silence fell.

A light breeze had sprung up, the whispering in the
trees, the rolling of the wheels in this night progress,
the pine-drugged air, sent Harz to sleep. When he
woke it was to the same tune, varied by Mr. Treffry's
uneasy snoring ; the reins were hanging loose, and,
peering out, he saw Dominique shuffling along at the
horses' heads. He joined him, and, one on each side,
they plodded up and up. A haze had begun to bathe
the trees, the stars burnt dim, the air was colder. Mr.
Treffry woke coughing. It was like some long nightmare, this interminable experience of muffled sounds
and shapes, of perpetual motion, conceived, and carried
out in darkness. But suddenly the day broke.
Heralded by the snuffle of the horses, light began glim-
mering over a chaos of lines and shadows, pale as
mother-o'-pearl. The stars faded, and in a smouldering
zigzag the dawn fled along the mountain tops, flinging
out little isles of cloud. From a lake, curled in a hollow
like a patch of smoke, came the cry of a water-bird.

A cuckoo started a soft mocking; and close to the carriage a lark flew up. Beasts and men alike stood still, drinking in the air—sweet with snows and dew, and vibrating faintly with the running of the water and the rustling of the leaves.

The night had played sad tricks with Mr. Nicholas Treffry; his hat was grey with dust; his cheeks brownish-purple, there were heavy pouches beneath his eyes, which stared painfully.

" We'll call a halt," he said, " and give the gees their grub, poor things. Can you find some water, Mr. Harz ? There's a rubber bucket in behind. Can't get about myself this morning ; make that lazy fellow of mine stir his stumps."

Harz saw that he had drawn off one of his boots, and stretched the foot out on a cushion.

" You're not fit to go farther," he said ; " you're ill."

" Ill ! " replied Mr. Treffry ; " not a bit of it ! "

Harz looked at him, then catching up the bucket, made off in search of water. When he came back the horses were feeding from an india-rubber trough slung to the pole ; they stretched their heads towards the bucket, pushing aside each other's noses.

The flame in the east had died, but the tops of the larches were bathed in a gentle radiance ; and the peaks ahead were like amber. Everywhere were threads of water, threads of snow, and little threads of dewy green, glistening like gossamer.

Mr. Treffry called out : " Give me your arm, Mr. Harz ; I'd like to shake the reefs out of me. When one comes to stand over at the knees, it's no such easy matter, eh ? " He groaned as he put his foot down, and gripped the young man's shoulder as in a vice. Presently he lowered himself on to a stone.

" ' All over now ! ' as Chris would say when she was little ; nasty temper she had too—kick and scream on the floor ! Never lasted long though—' Kiss her ! take her up ! show her the pictures ! ' Amazing fond of pictures Chris was ! " He looked dubiously at Harz ; then took a long pull at his flask. " What would the doctor say ? Whisky at four in the morning ! Well ! Thank the Lord ! Doctors aren't always with us." Sitting on the stone, with one hand pressed against his side, and the other tilting up the flask, he was grey from head to foot.

Harz had dropped on to another stone. He, too, was worn out by the excitement and fatigue, coming so soon after his illness. His head was whirling, and the next thing he remembered was a tree walking at him, turning round, yellow from the roots up ; everything seemed yellow, even his own feet. Somebody oppo-osite to him was jumping up and down, a grey bear —with a hat—Mr. Treffry ! He cried : " Ha-alloo ! " And the figure seemed to fall and disappear. . . .

When Harz came to himself a hand was pouring liquor into his mouth, and a wet cloth was muffled round his brows ; a noise of humming and hoofs seemed familiar. Mr. Treffry loomed up alongside, smoking a cigar ; he was muttering : " A low trick, Paul—bit of my mind ! " Then, as if a curtain had been snatched aside, the vision before Harz cleared again. The carriage was winding between uneven, black-eaved houses, past doorways from which goats and cows were coming out, with bells on their necks. Black-eyed boys, and here and there a drowsy man with a long, cherry-stemmed pipe between his teeth, stood aside to stare.

Mr. Treffry seemed to have taken a new lease of

strength ; like an angry old dog, he stared from side to side. " My bone ! " he seemed to say : " let's see who's going to touch it ! "

The last house vanished, glowing in the early sunshine, and the carriage with its trail of dust became entombed once more in the gloom of tall trees, along a road that cleft a wilderness of moss-grown rocks, and dewy stems, through which the sun had not yet driven paths.

Dominique came round to them, bearing the appearance of one who has seen better days, and a pot of coffee brewed on a spirit lamp. Breakfast—he said—was served !

The ears of the horses were twitching with fatigue. Mr. Treffry said sadly : " If *I* can see this through, you can. Get on, my beauties ! "

As soon as the sun struck through the trees, Mr. Treffry's strength ebbed again. He seemed to suffer greatly ; but did not complain. They had reached the pass at last, and the unchecked sunlight was streaming down with a blinding glare.

" Jump up ! " Mr. Teffrey cried out. " We'll make a finish of it ! " and he gave the reins a jerk. The horses flung up their heads, and the bleak pass with its circling crown of jagged peaks soon slipped away.

Between the houses on the very top, they passed at a slow trot ; and soon began slanting down the other side. Mr. Teffrey brought them to a halt where a mule track joined the road.

" That's all I can do for you ; you'd better leave me here," he said. " Keep this track down to the river— go south—you'll be in Italy in a couple of hours. Get rail at Feltre. Money ? Yes ? Well ! " He held out his hand ; Harz gripped it.

" Give her up, eh ? "

Harz shook his head.

" No ? Then it's ' pull devil, pull baker,' between us.. Good-bye, and good luck to you ! " And mustering his strength for a last attempt at dignity, Mr. Treffry gathered up the reins.

Harz watched his figure huddled again beneath the hood. The carriage moved slowly away.

XVIII

At Villa Rubein people went about, avoiding each other as if detected in conspiracy. Miss Naylor, who for an inscrutable reason had put on her best frock, a purple, relieved at the chest with bird's-eye blue, conveyed an impression of trying to count a chicken which ran about too fast. When Greta asked what she had lost she was heard to mutter : " Mr.—Needlecase."

Christian, with big circles round her eyes, sat silent at her little table. She had had no sleep. Herr Paul coming into the room about noon gave her a furtive look and went out again ; after this he went to his bedroom, took off all his clothes, flung them passionately one by one into a footbath, and got into bed.

" I might be a criminal ! " he muttered to himself, while the buttons of his garments rattled on the bath.

" Am I her father ? Have I authority ? Do I know the world ? Bssss ! I might be a frog ! "

Mrs. Decie, having caused herself to be announced, found him smoking a cigar, and counting the flies on the ceiling.

" If you have really done this, Paul," she said in a restrained voice, " you have done a very unkind thing and what is worse, you have made us all ridiculous. But perhaps you have not done it ? "

" I have done it," cried Herr Paul, staring dreadfully : " I have done it, I tell you, I have done it———"

" Very well, you have done it—and why, pray ? What conceivable good was there in it ? I suppose you know that Nicholas has driven him to the frontier ? Nicholas is probably more dead than alive by this time ; you know his state of health."

Herr Paul's fingers ploughed up his beard.

" Nicholas is mad—and the girl is mad ! Leave me alone ! I will *not* be made angry ; do you understand ? I will *not* be worried—I am not fit for it." His prominent brown eyes stared round the room, as if looking for a way of escape.

" If I may prophesy, you will be worried a good deal," said Mrs. Decie coldly, " before you have finished with this affair."

The anxious, uncertain glance which Herr Paul gave her at these words roused an unwilling feeling of compunction in her.

" You are not made for the outraged father of the family," she said. " You had better give up the attitude, Paul ; it does not suit you."

Herr Paul groaned.

" I suppose it is not your fault," she added.

Just then the door was opened, and Fritz, with an air of saying the right thing, announced :

" A gentleman of the police to see you, sir."

Herr Paul bounded.

" Keep him out ! " he cried.

Mrs. Decie, covering her lips, disappeared with a rustling of silk ; in her place stood a stiff man in blue. . . .

Thus the morning dragged itself away without any one being able to settle to anything, except Herr Paul, who was settled in bed. As was fitting in a house that had lost its soul, meals were neglected, even by the dog.

About three o'clock a telegram came for Christian, containing these words : " All right ; self returns to-morrow. Treffry." After reading it she put on her hat and went out, followed closely by Greta, who, when she thought that she would not be sent away, ran up from behind and pulled her by the sleeve.

" Let me come, Chris—I shall not talk."

The two girls walked on together. When they had gone some distance Christian said :

" I'm going to get his pictures, and take charge of them ! "

" Oh ! " said Greta timidly.

" If you are afraid," said Christian, " you had better go back home."

" I am not afraid, Chris," said Greta meekly.

Neither girl spoke again till they had taken the path along the wall. Over the tops of the vines the heat was dancing.

" The sun-fairies are on the vines ! " murmured Greta to herself.

At the old house they stopped, and Christian, breathing quickly, pushed the door ; it was immovable.

" Look ! " said Greta, " they have screwed it ! " She pointed out three screws with a rosy-tipped forefinger.

Christian stamped her foot.

" We mustn't stand here," she said ; " let's sit on that bench and think."

"Yes," murmured Greta, " let us think." Dangling

286

an end of hair, she regarded Christian with her wide blue eyes.

" I can't make any plan," Christian cried at last, " while you stare at me like that."

" I was thinking," said Greta humbly, " if they have screwed it up, perhaps we shall screw it down again ; there is the big screw-driver of Fritz."

" It would take a long time ; people are always passing."

" People do not pass in the evening," murmured Greta, " because the gate at our end is always shut."

Christian rose.

" We will come this evening, just before the gate is shut."

" But, Chris, how shall we get back again ? "

" I don't know ; I mean to have the pictures."

" It is not a high gate," murmured Greta.

After dinner the girls went to their room, Greta bearing with her the big screw-driver of Fritz. At dusk they slipped downstairs and out.

They arrived at the old house, and stood, listening, in the shadow of the doorway. The only sounds were those of distant barking dogs, and of the bugles at the barracks.

" Quick ! " whispered Christian ; and Greta, with all the strength of her small hands, began to turn the screws. It was some time before they yielded ; the third was very obstinate, till Christian took the screw-driver and passionately gave the screw a starting twist.

" It is like a pig—that one," said Greta, rubbing her wrists mournfully.

The opened door revealed the gloom of the dank rooms and twisting staircase, then fell to behind them with a clatter.

Greta gave a little scream, and caught her sister's dress.

"It *is* dark," she gasped; "O Chris! it *is* dark!"

Christian groped for the bottom stair, and Greta felt her arm shaking.

"Suppose there is a man to keep guard! O Chris! suppose there are *bats!*"

"You are a baby!" Christian answered in a trembling voice. "You had better go home!"

Greta choked a little in the dark.

"I am—not—going home, but I'm afraid of bats. O Chris! aren't you afraid?"

"Yes," said Christian, "but I'm going to have the pictures."

Her cheeks were burning; she was trembling all over. Having found the bottom step she began to mount with Greta clinging to her skirts.

The haze above inspired a little courage in the child, who, of all things, hated darkness. The blanket across the doorway of the loft had been taken down, there was nothing to veil the empty room.

"Nobody here, you see," said Christian.

"No-o," whispered Greta, running to the window, and clinging to the wall, like one of the bats she dreaded.

"But they *have* been here!" cried Christian angrily. "They have broken this." She pointed to the fragments of a plaster cast that had been thrown down.

Out of the corner she began to pull the canvases set in rough, wooden frames, dragging them with all her strength.

"Help me!" she cried; "it will be dark directly."

They collected a heap of sketches and three large pictures, piling them before the window, and peering at them in the failing light.

288

Greta said ruefully :

" O Chris ! they *are* heavy ones ; we shall never carry them, and the gate is shut now ! "

Christian took a pointed knife from the table.

" I. shall cut them out of the frames," she said. " Listen ! What's that ? "

It was the sound of whistling, which stopped beneath the window. The girls, clasping each other's hands, dropped on their knees.

" Hallo ! " cried a voice.

Greta crept to the window, and, placing her face level with the floor, peered over.

" It is only Dr. Edmund ; he doesn't know, then," she whispered ; " I shall call him ; he is going away ! "

" Don't ! " cried Christian, catching her sister's dress.

" He would help us," Greta said reproachfully, " and it would not be so dark if he were here."

Christian's cheeks were burning.

" I don't choose," she said, and began handling the pictures, feeling their edges with her knife.

" Chris ! Suppose anybody came ? "

" The door is screwed," Christian answered absently.

" O Chris ! We screwed it unscrewed ; anybody who wishes shall come ! "

Christian, leaning her chin in her hands, gazed at her thoughtfully.

" It will take a long time to cut these pictures out carefully ; or, perhaps I can get them out without cutting. You must screw me up and go home. In the morning you must come early, when the gate is open, unscrew me again, and help carry the pictures."

Greta did not answer at once. At last she shook her head violently.

" I am afraid," she gasped.

289

"We can't both stay here all night," said Christian; "if any one comes to our room there will be nobody to answer. We can't lift these pictures over the gate. One of us *must* go back; you can climb over the gate—there is nothing to be afraid of."

Greta pressed her hands together.

"Do you want the pictures badly, Chris?"

Christian nodded.

"Very badly?"

"Yes—yes—yes!"

Greta remained sitting where she was, shivering violently, as a little animal shivers when it scents danger. At last she rose.

"I am going," she said in a despairing voice. At the doorway she turned.

"If Miss Naylor shall ask me where you are, Chris, I shall be telling her a story."

Christian started.

"I forgot that—O Greta, I am sorry! *I* will go instead."

Greta took another step—a quick one.

"I shall die if I stay here alone," she said; "I can tell her that you are in bed; you must go to bed here, Chris, so it shall be true after all."

Christian threw her arms about her.

"I am *so* sorry, darling; I wish I could go instead. But if you have to tell a lie, I would tell a straight one."

"Would you?" said Greta doubtfully.

"Yes."

"I think," said Greta to herself, beginning to descend the stairs, "I think I will tell it in *my* way." She shuddered and went on groping in the darkness.

Christian listened for the sound of the screws. It came slowly, threatening her with danger and solitude.

Sinking on her knees she began to work at freeing the canvas of a picture. Her heart throbbed distressfully; at the stir of wind-breath or any distant note of clamour she stopped, and held her breathing. No sounds came near. She toiled on, trying only to think that she was at the very spot where last night his arms had been round her. How long ago it seemed! She was full of vague terror, overmastered by the darkness, dreadfully alone. The new glow of resolution seemed suddenly to have died down in her heart, and left her cold.

She would never be fit to be his wife, if at the first test her courage failed! She set her teeth; and suddenly she felt a kind of exultation, as if she too were entering into life, were knowing something within herself that she had never known before. Her fingers hurt, and the pain even gave pleasure; her cheeks were burning; her breath came fast. They could not stop her now! This feverish task in darkness was her baptism into life. She finished; and rolling the pictures very carefully, tied them with cord. She had done something for him! Nobody could take that from her! She had a part of him! This night had made him hers! They might do their worst! She lay down on his mattress and soon fell asleep. . . .

She was awakened by Scruff's tongue against her face. Greta was standing by her side.

" Wake up, Chris! The gate is open! "

In the cold early light the child seemed to glow with warmth and colour; her eyes were dancing.

" I am not afraid now; Scruff and I sat up all night to catch the morning—I—*think* it was fun; and O Chris! " she ended with a rueful gleam in her eyes, " *I told it.*"

Christian hugged her.

" Come—quick ! There is nobody about. Are those the pictures ? "

Each supporting an end, the girls carried the bundle downstairs, and set out with their corpse-like burden along the wall-path between the river and the vines.

XIX

Hidden by the shade of rose-bushes Greta lay stretched at length, cheek on arm, sleeping the sleep of the unrighteous. Through the flowers the sun flicked her parted lips with kisses, and spilled the withered petals on her. In a denser islet of shade, Scruff lay snapping at a fly. His head lolled drowsily in the middle of a snap, and snapped in the middle of a loll.

At three o'clock Miss Naylor too came out, carrying a basket and a pair of scissors. Lifting her skirts to avoid the lakes of water left by the garden hose, she stopped in front of a rose-bush, and began to snip off the shrivelled flowers. The little lady's silvered head and thin, brown face sustained the shower of sunlight unprotected, and had a gentle dignity in their freedom.

Presently, as the scissors flittered in and out of the leaves, she began talking to herself.

" If girls were more like what they used to be, this would not have happened. Perhaps we don't understand ; it's very easy to forget." Burying her nose and lips in a rose, she sniffed. " Poor dear girl ! It's such a pity his father is—a——"

" A farmer," said a sleepy voice behind the rosebush.

Miss Naylor leaped. " Greta ! How you startled me ! A farmer—that is—an—an agriculturalist ! "

" A farmer with vineyards—he told us, and he is not ashamed. Why is it a pity, Miss Naylor ? "

Miss Naylor's lips looked very thin.

" For many reasons, of which you know nothing."

" That is what you always say," pursued the sleepy voice ; " and that is why, when I am to be married, there shall also be a pity."

" Greta ! " Miss Naylor cried, " it is not proper for a girl of your age to talk like that."

" Why ? " said Greta. " Because it is the truth ? "

Miss Naylor made no reply to this, but vexedly cut off a sound rose, which she hastily picked up and regarded with contrition. Greta spoke again :

" Chris said : ' I have got the pictures, I shall tell her ' ; but *I* shall tell you instead, because it was I that told the story."

Miss Naylor stared, wrinkling her nose, and holding the scissors wide apart.

" Last night," said Greta slowly, " I and Chris went to his studio and took his pictures, and so, because the gate was shut, I came back to tell it ; and when you asked me where Chris was, I told it ; because she was in the studio all night, and I and Scruff sat up all night, and in the morning we brought the pictures, and hid them under our beds, and that is why—we —are—so—sleepy."

Over the rose-bush Miss Naylor peered down at her ; and though she was obliged to stand on tiptoe this did not altogether destroy her dignity.

" I am surprised at you, Greta ; I am surprised at Christian, more surprised at Christian. The world seems upside down."

Greta, a sunbeam entangled in her hair, regarded her with inscrutable, innocent eyes.

" When you were a girl, I think you would be sure to be in love," she murmured drowsily.

Miss Naylor, flushing deeply, snipped off a particularly healthy bud.

" And so, because you are not married, I think——"
The scissors hissed.

Greta nestled down again. " I think it is wicked to cut off all the good buds," she said, and shut her eyes.

Miss Naylor continued to peer across the rosebush ; but her thin face, close to the glistening leaves, had become oddly soft, pink, and girlish. At a deeper breath from Greta, the little lady put down her basket, and began to pace the lawn, followed dubiously by Scruff. It was thus that Christian came on them.

Miss Naylor slipped her arm into the girl's and though she made no sound, her lips kept opening and shutting, like the beak of a bird contemplating a worm.

Christian spoke first :

" Miss Naylor, I want to tell you please——"

" Oh, my dear ! I know ; Greta has been in the confessional before you." She gave the girl's arm a squeeze. " Isn't it a lovely day ? Did you ever see ' Five Fingers ' look so beautiful ? " And she pointed to the great peaks of the *Funffingerspitze* glittering in the sun like giant crystals.

" I like them better with clouds about them."

" Well," agreed Miss Naylor nervously, " they certainly are nicer with clouds about them. They look almost hot and greasy, don't they. . . . My dear ! " she went on, giving Christian's arm a dozen little squeezes, " we all of us—that is, we all of us——"

Christian turned her eyes away.

" My dear," Miss Naylor tried again. " I am far—that

294

is, I mean, to all of us at some time or another—and then you see—well—it is hard ! "

Christian kissed the gloved hand resting on her arm. `Miss Naylor bobbed her head ; a tear trickled off her nose.

" Do let us wind your skein of wool ! " she said with resounding gaiety.

Some half-hour later Mrs. Decie called Christian to her room.

" My dear ! " she said ; " come here a minute ; I have a message for you."

Christian went with an odd, set look about her mouth.

Her aunt was sitting, back to the light, tapping a bowl of goldfish with the tip of a polished finger-nail ; the room was very cool. She held a letter out. " Your uncle is not coming back to-night." Christian took the letter. It was curtly worded, in a thin, toppling hand :

" Dear Con,—Can't get back to-night. Sending Dominique for things. Tell Christian to come over with him for night if possible.—Yr. aff. brother,
Nchls. Treffry."

" Dominique has a carriage here," said Mrs. Decie. " You will have nice time to catch the train. Give my love to your uncle. You must take Barbi with you, I insist on that." She rose from her chair and held Christian's hand: " My dear ! You look very tired— very ! Almost ill. I don't like to see you look like that. Come ! " She thrust her pale lips forward, and kissed the girl's paler cheek.

Then as Christian left the room she sank back in her chair, with creases in her forehead, and began languidly to cut a magazine. ' Poor Christian ! ' she thought, ' how hardly she does take it ! I am sorry for her ; but perhaps it's just as well, as things are turning out. Psychologically it is interesting ! '

Christian found her things packed, and the two servants waiting. In a few minutes they were driving to the station. She made Dominique take the seat opposite.

" Well ? " she asked him.

Dominique's eyebrows twitched, he smiled deprecatingly.

" M'mselle, Mr. Treffry told me to hold my tongue."

" But you can tell *me*, Dominique ; Barbi can't understand."

" To you, then, M'mselle," said Dominique, as one who accepts his fate ; " to you, then, who will doubtless forget all that I shall tell you—my master is not well ; he has terrible pain here ; he has a cough ; he is not well at all ; not well at all."

A feeling of dismay seized on the girl.

" We were a caravan for all that night," Dominique resumed. " In the morning by noon we ceased to be a caravan ; Signor Harz took a mule path ; he will be in Italy—certainly in Italy. As for us, we stayed at San Martino, and my master went to bed. It was time ; I had much trouble with his clothes, his legs were swollen. In the afternoon came a signor of police, on horseback, red and hot ; I persuaded him that we were at Paneveggio, but as we were not, he came back angry—*Mon Dié !* as angry as a cat. It was not good to meet him—when he was with my master I was outside. There was much noise. I do not know what passed, but at last the signor came out through the door, and went away in a hurry." Dominique's features were fixed in a sardonic grin ; he rubbed the palm of one hand with the finger of the other. " Mr. Treffry made me give him whisky afterwards, and he had no money to pay the bill—that I know because I paid it. Well, M'mselle, to-day he would be dressed and very slowly we came as far as Auer ; there he could do no more, so went to bed. He is not well at all."

Christian was overwhelmed by forebodings ; the rest of the journey was made in silence, except when Barbi, a country girl, filled with the delirium of railway travel, sighed : " *Ach ! gnädige Fräulein !* " looking at Christian with pleasant eyes.

At once, on arriving at the little hostel, Christian went to see her uncle. His room was darkened, and smelt of beeswax.

" Ah ! Chris," he said, " glad to see you."

In a blue flannel gown, with a rug over his feet, he was lying on a couch lengthened artificially by chairs ; the arm he reached out issued many inches from its sleeve, and showed the corded veins of the wrist. Christian, settling his pillows, looked anxiously into his eyes.

" I'm not quite the thing, Chris," said Mr. Treffry. " Somehow, not quite the thing. I'll come back with you to-morrow."

" Let me send for Dr. Dawney, Uncle ? "

" No—no ! Plenty of him when I get home. Very good young fellow, as doctors go, but I can't stand his puddin's—slops and puddin's, and all that trumpery medicine on the top. Send me Dominique, my dear— I'll put myself to rights a bit ! " He fingered his un-shaven cheek, and clutched the gown together on his chest. " Got this from the landlord. When you come back we'll have a little talk ! "

He was asleep when she came into the room an hour later. Watching his uneasy breathing, she wondered what it was that he was going to say.

He looked ill ! And suddenly she realised that her thoughts were not of him. . . . When she was little he would take her on his back ; he had built cocked hats for her and paper boats ; had taught her to ride ; slid her between his knees ; given her things without number ; and taken his payment in kisses. And now he was ill, and she was not thinking of him ! He had been all that was most dear to her, yet before her eyes would only come the vision of another.

Mr. Treffry woke suddenly. " Not been asleep; have I ? The beds here are infernal hard."

" Uncle Nic, won't you give me news of him ? "

Mr. Treffry looked at her, and Christian could not bear that look.

" He's safe into Italy ; they aren't very keen after him, it's so long ago ; I squared 'em pretty easily. Now, look here, Chris ! "

Christian came close ; he took her hand.

" I'd like to see you pull yourself together. ' Tisn't so much the position ; 'tisn't so much the money ; because after all there's always mine——" Christian shook her head. " But," he went on with shaky emphasis, " there's the difference of blood, and that's a serious thing ; and there's this anarch—this political affair ; and there's the sort of life, an' that's a serious thing ; but—what I'm coming to is this, Chris— there's the man ! "

Christian drew away her hand. Mr. Treffry went on :

" Ah ! yes. I'm an old chap and fond of you, but I must speak out what I think. He's got pluck, he's strong, he's in earnest ; but he's got a damned hot

298

temper, he's an egotist, and—he's not the man for you. If you marry him, as sure as I lie here, you'll be sorry for it. You're not your father's child for nothing ; nice fellow as ever lived, but soft as butter. If you take this chap, it'll be like mixing earth and ironstone, and they don't blend ! " He dropped his head back on the pillows, and stretching out his hand, repeated wistfully : " Take my word for it, my dear, he's not the man for you."

Christian, staring at the wall beyond, said quietly : " I *can't* take any one's word for that."

" Ah ! " muttered Mr. Treffry, " you're obstinate enough, but obstinacy isn't strength. You'll give up everything to him, you'll lick his shoes ; and you'll never play anything but second fiddle in his life. He'll always be first with himself, he and his work, or whatever he calls painting pictures ; and some day you'll find that out. You won't like it, and I don't like it for you, Chris, and that's flat."

He wiped his brow where the perspiration stood in beads.

Christian said : " You don't understand ; you don't believe in him ; you don't see ! If I do come after his work—if I do give him everything, and he can't give all back—I don't care ! He'll give what he can ; I don't want any more. If you're afraid of the life for me, uncle, if you think it'll be too hard——"

Mr. Treffry bowed his head. " I do, Chris."

" Well, then, I hate to be wrapped in cotton wool ; I want to breathe. If I come to grief, it's my own affair ; nobody need mind."

Mr. Treffry's fingers sought his beard. " Ah ! yes. Just so ! "

Christian sank on her knees.

" Oh ! Uncle ! I'm a selfish beast ! "

Mr. Treffry laid his hand against her cheek. " I think I could do with a nap," he said.

Swallowing a lump in her throat, she stole out of the room.

XX

By a stroke of Fate Mr. Treffry's return to Villa Rubein befell at the psychological moment when Herr Paul, in a suit of rather too bright blue, was starting for Vienna.

As soon as he saw the carriage appear between the poplars he became as pensive as a boy caught in the act of stealing cherries. Pitching his hatbox to Fritz, he recovered himself, however, in time to whistle while Mr. Treffry was being assisted into the house. Having forgotten his anger, he was only anxious now to smooth out its after effects ; in the glances he cast at Christian and his brother-in-law there was a kind of shamed entreaty which seemed to say : " For goodness' sake, don't worry me about that business again ! Nothing's come of it, you see ! "

He came forward : " Ah ! *Mon cher !* So you return ; I put off my departure, then. Vienna must wait for me—that poor Vienna ! "

But noticing the extreme feebleness of Mr. Treffry's advance, he exclaimed with genuine concern :

" What is it ? You're ill ? My God ! " After disappearing for five minutes, he came back with a whitish liquid in a glass.

" There ! " he said, " good for the gout—for a cough —for everything ! "

Mr. Treffry sniffed, drained the glass, and sucked his moustache.

" Ah ! " he said, " No doubt ! But it's uncommonly like gin, Paul." Then turning to Christian, he said : " Shake hands, you two ! "

Christian looked from one to the other, and at last held out her hand to Herr Paul, who brushed it with his moustache, gazing after her as she left the room with a queer expression.

" My dear ! " he began, " you support her in this execrable matter ? You forget my position, you make me ridiculous. I have been obliged to go to bed in my own house, absolutely to go to bed, because I was in danger of becoming funny."

" Look here, Paul ! " Mr. Treffry said gruffly, " if any one's to bully Chris, it's I."

" In that case," returned Herr Paul sarcastically, " I will go to Vienna."

" You may go to the devil ! " said Mr. Treffry ; " and I'll tell you what—in my opinion it was low to set the police on that young chap ; a low, dirty trick."

Herr Paul divided his beard carefully in two, took his seat on the very edge of an arm-chair, and placing his hands on his parted knees, said : " I have regretted it since—*mais, que diable !* He called me a coward—it is very hot weather !—there were drinks at the *Kurhaus*— I am her guardian—the affair is a very beastly one— there were more drinks—I was a little—*enfin !* " He shrugged his shoulders. " Adieu, my dear ; I shall be some time in Vienna ; I need rest ! " He rose and went to the door ; then he turned, and waved his cigar. " Adieu ! Be good ; get well ! I will buy you some cigars up there." And going out, he shut the door on any possibility of answer.

Mr. Treffry lay back amongst his cushions. The clocked ticked; pigeons cooed on the veranda; a door opened in the distance, and for a moment a treble voice was heard. Mr. Treffry's head drooped forward; across his face, gloomy and rugged, fell a thin line of sunlight.

The clock suddenly stopped ticking, and outside, in mysterious accord, the pigeons rose with a great fluttering of wings, and flew off. Mr. Treffry made a startled heavy movement. He tried to get on to his feet and reach the bell, but could not, and sat on the side of the couch with drops of sweat rolling off his forehead, and his hands clawing his chest. There was no sound at all throughout the house. He looked about him, and tried to call, but again could not. He tried once more to reach the bell, and, failing, sat still, with a thought that made him cold.

" I'm done for," he muttered. " By George! I believe I'm done for this time ! " A voice behind him said :

" Can we have a look at you, sir ? "

" Ah ! Doctor, bear a hand, there's a good fellow."

Dawney propped him against the cushions, and loosened his shirt. Receiving no answer to his questions, he stepped alarmed towards the bell. Mr. Treffry stopped him with a sign.

" Let's hear what you make of me," he said.

When Dawney had examined him, he asked :

" Well ? "

" Well," answered Dawney slowly, " there's trouble, of course,"

Mr. Treffry broke out with a husky whisper : " Out with it, Doctor ; don't humbug me."

Dawney bent down, and took his wrist.

" I don't know how you've got into this state, sir,"
he said with the brusqueness of emotion. " You're
in a bad way. It's the old trouble ; and you know
what that means as well as I. All I can tell you is, I'm
going to have a big fight with it. It shan't be my
fault, there's my hand on that."

Mr. Treffry lay with his eyes fixed on the ceiling ;
at last he said :

" I want to live."

" Yes—yes."

" I feel better now ; don't make a fuss about it.
It'll be very awkward if I die just now. Patch me
up, for the sake of my niece."

Dawney nodded. " One minute, there are a few
things I want," and he went out.

A moment later Greta stole in on tiptoe. She bent
over till her hair touched Mr. Treffry's face.

" Uncle Nic ! " she whispered. He opened his
eyes.

" Hallo, Greta ! "

" I have come to bring you my love, Uncle Nic, and
to say good-bye. Papa says that I and Scruff and Miss
Naylor are going to Vienna with him ; we have had to
pack in half an hour ; in five minutes we are going to
Vienna, and it is my first visit there, Uncle Nic."

" To Vienna ! " Mr. Treffry repeated slowly. " Don't
have a guide, Greta ; they're humbugs."

" No, Uncle Nic," said Greta solemnly.

" Draw the curtains, old girl, let's have a look at you.
Why, you're as smart as ninepence ! "

" Yes," said Greta with a sigh, touching the buttons
of her cape, " because I am going to Vienna ; but I
am sorry to leave you, Uncle Nic."

" Are you, Greta ? "

" But you will have Chris, and you are fonder of Chris than of me, Uncle Nic."

" I've known her longer."

" Perhaps when you've known me as long as Chris, you shall be as fond of me."

" When I've known you as long—may be."

" While I am gone, Uncle Nic, you are to get well, you are not very well, you know."

" What put that into your head ? "

" If you were well you would be smoking a cigar—it is just three o'clock. This kiss is for myself, this is for Scruff, and this is for Miss Naylor."

She stood upright again ; a tremulous, joyful gravity was in her eyes and on her lips.

" Good-bye, my dear ; take care of yourselves ; and don't you have a guide, they're humbugs."

" No, Uncle Nic. There is the carriage ! To Vienna, Uncle Nic ! " The dead gold of her hair gleamed in the doorway. Mr. Treffry raised himself upon his elbow.

" Give us one more, for luck ! "

Greta ran back.

" I love you very much ! " she said, and kissing him backed slowly, then, turning, flew out like a bird.

Mr. Treffry fixed his eyes on the shut door.

XXI

After many days of hot, still weather, the wind had come, and whirled the dust along the parched roads. The leaves were all astir, like tiny wings. Round Villa Rubein the pigeons cooed uneasily, all the other birds were silent. Late in the afternoon Christian came out on the veranda, reading a letter :

" DEAR CHRIS,—We are here now six days, and it is a very large place with many churches. In the first place then we have been to a great many, but the nicest of them is not St. Stephan's Kirche, it is another, but I do not remember the name. Papa is out nearly all the night ; he says he is resting here, so he is not able to come to the churches with us, but I do not think he rests very much. The day before yesterday we, that is, Papa, I, and Miss Naylor, went to an exhibition of pictures. It was quite beautiful and interesting (Miss Naylor says it is not right to say ' quite ' beautiful, but I do not know what other word could mean ' quite ' except the word ' quite,' because it is not exceedingly and not extremely). And O Chris ! there was one picture painted by *him* ; it was about a ship without masts—Miss Naylor says it is a barge, but I do not know what a barge is—on fire, and floating down a river in a fog. I think it is extremely beautiful. Miss Naylor says it is very impressionistick—what is that ? and Papa said ' Puh ! ' but he did not know it was painted by Herr Harz, so I did not tell him.

" There has also been staying at our hotel that Count Sarelli who came one evening to dinner at our house, but he is gone away now. He sat all day in the winter garden reading, and at night he went out with Papa. Miss Naylor says he is unhappy, but *I* think he does not take enough exercise ; and O Chris ! one day he said to me, ' That is your sister, Mademoiselle, that young lady in the white dress ? Does she always wear white dresses ? ' and I said to him : ' It is not always a white dress ; in the picture, it is green, because the picture is called " Spring." ' But I did not tell him the colours of all your dresses because he looked so tired. Then he said to me : ' She is very charming.' So I tell you

305

this, Chris, because I think you shall like to know. Scruff has a sore toe; it is because he has eaten too much meat.

" It is not nice without you, Chris, and Miss Naylor says I am improving my mind here, but I do not think it shall improve very much, because at night, I like it always best, when the shops are lighted and the carriages are driving past; then I am wanting to dance. The first night Papa said he would take me to the theatre, but yesterday he said it was not good for me; perhaps to-morrow he shall think it good for me again.

" Yesterday we have been in the Prater, and saw many people, and some that Papa knew; and then came the most interesting part of all, sitting under the trees in the rain for two hours because we could not get a carriage (very exciting).

" There is one young lady here, only she is not any longer very young, who knew Papa when he was a boy. I like her very much; she shall soon know me quite to the bottom and is very kind.

" The ill husband of Cousin Teresa who went with us to Meran and lost her umbrella and Dr. Edmund was so sorry about it, has been very much worse, so she is not here but in Baden. I wrote to her but have no news, so I do not know whether he is still living or not, at any rate he can't get well again so soon (and I don't think he ever shall). I think as the weather is very warm you and Uncle Nic are sitting much out of doors. I am sending presents to you all in a wooden box and screwed very firm, so you shall have to use again the big screw-driver of Fritz. For Aunt Constance, photographs; for Uncle Nic, a green bird on a stand with a hole in the back of the bird to put his ashes in; it is a good green and not expensif please tell him, because he does not like expensif presents (Miss Naylor says the bird has an inquiring eye—it is a parrat) ; for you, a little brooch of turquoise because I like them best ; for Dr. Edmund a machine to weigh medicines in because he said he could not get a good one in Botžen ; this is a very good one, the shopman told me so, and is the most expensif of all the presents —so that is all my money, except two gulden. If Papa shall give me some more, I shall buy for Miss Naylor a parasol, because it is useful and the handle of hers is ' wobbley ' (that is one of Dr. Edmund's words and I like it).

" Good-bye for this time. Greta sends you her kiss.

" *PS*.—Miss Naylor has read all this letter (except about the parasol) and there are several things she did not want me to put, so I have copied it without the things, but at the last I have kept that copy myself, so that is why this is smudgy and several words are not spelt well, *but all the things are here*."

Christian read, smiling, but to finish it was like dropping a talisman, and her face clouded. A sudden draught blew her hair about, and from within, Mr. Treffry's cough mingled with the soughing of the wind ; the sky was fast blackening. She went indoors, took a pen and began to write :

" MY FRIEND,—Why haven't you written to me ? It is so long to wait. Uncle says you are in Italy—it is dreadful not to know for certain. I feel you would have written if you could ; and I can't help thinking of all the things that may have happened. I am unhappy. Uncle Nic is ill ; he will not confess it, that is his way ;

but he is *very* ill. Though perhaps you will never see this, I must write down all my thoughts. Sometimes I feel that I am brutal to be always thinking about you, scheming how to be with you again, when he is lying there so ill. How good he has always been to me; it is terrible that love should pull one apart so. Surely love should be beautiful, and peaceful, instead of filling me with bitter, wicked thoughts. I love you—and I love him; I feel as if I were torn in two. Why should it be so? Why should the beginning of one life mean the ending of another, one love the destruction of another? I don't understand. The same spirit makes me love you and him, the same sympathy, the same trust—yet it sometimes seems as if I were a criminal in loving you. You know what he thinks— he is too honest not to have shown you. He has talked to me; he likes you in a way, but you are a foreigner— he says—your life is not my life. ' He is not the man for you!' Those were his words. And now he doesn't talk to me, but when I am in the room he looks at me—that's worse—a thousand times; when he talks it rouses me to fight—when it's his eyes only, I'm a coward at once; I feel I would do anything, anything, only not to hurt him. Why can't he see? Is it because he's old and we are young? He may consent, but he will never, never see; it will always hurt him.

" I want to tell you everything; I have had worse thoughts than these—sometimes I have thought that I should never have the courage to face the struggle which you have to face. Then I feel quite broken; it it like something giving way in me. Then I think of you, and it is over; but it has been there, and I am ashamed—I told you I was a coward. It's like the feeling one would have going out into a storm on a dark night, away from a warm fire—only of the spirit not the body—which makes it worse. I had to tell you this ; you mustn't think of it again, I mean to fight it away and forget that it has ever been there. But Uncle Nic—what am I to do ? I hate myself because I am young, and he is old and weak—sometimes I seem even to hate him. I have all sorts of thoughts, and always at the end of them, like a dark hole at the end of a passage, the thought that I ought to give you up. Ought I ? Tell me. I want to know, I want to do what is right ; I still want to do that, though sometimes I think I am all made of evil.

" Do you remember once when we were talking, you said : ' Nature always has an answer for every question ; you cannot get an answer from laws, conventions, theories, words, only from Nature.' What do you say to me now ; do you tell me it is *Nature* to come to you in spite of everything, and so, that it must be right ? I think you would ; but can it be Nature to do something which will hurt terribly one whom I love and who loves me ? If it is—Nature is cruel. Is that one of the ' lessons of life ' ? Is that what Aunt Constance means when she says : ' If life were not a paradox, we could not get on at all ' ? I am beginning to see that everything *has* its dark side ; I never believed that before.

" Uncle Nic dreads the life for me ; he doesn't understand (how should he ?—he has always had money) how life can be tolerable without money—it is horrible that the accident of money should make such difference in our lives. I am sometimes afraid myself, and I can't outface that fear in him ; he sees the shadow of his fear in me—his eyes seem to see everything that is in me now; the eyes of old people are the saddest things in the world. I am writing like a wretched coward, but you will never see this letter I suppose, and so it doesn't matter; but if you do, and I pray that you may—well, if I am only worth taking at my best, I am not worth taking at all. I want you to know the worst of me—you, and no one else.

"With Uncle Nic it is not as with my stepfather; his opposition only makes me angry, mad, ready to do anything, but with Uncle Nic I feel so bruised—so sore. He said : ' It is not so much the money, because there is always mine.' I could never do a thing he cannot bear, and take his money, and you would never let me. One knows very little of anything in the world till trouble comes. You know how it is with flowers and trees ; in the early spring they look so quiet and self-contained ; then all in a moment they change—I think it must be like that with the heart. I used to think I knew a great deal, understood why and how things came about; I thought self-possession and reason so easy ; now I know nothing. And nothing in the world matters but to see you and hide away from that look in Uncle Nic's eyes. Three months ago I did not know you, now I write like this. Whatever I look at, I try to see as you would see ; I feel, now you are away even more than when you were with me, what your thoughts would be, how you would feel about this or that. Some things you have said seem always in my mind like lights——"

A slanting drift of rain was striking the veranda tiles with a cold, ceaseless hissing. Christian shut the window, and went into her uncle's room.

He was lying with closed eyes, growling at Domnique, who moved about noiselessly, putting the room ready for the night. When he had finished, and with a compassionate bow had left the room, Mr. Treffry opened his eyes, and said :

" This is beastly stuff of the doctor's, Chris, it puts my monkey up ; I can't help swearing after I've taken it ; it's as beastly as a vulgar woman's laugh, and I don't know anything beastlier than that ! "

" I have a letter from Greta, Uncle Nic ; shall I read it ? "

He nodded, and Christian read the letter, leaving out the mention of Harz, and for some undefined reason the part about Sarelli.

" Ay ! " said Mr. Treffry with a feeble laugh, " Greta an' her money ! Send her some more, Chris. Wish I were a youngster again ; that's a beast of a proverb about a dog and his day. I'd like to go fishing again in the West Country ! A fine time we had when we were youngsters. You don't get such times these days. 'Twasn't often the fishing-smacks went out without us. We'd watch their lights from our bed-room window ; when they were swung aboard we were out and down to the quay before you could say ' knife.' They always waited for us ; but your Uncle Dan was the favourite, he was the chap for luck. When I get on my legs, we might go down there, you and I ? For a bit, just to see ? What d'you say, old girl ? "

Their eyes met.

" I'd like to look at the smack lights going to sea on a dark night ; pity you're such a duffer in a boat—we might go out with them. Do you a power of good ! You're not looking the thing, my dear."

His voice died wistfully, and his glance, sweeping

her face, rested on her hands, which held and twisted Greta's letter. After a minute or two of silence he boomed out again with sudden energy :

" Your aunt'll want to come and sit with me, after dinner ; don't let her, Chris, I can't stand it. Tell her I'm asleep—the doctor'll be here directly ; ask him to make up some humbug for you—it's his business."

He was seized by a violent fit of pain which seemed to stab his breath away, and when it was over signed that he would be left alone. Christian went back to her letter in the other room, and had written these words, when the gong summoned her to dinner :

" I'm like a leaf in the wind, I put out my hand to one thing, and it's seized and twisted and flung aside. I want you—I want you ; if I could see you I think I should know what to do——"

XXII

The rain drove with increasing fury. The night was very black. Nicholas Treffry slept heavily. By the side of his bed the night-lamp cast on to the opposite wall a bright disc festooned by the hanging shadow of the ceiling. Christian was leaning over him. For the moment he filled all her heart, lying there, so helpless. Fearful of waking him she slipped into the sitting-room. Outside the window stood a man with his face pressed to the pane. Her heart thumped ; she went up and unlatched the window. It was Harz, with the rain dripping off him. He let fall his hat and cape.

" You ! " she said, touching his sleeve. " You ! You ! "

He was sodden with wet, his face drawn and tired ; a dark growth of beard covered his cheeks and chin.

312

" Where is your uncle ? " he said ; " I want to see him."

She put her hand up to his lips, but he caught it and covered it with kisses.

" He's asleep—ill—speak gently ! "

" I came to him first," he muttered.

Christian lit the lamp ; and he looked at her hungrily without a word.

" It's not possible to go on like this ; I came to tell your uncle so. He is a *man*. As for the other, I want to have nothing to do with him ! I came back on foot across the mountains. It's not possible to go on like this, Christian."

She handed him her letter. He held it to the light, clearing his brow of raindrops. When he had read to the last word he gave it her back, and whispered : " Come ! "

Her lips moved, but she did not speak.

" While this goes on I can't work ; I can do nothing. I can't—I won't bargain with my work ; if it's to be that, we had better end it. What are we waiting for ? Sooner or later we must come to this. I'm sorry that he's ill, God knows ! But that changes nothing. To wait is tying me hand and foot—it's making me afraid ! Fear kills ! It will kill you ! It kills work, and I must work, I can't waste time—I won't ! I will sooner give you up." He put his hands on her shoulders. " I love you ! I want you ! Look in my eyes and see if you dare hold back ! "

Christian stood with the grip of his strong hands on her shoulders, without a movement or sign. Her face was very white. And suddenly he began to kiss that pale, still face, to kiss its eyes and lips, to kiss it from its chin up to its hair ; and it stayed pale, as a white flower, beneath those kisses—as a white flower, whose stalk the fingers bend back a little.

There was a sound of knocking on the wall; Mr. Treffry called feebly. Christian broke away from Harz.

" To-morrow ! " he whispered, and picking up his hat and cloak, went out again into the rain.

XXIII

It was not till morning that Christian fell into a troubled sleep. She dreamed that a voice was calling her, and she was filled with a helpless, dumb dream terror.

When she woke the light was streaming in; it was Sunday, and the cathedral bells were chiming. Her first thought was of Harz. One step, one moment of courage ! Why had she not told her uncle ? If he had only asked ! But why—why should she tell him ? when it was over and she was gone, he would see that all was for the best.

Her eyes fell on Greta's empty bed. She sprang up, and bending over, kissed the pillow. ' She will mind at first; but she's so young ! Nobody will really miss me, except Uncle Nic ! ' She stood a long while in the window without moving. When she was dressed she called out to her maid :

" Bring me some milk, Barbi ; I'm going to church."

" *Ach ! gnädiges Fräulein*, will you no breakfast have ? "

" No, thank you, Barbi."

" *Liebes Fräulein*, what a beautiful morning after the rain it has become ! How cool ! It is for you good—

314

for the colour in your cheeks; now they will bloom again!" and Barbi stroked her own well-coloured cheeks.

Dominique, sunning himself outside with a cloth across his arm, bowed as she passed, and smiled affectionately:

"He is better this morning, M'mselle. We march —we are getting on. Good news will put the heart into you."

Christian thought: 'How sweet every one is to-day!'

Even the Villa seemed to greet her, with the sun aslant on it; and the trees, trembling and weeping golden tears. At the cathedral she was early for the service, but here and there were figures on their knees; the faint, sickly odour of long-burnt incense clung in the air; a priest moved silently at the far end. She knelt, and when at last she rose the service had begun. With the sound of the intoning a sense of peace came to her—the peace of resolution. For good or bad she felt that she had faced her fate.

She went out with a look of quiet serenity and walked home along the dyke. Close to Harz's studio she sat down. Now—it was her own; all that had belonged to him, that had ever had a part in him.

An old beggar, who had been watching her, came gently from behind. "Gracious lady!" he said, peering at her eyes, "this is the lucky day for you. I have lost *my* luck."

Christian opened her purse, there was only one coin in it, a gold piece; the beggar's eyes sparkled.

She thought suddenly: 'It's no longer mine; I must begin to be careful,' but she felt ashamed when she looked at the old man.

315

" I am sorry," she said; "yesterday I would have given you this, but—but now it's already given."

He seemed so old and poor—what could she give him? She unhooked a little silver brooch at her throat. "You will get something for that," she said; "it's better than nothing. I am very sorry you are so old and poor."

The beggar crossed himself. "Gracious lady," he muttered, "may you never want!"

Christian hurried on; the rustling of leaves soon carried the words away. She did not feel inclined to go in, and crossing the bridge began to climb the hill. There was a gentle breeze, drifting the clouds across the sun; lizards darted out over the walls, looked at her, and whisked away.

The sunshine, dappling through the tops of trees, flashed down on a torrent. The earth smelt sweet, the vineyards round the white farms glistened; everything seemed to leap and dance with sap and life; it was a moment of Spring in mid-summer. Christian walked on, wondering at her own happiness.

' Am I heartless?' she thought. ' I am going to leave him—I am going into life; I shall have to fight now, there'll be no looking back.'

The path broke away and wound down to the level of the torrent; on the other side it rose again, and was lost among trees. The woods were dank; she hastened home.

In her room she began to pack, sorting and tearing up old letters. ' Only one thing matters,' she thought; ' singleness of heart; to see your way, and keep to it with all your might.'

She looked up and saw Barbi standing before her with towels in her hands, and a scared face.

" Are you going a journey, *gnädiges Fräulein* ? "

" I am going away to be married, Barbi," said Christian at last ; " don't speak of it to any one, please."

Barbi leant a little forward with the towels clasped to the blue cotton bosom of her dress.

" No, no ! I will not speak. But, dear Fräulein, that is a big matter ; have you well thought ? "

" Thought, Barbi ? Have I not ! "

" But, dear Fräulein, will you be rich ? "

" No ! I shall be as poor as you."

" *Ach !* dear God ! that is terrible. Katrina, my sister, she is married ; she tells me all her life ; she tells me it is very hard, and but for the money in her stocking it would be harder. Dear Fräulein, think again ! And is he good ? Sometimes they are not good."

" He is good," said Christian, rising ; " it is all settled ! " and she kissed Barbi on the cheek.

" You are crying, *liebes Fräulein !* Think yet again, perhaps it is not quite all settled ; it is not possible that a maiden should not a way out leave ? "

Christian smiled. " I don't do things that way, Barbi."

Barbi hung the towels on the horse and crossed herself.

XXIV

Mr. Treffry's gaze was fixed on a tortoise-shell butterfly fluttering round the ceiling. The insect seemed to fascinate him, as things which move quickly always fascinate the helpless. Christian came softly in.

" Couldn't stay in bed, Chris," he called out with an air of guilt. " The heat was something awful. The doctor piped off in a huff, just because o' this." He motioned towards a jug of claret-cup and a pipe on the table by his elbow. " I was only looking at 'em."

Christian, sitting down beside him, took up a fan.

" If I could get out of his heat——" he said, and closed his eyes.

' I must tell him,' she thought ; ' I can't slink away.'

" Pour me out some of that stuff, Chris."

She reached for the jug. Yes ! She must tell him ! Her heart sank.

Mr. Treffry took a lengthy draught. " Broken my promise ; don't matter—won't hurt any one but me." He took up the pipe and pressed tobacco into it. " I've been lying here with this pain going right through me, and never a smoke ! D'you tell me anything the parsons say can do me half the good of this pipe ? " He leaned back, steeped in a luxury of satisfaction. He went on, pursuing a private train of thought : " Things have changed a lot since my young days. When I was a youngster, a young fellow had to look out for peck and perch—he put the future in his pocket. He did well or not, according as he had stuff in him. Now he's not content with that, it seems—trades on his own opinion of himself ; thinks he is what he says he's going to be."

" You are unjust," said Christian.

Mr. Treffry grunted. " Ah, well ! I like to know where I am. If I lend money to a man, I like to know whether he's going to pay it back ; I may not care whether he does or not, but I like to know. The same with other things. I don't care what a man has— though, mind you, Chris, it's not a bad rule that measures men by the balance at their banks ; but when it comes to marriage, there's a very simple rule, What's not enough for one is not enough for two. You can't talk black white, or bread into your mouth. I don't care to speak about myself, as you know, Chris, but I tell you this—when I came to London I wanted to marry —I hadn't any money, and I had to want. When I had the money—but that's neither here nor there ! " He frowned, fingering his pipe. " I didn't ask her, Chris ; I didn't think it the square thing ; it seems that's out of fashion ! "

Christian's cheeks were burning.

" I think a lot while I lie here," Mr. Treffry went on ; " nothing much else to do. What I ask myself is this : What do you know about what's best for you ? What do you know of life ? Take it or leave it, life's not all you think ; it's give and get all the way, a fair start is everything."

Christian thought : ' Will he never see ? '

Mr. Treffry went on :

" I get better every day, but I can't last for ever. It's not pleasant to lie here and know that when I'm gone there'll be no one to keep a hand on the check string ! "

" Don't talk like that, dear ! " Christian murmured.

" It's no use blinking facts, Chris. I've lived a long time in the world ; I've seen things pretty well as they are ; and now there's not much left for me to think about but you."

" But, Uncle, if you loved him, as I do, you couldn't tell me to be afraid ! It's cowardly and mean to be afraid. You must have forgotten ! "

Mr. Treffry closed his eyes.

" Yes," he said ; " I'm old."

The fan had dropped into Christian's lap ; it rested on her white frock like a large crimson leaf ; her eyes were fixed on it.

Mr. Treffry looked at her. " Have you heard from him ? " he asked with sudden intuition.

" Last night, in that room, when you thought I was talking to Dominique——"

The pipe fell from his hand.

" What ! " he stammered : " Back ? "

Christian, without looking up, said :

" Yes, he's back ; he wants me—I *must* go to him, Uncle."

There was a long silence.

" You must go to him ? " he repeated.

She longed to fling herself down at his knees, but he was so still, that to move seemed impossible ; she remained silent, with folded hands.

Mr. Treffry spoke :

" You'll let me know—before—you—go. Good-night ! "

Christian stole out into the passage. A bead curtain rustled in the draught ; voices reached her.

" My honour is involved, or I would give the case up."

" He is very trying, poor Nicholas ! He always had that peculiar quality of opposition ; it has brought him to grief a hundred times. There is opposition in our blood ; my family all have it. My eldest brother died of it ; with my poor sister, who was as gentle as a lamb, it took the form of doing the right thing in the wrong place. It is a matter of temperament, you see. You must have patience."

" Patience," repeated Dawney's voice, " is one thing ; patience where there is responsibility is another. I've not had a wink of sleep these last two nights."

There was a faint, shrill swish of silk.

" Is he so very ill ? "

Christian held her breath.   The answer came at last.
" Has he made his will ?   With this trouble in the
side again, I tell you plainly, Mrs. Decie, there's little or
no chance."

Christian put her hands up to her ears, and ran out
into the air. What was she about to do, then—to
leave him dying !

XXV

On the following day Harz was summoned to the
Villa.   Mr. Treffry had just risen, and was garbed in
a dressing-suit, old and worn, which had a certain air
of magnificence. His seamed cheeks were newly
shaved.

" I hope I see you well," he said majestically.   Thinking of the drive and their last parting, Harz felt sorry
and ashamed.   Suddenly Christian came into the room ;
she stood for a moment looking at him, then sat down.

" Chris ! " said Mr. Treffry reproachfully.   She
shook her head, and did not move ; mournful and intent, her eyes seemed full of secret knowledge.

Mr. Treffry spoke :

" I've no right to blame you, Mr. Harz, and Chris
tells me you came to see me first, which is what I
would have expected of you ; but you shouldn't have
come back."

" I came back, sir, because I found I was obliged.
I must speak out."

" I ask nothing better," Mr. Treffry replied.

Harz looked again at Christian ; but she made no
sign, sitting with her chin resting on her hands.

" I have come for her," he said ; " I can make my
living—enough for both of us.   But I can't wait."

321

" Why ? "

Harz made no answer.

Mr. Treffry boomed out again : " Why ?   Isn't she worth waiting for ?   Isn't she worth serving for ? "

" I can't expect you to understand me," the painter said.   " My art is my life to me.   Do you suppose that if it wasn't I should ever have left my village ;   or gone through all that I've gone through, to get as far even as I am ?   You tell me to wait.   If my thoughts and my will aren't free, how can I work ?   I shan't be worth my salt.   You tell me to go back to England— knowing she is here, amongst you who hate me, a thousand miles away.   I shall know that there's a death- fight going on in her and outside her against me—you think that I can go on working under these conditions. Others may be able, I am not.   That's the plain truth. If I loved her less——"

There was a silence, then Mr. Treffry said :

" It isn't fair to come here and ask what you're ask- ing.   You don't know what's in the future for you, you don't know that you can keep a wife.   It isn't pleasant, either, to think you can't hold up your head in your own country."

Harz turned white.

" Ah ! you bring that up again ! " he broke out. " Seven years ago I was a boy and starving ; if you had been in my place you would have done what I did. My country is as much to me as your country is to you. I've been an exile seven years, I suppose I shall always be—I've had punishment enough ; but if you think I am a rascal, I'll go and give myself up."   He turned on his heel.

" Stop ! I beg your pardon ! I never meant to hurt you. It isn't easy for me to eat my words," Mr.

Treffry said wistfully, " let that count for something."
He held out his hand.

Harz came quickly back and took it. Christian's
gaze was never for a moment withdrawn ; she seemed
trying to store up the sight of him within her. The
light darting through the half-closed shutters gave her
eyes a strange, bright intensity, and shone in the folds
of her white dress like the sheen of birds' wings.

Mr. Treffry glanced uneasily about him. " God
knows I don't want anything but her happiness," he
said. " What is it to *me* if you'd murdered your
mother ? It's *her* I'm thinking of."

" How can you tell what is happiness to her ? You
have your own ideas of happiness—not hers, not mine.
You can't dare to stop us, sir ! "

" Dare ? " said Mr. Treffry. " Her father gave her
over to me when she was a mite of a little thing ; I've
known her all her life. I've—I've loved her—and
you come here with your ' dare ' ! " His hand
dragged at his beard, and shook as though palsied.

A look of terror came into Christian's face.

" All right, Chris ! I don't ask for quarter, and
I don't give it ! "

Harz made a gesture of despair.

" I've acted squarely by you, sir," Mr. Treffry went
on, " I ask the same of you. I ask you to wait, and
come like an honest man, when you can say, ' I see my
way—here's this and that for her.' What makes this
art you talk of different from any other call in life ? It
doesn't alter facts, or give you what other men have no
right to expect. It doesn't put grit into you, or keep
your hands clean, or prove that two and two make
five."

Harz answered bitterly :

323

" You know as much of art as I know of money. If we live a thousand years we shall never understand each other. I am doing what I feel is best for both of us."

Mr. Treffry took hold of the painter's sleeve.

" I make you an offer," he said. " Your word not to see or write to her for a year ! Then, position or not, money or no money, if she'll have you, I'll make it right for you."

" I could not take your money."

A kind of despair seemed suddenly to seize on Mr. Nicholas Treffry. He rose, and stood towering over them.

" All my life——" he said ; but something seemed to click deep down in his throat, and he sank back in his seat.

" Go ! " whispered Christian, " go ! " But Mr. Treffry found his voice again : " It's for the child to say. Well, Chris ! "

Christian did not speak.

It was Harz who broke the silence. He pointed to Mr. Treffry.

" You know I can't tell you to come with—*that*, there. Why did you send for me ? " And, turning, he went out.

Christian sank on her knees, burying her face in her hands. Mr. Treffry pressed his handkerchief with a stealthy movement to his mouth. It was dyed crimson with the price of his victory.

XXVI

A telegram had summoned Herr Paul from Vienna. He had started forthwith, leaving several unpaid accounts to a more joyful opportunity, amongst them a chemist's bill, for a wonderful quack medicine of which he brought six bottles.

He came from Mr. Treffry's room with tears rolling down his cheeks, saying :

" Poor Nicholas ! Poor Nicholas ! *Il n'a pas de chance !* "

It was difficult to find any one to listen ; the women were scared and silent, waiting for the orders that were now and then whispered through the door. Herr Paul could not bear this silence, and talked to his servant for half an hour, till Fritz also vanished to fetch something from the town. Then in despair Herr Paul went to his room. It was hard not to be allowed to help—it was hard to wait ! When the heart was suffering, it was frightful ! He turned and, looking furtively about him, lighted a cigar. Yes, it came to every one —at some time or other ; and what was it, that death they talked of ? Was it any worse than life ? That frightful jumble people made for themselves ! Poor Nicholas ! After all, it was he that had the luck !

His eyes filled with tears, and drawing a pen-knife from his pocket, he began to stab it into the stuffing of his chair. Scruff, who sat watching the chink of light under the door, turned his head, blinked at him, and began feebly tapping with a claw.

It was intolerable, this uncertainty—to be near, and yet so far, was not endurable !

Herr Paul stepped across the room. The dog, following, threw his black-marked muzzle upwards with a gruff noise, and went back to the door. His master was holding in his hand a bottle of champagne.

Poor Nicholas ! *He* had chosen it. Herr Paul drained a glass.

Poor Nicholas ! The prince of fellows, and of what use was one ? They kept him away from Nicholas !

Herr Paul's eyes fell on the terrier. " *Ach !* my dear," he said, " you and I, we alone are kept away ! "

He drained a second glass.

What was it ? This life ! Froth—like that !

He tossed off a third glass. Forget ! If one could not help, it was better to forget !

He put on his hat. Yes. There was no room for him there ! He was not wanted !

He finished the bottle, and went out into the passage. Scruff ran and lay down at Mr. Treffry's door. Herr Paul looked at him. " *Ach !* " he said, tapping his chest, " ungrateful hound ! " And opening the front door he went out on tiptoe. . . .

Late that afternoon Greta stole hatless through the lilac bushes ; she looked tired after her night journey, and sat idly on a chair in the speckled shadow of a lime-tree.

' It is not like home,' she thought ; ' I am unhappy. Even the birds are silent, but perhaps that is because it is so hot. I have never been sad like this—for it is not fancy that I am sad this time, as it is sometimes. It is in my heart like the sound the wind makes through a wood, it feels quite empty in my heart. If it is always like this to be unhappy, then I am sorry for all the unhappy things in the world ; I am sorrier than I ever was before.'

A shadow fell on the grass, she raised her eyes, and saw Dawney.

" Dr. Edmund ! " she whispered.

Dawney turned to her ; a heavy furrow showed between his brows. His eyes, always rather close together, stared painfully.

"Dr. Edmund," Greta whispered, "is it true?"

He took her hand, and spread his own palm over it.

"Perhaps," he said; "perhaps not. We must hope."

Greta looked up, awed.

"They say he is dying."

"We have sent for the best man in Vienna."

Greta shook her head.

"But you are clever, Dr. Edmund; and *you* are afraid."

"He is brave," said Dawney; "we must all be brave, you know. You too!"

"Brave?" repeated Greta; "what is it to be brave? If it is not to cry and make a fuss—that I can do. But if it is not to be sad in here," she touched her breast, "that I cannot do, and it shall not be any good for me to try."

"To be brave is to hope; don't give up hope, dear."

"No," said Greta, tracing the pattern of the sunlight on her skirt. "But I think that when we hope, we are not brave, because we are expecting something for ourselves. Chris says that hope is prayer, and if it is prayer, then all the time we are hoping, we are asking for something, and it is not brave to ask for things."

A smile curved Dawney's mouth.

"Go on, Philosopher!" he said. "Be brave in your own way, it will be just as good as anybody else's."

"What are you going to do to be brave, Dr. Edmund?"

"I? Fight! If only we had five years off his life!"

Greta watched him as he walked away.

"I shall never be brave," she mourned; "I shall

always be wanting to be happy." And, kneeling down, she began to disentangle a fly, imprisoned in a cobweb. A plant of hemlock had sprung up in the long grass by her feet. Greta thought, dismayed : ' There are weeds ! '

It seemed but another sign of the death of joy.

' But it's very beautiful,' she thought, ' the blossoms are like stars. I am not going to pull it up. I will leave it ; perhaps it will spread all through the garden ; and if it does I do not care, for now things are not like they used to be and I do not think they ever shall be again.'

XXVII

The days went by ; those long, hot days, when the heat haze swims up about ten of the forenoon, and, as the sun sinks level with the mountains, melts into golden ether which sets the world quivering with sparkles.

At the lighting of the stars those sparkles die, vanishing one by one off the hillsides ; evening comes flying down the valleys, and life rests under her cool wings. The night falls ; and the hundred little voices of the night arise.

It was near grape-gathering, and in the heat the fight for Nicholas Treffry's life went on, day in, day out, with gleams of hope and moments of despair. Doctors came, but after the first he refused to see them.

" No," he said to Dawney—" throwing away money. If I pull through it won't be because of them."

For days together he would allow no one but Dawney, Dominique, and the paid nurse in the room.

" I can stand it better," he said to Christian, " when

I don't see any of you ; keep away, old girl, and let me get on with it ! "

To have been able to help would have eased the tension of her nerves, and the aching of her heart.   At his own request they had moved his bed into a corner so that he might face the wall.   There he would lie for hours together, not speaking a word, except to ask for drink.

Sometimes Christian crept in unnoticed, and sat watching, with her arms tightly folded across her breast. At night, after Greta was asleep, she would toss from side to side, muttering feverish prayers.   She spent hours at her little table in the schoolroom, writing letters to Harz that were never sent.   Once she wrote these words : " I am the most wicked of all creatures —I have even wished that he may die ! "   A few minutes afterwards Miss Naylor found her with her head buried on her arms.   Christian sprang up ; tears were streaming down her cheeks.   " Don't touch me ! " she cried, and rushed away.   Later, she stole into her uncle's room, and sank down on the floor beside the bed.   She sat there silently, unnoticed all the evening.   When night came she could hardly be persuaded to leave the room.

One day Mr. Treffry expressed a wish to see Herr Paul ; it was a long while before the latter could summon courage to go in.

" There's a few dozen of the Gordon sherry at my Chambers, in London, Paul," Mr. Treffry said ; " I'd be glad to think you had 'em.   And my man Dominique, I've made him all right in my will, but keep your eye on him ; he's a good sort for a foreigner, and no chicken, but sooner or later, the women'll get hold of him.   That's all I had to say.   Send Chris to me."

Herr Paul stood by the bedside speechless. Suddenly he blurted out.

" Ah! my dear! Courage! We are all mortal. You will get well!" All the morning he walked about quite inconsolable. "It was frightful to see him, you know, frightful! An iron man could not have borne it."

When Christian came to him, Mr. Treffry raised himself and looked at her a long while.

His wistful face was like an accusation. But that very afternoon the news came from the sick-room that he was better, having had no pain for several hours.

Every one went about with smiles lurking in their eyes, and ready to break forth at a word. In the kitchen Barbi burst out crying, and, forgetting to toss the pan, spoiled a *Kaiser-Schmarn* she was making. Dominique was observed draining a glass of Chianti, and solemnly casting forth the last drops in libation. An order was given for tea to be taken out under the acacias, where it was always cool; it was felt that something in the nature of high festival was being held. Even Herr Paul was present; but Christian did not come. Nobody spoke of illness; to mention it might break the spell.

Miss Naylor, who had gone into the house, came back, saying :

" There is a strange man standing over there by the corner of the house."

" Really!" asked Mrs. Decie; " what does he want ? "

Miss Naylor reddened. "I did not ask him. I—don't—know—whether he is quite respectable. His coat is buttoned very close, and he—doesn't seem—to have a—collar."

" Go and see what he wants, dear child," Mrs. Decie said to Greta.

" I don't know—I really do not know——" began Miss Naylor ; " he has very—high—boots," but Greta was already on her way, with hands clasped behind her, and demure eyes taking in the stranger's figure.

" Please ? " she said, when she was close to him.

The stranger took his cap off with a jerk.

" This house has no bells," he said in a nasal voice ; " it has a tendency to discourage one."

" Yes," said Greta gravely, " there is a bell, but it does not ring now, because my uncle is so ill."

" I am very sorry to hear that. I don't know the people here, but I am very sorry to hear that. I would be glad to speak a few words to your sister, if it is your sister that I want."

And the stranger's face grew very red.

" Is it," said Greta, " that you are a friend of Herr Harz ? If you are a friend of *his*, you will please come and have some tea, and while you are having tea I will look for Chris."

Perspiration bedewed the stranger's forehead.

" Tea ? Excuse me ! I don't drink tea."

" There is also coffee," Greta said.

The stranger's progress towards the arbour was so slow that Greta arrived considerably before him.

" It is a friend of Herr Harz," she whispered ; " he will drink coffee. I am going to find Chris."

" Greta ! " gasped Miss Naylor.

Mrs. Decie put up her hand.

" Ah ! " she said, " if it is so, we must be very nice to him for Christian's sake."

Miss Naylor's face grew soft.

" Ah, yes ! " she said ; " of course."

" Bah ! " muttered Herr Paul, " that recommences."

" Paul ! " murmured Mrs. Decie, " you lack the elements of wisdom."

Herr Paul glared at the approaching stranger.

Mrs. Decie had risen, and smilingly held out her hand.

" We are so glad to know you ; you are an artist too, perhaps ?   I take a great interest in art, and especially in that school which Mr. Harz represents."

The stranger smiled.

" He is the genuine article, ma'am," he said.   " He represents no school, he is one of that kind whose corpses make schools."

" Ah ! " murmured Mrs. Decie, " you are an American.   That is so nice.   Do sit down !   My niece will soon be here."

Greta came running back.

" Will you come, please ? " she said.   " Chris is ready."

Gulping down his coffee, the stranger included them all in a single bow, and followed her.

" *Ach !* " said Herr Paul, " *garcon tres chic, celui-la !* "

Christian was standing by her little table.   The stranger began.

" I am sending Mr. Harz's things to England ; there are some pictures here.   He would be glad to have them."

A flood of crimson swept over her face.

" I am sending them to London," the stranger repeated ; " perhaps you could give them to me to-day."

" They are ready ; my sister will show you."

Her eyes seemed to dart into his soul, and try to drag something from it.   The words rushed from her lips :

332

" Is there any message for me ? "

The stranger regarded her curiously.

" No," he stammered, " no ! I guess not.   He is well. . . . I wish——" He stopped ; her white face seemed to flash scorn, despair, and entreaty on him all at once.   And turning, she left him standing there.

XXVIII

When Christian went that evening to her uncle's room he was sitting up in bed, and at once began to talk. " Chris," he said, " I can't stand this dying by inches.   I'm going to try what a journey'll do for me. I want to get back to the old country.   The doctor's promised.   There's a shot in the locker yet ! I believe in that young chap ; he's stuck to me like a man. . . . It'll be your birthday on Tuesday, old girl, and you'll be twenty.   Seventeen years since your father died. You've been a lot to me. . . . A parson came here to-day.   That's a bad sign.   Thought it his duty ! Very civil of him ! I wouldn't see him, though.   If there's anything in what they tell you, I'm not going to sneak in at this time o' day.   There's one thing that's rather badly on my mind.   I took advantage of Mr. Harz with this damned pitifulness of mine.   You've a right to look at me as I've seen you sometimes when you thought I was asleep.   If I hadn't been ill he'd never have left you.   I don't blame you, Chris—not I ! You love me ? I know that, my dear.   But one's alone when it comes to the run-in.   Don't cry ! Our minds aren't Sunday-school books ; you're finding it out, that's all ! " He sighed and turned away.

The noise of sun-blinds being raised vibrated through

the house. A feeling of terror seized on the girl; he lay so still, and yet the drawing of each breath was a fight. If she could only suffer in his place ! She went close, and bent over him.

"It's air we want, both you and I ! " he muttered. Christian beckoned to the nurse, and stole out through the window.

A regiment was passing in the road; she stood half-hidden amongst the lilac bushes watching. The poplar leaves drooped lifeless and almost black above her head, the dust raised by the soldiers' feet hung in the air; it seemed as if in all the world no freshness and no life were stirring. The tramp of feet died away. Suddenly within arm's length of her a man appeared, his stick shouldered like a sword. He raised his hat.

"Good-evening ! You do not remember me ? Sarelli. Pardon ! You looked like a ghost standing there. How badly those fellows marched ! We hang, you see, on the skirts of our profession and criticise; it is all we are fit for." His black eyes, restless and malevolent like a swan's, seemed to stab her face. "A fine evening ! Too hot. The storm is wanted; you feel that ? It is weary waiting for the storm; but after the storm, my dear young lady, comes peace." He smiled, gently, this time, and baring his head again, was lost to view in the shadow of the trees.

His figure had seemed to Christian like the sudden vision of a threatening, hidden force. She thrust out her hands, as though to keep it off.

No use; it was within her, nothing could keep it away ! She went to Mrs. Decie's room, where her aunt and Miss Naylor were conversing in low tones. To hear their voices brought back the touch of this world of everyday which had no part or lot in the terrifying powers within her.

Dawney slept at the villa now. In the dead of night he was awakened by a light flashed in his eyes. Christian was standing there, her face pale and wild with terror, her hair falling in dark masses on her shoulders.

" Save him ! Save him ! " she cried. " Quick ! The bleeding ? "

He saw her muffle her face in her white sleeves, and seizing the candle, leaped out of bed and rushed away.

The internal hæmorrhage had come again, and Nicholas Treffry wavered between life and death. When it had ceased, he sank into a sort of stupor. About six o'clock he came back to consciousness ; watching his eyes, they could see a mental struggle taking place within him. At last he singled Christian out from the others by a sign.

" I'm beat, Chris," he whispered. " Let *him* know, I want to see him."

His voice grew a little stronger. " I thought that I could see it through—but here's the end." He lifted his hand ever so little, and let it fall again. When told a little later that a telegram had been sent to Harz his eyes expressed satisfaction.

Herr Paul came down in ignorance of the night's events. He stopped in front of the barometer and tapped it, remarking to Miss Naylor : " The glass has gone downstairs ; we shall have cool weather—it will still go well with him ! "

When, with her brown face twisted by pity and concern, she told him that it was a question of hours, Herr Paul turned first purple, then pale, and sitting down, trembled violently. " I cannot believe it," he exclaimed almost angrily. " Yesterday he was so well ! I cannot believe it ! Poor Nicholas ! Yesterday he spoke to me ! " Taking Miss Naylor's hand, he clutched it in his own. " Ah ! " he cried, letting it go suddenly, and striking at his forehead, " it is too terrible ; only yesterday he spoke to me of sherry. Is there nobody, then, who can do good ? "

" There is only God," replied Miss Naylor softly.

" God ? " said Herr Paul in a scared voice.

" We—can—all—pray to Him," Miss Naylor murmured ; little spots of colour came into her cheeks. " I am going to do it—now."

Herr Paul raised her hand and kissed it.

" Are you ? " he said ; " good ! I too." He passed through his study door, closed it carefully behind him, then for some unknown reason set his back against it. Ugh ! Death ! It came to all ! Some day it would come to him. It might come to-morrow ! One must pray !

The day dragged to its end. In the sky clouds had mustered, and, crowding close on one another, clung round the sun, soft, thick grey-white, like the feathers on a pigeon's breast. Towards evening faint tremblings were felt at intervals, as from the shock of immensely distant earthquakes.

Nobody went to bed that night, but in the morning the report was the same : " Unconscious—a question of hours." Once only did he recover consciousness, and then asked for Harz. A telegram had come from him, he was on the way. Towards seven of the evening the long-expected storm broke in a sky like ink. Into the valleys and over the crests of mountains it seemed as though an unseen hand were spilling goblets of pale wine, darting a sword-blade zigzag over trees, roofs, spires, peaks, into the very firmament, which answered every thrust with great bursts of groaning. Just beyond the veranda Greta saw a glow-worm shining, as it might be a tiny bead of the fallen lightning. Soon the rain covered everything. Sometimes a jet of light brought the hilltops, towering, dark, and hard, over the house, to disappear again behind the raindrops and shaken leaves. Each breath drawn by the storm was like the clash of a thousand cymbals; and in his room Mr. Treffry lay unconscious of its fury.

Greta had crept in unobserved, and sat curled in a corner, with Scruff in her arms, rocking slightly to and fro. When Christian passed, she caught her skirt, and whispered: "It is your birthday, Chris!"

Mr. Treffry stirred.

"What's that? Thunder?—it's cooler. Where am I? Chris!"

Dawney signed for her to take his place.

"Chris!" Mr. Treffry said. "It's near now." She bent across him, and her tears fell on his forehead.

"Forgive!" she whispered; "love me!"

He raised his finger, and touched her cheek.

For an hour or more he did not speak, though once or twice he moaned, and faintly tightened his pressure on her fingers. The storm had died away, but very far off the thunder was still muttering.

His eyes opened once more, rested on her, and passed beyond, into that abyss dividing youth from age, conviction from conviction, life from death.

At the foot of the bed Dawney stood covering his face; behind him Dominique knelt with hands held upwards; the sound of Greta's breathing, soft in sleep, rose and fell in the stillness.

337

XXIX

One afternoon in March, more than three years after Mr. Treffry's death, Christian was sitting at the window of a studio in St. John's Wood. The sky was covered with soft, high clouds, through which shone little gleams of blue. Now and then a bright shower fell, sprinkling the trees, where every twig was curling upwards as if waiting for the gift of its new leaves. And it seemed to her that the boughs thickened and budded under her very eyes; a great concourse of sparrows had gathered on those boughs, and kept raising a shrill chatter. Over at the far side of the room Harz was working at a picture.

On Christian's face was the quiet smile of one who knows that she has only to turn her eyes to see what she wishes to see; of one whose possessions are safe under her hand. She looked at Harz with that possessive smile. But as into the brain of one turning in his bed grim fancies will suddenly leap up out of warm nothingness, so there leaped into her mind the memory of that long ago dawn, when he had found her kneeling by Mr. Treffry's body. She seemed to see again the dead face, so gravely quiet, and furrowless. She seemed to see her lover and herself setting forth silently along the river wall where they had first met; sitting down, still silent, beneath the poplar-tree where the little bodies of the chafers had lain strewn in the Spring. To see the trees changing from black to grey, from grey to green, and in the dark sky long white lines of cloud flighting to the south like birds; and, very far away, rosy peaks watching the awakening of the earth. And now once again, after all that time, she felt her spirit shrink away

338

from his ; as it had shrunk in that hour, when she had seemed hateful to herself. She remembered the words she had spoken : " I have no heart left. You've torn it in two between you. Love is all self—I wanted him to die." She remembered too the raindrops on the vines like a million tiny lamps, and the throstle that began singing. Then, as dreams die out into warm nothingness, recollection vanished, and the smile came back to her lips.

She took out a letter.

" . . . O Chris ! We are really coming ; I seem to be always telling it to myself, and I have told Scruff many times, but he does not care, because he is getting old. Miss Naylor says we shall arrive for breakfast, and that we shall be hungry, but perhaps she will not be very hungry, if it is rough. Papa said to me : ' *Je serai inconsolable, mais inconsolable !* ' But I think he will not be, because he is going to Vienna. When we are come, there will be nobody at Villa Rubein ; Aunt Constance has gone a fortnight ago to Florence. There is a young man at her hotel ; she says he will be one of the greatest playwriters in England, and she sent me a play of his to read ; it was only a little about love, I did not like it very much. . . . O Chris ! I think I shall cry when I see you. As I am quite grown up, Miss Naylor is not to come back with me ; sometimes she is sad, but she will be glad to see you, Chris. She seems always sadder when it is Spring. To-day I walked along the wall ; the little green balls of wool are growing on the poplars already, and I saw one chafer ; it will not be long before the cherry blossom comes ; and I felt so funny, sad and happy together, and once I thought that I had wings and could fly away up the valley to Meran—but I had none, so I sat on the bench where we sat the day we took the pictures, and I thought and thought; there was nothing came to me in my thoughts, but all was sweet and a little noisy, and rather sad; it was like the buzzing of the chafer, in my head; and now I feel so tired and all my blood is running up and down me. I do not mind, because I know it is the Spring.

"Dominique came to see us the other day; he is very well, and is half the proprietor of the Adler Hotel, at Meran; he is not at all different, and he asked about you and about Alois—do you know, Chris, to myself I call him Herr Harz, but when I have seen him this time I shall call him Alois in my heart also.

" I have a letter from Dr. Edmund; he is in London, so perhaps you have seen him, only he has a great many patients and some that he has ' hopes of killing soon ! ' especially one old lady, because she is always wanting him to do things for her, and he is never saying ' No,' so he does not like her. He says that he is getting old. When I have finished this letter I am going to write and tell him that perhaps he shall see me soon, and then I think he will be very sad. Now that the Spring is come there are more flowers to take to Uncle Nic's grave, and every day, when I am gone, Barbi is to take them so that he shall not miss you, Chris, because all the flowers I put there are for you.

"I am buying some toys without paint on for my niece.

"O Chris ! this will be the first baby that I have known.

"I am only to stay three weeks with you, but I think when I am once there I shall be staying longer. I send a kiss for my niece, and to Herr Harz, my love—

that is the last time I shall call him Herr Harz ; and to you, Chris, all the joy that is in my heart.—Your loving   " GRETA."

Christian rose, and, turning very softly, stood, leaning her elbows on the back of a high seat, looking at her husband.

In her eyes there was a slow, clear, faintly smiling, yet yearning look, as though this strenuous figure bent on its task were seen for a moment as something apart, and not all the world to her.

" Tired ? " asked Harz, putting his lips to her hand.

" No, it's only—what Greta says about the Spring ; it makes one want more than one has got."

Slipping her hand away, she went back to the window. Harz stood, looking after her ; then, taking up his palette, again began painting.

In the world, outside, the high soft clouds flew by ; the trees seemed thickening and budding.

And Christian thought :

' Can we never have quite enough ? '

December 1899.